Ashen

H. L. Burke

Uncommon Universes Press LLC
1052 Cherry St.
Danville, PA 17821
www.uncommonuniverses.com

This is a work of fiction. Names, characters, businesses, places, events, and incidents are either the products of the author's imagination or used in a fictitious manner. Any resemblance to actual persons, living or dead, or actual events is purely coincidental.

Editing: Janeen Ippolito – www.janeenippolito.com
Proofreading: Hannah Wilson
Formatting: Sarah Delena White

Cover Design: Julia Busko

ISBN-13: 978-1-948896-24-5

To those who would belong

Chapter One

The scents of roasting cliffpigeon and potatoes wafted around the kitchen like beckoning fingers.

I'll get my turn once the evening rush is over, Lizbete thought. She bent over the cauldron of fish stew, stirring furiously. Her metal spoon clanked against the sides of the cast iron cooking pot—her guardian's favorite, heavy as a boulder and black as the caverns that honeycombed the mountain side.

The two village boys, who acted as table runners, rushed from the steaming hot kitchen to the more breathable common room. Every time they pushed through the swinging doors, they allowed them to clack noisily back into place. Every time, Lizbete winced. Did it take so much effort to ease the door into place rather than let it swing as wildly as a sheepdog's tail?

Steam rose off the stew and twined up her arms. She paused to savor the heat. Her eyes fell shut, and she swayed on her feet as the warmth trickled into her. It had been a long shift.

A particularly drizzly day had drawn more than the usual clientele into the tavern. Of course, there were the regulars. Fishermen lounged by the fires, thawing out after a day being battered by the cold ocean spray. Tradesmen crowded tables, eager to relax with a dose of burning wine. Auntie Katryn considered this liquor the tavern's signature drink, brewed from potato mash and caraway seeds and carrying a delightful taste of citrus and licorice.

Today, though, a group of merchants had stomped their way over the In-Land plains from the distant capital to make the last of the season's trades. The village had swarmed the fresh faces, begging for outside news. Like as not, the winter snows would have the high passes closed before the end of the week. While the village was self-sufficient in terms of food and shelter, luxuries from the lands beyond the coastal peaks were greatly prized, as was any gossip from the larger villages with their scandalous politicians and occasional feuds. Lizbete could do without both. After all, the luxuries rarely came the way of a cook's foundling assistant, and it wasn't as if the village of Brumehome didn't produce enough gossip without outside assistance.

Lizbete raised the spoon to her lips. The steaming liquid stung her tongue for a split second, but she'd found out long ago that she was immune to burning. Her blood absorbed the warmth, turning the broth to the perfect temperature. She concentrated on the way the individual flavors played off each other: warm butter, mild white fish, aromatic onions, and a bit of crisp white wine she'd stolen from behind the tavern's bar. While the recipe was Auntie's, Lizbete enjoyed making things her own by throwing in something unexpected, in this case, the wine. She just had a feeling that the oily fish and creamy base needed something to brighten it up, like sun shining through the edges of a cloud.

The warmth rising from the pot continued to ease its way into her bones. Her head nodded, though she continued stirring. True, down-to-the-marrow warmth was a rare treat. The villagers harnessed energy from volcanic steamvents to warm their houses and power some basic machinery. Still, Lizbete never felt the warmth of the steam made a dent against the inclement weather and the constant freezing winds that swept off the sea.

Oh, to be truly warm…

The stew began to push against her stirring. Brow furrowed, she opened her eyes. Had it simmered too long and begun to thicken and burn? Horror filled her chest. The top of the stew crusted with ice crystals.

Not again.

She let go of her spoon and staggered back. The fire beneath the pot still crackled. She cast a frantic glance around the kitchen. Auntie Katryn had left her in charge of the stew so that the older woman—and owner of the tavern—could see to her guests. The serving boys still dashed in and out, but neither gave Lizbete a second glance.

Trying to force her body to draw heat from the steam floating around her rather than through her hand, Lizbete poked at the frozen surface of the stew with the tip of the spoon. Maybe the broth would thaw before it was needed? The few times she'd allowed her attention to lapse to the point of freezing food items, there'd always been time to thaw it. Having it happen in the middle of the dinner rush was inconvenient, but it would thaw. It had to thaw. If only they didn't need it soon.

"Hey, Ash Lizard!"

She jumped and spun about, the spoon clattering on top of the ice in the pot.

A blurry figure approached her. Her near-sighted eyes only perceived an indistinct red face topped with a blur of flame she assumed to be hair. He stepped right up to her, finally coming into focus as Tieren, the older of the two serving boys. Tieren gave her a mean-spirited grin. Severe wind and sunburn scorched his otherwise pale cheeks, nose, and forehead, almost matching his flame-orange hair. He was perhaps a year younger than her, but like most of the villagers, far taller and stronger than she could ever hope to be.

Frail and thin, Lizbete sported ashen skin that resembled the silver-scaled cave lizards that lurked in the warmth of the steam-vents, only emerging from their caves to eat flies. The comparison of her complexion, combined with the unfortunate first syllable of her name and the way she always clung to sources of heat like a lizard, had been the cause of her cruel moniker. As much as Auntie had tried to discourage "Ash Lizard", not allowing it to be spoken in her presence, the town was more like to call Lizbete that than her actual name.

A shiver cut through her. If Tieren saw the frozen stew, he'd ask questions, questions she couldn't—or at least didn't want to—answer.

Moving to block his view of the icy stew, Lizbete squared her shoulders. "Madam Katryn doesn't like it when you call me that."

His lips curled back over yellowed teeth. "Madam Katryn isn't here now, is she?"

Lizbete opened her mouth to snap that she'd tell on him, only to immediately clamp it shut.

Tieren was only a temporary employee, on loan to Katryn while her usual waitress, Falla, was abed after childbirth. The threat of firing didn't hold much fear for the boy in the short run, and in the long run, he would likely remember the ill-turn and use it as an excuse to torment Lizbete. His father was the local butcher, someone she had to do business with on Katryn's behalf on a regular basis.

The likelihood of seeing Tieren outside of Katryn's protection was too high to risk his wrath.

"Whatever." She'd put up with him, but she didn't have to be pleasant about it. "Did you want something?"

"The guests are hungry and the roast ewe is almost gone. The boss wants you to get the stew ready to serve, then put what's left of the ewe in the big pot to boil down for stock."

Lizbete's shoulders tensed.

"All—all right," she stammered.

Tieren narrowed his eyes. "Get a move on it, Ash Lizard." He turned away.

Lizbete fished the spoon out of the pot, an easy enough task as the utensil lay on the frozen surface of the stew. She hit the spoon against the top of the stew, breaking off ice crystals. If she could crack the broth into smaller pieces, it might thaw faster. "Blast it all…"

Auntie Katryn would never serve cold stew, let alone frozen stew. Why did those vent-blasted patrons have to eat so much so quickly? The spoon clinked against the solid stew, barely denting it.

"Oh, Skywatcher, not now!" she groaned. If the Skywatcher deity was listening, he didn't immediately answer. She tossed log onto the flames beneath the pot. The fire roared to new life, but while the edges of the chunk of stew began to sweat, the middle remained unchanged.

"Three orders for fish stew!" Dori, the other serving boy, shouted from the door.

Lizbete groaned inwardly. She needed to get Katryn.

Setting the spoon in a bracket attached to the hearth, she crept through the kitchen towards the noisy, smoky common room. Her shoulders hunched towards her ears. Auntie Katryn wouldn't be mad. Auntie was rarely mad, but the frozen stew would set the evening back a bit. Customers might complain, forcing her to compensate with free food, which would cost her money. Auntie already put up with enough inconvenience and local derision for having Lizbete under her care. Lizbete didn't want to cause her more trouble.

Still, the longer Lizbete waited to tell her guardian, the worse things would get. With a deep breath, she pushed her way through the swinging double doors and out into the press of the dinner rush.

She bounced off Tieren's chest. The young man dropped the stack of empty wooden bowls he'd been rushing to the kitchen to fill. He staggered back a step, scowling.

"What are you doing out of your steamvent, you dirty, sooty thing?"

Eyes darted to them, and a hush fell across the room. Lizbete cringed. She had hoped to sneak through unnoticed. A murmur of "Ash Lizard" rose from the nearest table at a volume they probably assumed would go unnoted—and for anyone but Lizbete, they would've been right. For whatever reason, Lizbete's senses had decided to compensate for her awful eyesight by giving her acute hearing. As someone often on the receiving end of malicious whispering, she could've done without this ability.

The majority of Brumehome villagers had ruddy complexions and tall, broad-shouldered frames, but with Lizbete's poor vision, they blurred together into one intimidating swoosh of browns, reds, pinks, and the occasional blond. From the patrons close enough to see, however, she could tell that everyone was staring at her.

Behind the bar, the rounded shape of Auntie Katryn stood out from the rest of the throng, made further visible by the red kerchief she constantly wore in her hair. She paused in her work of pouring burning wine into wooden tumblers for the line of boisterous guests.

"Lil' Liz!" The middle-aged woman bustled around the bar. The various patrons scattered to avoid being mowed down by her considerable girth. By the time she reached Lizbete, she was red-faced and puffing. Her blue eyes watered and her graying brown hair was coming loose from its braids. Auntie stopped short of bowling the much smaller Lizbete over, worry furrowing her brow.

Lizbete dropped her gaze to the stone tiles of the floor. Warmth filtered through the thin soles of her skin shoes. Like many of the finer homes and businesses within Brumehome, the tavern was heated by steamvents that traced throughout the town like veins through flesh. Lizbete concentrated on this warmth and tried to find her courage.

"There's a problem with the stew," she said in a hoarse whisper.

Auntie set her hand on the girl's shoulder. "A problem is only a solution waiting to happen."

They entered the kitchen. Tieren craned his neck over Auntie Katryn's head, trying to look around her. She shooed him back into the common room and let the door snap shut behind him.

Together they crossed to the hearth. Lizbete prayed that when she looked this time, the frozen stew would have returned into bubbling, steaming liquid. No such luck. Auntie tapped at the brick of iced food with her finger and gave a low whistle. The stew ice sank a little bit, squelching within the pot.

"I see." She clicked her tongue. "Lil' Liz, Lil' Liz, how did you manage..." Her gaze fell on the spoon in its bracket. "Ah, you used a metal spoon to stir it?"

Lizbete flushed. *Of course.* She had been so panicked, she hadn't even considered that detail. "The wooden ones all needed to be washed after the afternoon's cooking. I thought it would be all right since the room is so warm."

"Metal draws in heat, and your body always takes from the easiest source. If you'd used the wooden spoon, you probably would've drawn from the air, but instead the heat got lapped up like milk by a cat." Auntie continued to poke at the stew. She then pointed to the other fireplace where the remains of the roasted ewe still spun on a spit, waiting for Lizbete to gather up the scraps and simmer the bones for stock. "Get the drippings from the pan beneath it. They should still be plenty hot."

Lizbete ran and snatched up the pan. The immediate contact with the heated metal stung, but only for a heartbeat. Her body absorbed the excess heat and the surface cooled to a manageable temperature. Lizbete hurried to give the vessel to Auntie, lest Lizbete's pulling of the heat had frozen the drippings.

Auntie Katryn mixed the drippings into the stew. The surface spluttered, hissed, and steamed. Then the ice broke apart. She took up the metal spoon and stirred. The solid chunks became smaller and smaller until they disappeared altogether.

"Give it a few minutes so we don't serve cold stew, then have the boys ladle it out." She set her hands on her broad hips and gave a hearty laugh. "Actually, it might improve the flavor. Mutton-enhanced fish stew. I'm going to call it a special!"

Relief eased the tension between Lizbete's shoulders. She should've known Auntie would be able to fix everything. She always managed.

Auntie examined Lizbete's face, then reached into her apron pocket for a handkerchief. "You've managed to get ashes smudged on your face again, Lil' Liz." She brushed her finger across Lizbete's cheek.

Embarrassed, Lizbete took the square of cloth and rubbed fiercely at her skin. "It's warm among the ashes."

"It's also warm in the dining room near the fire." Auntie squeezed Lizbete's shoulder. "You've spent enough time in this lonely kitchen. Come sit at the bar while I pour out. The boys can handle the rest of the meal."

Lizbete hesitated, remembering the ugly whispers her brief appearance in the common room had evoked.

A sad smile crossed Auntie's face, and her voice dropped to a sympathetic murmur. "You can't hide away in the smoke and steam forever, Lil' Liz."

"I wouldn't mind a bowl of stew." Liz forced a grin. "Especially knowing it's a special."

Auntie guffawed and served her a wooden bowl.

With the non-conductive wood holding her stew, Lizbete was able to take her time getting to the bar without fear of her blood cooling her dinner too much. She smushed herself into the corner where the bar met the wall, both to avoid the crowd and absorb the heat rising through the steam pipes running through that section of the wall. She took a bite of her stew. The fishy flavor contrasted nicely with the fresh herbs from Auntie's garden box, along with the unctuous and savory hint of mutton fat. She held the stew in her mouth until her blood absorbed all its heat, then swallowed it down.

One of the merchants brought out a bone flute prompting Baldric, the town's minstrel, to produce his boxy, horse-hair harp. The other patrons cleared a space around them as the two men began an "impromptu" duet too good for it to be spontaneous—especially too good for Lizbete, who had heard them through the walls earlier that night, planning out their spectacle. Even so, it didn't take away from the skill of both men, or the way the happy, lilting tune waltzed through her soul. She leaned against the wall, heart lightening. No one looked in her direction, but as the audience began to sway as one, some clapping their hands in time to the beat, she felt less alone. For a moment, she was part of the revelry, if only as an unwelcome guest.

Before she could lose herself completely in the bliss, a trio of young people pushed their way to the open seats midway down the bar. Lizbete tensed. She recognized one of the boy's height and dark hair almost immediately. Squinting to better her vision, she managed to confirm that the features belonged to the handsome but haughty face of Einar, the mayor's second son. The girl on his arm was the shapely Marget, who was the same age as Lizbete but with far more curves to show for it. The daughter of a local fisherman who had expanded his fleet to three boats and employed a crew for each, she was the closest thing Brumehome had to a princess. The third youth wasn't familiar to Lizbete, and his road-worn clothes and olive complexion suggested a traveler.

None of them took any notice of Lizbete, though Einar's gaze darted about the room like an owl on the hunt.

"Where are the servers?" He crossed his arms.

"They're probably shorthanded." Marget tossed her auburn waves from one shoulder to the next. "That lazy waitress your aunt employs is still out with child. You'd think she have learned to shove her husband out of bed by this point. Six children is far more than I'd personally like."

"I'm not in a hurry," the stranger said in a pleasantly exotic accent, rolling his r's. "Good music and good company."

"I didn't bring you to my family's establishment to wait." Putting both hands on the bar top, Einar vaulted over it. The bar shook under his weight, and a few of the nearby patrons shot him dirty looks. Einar snatched an unopened bottle of burning wine off the shelf and proceeded to pour himself and his companions drinks.

The stranger took a sip and then coughed. "This is what you drink here?"

Einar knocked back his tumbler with exaggerated relish. Ironic considering how many times Lizbete had seen him puking his guts out after an evening of drinking. "It warms you up." He smirked. "We need something fiercer than you folks of sunnier lands."

"I prefer a sweet red wine." The stranger shrugged.

"Got mead." Einar exhibited a smaller bottle.

A smile blossomed on the stranger's face. "That'll do."

The three sipped in silence. Lizbete considered slipping further from them. While Einar hadn't noticed her yet, he would, and he never passed up an opportunity to call her names or push her around.

"So, Chiro…" Marget turned her tumbler in a slow circle. "You said you'd run into someone from our village while on your journey?"

"Yes, at the next village over." The stranger—Chiro apparently—wiped his mouth with the back of his hand. "He was consulting with the local healer. When he found we were headed in this direction, he asked us to bring word to his family that he'd be returning within two days. This is why I sought you out, Einar, while my fellow merchants were unloading."

Lizbete stiffened. Could it be?

Einar scoffed. "Sounds like Brynar. Still messing around with quacks and charlatans, trying to stop the inevitable for our sister."

"It's rather heroic of him, don't you think?" Marget gave a dreamy sigh.

Lizbete rather thought so too, as much as she hated to agree with Marget.

"My brother's a fool who wastes time seeking a cure that doesn't exist, when he should be preparing to take my father's place. It only draws out hope and therefore pain." Einar's scowl deepened, and for a moment, Lizbete thought she could hear distress in his voice—though that would require an emotional depth she wouldn't have attributed to the vain and selfish youth. "Let him stay away. The village runs fine without him."

"You're just saying that because you know the local girls won't give you a second glance if your brother is there to distract them." Marget sniffed.

"Only the foolish ones. My father is wealthy enough to set me up in whatever trade or business I'd like." Einar's chin shot into the air, his arrogance chasing away the trace of grief that had almost humanized him to Lizbete. "My brother? He'll never be anything but the next mayor."

"Oh, yes, *only* a lowly mayor." Marget rolled her eyes.

Lizbete pushed the last few bites of stew around her bowl. She hadn't seen Brynar in over three months, and that in passing, as he hurried after his father on official business. The last time they'd actually talked . . . it had been at least a year. An emptiness formed in the pit of her stomach in spite of the large serving of satisfying stew. Brynar had been one of the few villagers who would talk to her. Until he wouldn't. She missed their talks, him listening to her worries as he helped her carry water back from the well, and especially the way his eyes lit up when he laughed. She'd tried to tell herself he was just busy, and he obviously was. Still, a few moments to drop by the tavern didn't seem too much to ask.

"You should know from watching your father that a savvy fisherman can gather far more wealth than my father has the ability to," Einar said.

"I prefer a man who doesn't stink of fish." She shuddered.

Chiro eased closer to her. "Perhaps a merchant, then? Exotic lands provide us many chances to make our fortune."

Marget fluttered her eyelashes at him.

"Hey!" Einar shouldered his way between the two. "Get away from my girl."

Lizbete bit back a contemptuous laugh. While Einar spent the most time around Marget, he was an equal opportunity flirt. According to Brynar, Einar would've been much worse had their father not taken both young men aside at an early age and told them if they ever got a girl with child, they'd be required to marry her immediately.

"If you can't take a little competition, I'm sure I can find other suitable females." Chiro's gaze swept the gathered crowds. Lizbete dropped her own stare to the bar-top, not wanting to be caught watching Einar and his friends. "What about that little one there in the corner? I've never seen someone so pale. It's rather exotic."

Lizbete's stomach flip-flopped as she realized he was referring to her. Boys never noticed her.

"If you think cradling a corpse would be alluring." Einar made a face. "I've seen week-dead bodies with more color and life than Ash Lizard."

Shame rippled through her.

"Ash Lizard?" Confusion flavored Chiro's tone.

"That's what we call the little monster," Marget said in a disdainful hiss. "The girl is cursed by dark spirits. In fact, some say she might be one of them. You get too close, she'll suck out your soul and leave you an empty husk."

16

Chiro chuckled. "Really, now. I may be a stranger to your lands, but I'm not an idiot you can scare with wild tales." Lizbete slowly raised her head. Unwilling to look directly at them, her vision weakened further. Still, she could see their movements. They drew together even as their voices dropped to whispers.

"No, it's true." Marget grasped Chiro's arm. "Sixteen years ago she was left on the meeting hall's doorstep in the dead of winter. By the time a local herdsman found her, she was stiff and cold—he thought dead. However, he brought her in and laid her by the hearth and she came back to life. Started squawking like a rooster running from the axe."

"A strange tale, but hardly frightening." Chiro shrugged.

"Aye, but that night, not having a place to keep her—herdsman here often live in temporary structures out with their flocks—he brought her into the heated barn he kept for his birthing animals." Marget gave an exaggerated shudder.

Einar placed his hand by his mouth. "The next morning half the sheep in the barn were blue and stiff, frozen solid. That little gray maggot lay beside them, as hale and whole as ever."

Lizbete's chest tightened, and her dinner threatened to force its way back up her throat. She'd heard the story before, though Auntie had tried to shelter her from it. She didn't like the idea that she'd killed that many animals, even if she hadn't known what she was doing at the time or couldn't remember the deed.

"If she's such a foul creature, why is she here?" Chiro asked.

"Oh, some in the village wanted to kill the little beast the moment the deaths were discovered, but my father has some strange ideas about justice. He says spirits and curses are all superstitious nonsense, and he wouldn't let a baby be killed based solely on such irrational notions." Einar grunted in agitation. "So he gave her to my aunt. Aunt Katryn has always had a thing for strays."

"Since then, nothing else has died around her, though if you're near her, you get an uneasy feeling. No one likes it. No one chooses to be around her long."

Lizbete bristled. That wasn't completely true. Auntie chose to be around her, and Falla didn't mind her so much. There was also little Elin, Einar's own sister. And of course, Brynar.

"Your siblings do," Marget pointed out, perhaps just for the joy of contradicting Einar.

"Elin is practically a ghost herself. One hand grasping this life even as the rest of her is drawn into the spirit world. Brynar, he used to rub elbows with the girl from time to time, but even he cut it off. After all, wouldn't do for the future mayor to have such disreputable connections."

Lizbete froze. Brynar had cut her off? No, Einar had to be just saying that. Yes, Brynar had stopped visiting with her, rather suddenly at that, but he'd always been kind to her, often when no one else would be. He'd just gotten busy, that was all. It wasn't intentional.

It couldn't be.

She remembered Brynar's kind smile and clear blue eyes, always so sincere and intent. Always ready to listen to her, ready to acknowledge her when the rest of the town would rather pretend she didn't exist. No, he wouldn't have just abandoned her. That wasn't who he was.

Or was it?

"If you want female companionship that's a little less likely to kill you, I have a cousin." Marget stood and offered Chiro her hand. "It's too bad you will be leaving so soon. She needs someone to take her to the festival of the First Frost. All of us will be there. It wouldn't do to have a cousin of mine go without an escort, but her worthless boyfriend . . . it's a long story. I'll tell you it after this dance."

"Hey now!" Einar burst to his feet. His girl and his guest were already striding into the center of the room. Momentary pleasure at his humiliation warmed Lizbete's chest, only to fade as quickly as it had sprung up.

She'd never been to the Festival of First Frost, though she'd stared at the glow of the lights and listened to the lilting, lovely music from her bedroom window. The idea of being in the center of that joyous gathering, rather than watching from a distance, filled her with a quiet longing. Last year she'd almost gone, if only to sit on the sidelines. She'd lost her nerve hours before the music started. Even Auntie had encouraged her to make an appearance, and Brynar had said he'd save her a seat at the feasting table.

Brynar...

Loneliness squeezed her heart. She tried to recollect the last time she'd spoken with Brynar. He'd been preparing for a journey, but he'd also been acting awkward rather than his usual easygoing self. Was Einar telling the truth? They were brothers, after all, and while different in almost every way, still flesh and blood.

But she couldn't believe that about Brynar. If he had rejected her, that cut her circle of true friends nearly in half. Taking up her bowl, she retreated to the kitchen, now empty except for a simmering pot filled with the bones of that evening's ewe roast. She pressed her back against the large ovens that were cooling after a day of bread making and closed her eyes. She was so tired of being alone. Yes, Auntie Katryn was family, but she would've done anything for one friend her own age to talk to.

"Oh, Skywatcher," she breathed into the dark, "is it really so much to ask? Just someone to talk to who doesn't see me as a monster or a freak?"

The kitchen was silent except for the bubbles popping at the surface of the simmer pot. Her hands smoothed the ashes at the edge of the hearth, feather soft, leaving her pale gray skin smudged once more. Well, it wasn't as if she needed to be presentable for customers anyway. With a sigh, she sank to the floor, pressed her cheek against the oven as if it were the softest of pillows, and tried to forget what Einar had said about Brynar.

Chapter Two

Lizbete worked the handle of the old pump behind the tavern and watched as the steaming water spurted into her bucket. The water had a distinct smell of sulfur. Years of mineral deposit had crusted the surface of the pump with rough, grayish-white bubbles. Auntie Katryn claimed the minerals in it had healing properties which was why sickness was relatively rare in Brumehome—though Lizbete wasn't sure what Auntie was using for comparison, having never lived elsewhere. Lizbete leaned into the steam rising from the water, soaking in its heat. She generally disliked chores that took her outside of the tavern, even for a few minutes. At the height of summer, when the world around Brumehome was green and the sun shone upon the stone streets and chased away the constant fog, it wasn't so bad, but that was a small window of time. Now as winter approached and more and more days were overcast, she longed to stay beside her ovens and fireplaces.

However, the hot spring feeding the tavern's water pump made the area around it almost as warm as the kitchen, even in winter. The rocks beneath her feet heated the soles of her shoes. Steam caressed her skin like tender hands. When the water splashed against her, it hissed and scalded but not painfully. Lizbete never found heat painful.

As she waited for the bucket to fill, she allowed her gaze to wander over the vicinity. The back of the tavern sat up against a rock wall. The hot spring poured from somewhere behind the wall, but had been channeled into various pipes for use in the tavern generations ago. The narrow alleyway between the rock wall and the tavern itself resembled a spider's web, but with copper pipes rather than threads of webbing. The pipes cast odd shadows over the nook with the pump.

"Hey, Liz!"

Lizbete started and bumped into the bucket. It splashed water over the stones beneath her with a hiss. Shaking her head, she took a few steps closer to where the voice had come from. A person came into focus. Large eyes set in a thin face peered through a gap between two pipes.

A faint smile crossed Lizbete's face. "Elin, don't sneak up on me like that."

The ten-year-old wriggled between the pipes. "I try to stamp my feet, but I'm just not that heavy." She straightened her sack-like brown smock that had gotten twisted as she'd squeezed through the cracks. "Einar says I glide about like a dark spirit and it's unnerving."

"It doesn't take much to unnerve Einar." Lizbete sniffed.

Elin brushed her stringy brown hair back from her face. "Yeah. It's fun to make him nervous, though. I once spent a whole dinner staring at the space above his head until he lost it and started shouting at me to stop. Brynar thought that was hilarious."

Lizbete clicked her tongue. "You know, for such a seemingly

harmless thing, you're a little bit evil."

"I know." Elin smirked. She took a step forward but tripped and stumbled.

"Easy!" Lizbete grabbed her arm. Immediately heat rose from Elin into her. "You all right? You feel feverish."

The girl's cheeks flushed, and she drew a deep breath. "I'm always feverish. Comes of being touched by a dark spirit, you know." She rolled her eyes.

This was true, but it felt worse than usual. Elin's eyes were sunken in, her cheeks hollow.

Lizbete bit her bottom lip and focused on pulling heat from the girl.

The lines in Elin's forehead eased. "Oh, that feels better. One day you're going to have to tell me how you do that."

"No, I'm not going to, and you're not going to tell anyone that I do it." Lizbete released her before she accidentally siphoned off too much heat. "You really shouldn't be wandering around the village when your fever is spiking like that."

"I hate being cooped in all day." Elin crossed her arms. "Especially not today. Brynar's just come home."

Lizbete's breath caught in her chest. "He did? When?"

"He got in late last night and has spent the morning in the town square catching up with all his friends. All except one friend who was nowhere to be seen." Elin glared at Lizbete meaningfully.

Lizbete's heart dropped into her stomach. "I'm sure he's busy. The whole town is going to want to hear about his journey and the things he saw. We don't get outside news all that often, and Brynar has always been the village's favorite son." She took up the bucket of water. "I'd just as soon avoid that crowd." And maybe Brynar, too. The more she'd considered Einar's assertion that Brynar had cut their friendship off, the more likely she felt it was true. If so, he didn't really want to see her, and pushing her way into his circle again would only hasten the rejection. Also, even if Brynar's presence usually prevented the other village youth from openly bullying her, no one wanted her around.

"But he's your friend too!" Elin wrinkled her nose. "Are you mad at him for something? Did he do something to you? Do I need to yell at him?"

A barking laugh escaped Lizbete. Immediately, the heaviness in her belly lightened. It was good to have at least Elin on her side. "No, it's not—well, I mean, you know how it is, Elin. Brynar is the local hero, and I'm the Ash Lizard."

"The same people who call you Ash Lizard call me spirit-touched and a walking ghost." Elin frowned. "They're just idiots."

"Maybe, but there are a lot of them."

"Yeah, honestly the village could use a swift plague."

Lizbete's jaw dropped. "Elin!"

"I'm kidding!" Elin groaned. "I don't want them to die . . . though if they got some sort of very specific disease that made them mute, *that* I'd root for."

Lizbete shook her head. "You're definitely a little bit evil. I'm fine though. I've got work to do that'll keep me at the tavern all day, and Brynar? Well, we're not as close as we used to be." Regret ate at Lizbete's soul, along with a longing for what had once been, but she pushed forward. "I can't really blame him for wanting to stay away. The town hates me, and he's destined to lead the town when your father retires. He can't be associated with the local pariah."

Elin stiffened. "Then I can't be associated with him."

"It's not his fault," Lizbete quickly added. "It's just how things are. Besides, he's your brother."

"He may be my brother, but you're my friend, and *his* friend." Elin set her jaw hard. "If he can't see that, then he's as big a fool as Einar."

Lizbete arched an eyebrow. "Harsh words indeed." She shifted the bucket from one hand to the other then nodded in the direction of the tavern entrance. "Do you want to come inside with me? It's pie-making day. Auntie Katryn will probably let you eat the apple peels."

"No." Elin edged away from Lizbete. "I've got something I need to do." She cast a nervous glance around the alley. "Goodbye!" She rushed off as if a dark spirit were chasing her.

Lizbete laughed uneasily. She adored Elin. For all her brashness, the girl was honest and good-hearted. Still, sometimes the workings of her mind worried Lizbete. There was no telling what the girl would get up to if left to her own devices.

Returning to the warm kitchen, Lizbete emptied the still-steaming water into the basin beside the tower of unwashed dishes. Tieren cast her a dirty look as she did so. Lizbete just smiled. It wasn't her fault that the boy had been assigned dish duty—but she could still relish the idea of his fingers pruning as he labored through the mountain of crusty bowls and grimy tankards.

She walked around the ovens to the corner where Katryn had set up a workstation for pie day. Three baskets filled with the last of the year's apple harvest sat next to a table with paring knives, bags of flour, jars of lard, and all the makings of an excellent batch of pies. This included exotic ingredients like cinnamon and cloves purchased off foreign merchants. Even though they hadn't started yet, the smell of apples and spices circled around the room in a tantalizing perfume.

Katryn stood up from the end of the table and held out a knife.

"Peel or slice?"

"Peel," Lizbete answered firmly. Peeling was by far the preferable task. She enjoyed watching the outside of the apple slip away to reveal the pure white interior.

Taking her seat, Lizbete focused on trying to peel the apple in a single long strip. She'd let the peel fall into the basket before passing the pale, naked fruit to Katryn to chop into small pieces. Sometimes Lizbete would stick a peel in her mouth to chew on as she worked. The peels she didn't eat, Katryn would use to make apple tea or to flavor mulled wine. The knife slid easily under the green skin of the fresh apple. The juice misted about her, bringing with it a sweet-sour smell, fresh and full.

With the motion so repetitive, Lizbete sank into her own thoughts. Hopefully Elin would have the common sense to leave well enough alone with Brynar. Whatever his reasons for breaking off their friendship, he'd made his choice. It wasn't as if his rejection of Lizbete would influence Lizbete's relationship with Elin. If anything, Elin was the only reason he'd befriended Lizbete in the first place.

Not that Brynar had ever been cruel to Lizbete. However, they had so little in common. Elin had started visiting when she was a sickly toddler, spending time with her aunt, Katryn, to give her often-exhausted mother a rest. Seeing if Lizbete's abilities could soothe the child's constant fevers had been Katryn's idea, but somehow the practice had evolved into Elin following Lizbete about the tavern as she did her chores.

Elin's mother had tried to object. The rumor of Lizbete's part in the death of multiple animals frightened most village mothers to the point where Lizbete was never allowed unsupervised with younger children. As with most things, Elin became the exception to that rule, and Brynar had followed.

At first he just worriedly hovered over his little sister, then grew to appreciate that Elin obviously felt better when in Lizbete's presence. They'd talked, laughed, and he'd carried loads for her when she needed assistance. He'd confided in her over the worries for Elin's health, of the stresses of being the future leader of their village, and of his younger brother's constant troublemaking.

In return she'd had someone to talk to, someone who stood up for her on occasion. She didn't tell him about every frustration, every time someone chucked mud in her direction or hissed 'Ash Lizard' as she walked by. If he were around, those things just didn't happen. If anyone even started, he'd give the offending party a cold, disappointed stare, and they'd fall silent.

Her keen hearing often made her party to the whispers of other village girls, their giggled gossip about what exactly made Brynar the most desirable match in town. The son of the mayor and likely the future mayor. Handsome. Well-liked. Strong. Tall. Intelligent. However, Lizbete had never heard any of them list the quality that truly made Brynar the one shining star to pierce the darkness of their small town. Brynar was *kind*. He was kind to her when he didn't have to be, and she'd truly missed that part of him in his time away. Of course the handsome, likeable, and intelligent aspects of him were nice too.

Her knife slipped through the peel of her current apple too early, and a half-apple length fell into the bucket. She clicked her tongue.

Need to stop daydreaming on the job.

A door opened in the distance, and footsteps tapped upon the stone floors of the common room beyond.

Auntie Katryn put aside her knife with a sigh. "I'd best see who that is. It's close enough to midday that some people might be look-ing for an early meal."

"Let Tieren handle it." Lizbete pointed her chin in the direction of the dishwashing station.

"And have him sour the customers' appetites with his sullen face?" Auntie shuddered. "No. Besides, I need him to run to his father's shop for me. We could use some bacon to season the potato mash tonight." She stomped in the direction of the boy. "Come on. I have work for you."

Lizbete returned to her work as the swinging door shut behind Auntie and Tieren. Murmured voices—too faint for even her ears—rose from the common room. Lizbete popped another peel into her mouth.

The door opened again and footsteps approached.

"Was it not a customer?" she asked.

"Nah, just an old friend." The pleasant, masculine voice sent Lizbete's heart into her mouth. She swallowed the peel so fast the edges scraped her throat and she burst out coughing.

"Hey! Easy there!" A broad hand patted her between the shoul-ders. Immediately her blood reached for his heat, and she instinc-tively jerked away. Her apple hit the floor.

Leaping to her feet, she spun to face him. "Brynar? What are you doing here?"

His pale eyebrows arched towards his hairline. He bent and picked up the apple. "Visiting you." He settled in Auntie Katryn's seat.

Lizbete scrambled to make sense of this. "Visiting your aunt, you mean?"

"No. My aunt made a point of dropping by to visit me this morning." He crossed his legs and leaned back in the chair. Brynar was tall and handsome in a way even her poor vision couldn't ignore, with a straight nose, a strong chin, and limpid blue eyes. A few times during their friendship, she'd caught herself staring at him, only to have butterflies attack her insides when he made eye contact. Even now, his smile made her feel all twisted up inside, like she was hungry but knew she'd have to wait until the end of the dinner rush for her own meal. "She brought some excellent tartberry muffins to share, asked me about my trip, and caught me up on tavern gossip. In fact, I haven't had a moment to myself all morning. Pretty much every friend or relation I have in the village—practically the whole village, in fact—has managed to see me at least in passing since I got in last night. Or should I say every friend but one?"

Her stomach flip-flopped. "Yes, well . . . I didn't want to get in the way, you know."

"I figured, which is why I came here." One corner of his mouth curled into a roguish grin. Ironic considering he was the least roguish person she'd ever met. She suspected he'd learned the expression from Elin.

Elin.

She narrowed her eyes at him. "Are you sure the reason you are here isn't because a certain sharp-tongued little lass told you if you didn't come see me, she'd give you an earful?"

He laughed. "Well, Elin did give me a gentle reminder that you might not be comfortable coming down to our father's house."

"Gentle?" She tilted her head to one side.

"Gentle in that she threatened to pinch my ears off rather than flay my skin and leave me for the cliffpigeons to pick the flesh from my bones. So, Elin-gentle."

"Huh." She sat back down and reclaimed her paring knife. Gentle or not, it still meant he was there because Elin had told him to be, not because he wanted to be. "It was nice of you to drop by."

"I missed you and wanted to see you again, too. It wasn't just Elin, though I do admit I was hoping you'd stop by and see me. The roads go both ways, you know." He rolled the apple she'd dropped between his hands, then offered it to her.

"I can't use that. It's been on the floor." She frowned.

"I guess. Seems a waste, though." He picked up Auntie Katryn's knife and sliced off a sliver of apple. He popped it into his mouth. "Still tastes fine."

"Go ahead and eat it then." She started to peel a new apple.

The room fell silent other than the swish of Lizbete's knife working its way through the apple's skin and the crackle of the fires. Lizbete avoided looking at Brynar. Why had he even come back? Chances are, he was just going to leave again. The future mayor couldn't be seen socializing with the Ash Lizard. That wasn't how things worked in Brumehome. She had her place. He had his. They weren't together.

"This for apple pies?" He nodded towards the chopped-up apples.

"Yes. Last of this year's batch."

"I remember when Aunt Katryn used to have me and Einar over for pie day. She'd put us to work right alongside you. I'd smell of apples for the rest of the week, but the pies were worth it."

Her chest tightened. "Einar never did much work. Mostly sulking." *It was mostly me and you.*

"Yeah, some things never change." Brynar grimaced.

Lizbete's movement slowed. Those days were some of her favorites, laughing and working with Brynar. Sometimes he'd carve funny faces into the apples and she'd make up voices for them. The work always went fast, leaving her sorry when the pies were in the oven.

"Did you—did you find what you were hoping on this last journey?" She hazarded a look up at him.

The wrinkles on his forehead deepened, and he fiddled aimlessly with the knife. "No, but I found some things that might lead to what I was looking for. I visited every town healer along the Merchant Path. Most gave me the same nonsense: dark spirits touch who they touch and there's nothing we mortals can do about it."

"But some said something else?"

"Oh, a few wanted to sell me their miracle cures, but I've dealt with enough quacks and charlatans to be able to sniff out when someone just wants my coin." He sat up a little straighter. "There were a few suggestions of herbal remedies I want to get Mother to try, but the one that really intrigued me was this old woman in Herdrest. She said her grandmother used to tell a story of magical blood-red crystals that could expel foul spirits from the body. She said they grew deep in some caves, that they had a prickling energy that could heal all sorts of sicknesses, but especially those attributed to evil spirits."

Lizbete bit her bottom lip. She didn't want to take away his last hope.

"You look skeptical?"

"Magic crystals sound a lot like a miracle cure," she pointed out. "How do you know this isn't more quackery?"

"Mainly because she admitted she'd never seen one of the crystals and didn't have any to sell to me." He took another sliver off the apple and ate it. His teeth crunched through the firm flesh. "Quacks want your money. They'll sell you any hope for coin. That she wasn't asking for coin means she has no reason to lie to me." His shoulders slumped. "Of course, she also didn't know if it was real. Could simply be a story her grandmother told her."

"But you're right, it's hope." Lizbete forced a smile. She'd seen disappointment in Brynar's eyes too many times regarding his sister's health.

"I guess. Honestly, if this falls through, my father isn't going to allow me to make another journey specifically to look for a cure. He says it's false hope, and we as a family need to be preparing for the inevitable, not living in denial."

"She seems to be doing all right," Lizbete said, wishing she could offer more concrete comfort. "At least, she's still getting around the village just fine."

"She has her good days and bad." His shoulders slumped. "Perhaps I need to accept that she'll never be as strong as other children, but it's so hard when she wants to play and run, but she can't. She has so much spirit, Liz. Right from birth, fighting to live when the midwife said she wouldn't last the first night. If there's even a slight chance that I can help her, that I can keep her with us, give her a full life—what sort of brother would I be if I didn't chase that down like a hound on a scent?"

"Einar," Lizbete said matter-of-factly. "You'd be Einar."

Brynar guffawed. "Yeah, well, we all deal with grief in our own ways." His expression darkened. "I wish he wouldn't mourn her while she is still here, though. She lives under enough of a shadow as it is."

"She's a strong kid, though." Lizbete leaned over the table. She longed to hug him, but even if she'd known for sure he'd accept the affection, she couldn't risk her blood stealing his warmth.

"Yeah, she is." He turned the apple slowly in his hands before giving her a smile that sent her insides fluttering. "I wish I could bottle whatever you do for her, whatever secret the two of you are keeping. She won't tell me why, but she's always better after she visits with you."

Lizbete dropped her gaze from him. Even if healing Elin was a good thing, the other aspects of her nature were despicable enough that it would kill her if Brynar found out. The room fell silent for a long moment before Brynar tilted his head to one side, gazing intently at her.

"But enough about me. How've you been? I can't remember the last time we really talked."

She could.

She could also remember the aching weeks that had followed that encounter when she'd looked for him. Jumping every time the tavern door opened, hoping it was him, only to be disappointed over and over again. Her gaze fell to her lap. "Oh, same old, same old."

"You picked up any admirers from among the village boys yet? Anyone invited you to the First Frost?" With anyone else she would've assumed this to be sarcastic.

"Boys don't want to cradle a corpse." Einar's bitter words slipped easily from her lips.

"Hey!" Brynar's tone sharpened. He reached across the table and placed his hand on her wrist.

She froze at his touch. Instinct told her to pull away before something happened, but something else, something she didn't want to think about and therefore couldn't name, held her in place. She stared at him.

"Liz, there are enough idiots spouting nonsense like that without you adding to the noise," he whispered, his hold on her tightening.

The warmth and pressure of his hand on her skin entranced her. She couldn't move. Couldn't speak.

A door slammed.

"Brynar?" a masculine voice barked.

"Oh, hello, brother," Auntie Katryn responded.

Brynar leaped to his feet. He shivered and turned up the collar of his coat. "Is there a draft in here?"

Shame flashed through Lizbete.

She was the draft. She'd pulled from his heat.

The swinging doors burst open and a dark-bearded man with Brynar's eyes and Einar's scowl pushed into the kitchen. Auntie Katryn hustled behind him, sweat beading on her brow.

Mayor Sten. Lizbete wanted to slide under the table and disappear.

"Brynar, what are you doing, hiding back here?" His father stomped towards him. While known as a fair man, the mayor was imposing, able to hold his own against the brawny tradesmen and grizzled fishermen who made up the majority of his constituents. His broad chest filled out his homespun worker's shirt, which he wore in spite of his status. Though Brynar was a few inches taller than his father, he still seemed small in comparison. Now the young man drew himself up to his full height.

"I'm not hiding," he said, a defensive edge to his tone.

"You have guests waiting for you back at the house. Your mother is planning a dinner in honor of your return, and where are you?" Lizbete shrank a little smaller with every word. Thankfully Sten focused purely on Brynar, seeming unaware of her presence.

"I wanted to take a minute to visit . . . Aunt Katryn."

Lizbete swallowed. Was he lying to protect her? Or to save face because he didn't want his father knowing they were speaking again?

"It's my fault, brother," Auntie Katryn soothed, her words coming out clipped as if she were short of breath. "I didn't realize he was needed and set him to work like I would have in his youth."

"Hmph." Sten sized up Brynar who returned his stare, cold determination for fiery scorn. "You're not a boy anymore, Brynar. At eighteen I was already well-set on my path to my current position. You can't waste time doing tasks beneath your status, nor chasing goals that don't lead to your destiny as my son and heir. Understand?"

Brynar's jaw tensed. "Perfectly."

Sten gave a brief nod. "Let's go then."

"I'll be with you in a moment, Father." Brynar turned away from him. "You can get started. I'll catch up."

Sten's lower lip slackened before he gave a curt nod and stormed out of the room. Auntie Katryn exhaled a great breath then hurried after her brother. Even though the mayor had never threatened her—and rarely acknowledged her existence for that matter—Lizbete couldn't help but be relieved at his departure.

Lizbete stood. "Are you all right?"

"I'm fine." Brynar set the paring knife down amongst the chunks of apple. "Father thinks he can guide me like a weaver guides a shuttle, is all. In some ways, maybe he's right." He shook his head. "Still, I have a little independence left, and who I spend my free time with is up to me, not him."

"Don't upset him on . . . Just don't." She almost said, "On my account," but it seemed vain that she would even be a consideration for Brynar.

"Some things are worth fighting over." A faint smile crossed his lips. "While we're on the subject, I'm going to consult Widow Gri about the crystals tomorrow. Would you like to come?"

Lizbete drew back. "Widow Gri . . . the witch?"

"She's as much a witch as you're an Ash Lizard or Elin is a ghost." Brynar chuckled. "She also knows more about healing than any in the village. I've talked with her about Elin before."

Lizbete hesitated. Widow Gri's late husband had been a merchant who had returned with her, a foreign bride, decades before—only to die a short time afterwards. This had led to rumors that she'd killed her unwitting husband. The villagers claimed she practiced foul magic, consorted with dark spirits, and had magical lenses she could use to gaze into the spirit realm.

As a child Lizbete had been terrified of the tales, and even now she'd never dared to approach her. Instead, she'd only seen the old woman at a distance, lurking at the edge of town, shopping in the early morning when no one else was about—also when Lizbete preferred to do her own errands. Fewer people to mock her.

Maybe Brynar was right. Besides, it would be an excuse to spend time with him, before his duties as the mayor's son inevitably stole him away from her again.

"If you really want me to, I'll go with you."

"Great. I'll meet you here after breakfast." He passed her the apple he'd been picking at through their whole discussion. "It's truly good to see you again, Liz."

"And you as well," she managed to get the words out in a squeak.

With one last laugh, he left the kitchen.

Lizbete glanced down at the apple. A knob-nosed, wide-eyed face with a jagged line for a mouth stared back up at her. Her throat tightened, but she pushed the carved apple into the pile with the other fruit waiting to be chopped. Time didn't go backwards, and neither could she.

Chapter Three

The morning after Brynar's return, Lizbete had intended to go about her routine as if nothing had changed. Yet, she couldn't stop herself from waking up while the sky outside was still pale blue with the last few fading stars, before even early-riser Auntie Katryn was up. She also couldn't force herself back to sleep. Instead, she lay wide-eyed and worried in bed, bundled in blankets and tied up in knots. What if Brynar didn't come? What if he did but she made a fool of herself? What if the witchy widow put a curse on her?

Finally she heard the scraping and rattling of pans as Auntie began her daily chores. Lizbete's room was built above the kitchens, small but strategically placed so the heat from the ovens kept the temperature high all day and far into the night. This also meant Auntie's reliable early morning arrival, with clattering crockery and starting the stoves, served as a wake-up call as good as any rooster.

As soon as she heard Auntie bustling beneath her, she leaped out of bed to dress. She pulled on her woolen stockings and slid into the gray smock—almost the same color as her loathed skin— that she wore over her thick leggings and close-fitting, long-sleeved undershirt. Most of the women in village wore similar garments, warmth being more of a priority than fashion. However, unlike Lizbete, they added colored sashes tied about the middle to hint at an hourglass silhouette, colored kerchiefs, and if they were truly fancy, embroidery of flowers, stars, and birds about the collars. The one time Lizbete had tried to approximate this look, borrowing some of Auntie's colorful trimmings, a group of boys had followed her about the town, shouting about how the corpse had prettied herself up and wondering if the lizard had shed her skin. Lizbete had decided she could do without the added attention.

Now, however, she cast a longing gaze over the purple sash hanging on her wardrobe door. Auntie had presented her with the cloth last year on Gifting Day, a holiday where everyone in the village exchanged small tokens with those closest to them. Brynar had never seen her in that sash.

As quickly as the idea presented, she kicked it into the dirt and ground it into submission with a heel made of practicality. She had no business trying to impress Brynar. He probably wouldn't even show up, and she'd be sitting there in the kitchen, wearing that stupid scarf. What if he'd told his other friends—his *real* friends—about his joke, asking the Ash Lizard to accompany him to see the witch? What if they were laughing at her? What if they saw her in the sash and put together why?

The thought froze her in place, and she almost jumped back in bed to hide beneath the blankets once more.

"He wouldn't do that," she whispered to the emptiness of her bedroom. No matter how their friendship had ended, Brynar had never been cruel.

She turned her back on the sash before it could tempt her further, shoved her feet into her worn shoes, and tramped down the narrow stairs towards the kitchen.

Auntie Katryn grinned at her appearance and burbled out a greeting Lizbete barely heard and only nodded in response to. Instead, Lizbete buried herself in her morning chores: starting fires, brewing tartberry tea, making sure all the dishes were clean and stacked. When this was accomplished, she filled a wooden bowl with thick, gooey porridge, and settled beside the roaring fire to eat.

Normally Lizbete gulped her breakfast. One of the few good things about her "condition" was that she could wolf down food that would've scalded weaker throats. Today, however, she took her time, not wanting to appear in a hurry or eager for a meeting that probably wouldn't come.

Even so, when the door to the tavern creaked open, her throat tightened, preventing her from swallowing the bite of porridge she held in her mouth. Auntie Katryn, who had been kneading dough for the day's bread, dusted the flour off her hands and hurried into the common room.

"Brynar!" she called.

The greeting made it even harder for Lizbete to get the bite down. She managed, but her throat hurt from the effort.

"Two days in a row?" Auntie continued. "What an excellent surprise!"

"I'm only here for a moment. I asked Lizbete if she wanted to run an errand with me this morning, and she said yes." The floorboards creaked as if Brynar was shifting from foot to foot. Lizbete's sensitive ears twitched. "Is she here?"

"Oh, I'm sure that big-eared little rabbit is listening in on us as we speak. Lil' Liz!" Katryn scarcely raised her voice from her speaking tone.

Blushing, Lizbete placed her bowl on the hearth, dusted the

ashes from her skirt, and scrambled into the common room.

Brynar smiled at her approach. "Ready to go?"

"I . . . I . . . sure." Her shoulders hunched. She sounded like a gibbering idiot.

"Let me get your cloak!" Auntie Katryn rushed from the room. She returned a moment later carrying a thick woolen garment that actually belonged to her, not Lizbete.

"You need to stay warm," she whispered as she fitted it around Lizbete's shoulder.

Lizbete cringed. It probably seemed an off-hand remark to Brynar, but to Lizbete, it served as a reminder of her weakness. "I'll be careful," she assured her guardian. "We're not going far."

"Just pace yourself. If you start to feel a chill, step inside some business or other and wait until you're fully warm again, all right?" Auntie's eyes widened with concern.

"I promise," Lizbete assured her.

"Shall we?" Brynar offered her his hand.

Lizbete stared at the extended appendage. Her imagination bombarded her with visions of Brynar, stiff with cold, lips blue, eyes lifeless. She shoved her hands into the pockets of her smock. "Yes, let's get started."

He blinked but nodded and lowered his hand. "It's not far. No need to hurry."

Something within her ached. She hated how she couldn't even touch him. He must think her cold and standoffish, but she couldn't risk it. If she hurt him, she'd never forgive herself.

Instead of taking the broad, shop-lined street that cut through the center of Brumehome, Brynar slipped into an alleyway between the inn and the blacksmith's and then proceeded to skirt the village houses. In spite of his assurances that Widow Gri was no more a witch than Lizbete was an Ash Lizard, he certainly seemed keen to avoid anyone seeing him headed to her hut. Her mind spun with every story the villagers had ever whispered about the widow. Stories of curses, hexes, men turned to toads—all far too fanciful to be real. Still, the woman kept to herself. If she'd wanted to keep dark secrets, she definitely could.

However, after a few minutes tramping through the narrow walkways and back alleys, more practical concerns presented. Lizbete started shivering. She could feel the heat rising from her like water evaporating into steam. She focused inward trying to ignore the cold, pulled Auntie's cloak tighter about her body and clenched her jaw to keep her teeth from chattering.

A blanket of gray covered the sky. The clouds were too high and light for her to fear immediate rain or sleet, but they blocked the sun and so deprived her of one potential heat source. Some of the larger homes they passed had steampipes running into them. She edged near these and managed to get a quick injection of heat. It didn't last, and Brynar's pace prevented her from lingering long enough to reclaim any considerable warmth.

Her leg muscles stiffened. Her toes grew numb. Her bones ached.

A spasm cut through her, and her jaw unclenched. Her teeth chattered painfully, knocking together like an infant shaking a bone-rattle.

Brynar paused midstride. "Are you cold?" He'd unbuttoned his coat, exposing his off-white linen tunic and sturdy work trousers. Apparently not bothered enough by the temperature to need the garment.

"I'll be fine." She managed to get her shivering under control long enough to spit the words out.

His brow furrowed. "You don't look fine." He stepped closer to her. Even before he touched her, his warmth called to her. Her blood rushed to the surface, and her skin tingled. His hand brushed her wrist. "You feel like ice." Heat flowed through the contact, and her seized muscles relaxed.

"No!" she gasped. She wrenched away and hid her hands under her cloak.

His eyes widened. "I . . . I'm sorry." He cleared his throat. "I didn't think. I won't touch you again." He dropped his gaze to his feet and trudged along.

Lizbete's heart shriveled.

Don't be silly, she chided herself. *You don't want him to touch you. It could hurt him, or he could feel me stealing his warmth and figure things out.*

Even if they weren't friends anymore, the thought of Brynar realizing her true nature sickened her. Maybe their friendship couldn't return to the way it had been, but at least he didn't see her as a monster, as something to fear and revile. If he knew, he would. She set her jaw hard and hurried after him.

Brumehome hugged the cliffs around a broad bay overshadowed by the dark-stone peak that was Ash Mountain. As they left the last of the closely huddled houses, Brynar turned onto a narrow path that wound up the side of the cliff towards the plateau where the herdsmen watched their flocks and farmers planted crops. A fog obscured the path before them and mist beaded on Lizbete's hair and skin. Between the haze and her own poor eyesight, she couldn't be quite sure where the edge of the path was. Fearing the drop off, she clung to the cliff side, tracing the cold stone with her hand.

A cold breeze whistled around them, and Lizbete's shoulders hunched towards her ears. Her body ached. They had to be close to the Widow Gri's home. There was bound to be a fire there. She'd huddle beside it and warm herself anew.

Brynar drew closer to her and narrowed his eyes. "Are you sure you're all right? You look like you're freezing."

"That's just my complexion. Walking corpse, remember?" She pushed past him.

"No, you look grayer than usual, and your lips…" He jogged to catch up with her. "Would you take my coat, please? I don't need it."

Lizbete hesitated before nodding. He didn't need it, true, but it likely wouldn't help her much. A coat kept in heat. It didn't produce it.

However, the moment he draped the coat about her shoulders, a trace of warmth, faint as a breath, settled into her skin. The heat had an odd familiarity to it.

It's his body heat, caught in the cloth. She'd never noticed before, but there was a signature to his warmth, unlike the fierce, sickly heat she drew from Elin's fevers or the comforting, bustling heat that she sometimes accidentally took from Auntie Katryn. No, this heat was calming but also strengthening, like his serious but sincere gaze.

What would it be like to completely bask in his delicious warmth?

"How much farther?" she stammered, pushing away the thought.

"Not far at all." They reached the top of the path, and the verdant green hills of the In-lands stretched before them. Blue lakes glimmered in the distance, and jagged outcroppings of rock burst the surface of the meadows. In the distance, she could see a few blockier shapes that might've been structures, probably farmhouses and barns. Her heart faltered. All seemed impossibly remote when her toes already felt stiff and numb within her sheepskin shoes. However, rather than take the broad road that twisted through the valley towards the farms, Brynar turned to follow the cliff along a barely visible path, a worn strip of earth winding through the grass and bushes. This continued down a slight slope and into a hollow with a large green mound at the center. Smoke wafted from the top of this mound. At least she thought it was smoke. More steamvents?

They circled the mound, Lizbete following as close to Brynar as she dared. On the other side of the mound was an opening beneath two boards bound together at the top to form a triangular arch.

"This is a house?" She swallowed.

"They're called pithouses. They don't make much sense to build down by the village where we have plenty of steam to heat our homes. Up here, with the cold winds racing across the In-lands, they provide much needed shelter." Brynar stooped under the arch and rapped upon the wooden door with his fingers. It creaked open.

"Brynar Stenson," an airy voice rose from the darkness beyond, "it has been a while since you darkened my door."

"I've been away, seeking wisdom." Brynar beckoned Lizbete closer. "I brought a friend."

Smoke and heat drifted through the opened door. In spite of her fear, Lizbete longed to rush inside and hide herself from the cold.

Instead she came to Brynar's side and tried not to shiver.

A bent figure hobbled out. At first her face was a brown blur surrounded by a halo of gray, but then she stepped into Lizbete's field of vision.

A maze of wrinkles marked Widow Gri's face. Her skin was dark and weathered. A kerchief barely kept down her wild gray curls. Two strange glass circles held together by wire sat upon her broad nose, and behind those circles blinked lively brown eyes. Her gaze fixed upon Lizbete, and the woman's lips parted in a gasp.

"Oh, the Spirit Girl. I had always hoped to make your acquaintance." She stepped back and opened her arms in a welcoming gesture. "Come in, both of you."

Lizbete staggered the last few feet into the pithouse. Her knees weakened as warmth curled around her like a kitten circling her ankles.

"It is good, the fire, yes?" Widow Gri crooned.

Lizbete started. "Y-yes, it is good."

The widow pulled a chair that appeared to be made out of various pieces of driftwood, gnarled in shape but worn smooth by the waters. She slid this across the packed dirt floor of her home to rest in front of the crackling fire.

"Sit, sit. Thaw your blood. Take as much as you need."

Take? Lizbete shuddered. What did this strange woman know? Still, she needed that fire.

"Thank you," she said, sitting down.

Brynar and the Widow retreated into the far corner of the house, lit by a single oil lamp. That area was filled with crowded shelves, though the contents of the shelves might as well have been rocks and mud for all Lizbete could make of them. Widow Gri dropped her voice to a conspiratorial whisper Lizbete probably wasn't meant to hear. "You wish to know about the Spirit Girl? I can tell you much."

Lizbete went rigid. Widow Gri inhaled sharply, her gaze darting back towards Lizbete. Lizbete quickly angled towards the fire and pretended she wasn't listening.

"No, not at all," Brynar replied, his voice also low. "She's just here because . . . I wanted her to be here, that's all. I wanted to talk to you about my sister."

"You need more blue moss?" There was the grating of a jar lid opening. "It eases fevers."

"Only for a night, and it makes her sleepy." Brynar sighed.

Content that they were no longer looking at her, Lizbete kicked off her shoe and stocking and slid her foot into the fire, letting the flames lap over her frozen toes. After a moment of painful tingling, her toes began to thaw. Warmth ran through the veins in her legs, up into her chest, melting her stiff muscles and easing her aches away.

The rustle of stocking feet upon the floor jolted her back to awareness.

Widow Gri grinned toothily at her. "Feeling better, dearie?" Her gaze dropped meaningfully to Lizbete's foot. The firelight reflected eerily on the lenses over her eyes.

Lizbete yanked her foot from the flames. "Yes, thank you."

The widow had obviously seen, yet she continued to grin. Lizbete searched her face, looking for signs of fear or repulsion, but found none.

"So—" Widow Gri spun on her heels and faced Brynar who still stood in the corner, just out of range where Lizbete could see him clearly. "If you aren't here for my moss, what do you need?"

Brynar crossed the room and settled on a wooden footstool near Lizbete. His brow furrowed before he launched into his tale of visiting various charlatans and hopeful healers on his journey. When he brought up the crystals, Widow Gri's eyes lit up.

"Ah, I have heard of those miraculous things. I even handled one once, a long, long time ago."

Brynar sat up straighter. "So they are real?"

"Oh, yes, but rare in the Upper-World." Widow Gri skirted around the firepit, picked up a kettle, and hung it from a hook over the blaze.

"Upper-World?" The hair on the back of Lizbete's neck stood on end. The phrase had a strange familiarity, though at the same time she couldn't remember ever having heard it. "What does that mean?"

Widow Gri pushed the lenses further up her nose, a sly smile on her lips. "It's just a term for everything that the sun touches, as opposed to the other realms such as the Under-Sea and the Within-Earth. Those crystals grow Within-Earth, in the caves and chasms around volcanoes, specifically."

Brynar leaned forward. "Like in the steamvents around Brume-home?"

"Maybe. It seems to meet all the necessary conditions."

The kettle roiled as Widow Gri set out an earthenware tea set. "Tartberry tea?" She arched an eyebrow.

"Yours is the best." Brynar smiled.

Lizbete bit her bottom lip. "The steamvents are dangerous, though. Dark. Sometimes stifling and, well, we don't know what lives in them."

She didn't want to seem like a superstitious fool for fearing dark spirits, but the stories of them stealing livestock, kidnapping children, and leaving their victims as empty, soulless husks had always given her nightmares. Sitting beside the comforting fires in Auntie Katryn's kitchen, it was easy to dismiss such things as silly stories. Here, in the gloomy light of the tiny, burrow-like hut under the unnerving gaze of the widow, the existence of such monsters seemed far too plausible.

"Every realm has its dangers. A walk across the plains of the

Upper-World can lead to death from exposure. Fall into the Under-Sea, and you will drown." After wrapping her hand in a thick cloth, the widow took the kettle from the flames and poured the boiling water over the dried herbs and berries waiting in her clay pot. "However, the dangers of the Within-Earth are not impassable. You will need a light, some method to find your way home, and an awareness of your surroundings. If the air becomes toxic or the atmosphere too hot, you must retreat before you are baked or poisoned." She poured the tea into the two cups and passed the first, still steaming, to Lizbete. Her gaze drilled into the girl's as if waiting to see what she would do.

From the heat leaching through the sides of the cup into her hands, Lizbete could tell the water was far too hot still for an average person to drink. However, Widow Gri obviously had already pinpointed that there was something odd about Lizbete, and she didn't seem put off by it. If this was a test, Lizbete was going to pass.

She took a quick swig. The scalding water rushed harmlessly over her tongue and down her throat, and her insides gurgled with pleasure. If she had it her way, she'd eat all her meals at this temperature, but people tended to cast her weird looks when she did.

Widow Gri emitted a pleased hum, almost a purr. "Interesting. I am glad we finally got to meet. You are a fascinating subject."

Annoyance stirred within Lizbete. While she was happy not to be looked upon as an object of fear and scorn, being observed like a dead fish cut up by a curious lad didn't suit her much either. Two could play at this game.

"So, are you a witch?" She tilted her head quizzically to one side.

Brynar coughed.

"Liz," he hissed.

Widow Gri chuckled. "I consider myself more a scholar. I observe. I take note. I draw conclusions. This often leads me to knowledge that may seem mystical or even dangerous to those who have not taken the time to do the same."

"Those bits of glass in front of your eyes." Lizbete nodded towards them. "The villagers say you can see the spirit world through them. Can you?"

Brynar's mouth contorted as if he'd just bit into an unripe tartberry, but Lizbete pushed aside any desire to placate him. Maybe he hadn't caught onto what Widow Gri was up to, or maybe he just didn't care. Either way, this wasn't his business. It was between Lizbete and the witch.

Still laughing quietly, Widow Gri slipped the lenses from her face and held them out. "Why don't you see for yourself?"

Lizbete hesitated. Fear gripped her heart. Yes, she'd poked the wolf, but she hadn't expected—well, she wasn't sure what she expected, but not an offer to potentially gaze into the spirit world.

The lenses aren't hurting the widow. They won't hurt me, she assured herself.

She took the lenses. The wire frame that held the lenses in place had two arms that had appeared to rest on the widow's ears. Lizbete held the lenses by these and carefully settled them in place over her eyes.

Her breath escaped her.

Everything came into focus. The red blur that was the flame of the fire became individual tongues and embers. The lumps and bumps on the shelf at the back wall solidified into jars, boxes, and baskets. Her gaze snapped to Brynar. While he'd been close enough that she could read his expression, now she could see the threads of gray and green that twined through the blue of his eyes, each individual sweeping lash, the faint freckles that crossed his nose.

Her mouth dropped open.

"Liz?" Brynar leaped up and placed his hand on her shoulder. "Are you all right?"

"I—I can see!" she stammered.

Confusion clouded his face. "You couldn't before?"

She shook her head. "Not like this." She faced the widow. "Where did you get these?"

"A lens grinder in my homeland, before I came here. He specialized in telescopes and microscopes—" If the widow noted Lizbete's confusion at the strange words, she didn't react to it. "But occasionally he worked on spectacles like mine." She crossed to the shelf and felt about until she found a velvet pouch. With this, she returned to Lizbete and put out her hand.

Reluctantly, Lizbete returned the lenses. The spectacles. *What an odd word.*

Widow Gri redonned her spectacles then held the velvet pouch out to Lizbete. Lizbete's heart quickened as the woman continued. "Before I left my homeland to marry my beloved, I made certain to commission a spare set. They are delicate, and I knew if they broke, I would be hard-pressed to find replacements. However, I am extremely careful, and therefore my replacements have sat, unused, for decades. Perhaps they were waiting for you this whole time."

Lizbete reached into the pouch and slipped out a pair of spectacles identical to Widow Gri's. "I . . . I can have them?"

"You may. Better they see use on your face than go to waste sitting on my shelf."

Lizbete gratefully donned the new spectacles.

Brynar blinked at her. "Wow, those make you look different."

Her enthusiasm flagged. "Different meaning strange?"

"No, you're actually . . . I like them." He smiled. "They suit you."

The widow passed Brynar the remaining cup of tea. "Should be cold enough to drink now." With her guests sipping their tea, she pulled up a chair and sat with eyes half-lidded as if deep in thought. Finally, she spoke again. "The steamvents may have the crystals you seek, or they may not. Unfortunately, I am too old to accompany you, but don't go alone."

Brynar turned his earthenware cup slowly in his hands. "I would hate to ask anyone to accompany me somewhere so dangerous."

Lizbete squirmed in her seat. She didn't want to go, and she didn't want Brynar to go, but she would prefer to go with him than for him to go alone.

"Whatever you decide, keep your eyes open. If you do find the crystals, I would very much like to see them." The widow filled a third cup with tea.

"I will likely need your help learning to use them medicinally." Brynar frowned. "Potions and salves I have experience with, but how does one administer a crystal?"

"I would happily assist with that, though I'm sure you could figure it out on your own." Widow Gri nodded at Lizbete and then Brynar. "He'd never let on, but this young man has learned as much about healing in the last two years as any student in the great universities of my homeland might in the same time—and without the resources of the libraries."

"That's a bit of an exaggeration." Brynar hid his expression behind his teacup.

"Oh, maybe you don't know the book knowledge they would, but in terms of practical application, I'd say you are further on the path to a full-fledged healer than you think. If you devoted yourself to it fully, you'd be a spectacular healer, my boy."

"Well, for better or worse, that doesn't seem to be where my life has been directed." A look of resignation passed over his face. He stood. "Speaking of which, I'd like to get back to the village before people start wondering where I am. Are you ready to go, Liz?"

Liz drew a deep breath. It would be hard to leave the warmth of the tiny hut to face the cold walk home, but she couldn't exactly stay there forever. "Yes." She stood and pulled her two outer garments—Auntie Katryn's cloak and Brynar's coat—closer about her. "I should hurry back, too. I'm sure Auntie has work for me to do."

Brynar thanked Widow Gri for her time and ducked out the door. Lizbete moved to follow him, but a hand clamped down on her arm. She whirled about and faced the widow. The older woman's vise-like grip kept Lizbete from wrenching free. Though in her currently warm state the draw was lessened, heat still drifted from the widow into Lizbete's blood. With it came a sensation of age, of grief, and much curiosity.

"Fascinating," the widow breathed. "Do you know what you are, girl?"

Lizbete's throat closed in on itself, but she managed to choke out, "Do you?"

"No, which is why I asked."

Lizbete cleared her throat. "Then what makes you think I'm anything?"

The widow cackled. "Oh, anyone can see you are something. You hear what you should not. You draw heat. You resist burning." She released Lizbete. "You are something, and I would give my remaining spectacles to know what."

"Liz?" Brynar poked his head into the hut. "Are you coming?"

"Y-yes." Lizbete took a step in his direction.

"Whatever you are, it's for a purpose, girl," the widow whispered, too low for Brynar to hear, but to Lizbete it might as well have been a shout. "But you'll never find answers if you choose not to look."

I don't want to look because there's nothing to find, Lizbete tried to quiet her panic with the thought, but the strangeness of the widow's words clung to her like the ash that smudged her skin.

Pulse pounding, Lizbete burst out of the hut, colliding with Brynar.

"Easy." He caught her by the shoulders. "Are you all right?"

Her new spectacles slipped down her nose, and she pushed them back up. In the gray light of the cloudy day with Brynar before her, the widow's strange words seemed little more than a bad dream.

"I'm fine. Let's get home."

Chapter Four

The clarity of the world overwhelmed Lizbete. She paused every few feet to admire individual blades of grass or pebbles on the path. Then she staggered forward, looking every way but where she was going, until her gaze fell on Brynar and his amused smile. Embarrassment rushed through her. She put her eyes to the path and quickened her pace.

However, when they reached the edge of the cliff and the path winding down to the village, she stopped cold. Brumehome rested below her like a map rolled out on a table. The steady wind coming off the sea cleared the last remnants of the morning fog, and she could see every detail, every roof, every road, every garden patch. Perfect squares on a living quilt.

The village had been her home for her whole life. She'd never gone much farther than a short walk from it. To see it laid out before her now, her entire world visible at a glance, made her feel small. She'd so rarely dared to step outside of Brumehome. Now she could tell it was just a speck on the surface of a much bigger reality.

While there were more structures below her than she could

quickly count, the town still seemed tiny. She'd somehow expected it to be much bigger, stretching over the entire shoreline as far as the eye could see. Instead the grouping of homes and businesses clung to a small section of the cliff. A haze of smoke and steam gave the view a ghostly pall, as if she were looking through frosted glass or holding the image only in her imagination. A rickety pier stuck out into the water, surrounded by a dozen or so bobbing boats and one or two larger ships. Beyond that, white-capped waves danced over slate gray waters above which swooped gulls and cliffpigeons.

"Quite a view, huh?" Brynar chuckled, easing alongside her. His warmth called to her, but she forced her mind from it.

"It's so small." She swept her eyes along the coastline, noting a few more docks and fishing huts away from the whole. She froze. Beneath the shadow of Mount Ash, a great white cloud obscured a section of the shore. Something glowed within the haze, though, something red and hot.

"What's that?" She pointed.

"Huh?" Brynar craned his neck, following her indicating finger. "Oh. That's the Fire Flow. At the foot of Mount Ash there are crevices that ooze lava constantly, like blood from an open wound. When the Flow hits the cold waters of the bay, it steams and hardens into rock."

"It must be warm there," she whispered.

"Warm?" He arched an eyebrow. "If by warm you mean scalding, sure. My father likes to tell of a cousin of his who sailed too close. The steam cooked him alive in his boat. By the time his vessel drifted out of the haze so we could claim it . . . let's just say it wasn't pretty."

Lizbete tightened her garments about her. With her ability to withstand temperatures others could not, she might be able to walk in that steam. It might even keep her warm. However, she kept quiet and followed Brynar back down the path towards the village.

As they approached Brumehome, Lizbete's eyes began to ache for staying open so wide. Everything she passed seemed brand new. She'd never noticed the flower boxes in the upper-story windows of the various houses, the speckled pattern on the breasts of the wrens that picked at the cracks between cobblestones. The clouds that floated overhead had a distinct texture. They weren't a smooth blanket as she'd always perceived them, but in fact a varied landscapes of bulges and dips with lighter and darker patches.

They passed the first house, and Lizbete inhaled sharply. There, leaning up against the back of the second building, was Einar. The young man wore his typical sulky expression, but also a strange, determined look, as if he were waiting and planning something. Lizbete hunched in on herself.

Brynar paused and whispered to her, his eyes never leaving his brother. "Don't worry. He won't do anything to you as long as I'm here. He knows I won't stand for it."

She swallowed, still dropping behind him as they approached Einar's position.

Einar's eyes flitted across her, his mouth puckered. Then he shook his head and stared fire at his brother. "Hopi, down at the docks, told me he saw you heading up the cliff to the witch's house."

Brynar came to a halt and scowled. "The people in this village talk too much."

"Maybe they just want someone to listen," Einar snapped.

Lizbete recoiled. Einar's tone held more righteous frustration than mean-spiritedness. Almost as if he were disappointed in Brynar. Had Widow Gri's spectacles cast some sort of weird spell on her that she was now seeing the world upside down?

"I was only gone for a couple hours, Einar," Brynar soothed. "I just got home from an eight-week journey. The town can do without me for one more morning."

"That's exactly the problem, though!" Einar's fists clenched. "They're already talking about how you care more about events abroad than here, how you are never here when Father needs you, how you spend more time consulting with healers than helping to run the town. You're not there when Father needs to settle disputes." He jabbed a finger at Brynar's chest. "You're not there when he needs to collect the taxes to send to the capital. You're not there for any of the dozen little emergencies that need attended to from week to week. You're off looking for a cure you'll never find in far off towns and even foreign lands. Even when you are home, you spend your time with the freaks of nature the rest of the town has had the good sense to reject—"

His words gripped Lizbete's soul like claws.

"Watch it!" Brynar's voice took on a warning tone.

"No, you watch yourself!" Einar stuck a finger in his brother's face. "How can you spend so much time off on your own tasks when there's a whole village here that needs you?"

"How can I do anything else?" Brynar's shoulders slumped. "As long as there's a chance I can find a cure for Elin—" Lizbete's heart when out to him and she longed to touch him, if only to put her hand on his shoulder. However, a breeze tickled the back of her neck, and she shivered. The need for heat was already growing within her again. Especially now, she couldn't risk contact with another human.

"Elin is one person, and you know what, Brynar? You can't save her. You've been trying since you came of age, and what has it got you?"

"At least I'm trying!" Brynar pulled himself up to his full height and took a menacing step towards the younger man. "The people here think that just because they've never seen something, it can't exist, but there's a whole world out there, Einar. There are great minds studying herbs and chemicals. There are philosophers pondering the mysteries of the earth, but this place? Everyone here assumes that if something doesn't fit their tiny preconceived notions of how the world works, it's at best nonsense and at worst evil."

The force of his words sent a quivering through Lizbete. His eyes carried a strange, desperate light she'd never noticed before. Her breath caught in her chest.

Then his shoulders slumped. "And maybe you're right. Maybe I am looking for something that doesn't exist, but at least I'm looking, and that's more than I can say for the rest of you."

For a moment Einar's mouth worked, opening and closing, with nothing coming out. Then his lips pursed, and he let out a contemptuous hiss. "You think you're too good for this village, too good for your home and your family with your big words and your travels and your holier-than-thou . . . Maybe you're not! Maybe this place is too good for you!"

He pushed past Brynar, clipping Lizbete with his shoulder. As he impacted against her, she drew a quick breath without thinking. His heat rushed into her—tense, angry. Hurt. He shivered noticeably as he stormed away, and regret flooded Lizbete.

"He's really upset," she breathed.

Brynar rubbed his forehead as if it hurt. "I know. And in some ways, he's not wrong."

Her hands shook, and she hid them between his coat.

His eyes widened. "You're cold again?"

"I—I get cold easily," she said. An understatement, but at least not a lie.

"Let's hurry then. If we cut across town square, we'll be at the tavern in no time." He grimaced. "Everyone will see us, but apparently everyone already knows what I've been up to today. Steamblast the gossips."

Lizbete stayed in Brynar's shadow as they crossed the courtyard. She pulled the coat's collar up around her face, hoping no one would recognize her and question why she was with Brynar. Or ask about her new spectacles. The thought of people staring at her chilled her further, so she pushed it out of mind. Instead she focused on Brynar's broad shoulders and on his quest to help his sister.

Was he really going to go into the steamvents? What if the stories about evil, soul-stealing spirits were true? Even if such superstitions were unfounded, dangers still haunted those passages. Molten stone, deadly gases, twisting passages one could lose oneself in forever. He couldn't go in there. Nothing was worth it.

But he would. If it gave him a chance to save his sister, he would. Nothing she, or anyone else, could say would stop him.

What if Widow Gri is right and my strangeness has a purpose? I'm resistant to steam and heat. Maybe I'd have some advantage in the vents. Maybe I could help him.

They reached the tavern, and Brynar opened the door for her. "I hope you don't mind if I don't come in. I want to see if I can sort things out with Einar, or at least stop him from telling Father about our fight."

"That's all right. Thanks for taking me with you. It was . . . interesting." She didn't think she'd forget a word that Widow Gri had spoken, not as long as she lived.

Brynar smiled. "Thank you for coming with me. It's good to

have someone who doesn't think I'm insane for pursuing this quest, plus I enjoy your company. I'm sorry I—" He hesitated, his smile fading. Confusion filled her. What was he sorry for? He'd been away because of Elin. She understood that. Instead of finishing his thought he shook his head and let out a long breath. "Stay warm, all right?"

An image of Brynar struggling to find the crystals below ground, all alone, in the dark filled her mind.

No, you idiot! Don't let him go!

"Brynar!" she gasped.

He spun to face her, eyebrows arching.

Her jaw clenched. Well, now or never. "If you go to the steam-vents, I want to go with you. I don't care if it is dangerous. I—I need to go too, all right?"

His expression softened. "Are you sure?"

She nodded. "Yes. More sure than I've ever been about anything."

He shifted from foot to foot. "I didn't want to ask that of you, but I'm so glad you—Thank you, Liz. I need to put a few things together. Would tomorrow after midday be too soon?"

"No, that's fine." Suddenly remembering that she was still wearing his coat, she slipped it off and held it out to him.

He waved it away. "No, you should keep it. I'm warm enough, and you might need it tomorrow."

She drew it to her chest and hugged it. "Thank you."

He put out his hand as if he were going to touch her, only to drop it back to his side. His mouth opened and closed as if he had something else to say. Instead, with one last smile, he turned away.

Lizbete stumbled into the warm, smoky tavern and closed her eyes.

"Oh, Skywatcher..." she prayed. "What have I gotten myself into?"

Chapter Five

Lizbete's knife slapped rhythmically against the wooden cutting board as she powered through the basket of vegetables Auntie Katryn needed stewed for the midday meal. The pile of orange disks of carrot, green bitterroot, and pale potatoes grew before her with every chop.

What if Brynar changes his mind and doesn't come to get me? What if he doesn't change his mind and we end up lost in the steamvents? What if he goes without me and gets lost all alone?

Worries looped in her brain, so she doubled down on her focus, trying to make the vegetable slices as uniform as possible. The more she concentrated on this mundane detail, the less mental space she'd have to imagine the terrible things that might lurk in the dark passages she'd agreed to explore.

The door to the common room swung open. Lizbete dropped her knife and spun about. Auntie Katryn pushed through, lugging a sack of flour almost as big as she was, her face flushed bright red.

"Here, let me help you!" Lizbete rushed to take the sack. It nearly bowled her over, but she widened her stance and staggered the last few feet to the prep table. Auntie Katryn leaned against the door frame, put her hand to her chest, and drew several deep breaths.

"Whew." She laughed, though her tone was strained. "I really need to lose some weight. If younger me saw how worked up I get just carrying supplies, she'd pity me like the fat old thing I've become."

"You're just well-insulated." Lizbete smiled.

Auntie pulled the kerchief from her hair and dabbed at her face. "That's one way of looking at it." She raised her eyebrows. "My, you certainly tore through those veggies in no time. Toss them in the simmer pot with the meat scraps from last night. It'll pad out the stew."

Lizbete scraped her pile off the prep table and onto a platter she could use to carry them to the simmer pot. "Do you think it'll be busy today?"

"Hard to say. It's fair weather, so the fishermen might stay out at sea a little longer—or they might get their work done faster and want to celebrate. You never can tell."

Lizbete tilted the platter so that the vegetables could slide into the simmer pot. They splashed into the brown broth, stirring up the scents of herbs and tender lamb. The steam from the pot fogged her spectacles, and she plucked them from her face for a quick wiping.

A banging rose from the common room. Lizbete quickly replaced her spectacles.

Auntie's brow furrowed. "We shouldn't have customers already. They know I don't unlatch the door until the meals are ready to eat."

Lizbete's shoulders tensed. Was Brynar early?

"I'll see who it is!" she burst out.

Auntie's eyes widened. "Really? You sure?"

Lizbete dropped her gaze to the floor. She rarely volunteered to face a customer on her own, but if it were Brynar, she wanted to see him first. She hadn't told Auntie Katryn about the steamvents and didn't want Brynar to let on what their errand actually was. Lizbete's guardian had enough to worry about with her busy tavern and her own health.

"I'll just tell them we aren't ready to serve yet." Lizbete set the empty platter back on the prep table and scurried out the door before Auntie could question her further.

Heart in her throat, she wove her way through the empty tables and chairs of the common room to the great wooden entrance. The person on the other side hammered again. Lizbete froze a few steps away. Brynar wasn't that impatient. Still, she'd agreed to open the door.

She pulled the cord to undo the latch and stepped back as the door swung inward. Behind it stood a thin-faced man with pale hair, gray eyes, and weathered clothes. He was familiar, but Lizbete's mind scrambled to find a name.

He narrowed his gaze at her. "Where's my sister?"

That jogged her memory.

"Hangur?" she stammered.

"Of course, you half-wit." The man pushed through and shouted, "Katryn? Kat! Where are you? I need a drink." Without waiting for a response, he stomped behind the bar and grabbed the nearest bottle of burning wine.

Lizbete shut the door behind her, staring at the intruder. Auntie Katryn had two brothers and two sisters. Her oldest sibling, Sten, was well-established as the town mayor, and her sisters all had families, businesses, and a certain degree of status amongst the villagers. Hangur, the youngest of the family, was a bit of a wastrel. As long as she could remember, he'd loitered about the village, doing odd jobs for his keep or relying on the charity of his better established siblings . . . only to disappear when their goodwill ran dry, either to roam the country or to take up work on merchant ships. This last absence had been particularly long. Lizbete couldn't remembered seeing him since she was thirteen.

Auntie Katryn stumbled into the room, eyes wide. "Hangur? What are you doing here?"

Hangur snorted, wrenched the cork from the bottle with his teeth, and spat the stopper on the ground. "A fine greeting for your little brother after all these years."

Auntie shook her head. "Last I heard you'd taken work as a herdsman near the capital, is all . . . and you had a wife?" She glanced around the room as if expecting the alluded-to female to form from the shadows and introduce herself.

"Both were temporary arrangements." Hangur chuckled. He took a long swig from the bottle before jerking his head in Lizbete's direction. "I see you're still keeping that stray about."

Lizbete glared at him. The villagers in general might hold her in contempt, but Hangur was little better than a vagrant. Him calling her a stray was like a pig criticizing a horse for its smell.

Auntie's cheeks turned crimson. "This is as much Liz's home as it is mine. I'll thank you to treat her with kindness while you're under my roof, brother."

Hangur made a clicking noise out of the corner of his mouth. "So sensitive, sister. When we were young, you and Sten would throw much worse at me. Called me thick-skulled and crook-ed-nosed."

"I . . . well, it was not something we should've done, and we're not children anymore. Any of us." She bustled around the bar and reached for the bottle. "Did you want something hot to eat? You can sit by the fire for a while. My customers will be here soon, but I'll always have a table for you."

Hangur angled his body so that the bottle remained just out of Katryn's reach.

Lizbete edged away from the door. Auntie was too nice. Hangur never paid for anything, and would live off Katryn's charity long as she allowed him to. Give him a meal and next thing she knew—

"A table and a room, I was hoping."

Lizbete stiffened. Her gaze shot to Auntie, praying the older woman would have the common sense to shut the door in the face of his suggestion.

"We only have four guest rooms, and I need them in case we get actual travelers. Can't you stay with—" Auntie Katryn shut her mouth, and Lizbete groaned inwardly. No one in Brumehome would want to give Hangur lodging, even for a few days. Might as well invite a family of rats or an infestation of fleas into one's home. They'd be easier to get rid of and less of an aggravation while they were there.

His mouth turned down into a pout.

Auntie shuddered and shook her head. "This is my livelihood, Hangur. I can't afford to give away a quarter of my rooms."

"I'll work for my keep!" Hangur set down the bottle. Auntie immediately snatched it up. "Sten always says you could use a man around the place."

"I do quite fine—"

The door, which Lizbete hadn't bothered to latch, swung open. Brynar strode in. He was dressed in his traveling clothes—a pale blue tunic, leather vest, and worn gray coat—with a pack on his back. His gaze immediately shot to the confrontation at the bar.

He blinked. "Uncle Hangur?"

Hangur frowned at him then recognition lit his face. "Ah, Einar! You've grown. How's your father?"

"He's fine." Brynar didn't correct his uncle's mistake, but his scowl deepened. "I didn't know you'd come home."

"Just got in. Hitched a ride with a farmer who was bringing some goods to market from the In-Lands."

"I hope your stay goes well. I'm sure Father will be interested in seeing you." Brynar approached Lizbete. "You ready to go?"

Lizbete hesitated. She didn't want to leave Auntie alone with Hangur, but it wasn't as if the man were dangerous, just annoying.

"Auntie, do you need anything else from me?" she asked.

"Nah, if she does, I'll help her out. You can run off and play." Hangur smirked.

Displeasure rippled in Lizbete's gut.

"I'll be fine, Lil' Liz," Auntie said before she could react. "Make sure she stays warm, all right, Brynar?"

"Yes, ma'am."

Lizbete fetched Brynar's coat. She'd hung it in the kitchen near the fireplace in hopes that it would gather warmth. When she slipped it over her shoulders, it did indeed carry a trace of heat—not Brynar's comforting warmth, but still pleasant. She tightened it around herself and returned to the common room.

"Ready to go," she told Brynar.

"Wait a moment!" Auntie said before Brynar could respond. She bustled up to Lizbete, handkerchief in hand, and rubbed at the girl's cheeks. "Always with the ashes." She clicked her tongue.

Lizbete fidgeted under her auntie's preening. "It's fine, Auntie. You don't need to fuss."

"Of course I do." Auntie grinned but backed off. "Behave yourselves, you two."

With one last skeptical glance at Hangur, Lizbete nodded to Brynar and followed him out into the village street.

Before they even turned the corner to lose sight of the tavern, however, Lizbete slowed her pace and looked back. "Do you think we should leave them alone?"

Brynar's mouth wrinkled, but he shrugged. "Aunt Katryn can look after herself. I'll let my father know Hangur's back, though. Father has a way of bringing the weight of the town's disdain down upon any target he chooses. He won't let Hangur get away with much, at least not for long."

Shaking off her doubts, Lizbete picked up the pace again. A blue sky stretched above them, filled with sunlight. Between that and her cloak, she hoped she could keep her warmth until they reached the steamvents. Once there, maybe it wouldn't be a problem.

They reached the square, alive with the bustle of market day. Lizbete pulled her hood over her head and prayed no one questioned why she was out of the tavern—or with Brynar. To her surprise Brynar steered them towards the main path leading out of town along the coastline.

"Shouldn't we be headed to the cliff face?" She pointed to their left.

He shook his head. "The vents that open there are smaller. We want the large ones closer to the Fire Flow. Those will be more likely to take us deep enough to find what we need." He gave out a long sigh. "If what we need exists at all."

Her chest tightened. She wished she had something comforting to say, but assurances that they would find the crystals felt hollow. She wasn't sure she believed they would, or that such things even existed, or if they did, that they'd actually be any help to Elin. All she could do was to be present for him in his search. She'd accept that.

They left the village and walked along the beach. The constant breeze rising off the ocean cut into Lizbete in spite of the warmth of her cloak. She clenched her jaw, worried that she'd start shivering and he'd insist on taking her back. Ahead, white wisps of mist drifted from the sheer cliff face towards the waiting water, and beyond even this, a wall of white mist.

"How close do we need to get to the Fire Flow?" she asked.

"Not dangerously so." He pointed towards the cliffs. Piles of driftwood, some made up of tree trunks far larger than any that grew near Brumehome, formed natural barriers and blocked their view. "There's a crevice right behind there that Einar and I used to dare each other to explore when we were children. We never went so deep that we couldn't see the light from the entrance, though." He shifted his pack from his shoulders and opened it. From within he withdrew a bronze lantern with rare glass panes. "I picked this up in the capital on one of my trips. They have glass factories there that make all sorts of vessels. Some of the larger houses even have glass windows." He lit the lantern with a tinderbox from the backpack before shouldering the pack again.

They strode around the pile of driftwood. A dark crack marred the cliff face like a tear in a curtain. Steam wafted from it like smoke from a chimney. A faint, sulfurous scent tickled Lizbete's nose.

"That's it," Brynar said.

Her throat tightened. "It looks so dark."

"It *is* dark." He smiled. "We're bringing a light for a reason."

The entrance to the cave was about as wide as Brynar's arm span and just high enough that he could enter without ducking. Beyond stretched a bare stone tunnel. The odor was stronger here, pungent but not unbearable. One thing, however, made putting up with the stench and the shadow fully worth it: delicious heat seeped from the passage before them. It curled around them, embracing Lizbete. Her stiff fingers loosened their hold on her cloak. The muscles in her back eased, and she sighed.

Brynar held up the lantern with one hand and reached into a pocket inside his leather vest with the other. He pulled out a nub of charcoal and proceeded to mark the wall with an arrow pointing towards the entrance.

"What's that for?" Lizbete frowned.

"To help us find our way out again, just in case we get turned around." He took a few steps forward and made a similar mark.

"But we can still see the way out." She pointed to the mouth of the cave and the sunlight pooling on the worn stone.

"Good to develop the habit now rather than when we can't." They moved deeper into the cave.

Lizbete traced her hand against the wall. Her fingertips came away damp. After a few minutes, the outside light faded behind them, leaving nothing but the glow from Brynar's lantern. She shrank closer to him.

"What exactly are we looking for?"

"I have to think I'll know it when I see it." Brynar let out a low whistle which echoed eerily down the path ahead of them.

Lizbete took a step forward and stumbled as the floor proved several inches lower than she anticipated.

"Easy!" Brynar grabbed her by the shoulder.

The warmth of their surroundings made it unlikely her blood would pull heat from him. Still, she shied away.

His face pinched, and he cleared his throat. "It's unlikely we'll find the crystals near the surface. We need to go deeper."

They walked in silence, save for the hollow tap of their feet against the stone floor. Every few steps, Brynar would make another mark with his charcoal. Lizbete's glasses fogged. She removed them and wiped them clean before scurrying to catch up with him.

The tunnel sloped steadily downward. Sometimes a side tunnel would open up. Brynar glanced down these, but always stayed on the main path. Jagged, teeth-like protrusions occasionally jutted from the floor or the ceiling.

"Careful!" Lizbete gasped as Brynar turned from making one of his marks and stepped towards such a dagger of stone, right at his head-height.

He wove around it. "Thanks. Need to look out for those."

Something rattled in the darkness in front of them. Lizbete inhaled sharply, and Brynar froze. In the quiet, Lizbete could hear his heart beating wildly.

However, he smiled bravely. "Our tramping around might've pried loose some rocks. Let's keep our voices down, all right?"

She nodded.

They rounded a bend.

"So…" he said in a low voice, "Any plans to attend the First Frost this year? I still remember you standing me up at the last one."

She hesitated. "No one wants me there."

"I did—do." He made another mark on the wall. "Even so, you want to go. I can see it in your eyes whenever people talk about it."

"No, I don't," she lied. "It's a silly dance and if I went everyone would just make fun of me. There's nothing there for me."

"There's music, good food, and laughter. Those are all things you like. You should consider it. I won't let anyone make fun of you."

"You can't protect me forever."

Especially not when you disappear for months at a time.

"One village dance is hardly forever, though I don't mind being your protector for longer periods." He flashed her his most winning smile, the one that always made her want to smile back, though now she could only stare at him.

"My protector?" Her throat tightened. What did he mean by that? Was he really offering to look out with her if she dared the dance?

"Um, yes." His cheeks reddened, then he cleared his throat. "After all, that's what Father is training me for: to look after Brumehome and its citizens."

"By 'citizens' he means the normal people. Not the local rejects." She angled away from him. Of course it was just his civic duty. Nothing personal. How had she dared to hope it was personal, that she was special to him? "Einar was right about that. Caring for me isn't good for your reputation."

"That doesn't mean I'm going to stop."

But you did. You went away for so, so long, and I was all alone.

"Well, I will need to learn to look after myself someday." She increased her pace, slipping outside the circle of lantern light. Immediately the darkness of the cave threatened to swallow her up. She almost retreated back to his side, but her pride bit at her, and she continued to walk, feeling her way with one hand on the slick tunnel wall.

After a few steps, her surroundings didn't seem so dark. She could see the shadowy outlines of more rock teeth, the looming barrier that was the ceiling, and a vague shape in the mouth of a side tunnel.

The shape darted away.

Lizbete's heart jumped into her throat. A muffled yelp escaped her.

"Liz!" Brynar leaped to her side. "What's wrong?"

The light from the lantern dazzled her, and she sat, blinking dumbly. "I—I thought I saw something move."

He held the lantern higher, and the circle of light expanded. "Where?"

She motioned to the side tunnel. He took a determined stride forward.

"No!" She grabbed his arm.

He paused. "What if there's something in there?"

"Exactly." She tightened her hold on him. "What if there's *something* in there?"

He let out a breath. "Our other option is to give up when we've barely gotten started. I don't want to do that. It could just be an animal. Foxes live in burrows. One might've wandered in here. It's probably nothing to be afraid of."

She would've felt a lot better about his assurance, except that she heard his heart hammering. Uncertain, she released him. As he moved forward, she pasted herself to his side, just far enough away to avoid taking his heat.

The light from the lantern fell into the side passage. Shadows stretched from the rock formations like arms reaching down the otherwise empty tunnel. The lack of lurking monsters did little to ease Lizbete's nerves. The hairs on the back of her neck prickled, and she shuddered.

"See," Brynar said brightly. "Nothing to worry about. The shadows catch you off guard, is all." His heart rate slowed. "Einar and I used to try and scare each other senseless in here."

They returned to the main tunnel.

"How deep do you think we'll have to go to find the crystals?" she asked.

"No idea." His voice remained buoyant, but his steps faltered. "There are a lot of passages to search, though. The whole coastline is peppered with caves like a ship's hull eaten away by worms. We could explore for a lifetime and never reach the end of them or uncover all their mysteries. I don't expect you to stay with me through all of that, though. It was kind of you just to come today. I couldn't ask you to—well, if you get tired and need to go home, just let me know."

Lizbete squeezed her bottom lip between her teeth. Of course. She was being foolish to think their quest would be over in a day. Foolish and selfish. After all, the cost if they failed was potentially Elin's life. "I'm happy you brought me along. I know how important the crystals are, and it means a lot that you trust me with this."

"Of all the folk in the village, you're the only one besides me who has never given up on Elin." He turned to face her. "Thank you for that."

"You're welcome." Her heart leaped into her throat and her words came out in a squeak. Embarrassment flooded her chest, prickling her neck and face. How did he keep doing that to her?

They continued on for a while in silence, Brynar occasionally marking the walls while Lizbete watched the shadows with suspicion. What was she even afraid of? Dark spirits weren't real. There was nothing here but stone and steam.

The air grew warmer the deeper they journeyed.

Brynar stopped to dab sweat from his brow with his sleeve. "I wish Widow Gri could've been more specific than just 'underground'." He eyed her. "Aren't you hot? If you want, you can put your cloak in my pack."

She tightened her hold on the edge of her garment. "I like it."

"All right, but remember, being too hot can be just as dangerous as being too cold. If you start to feel faint, let me know."

"I will." Lizbete couldn't imagine being "too hot." She could rarely remember feeling anything other than lukewarm, even on the brightest of days or when close to her fire.

Maybe Widow Gri was right, and I'm something . . . not human. But what could I be if I'm not human?

It wasn't as if humans as a race had been particularly kind to her, but they were all she knew. Also, the few meaningful connections she did have were of the human variety.

They turned a corner and stumbled into a blanket of warm mist. It churned gently in the light of their lantern. The smell of sulfur increased until Brynar's eyes visibly watered, but Lizbete remained unaffected. If anything, she was more comfortable, not having to cling to remnants of heat to keep from shivering. She swallowed.

I'm human. I'm definitely human. What else could I be but human?

Up ahead the pathway branched off into three different passages. A wide passage curved away to the right. The center passage dripped with stalagmites and progressed at an upward angle, but the third...

Lizbete gazed down the left-most passage as Brynar considered the other two. The light from the lantern only revealed the first few feet: narrow but tall and filled with twisting tendrils of fog and mist. Heat rose from it. Delicious heat. She extended her arm, and the change of temperature embraced her like the water from a hot bath. Everything in her body melted.

"We should go down this one," Brynar motioned towards the wide path on the right. "The second passage slopes up, which I don't like." He took a step forward.

"What about the third?" Lizbete frowned. "It's the only one that leads deeper."

Brynar stopped and blinked. "The third?" He turned and stared where she was pointing. A look of first confusion then amazement spread across his face. "I didn't see that one."

She coughed. "How didn't you see it? It's right here."

"I don't know." He stepped closer to the opening. "Now that you point it out, it seems so obvious."

"Because it *is* obvious." She narrowed her eyes at him. Was he teasing her?

Something stirred in the darkness behind them. A nearly imperceptible noise, even with her acute hearing, like cloth sliding across skin or the whisper of bird wings on the breeze. She stiffened.

"What?" He tilted his head.

"I don't know." She knew he hadn't heard the sound. She could almost imagine she hadn't heard it. Maybe he was right. Maybe they should go up the broader path, the one that didn't seethe with vapors. Something, however, pulled her into the heat and the steam. "I think our best chances are down there." She pointed into the third tunnel.

"Yeah, you're right. It at least goes downward." He shifted his pack on his shoulders and drew a deep breath. "Let's go."

The thick fog rose to their knees. Sweat beaded on Brynar's forehead, and his shirt stuck to his chest. Lizbete tried to hide the fact that she wasn't bothered by the heat—in fact, she savored it.

A little ways down the passage, Brynar grimaced. "This steam is making it hard to see the floor. We could be literally walking on the crystals and not know it." He stopped and leaned against the wall. "Ouch!" He pulled his hand away and stared at it. His palm reddened. "The stone is hot."

Worry pinched Lizbete's soul. She'd never been burnt, but she'd heard from others how much it hurt. Auntie Katryn had once burned her hand on the kitchen stove and been in pain for weeks, feverish for part of that. "Let me see."

Brynar stretched out his hand. She hesitated. Did she really want to risk this? Well, he wouldn't know what she was doing anymore than Elin did when Lizbete soothed her fevers. She held Brynar by the wrist and allowed her blood to breathe. A fierce heat, not Brynar's usual consoling energy, entered her body, bearing with it a tinge of pain. The skin on Brynar's hand returned to its normal, creamy coloring. She allowed her fingers to linger against him for a moment, savoring the contact. Her heart ached for more. Throat tightening, she jerked away.

"It doesn't look so bad. You'll be fine," she said with intentional flippancy.

His brow furrowed. "Yeah. I guess I was making a big deal out of nothing."

He shook his hand and they continued walking down the path. A gurgling noise caught Lizbete's ears and she jumped. "What was that?"

"Sorry, just my stomach." Brynar flushed. "I . . . I didn't think it was that loud." He sighed. "I don't have a way of marking time in here, but based on my hunger, it's growing near dinner. Maybe we should start out. If it took us this long to get this deep, by the time we get out, it'll be near nightfall."

Lizbete glanced down the narrow passage. It disappeared into darkness, never seeming to end. "But we haven't found the crystals yet."

"The chances of us finding them on our first search were slim." Bryanar unshouldered his pack and removed a small bundle wrapped in leather and string. Unwrapping this revealed dried fish and flatbread. He passed Lizbete half of the food before folding the flatbread around a large strip of fish and biting into it. "If they were that easy to find, they wouldn't be rare."

"I suppose not." She nibbled at the edge of the flat bread. She'd never really liked dried fish. In Auntie's cooking, the flavor mellowed and combined with seasoning to create something palatable, but when dried, the fishiness condensed, until all she could taste was the oil and the salt of the sea. Not wanting to appear ungrateful, she continued to pick at the meal. "So are we coming back then?"

"You don't have to. This is my quest, not yours, after all."

"I want to help. Elin is my friend," she pointed out.

"Yes, but it might be a while until Father lets me slip away for a full afternoon." He put his pack on again. "He wants me overseeing preparations for the First Frost Festival."

Her chest emptied out. Brynar would soon be caught up in the day-to-day business of the village, business she had no part of and wasn't welcome to participate in, like festivals and dances.

"Anyway, let's get back."

They turned around and strode back up the passage. As they reached the intersection of the three tunnels, Lizbete heard that strange sound again, soft and subtle. This time it came from the tunnel behind her, the one she'd just left.

Heart in her throat, she spun about.

Nothing. Not even shadows at the edge of the lantern light. Only empty tunnel and twisting mist and...

"What's that?" She narrowed her eyes. Something red glinted in the darkness.

Brynar turned. "Is that a light? Fire perhaps?"

Without thinking, Lizbete broke from the circle of lantern light and rushed through the mist to the glow. It rose from the ground, a patch of glowing crimson beneath the nebulous mist. Energy prickled through her, alive and warm, but also like the sensation she got biting into a peppercorn. She almost fled, but she needed to know what this was.

Jaw clenched, she shot her hand into the mist. Her fingers circled something small, about the size of her index finger, and filled with that strange energy. She drew it out of the steam: a rod of red glass—or was it crystal?—glowing with an inner light.

Brynar's jaw dropped. "How did we miss that?"

Lizbete's mouth went dry. They hadn't missed it. It hadn't been there moments before, but now . . . it was. Something had put it there. Or someone.

But who? And why?

Chapter Six

The crystal glimmered in Lizbete's hand. The energy within it called to her. It was warm, but more than that, it was a different sort of warmth. One she'd never felt before. Prickling, buzzing—it hummed like music, a living energy, fierce and potent.

"Are there any more?" Brynar swung the lantern into the mist, trying to get a clear look at the floor. "I don't know why, but I imagined them in clusters, not a single one just . . . there."

"No, this is the only one." The surety in her own voice surprised her, but somehow Lizbete knew that if there had been others, she'd feel them. She'd notice them. It wasn't that she had missed this one crystal. It simply hadn't been there before, until it was. Prying her eyes from the alluring crystal, she squinted down the path. "It didn't grow here. It was left after we passed by."

"Left by who? Or what?" Brynar laughed uncomfortably. "Nothing lives down here, unless you believe the old tales about dark spirits."

Lizbete shrugged. She didn't want to think about soul-sucking monsters right now, or what it meant that she was drawn to the crystals. To the warmth, to the darkness here under the earth.

Not human. Something else. Something . . . wrong.

She thrust the crystal at Brynar, afraid if she held onto it any longer she wouldn't be able to give it up. "Do you know what to do with this?"

"No, but I bet Widow Gri does." He tucked it into his pocket. His shoulders slumped, and he let out a long breath. "We actually did it."

Separated from the tantalizing energy of the crystal, Lizbete's focus snapped back to the present worries. Elin, primarily. "But we only found one crystal. How long will that help her for?"

"I don't know, but if there's one, there's more." He closed his eyes. "It's a start. Come on. If we hurry, we'll be home in time for dinner."

They didn't speak much on the walk back. Brynar focused on tracing their path from one of his charcoal marks to the next while Lizbete followed along silently. The feeling of eyes upon her never let up. Every few minutes she'd look over her shoulder, but never saw more than shadows and darkness. That didn't mean something wasn't there, though. The crystal proved something was there. Didn't it?

Finally, they turned a corner and found a small circle of pinkish light beckoning them. A grin broke out across Brynar's face, and his pace quickened. Lizbete pushed herself to keep up with him, but found her feet dragging. Every step closer to the surface made her blood grow colder, the air about her thinner and less like a comforting blanket. The noise of surf upon shore throbbed like the panting of a great beast punctuated by the harsh cries of seabirds.

Before her time spent in the silence of the caves, she hadn't realized how loud the surface world truly was. Every sound pierced her like a thorn. Something deep-seated but often ignored drew her towards the warm, dark quiet of the world beneath the world.

Don't be an idiot. You can't live in caves. Everyone you know, everyone you love, is on the surface.

"I can't hide from life," she whispered.

"What?" Brynar glanced at her.

"Nothing." She squared her shoulders. "Do you think Auntie will be worried with how long we were gone?"

Brynar extinguished the lantern, as the light from the cave's mouth now overwhelmed the flickering flame within it. "I hope not. She knows you're with me, and I like to think she trusts me."

"Oh, she does." They emerged onto the stony beach. Lizbete blinked rapidly to force her eyes to adjust. Pinks, purples, and oranges streaked the horizon before them. The sun slipped into the water beyond the bay, a bright orb of fire against a darkening world. Lizbete smiled. The upper world possessed so much beauty. What nonsense it was to crave the depths and the dark.

By the time they reached the tavern, twilight cloaked the world. Rowdy voices rose from the building, dinner obviously in full swing.

Brynar opened the door, and immediately voices called out to greet him. Lizbete hid behind him, not wanting to draw attention to Brynar spending time with her.

"Ah, Brynar, Lil' Liz! You're back!" Auntie rushed out of the crowd.

So much for avoiding attention.

Lizbete stepped out from behind Brynar and accepted Auntie Katryn's hug. "Do you need help with the dinner rush?"

"No, we're fine. The boys are running food, I'm cooking, and look!" Auntie withdrew and pointed to the bar. Lizbete's mouth dropped. Hangur swaggered behind it like a captain walking the deck of his ship, pouring drinks and chatting with customers.

"He's not making a nuisance of himself?" Brynar arched his eyebrows.

"On the contrary, he's the best barman I've ever had." Auntie grinned, but just as quickly displeasure crinkled the corners of her mouth. "Well, he is if he's kept accountable so he doesn't drink with the customers, but I have some help keeping an eye on him in that regard." She jabbed her elbow towards the end of the bar.

Brynar's face paled. His father sat, tankard in hand, staring straight at him . . . and Lizbete.

Lizbete's heart contracted. At Mayor Sten's side sat Einar. The mayor leaned over and whispered something to his younger son, who nodded and disappeared into the crowd.

Brynar cleared his throat. "I'm glad my father is helping out. I suppose I should get going."

He turned back towards the door, but Auntie grabbed his arm. "He wants to talk to you. I know he can be stubborn and single-minded, but he wants the best for you. For all of us."

"I know. Doesn't make dealing with him any easier, though." He turned to Lizbete and offered her his hand. "Thanks for coming with me today."

Lizbete stared at his offering hand. The tavern was warm and smoky. Her blood, which had chilled and stiffened on the walk home, absorbed the heat like a sponge taking on spilled wine. Still, she wasn't fully warm, and she might easily steal from him. But if she didn't accept, what would he think?

She shot her hand out, grasped his fingers, squeezed them once, then jerked away.

He gave an uncomfortable laugh. "I promise I don't bite."

But I might. Frost bite. In spite of her angst, the stupidity of her own thoughts made her smirk, then chuckle.

Brynar grinned. "That's what I like to see. Take care, Liz."

Her chest flooded with a different sort of warmth and she could barely stop herself from gawping at him like an idiot.

As Brynar shouldered through the crowd towards his father, Auntie Katryn placed her hand on Lizbete's shoulder.

"Come," she murmured. "Let's get you something warm to eat." She gently steered Lizbete towards the back of the room and the swinging doors to the kitchen.

Something squeezed at Lizbete's heart as she thought of disappearing into the dark kitchen, away from other people. Was it her cave? After all, wasn't it unnatural for a human to prefer the dim, smoky kitchen to the lively, well-lit common room filled with laughter and companionship? And she was human.

I'm human. I'm human and nothing else.

"Can I eat out here?"

Auntie Katryn blinked at her. "You want to?"

Lizbete's throat constricted, but she managed to nod.

A smile blossomed on Auntie's face. "A few outings with Brynar seems to have brought you out of your shell. I'm glad, Lil' Liz. You need to make more friends. Maybe at this rate you'll be willing to go to the First Frost."

Lizbete's shoulders hunched towards her ears. She almost rushed for the safety of the kitchen, but the pride glowing on Auntie's face held her in place.

"Small steps," she managed to squeak out. Auntie led her to an empty table near the bar. Resisting the urge to flee to a dark corner, Lizbete slipped into her seat. She could see Brynar and his father, though their backs were to her. Angled towards them, she managed to catch their voices over the general hubbub.

"Where were you all day?" Sten asked.

"Does it matter?" Brynar took up a tumbler from the bar. His father must have ordered him a drink already. "I made sure I wasn't needed before I left. Unless your schedule changed, you spent this afternoon playing *Fox and Hens* with Great Uncle Iver. Hardly something I was needed for. If you can take the time off to chat over a game with family, I can use the same time to pursue my own interests."

"Your own interests aren't necessarily in your best interests." Sten snorted and sipped his own drink.

"I think I'm old enough to make such decisions for myself, sir."

In spite of the obvious antagonism in his tone, Brynar's posture mirrored his father's. Their firm mouths had equal levels of determination. A smile quirked the corners of Lizbete's mouth. It was like watching two goats from the same herd banging their heads against each other.

"I actually did have a task for you today." Sten faced the crowd.

Afraid he'd see her looking, Lizbete shrunk in her seat. She needn't have worried. Sten quickly scanned the crowd, his gaze skipping over her as easily as he might ignore a pebble in the street. He focused on something behind her and beckoned.

Einar hurried through the crowd with another young person on his arm. A young woman. A *pretty* young woman.

While all the village girls were inarguably prettier than Lizbete, this girl made her feel like a lump of coal next to a lit candle. Her golden tresses fell down her back, and while she wore the same smock dress as most village girls, she'd embellished it with embroidery, sashes, and trim, all in a light blue that almost matched her eyes.

The blacksmith's daughter. Witta. While Lizbete knew her name and face, she had little more knowledge of the girl. Witta was a little older than her, maybe seventeen, but she was not a part of the aggressive clique of local young people who tormented Lizbete. No, the few times Lizbete specifically remembered seeing Witta, she'd been quietly going about her own business, at market with her mother or running errands for her father.

Even so, seeing her approach Brynar caused something petty and nasty to stir in Lizbete's gut, followed immediately by shame. Witta had never done anything to harm Lizbete. Why was Lizbete suddenly wishing to yank her flowing blonde hair from her head?

Brynar's brow furrowed as his brother and Witta approached him. Witta grinned and gave him a bobbing curtsy. "Hello! Did your father tell you about my ideas? I have so many ideas!"

Brynar's eyes darted from her to his father and back again, confused and slightly desperate. Lizbete's jealousy faded into bemused pity.

"Ideas for . . . ?"

Witta's smile faded. "Oh, you didn't tell him?"

"You spoke so eloquently on the matter this afternoon that I didn't wish to deprive you of the chance to make your case with equal fervency to my son." Sten smiled, a mischievous glint creeping into his eyes. "After all, you two will be planning and overseeing the First Frost Festival together this year."

A stone crashed into Lizbete's stomach.

Brynar dropped his tumbler. "We—we will?"

Sten straightened his posture and stepped away from the bar. "It's time you started taking on some actual responsibility in this village, Son. The First Frost is an important yearly tradition, but, as this charming young woman pointed out to me today, there are many ways it could be improved upon. I'll let her expound upon that. If you will excuse me and your brother—" He nodded mean-ingfully to Einar. "You and Witta will have much to discuss."

Brynar opened his mouth, shut it again, then scowled, and set-tled sulkily onto his bar stool as his father and brother drifted out of the tavern.

His father played him as well as the pieces in his Fox and Hen *matches,* Lizbete noted. *Brynar's no pushover, though. He won't let this girl—*

"I'm so glad we're finally getting to talk!" Witta scrambled on top of the barstool that Sten had abandoned. "I got a little carried away, talking to your father about all my ideas for the First Frost. You see, every year, we basically do the same thing, and it's won-derful. I would never disrespect the time-honored traditions of the First Frost. Still, there are things we could do that would make it so so so much better!"

"Here you go, Lil' Liz."

Lizbete gasped and jumped. Her chair wobbled, and she just managed to brace her feet against the floor to stop it from toppling over, taking her with it.

"Easy!" Auntie Katryn slammed a bowl of steaming stew onto the table then whirled and grabbed Lizbete by the shoulders. Brown gravy splashed across the tabletop.

"I'm fine!" Lizbete gasped. "You just startled me."

Auntie tilted her head. "Are you sure? You look . . . off."

"I'm fine," Lizbete repeated.

Her stupid, sensitive ears, however, could hear Witta chattering like a perky songbird.

"I would love to make it a masked ball. They have those in the royal court, and everything I've read about them sounds so brilliant! Can you imagine? A dance, but with everyone wearing fancy masks.

You wouldn't know who you are dancing with, and in a town as small as ours? Oh, that would be so mysterious…"

Lizbete picked up her spoon and loudly slurped a bite of stew.

Masks are silly. The First Frost is silly. People are silly.

Oh, I wish I were back in that cave.

Chapter Seven

Lizbete slipped through the side door and braced herself against the smack of cold, salty sea breeze. A quiet wailing echoed through the streets of Brumehome. Overhead, dark clouds hovered over the city like a tavern patron in a bad mood, just waiting for Lizbete to spill a drink so he could explode in a storm of anger.

Across the narrow pathway, the hens clucked anxiously in their coop. Always thinking of how she could make life easier for helpless creatures under her care, Auntie Katryn had built the chicken coop over a small steamvent. Even when the weather turned freezing, the birds would be toasty warm.

Lizbete took the feed bucket from its hook and filled it with grain for the restless fowls. Hopefully the coming storm wouldn't disrupt their laying. Her limbs stiffened, and she hugged herself as best she could while still holding the feed bucket. Even the smelly coop would be preferable to this chill.

She crossed to the door and set the bucket down to deal with the latch. A rash of fox and stoat sightings had prompted Auntie to tie the door shut with rough twine, besides depending the wooden latch. Lizbete's cold fingers fumbled with the knots. Finally, she managed to undo the last one.

The wind died down for a moment. A faint scratching jerked Lizbete's head in the direction of the back alley. She stared into the shadows.

Nothing.

The wind gusted with an even louder howl. She shook her head and entered the coop.

After dumping out the feed, she went over the remaining chicken-care tasks. Their water was still full and clean, and while stinking, their bedding could go a few more days before replacement. She plucked the five eggs, still warm to the touch, from the laying boxes and settled them carefully in the empty feed bucket, then did a head count.

"Grayfeather, Sharpbeak, Redwing, Scratcher—" She named each hen in turn. Wait, where was Clucky? She did another count. Eight hens, one rooster.

Yep. They were short one. She swallowed. The doors were all shut. The bedding was undisturbed, showing no signs that a predator had burrowed in from the outside. Her spectacles slipped down her nose, and she pushed them back up, blinking at the chickens as if the missing one might magically appear amongst them. Had Clucky even been inside the night before? Thinking back, Lizbete remembered doing a headcount before locking them in for the night. Clucky had definitely been among them, her coal black feathers gleaming in the light of the lantern as Lizbete bid all the fowls good night and refilled their water.

But if that were the case, what had happened to the hen?

Throat tightening as she thought about giving Auntie Katryn the bad news about Clucky's disappearance, Lizbete exited the hen-house. Her toe kicked at something that clattered across the cobblestones noisily enough to draw her attention.

A bright blue sphere about the size of a large onion rolled away from her. Almost dropping the bucket of eggs, she stooped and caught it before it escaped. It weighed heavily in her hands, shining brightly. Stone, polished to a mirror-like luster. Dark and light blues swirled upon its surface.

She looked around. It didn't seem to be the sort of thing someone would drop without noticing, even if someone had passed by in the short time she'd been inside.

"Hello?" she called out.

The wind carried away her voice. Placing the egg bucket on the ground, she clutched the lovely stone to her chest. Unlike the crystal she'd found for Brynar the day before, there was no strange, magical energy in this stone. It felt cool to the touch, smooth as glass, but mundane. Still, the strangeness of its appearance troubled her. She almost dropped it and ran.

No, that's silly. It's just a stone. It was probably already there when I went into the coop. I just didn't notice it. It's nothing strange. Nothing supernatural. Just a pretty stone.

But what if it had been left for her? Some gift? Her hold on it tightened. She loved presents, but got them rarely. This couldn't be for her. Oh, but she wanted it to be for her. Her mind spun, trying to figure out how it could be for her and who it could be from. Auntie wouldn't just leave a gift in the street, but Elin might. Yes, sneaking up on Lizbete and leaving something that would puzzle her but also please her was a very Elin thing to do. That had to be it.

"Elin?" Lizbete cupped her free hand around her mouth. "Elin, are you hiding back there?"

No one responded, but Elin wouldn't likely give up her prank that easily.

"Thank you!" Lizbete picked up her bucket again and entered the tavern.

Returning to the kitchen, she set the eggs in a basket before heading to the common room to search out Auntie Katryn. She pushed through the swinging doors and froze in her tracks.

Witta, the pristine blonde beauty, leaned across the bar, chattering merrily at Auntie Katryn. The tavern owner stood in bemused silence, rubbing down tumblers with a damp cloth.

"So that's what we'll be needing." Witta paused for a breath and poked a rolled-up piece of paper at Auntie.

Auntie shied away from the paper as if it had been a hot poker. "I don't see what is wrong with the fish fry we've always done for the First Frost. I was under the impression everyone liked it."

"Oh, of course! We love your fish fry, Miss Katryn." Witta's cheeks reddened. "I didn't mean to suggest that it was in any way wanting."

"It's not wanting, but you don't want it?"

Lizbete grimaced as she watched the thoughts churning in Auntie's brain, like milk about to thicken to cream. Auntie had always been proud of her fish fry. It was one of the selling points she'd used when trying to convince Lizbete to attend the infamous First Frost.

"Ah, you see, this year we are doing everything on *theme* and a fish fry is just . . . it's not." Witta ended firmly. "So if we could do the fruit pies and the roasted cliffpigeons instead?"

Auntie's eyes clouded over slightly. "But the whole village shows up for the First Frost. That would be—"

"My estimate is that we'll need roughly four hundred cliffpigeons, just in case people want seconds or some of them burn," Witta plowed forward. "I've already spoken to the local hunters about how many they'll need to bring in, and I can get children to do the plucking."

Lizbete sank against the doorframe, still clutching her found treasure. Witta certainly was a gale-strength wind, determined to drive everyone before her. How would poor, easygoing Brynar manage against her tenacity? The thought twisted Lizbete's stomach.

Well, Brynar could look after himself. On the other hand, Auntie Katryn was Lizbete's responsibility. She took a determined step forward.

The door to the tavern swung open, and as if summoned by her thoughts, Brynar strode in, grinning. However, when his gaze fell upon Witta, his bottom lip went slack.

She glanced over her shoulder and did a double take, then rushed to him, her smile radiant. Lizbete's hold tightened around her blue sphere.

"Just the person I was going to see next!" Witta clapped her hands. "Did you get a chance to look at the drawings I made of the decorations?"

"Um, yeah." He shifted from foot to foot. "They look great." Elin, who had been hiding in Brynar's shadow, stepped around her brother and wrinkled her nose

"He's lying. He didn't look. He doesn't know decorative table-cloths from nose-rags, so it wouldn't matter anyway."

Witta's face fell. "Oh."

"That's not true!" Brynar burst out. "I mean . . . the part about me not really knowing anything about decorations, sure. I don't, but I did look." He rubbed at the back of his neck. "I'm sure whatever you want to do is fine. Just let me know if you need help setting them up."

"But we're working on this together. I want you to be happy too.

This is a partnership." Witta's bottom lip quivered ever so slightly.

Lizbete imagined herself hurling her blue sphere in the general direction of the young woman's stupid pout.

"Is there something wrong with your lip?" Elin tilted her head all the way to one side. "You got a tic?"

Witta recoiled. "I—"

"Elin." Brynar used his warning tone.

"Oh, look! It's Lizbete!" Elin said brightly. She pushed past Witta and hurried to Lizbete. She pointed to the sphere. "What's that? It's pretty. Looks heavy enough to smash a skull with, too."

Witta paled.

Lizbete chuckled awkwardly. "You mean you didn't give—?" Or she did and this act was just part of the gag. Lizbete forced a confident smile. "Oh, this old thing? I just found it lying around."

Elin squinted at her. "Huh."

Lizbete considered Elin. The girl's face had a healthy color, not the pallor of weariness nor the shine of fever. "You look well."

"I feel well." Elin beamed. "Thanks to you and Brynar."

Witta's brow furrowed. She continued to address Brynar as if Lizbete wasn't even there. "I was hoping we could talk some more about the plans for the festival, but if it's a bad time. . ."

"It's a bad time," Elin said.

Witta recoiled, then glared at the girl.

"Actually, hold on." Auntie Katryn bustled around the bar and across the table room before disappearing into the kitchen. She emerged a moment later carrying a basket. "If you would be a dear and take these to your mother for me. I heard she was abed with a headache recently."

"Last week." Witta frowned. "She's fine—"

"Oh, but with these tartberry muffins she'll be so much better."

Auntie thrust the basket at Witta. "If you hurry, they'll still be warm when she gets them."

Witta opened her mouth, shut it again, then nodded. "She'll be happy to have them. Thank you, Miss Katryn." She glanced at Brynar. "We'll see each other soon? We have much to discuss."

"I'll make the time," Brynar promised.

Witta took the basket and swept from the room.

"Determined little thing." Auntie clicked her tongue.

Lizbete frowned at her guardian. "I thought those tartberry muffins were for Falla and her children."

"We can always bake more." Auntie shrugged. "That girl talked my ear off for half the morning about her menu for the First Frost, and I could tell she was just as eager to get her claws into Brynar. Also, I sensed Brynar and you have business." A faint smile crept across Auntie's lips only for her to wince and put her hand to her chest. "Woof! I'm short of breath again. If you young folk are all right without me, I'm going to put my feet up for a bit." She left the common room for a small side room that was sometimes used as a private dining room for meetings and parties.

Once Auntie was gone, Lizbete focused on Elin. "So, you're feeling better today?"

"Excellent. Thanks to this." Elin reached under her smock and pulled out the red crystal. Someone, probably Brynar, had crudely wrapped it in wire so that it could be hung from a chain around her neck. It glowed with a subtle light, like a coal in a dying fire. Lizbete pushed her spectacles back up her nose and squinted at it. She'd remembered it being brighter, but maybe that was just because she'd last seen it in a dark cave rather than a well-lit room.

Brow furrowed, Brynar pulled up two chairs in front of the fire. He motioned to one for Lizbete. She settled into it, holding her blue sphere in her lap. Her gaze, however, never left the crystal. A gentle humming energy rose from it, even over a few feet of distance. Still, the pulsing power wasn't as strong as she thought it had been in the cave.

"I wasn't sure how to administer a crystal as a cure, but I wanted to start right away, so I just decided to put it directly on her skin," Brynar said. "It worked almost immediately. Her fever broke, and she slept through the night like a baby."

"No, like a young woman who was very tired." Elin wrinkled her nose at him. "I'm not a baby."

"It's just an expression." He rolled his eyes. "The point is, you're normally a fitful sleeper. You're awake a lot, having bad dreams, unable to settle. Last night, you weren't."

"And this morning, I have all the energy!" Elin stretched her arms out wide and spun in a circle. She bumped into a nearby table.

"Maybe a little too much." Lizbete smirked.

Elin grimaced. "Nah, just the right amount." She began a skipping dance, hopping first on one foot, then the other, intentionally bumping into every table in the living room as she went.

Brynar took the chair opposite Lizbete. He tapped his fingers against his knee, a faraway look in his eyes. "I'm just glad to see her feeling better, even if it does mean she's running me ragged."

Lizbete chuckled. Seeing Elin with energy again was definitely encouraging.

He drew a deep breath. "Elin, do you mind if I talk to Liz alone for a while?"

Elin paused mid-hop. "Why'd you ask me to come with you if you were going to send me away?" Lizbete stopped herself from vocally agreeing with Elin. It did seem strange, but Brynar had been strange lately. He'd been hanging around her when he had better things to do, and arguing with his father who he'd always respected. Requesting a secret meeting with the local Ash Lizard wasn't that much odder for him.

He tilted his head like a begging puppy. "Please? I won't be long. I'll catch up with you before you reach home."

She pointed an accusing finger at him. "You're plotting to murder me together, aren't you?"

"Don't be ridiculous," Lizbete said. "We only plot murders under the cover of darkness. It's much too bright here."

"Hmph." Elin tossed her dark hair. "Well, I'm watching you . . . both of you." She then spun on her heel and pranced out the door.

Lizbete chuckled. The improvement of her health had also increased her attitude, and unlike her physical strength, the strength of the girl's sass had never been wanting.

She then focused on Brynar. "She's right, though. Why'd bring her if you didn't want her here?"

He sighed. "Two reasons. First, I wanted you to see that she was better. Second, I wanted you to get a look at the crystal without separating her from it when it's obviously doing her so much good." Wrinkles of worry formed around his clear blue eyes. "But it's dimming already. I noticed this morning that it didn't shine as brightly as it did the night before. What if it loses its potency and stops helping her?"

Lizbete tightened her hold on her sphere. "Then we go back and get another crystal. If there's one, there's bound to be more."

"Yes, but it took so long just to find this one, and if they only last a few days..." He shook his head. "What if I only found a temporary solution rather than a permanent cure?"

"You give up too easily." Lizbete reached for his hand without thinking. When her fingers brushed his wrist, warmth leaped into her blood, bringing with it that tantalizing taste of him. She jerked away as if burnt.

His eyes widened. He stared at her hand, following it with his gaze as she hid it behind her back.

Her stomach twisted. Had he felt her stealing from him? Would he say anything? She forced a calm tone, hoping he wouldn't question what had just happened. "We'll figure this out. Nothing you've tried before has had such an immediate or obvious result. You're almost to the finish line, Brynar. Don't give up and go home because of a few bumps in the path."

"Yeah, I know." He rubbed his forehead. "Things have just been . . . ah, I'm not going to bore you with my family drama."

"Because my life is so exciting in contrast." She forced a laugh. She would've loved to have a family to have drama with. Well, Auntie was family, but the woman had as much sense of drama as a bowl of porridge. "I'd be happy to go into the caves to look for more crystals for you. You wouldn't even have to come with me." After all, the caves were warm, dark, and quiet—if a little scary.

"I couldn't ask that of you." With a sad smile, he stood. "Though I wouldn't mind going together again sometime. I want to see how long this crystal lasts. It'll give me an idea of how many we need to collect and how sustainable this cure is in the long run." He glanced at the door. "I really should go after Elin, but I'm half afraid that Witta will be lying in wait."

"Like a fox waiting to spring upon you with table setting options." Lizbete gave an exaggerated shudder. She put her sphere on the table. It balanced perfectly, not rolling off the table as she had feared.

He laughed. "Yeah, exactly like that. Speaking of which, have you given any more thought to attending the First Frost with me?"

Her heart dropped into her stomach. "*With* you?" Was he asking her to go with him . . . as an escort? A First Frost invite was usually something exchanged between courting couples. Even the most flirtatious of the village boys would simply ask their favorites if they'd save them a dance, not if they'd go *with* them.

"Yes. I mean, we did agree you'd need protection, didn't we?" His eyes earnestly searched her face. "If you want me to, I'd be willing."

Embarrassment flooded her. No, he didn't mean it that way. It was an offer of security, not affection. How could she have even let herself think that the most desirable young man in the village would consider her as a romantic interest?

"Actually, I thought I said that I couldn't always count on you to protect me so I needed to learn to stand up for myself." She stood and crossed her arms, faking what she hoped was a defiant scowl.

A mischievous smile quirked his lips. "So you're going to escort yourself then? That pleases me almost as much. Just so long as you're there."

She gaped at him. "That wasn't what I—"

The ground rippled beneath her. She froze.

Brynar's eyes widened. "What was—"

The floor of the tavern trembled. Lizbete yelped and toppled into Brynar, who was also wobbling on his feet. Her sphere rolled from the table with a great bang. The walls vibrated. Crockery crashed in the kitchen. Auntie's shriek pierced Lizbete's ears along with distant echoes of screams from outside the tavern. The urge to run to her guardian grabbed Lizbete by the throat, but she couldn't get her footing on the undulating floor. Brynar gripped her harder, and somehow they managed to stay upright.

The world vibrated. Chaos assaulted Lizbete's ears: crashing, shouting, grinding of stone against stone—and within it all a hissing voice that shivered through her like cold water. Something alive, something angry, something hungry and demanding and unassailable. She whimpered. Her fingers clutched at Brynar's shirt.

Then it stopped.

Brynar clutched her closer, his chest rising and falling unevenly. His heart pounded in her ears.

"Are you all right?" he stammered.

Still too overwhelmed to speak, she managed to nod. Her grip on him tightened, helping her fight her fear. His warmth seeped into her. The realization that her blood was stealing from him shook Lizbete out of her terror, and she pulled away from him, gasping for breath. Disappointment crossed his face.

She shuddered. "What was that?"

He glanced around the room. "An earthquake. I've heard of them, even experienced one when I was five or so, but not that strong." He let out a whistling breath. "I don't think there is any major damage, but we should—"

Lizbete suddenly remembered the cries she'd heard during the quake. One cry in particular.

"Auntie!" She bolted for the door to the kitchen.

Pushing through, she skidded to a halt. Crockery and pans littered the floor. Apples rolled across the ground and Auntie . . . Auntie huddled beside the fireplace, gripping her chest with both hands, her face pinched in pain.

"Auntie!" Lizbete wailed, rushing to her side.

She collapsed next to her guardian. Sweat beaded the older woman's brow, though when Lizbete chanced to brush her hand across Auntie's cheek, she felt cold to the touch. "Auntie Katryn?" she whimpered

Auntie pried one open. "My chest hurts. The tavern—it shook. I thought it would fall down upon us." She inhaled sharply. "I can't breathe!"

Brynar's feet pounded across the kitchen floor before he knelt beside them. "Easy! Take deep breaths."

Lizbete swallowed, wanting to embrace Auntie, but knowing if she did, she risked drawing away her warmth. Well, if her blood had a better source to pull from, it might not take from Auntie.

Hoping Brynar didn't notice, Lizbete sneaked the fingers of one hand into the coals of the fireplace. The fire rushed into her like a gulp of wine. She wrapped her other arm around Auntie's waist and pulled her closer. The woman's bulky frame barely moved, so Lizbete slid nearer to her instead.

"I'll be fine, Lil' Liz," Auntie murmured, her words slurring as if she'd been drinking. "I was just frightened. It's over now. We'll all be okay."

Something banged in the common room behind them. "Katryn? Are you in here?"

Hangur. Lizbete winced. What did that waste of space want?

"She's in here, Uncle!" Brynar called out. "I need help moving her."

Hangur rushed in, eyes wide. Between him and Brynar, they managed to pick up Auntie Katryn and carry her out of the room. Lizbete shuffled behind them, afraid to get in the way but not wanting Auntie to leave her sight.

"I'll be . . . fine," Auntie huffed, her voice tight. "The quake just startled me, is all. I'm out of breath is all . . . Ouch."

"You need to lie down."

The men started up the narrow staircase, angling to the side with Auntie in between them, towards the bedrooms. Lizbete hung back.

Skywatcher, let her be all right. Let Auntie be all right. If I lose her, I have nobody.

Brynar jogged down the stairs, his face drawn.

Lizbete clutched at his sleeve. "Is she all right? Should we get someone to help? Maybe Widow Gri?"

Brynar sighed. "She's resting. Hangur's with her."

Lizbete started. "What good will Hangur do her?" Hangur was worse than useless. His incompetence might stress Auntie further and then—and then— Lizbete didn't want to think of it.

"He's a person who can watch over her and let me or someone else know if something happens." Brynar brushed his hand across his forehead. "I need to get Widow Gri, but I also need to make sure Elin got home safely and that no one else got hurt."

"I can get Widow Gri," Lizbete burst out. The walk would be cold, but she could make it. She'd just have to hurry so she reached her destination before her muscles seized from the cold.

"That would be a big help." He removed his coat and draped it about her shoulders.

She stiffened. Was he starting to piece together her "difficulties"?

"It's cold out. Fetching Widow Gri is important, but be careful on the path, all right? Don't take risks in your hurry. I don't want you getting hurt, especially if another quake hits."

Her tongue stuck to the roof of her mouth, but she managed to nod.

Gripping his coat tight about her, she rushed across the common room and out the door.

Chapter Eight

The whole of Brumehome looked as if a herd of wild oxen had run through it. All the structures on Lizbete's route appeared to be standing, but many showed obvious damage. Barrels and crates were toppled. Wares from market stands rolled about on the cobblestones.

Villagers stood in the street, clumping in small groups to talk over what had happened or staring at their homes and businesses, assessing potential repairs. None gave Lizbete a second glance as she darted through the streets.

By the time Liz reached the edge of town, her chest ached and her pulse pounded. She couldn't slow down, though. Every second counted, for she was racing both against potential ill befalling Auntie Katryn and her own fleeing heat. She made the path up the cliff face at a sprint. About halfway up, her pace began to flag. Her legs grew heavy, and picking her feet off the ground seemed to cost a great deal of strength. Pausing, she drew several deep breaths.

I can't stop now. Brynar and Auntie are depending on me.

She crested the top of the path and crowed in triumph. As if in response, a frigid sea breeze slapped her in the face. She whimpered as the clouds opened up, and rain poured from the heavens. Lizbete winced. In her terror over the earthquake and Auntie's health, she'd forgotten the approaching storm. Now it was here, and she was stuck out in it.

The cold air bit at her. It snaked through her body and chilled her blood. Her legs cramped, and she fell to her knees. She'd almost gotten there. She couldn't give up now.

Drawing on the last of her strength, she pushed herself to her feet and ran—or shambled quickly—down the path. The rain blinded her. She had to trust to her feet, feeling for the mud of the path rather than grass beneath her, to keep her way. Finally, the lump in the earth that was the widow's pit-house loomed before her.

She collapsed against the door and coughed out, "Widow Gri? Please, let me in."

The door popped open. Lizbete fell forward into the warm, smoky interior of the pit-house.

"Lizbete?" Widow Gri gasped. She grabbed Lizbete around the chest and pulled her into the house, towards the fire. Lizbete's blood drew in the widow's heat like a parched man gulping water. This time the warmth brought with it the taste of determination and worry.

"Let me go!" Lizbete gasped. Widow Gri ignored her. With a great push, she settled Lizbete into a chair beside the hearth then withdrew, teeth chattering. Lizbete hung her head. She'd taken so much so quickly. Would Widow Gri say anything?

"What dragged you up here in this weather, on your own?" the widow asked. "It must be urgent for you to risk freezing like this. Does it have something to do with that tremor we had a bit ago?"

"Yes. No. Sort of." Lizbete took a deep breath. "Auntie collapsed after the quake. She had trouble breathing and said her chest hurt. We got her into bed, but I'm worried."

Widow Gri's wrinkles deepened. "Ah, not good. I've seen how she huffs and puffs around the market. She can't handle that sort of shock to her system." Her mouth wrinkled. "I think I have some things that might help. Stay here. Thaw."

Lizbete cringed. Even if Widow Gri wasn't going to make an issue of her taking the heat, it was obvious she knew something about Lizbete's condition.

The widow bustled about the house, placing various jars and small pouches into a basket. At last, she gave a satisfied nod before taking a hooded cloak from a hook by the door and turning to face Lizbete. "Stay here. Don't try and go out until the storm has stopped."

A lump formed in Lizbete's throat. "But Auntie—"

"You freezing to death won't do her any good. There's kindling in a chest in the back corner and some food in the cabinet. Treat yourself to whatever you like, but stay warm and stay inside, understand me?" The widow wagged a finger at her.

Lizbete's heart sank, but she nodded.

With that, Widow Gri left, slamming the door behind her.

The wind whistled over the tiny pit-house, but the merry crackling of the fire combatted the eerie silence.

Still, with the storm raging outside and Lizbete's blood only just beginning to thaw, the cozy cottage might as well have been a cage, something she couldn't escape to return to her loved ones. She rubbed her arms. The motion eased the cramps in her tight muscles. To speed her warming, she stuck her hand into the fire. Normally she avoided this. It was just too strange, too . . . inhuman.

But maybe I'm not human. Widow Gri certainly seems to think I'm not, and now even Brynar suspects something. Does Auntie know what I am? Or does she at least know that I'm not human?

She sifted the hot coals in the fireplace between her fingers. They did little more damage to her than a splash of scalding water would, which was to say none at all. A temporary sting then her blood wicked away the excess heat and spread it throughout her body.

Auntie had never treated Lizbete as anything but a normal girl—all right, that wasn't completely true. She was more protective of her than she might've been had Lizbete not had her strange propensities. She also was always firm in that Lizbete needed to keep her heat stealing and fire resistance to herself. So at least to that extent, Auntie did realize that there was something not quite right with her charge, no matter how much she loved her.

If something happens to her, if she doesn't get better, I'll be so alone.

Sure, Brynar might *want* to help her, but his family would never let him stay with her or her with them. Lizbete didn't think she could keep up the tavern on her own.

"Oh, Skywatcher, what am I going to do?" she whispered to the silence. "Where did I even come from? Could I go back there?"

Finally warm, she stood and crossed to the door. Cold air seeped from around the door frame. The door shuddered as another gust of wind shook it, and hard raindrops pelted against the roof of the cottage like thrown pebbles. In fact, from the sound, the rain might've turned to sleet and ice. Lizbete winced. She'd never make it through that. Her only hope really was to wait until it let up and pray that Auntie would be all right.

Resigned to waiting, she settled back into the chair by the fire and closed her eyes.

Almost immediately, a faint scratching caught her ears, barely audible over the howling of the gale. Her eyes snapped open, and her head jerked in the direction of the noise.

The door?

She sat still. What was that? Had she imagined it?

The sound repeated, louder.

Was someone—or something—out there? In this weather?

"Hello?" she called out.

The noise stopped as suddenly as it had started.

The hair on the back of her neck prickled. The noise had stopped when she spoke. If it were just the wind, it wouldn't have done that, but if it were a person with good intent, why wouldn't whoever it was answer her?

Her heart pounded painfully. An animal? A fox or a stoat wouldn't be out in such a storm. No, it would need to be a bigger, sturdier animal. A bear?

Bears rarely came this close to human settlements. Lizbete had never seen one, but she'd heard stories of their size and ferocity. A storm would be nothing to a bear. No, not a bear. She wouldn't believe it was a bear. Something friendlier and small enough to be spooked by her shout. A lost dog? Yes, that could be it.

But what if it wasn't…

She shrank in on herself. Tales of dark spirits and bloodthirsty monsters sprang to mind, hideous fiends that roamed the frozen plains of the In-Lands searching for hot blood to drink.

"My blood is cold," she murmured to herself. *Of course, a beast won't know that until after it's spilled it.*

No. Monsters weren't real. There were no dangerous beasts this close to Brumehome. It was only the wind. Nothing more.

But if I don't look I'll never know, and I'll only keep imagining the worst.

With a deep breath, she crossed the room, set her hand to the latch, and yanked the door open. Thunder cracked, and she cowered against the doorframe.

An unearthly purple sky greeted her. Dark clouds and driving rain cast the world in deep shadow. The foolishness of her own plan struck Lizbete immediately. It was too dark to see clearly beyond a foot. Already raindrops splattered her spectacles, further obscuring her vision. Anything could be lurking within arm's length, and she wouldn't know it.

A flash of lightning split the sky, and in the white of the flash, something glinted on the doorstep.

Without thinking, she scooped it up and slammed the door shut behind her.

Water dripped from her. Cold water. She sprinted to the fire and stuck her empty hand into the flame. Only then did she glance down at the object she'd retrieved. It was a crystal. Not one of the magical red crystals that had been so helpful to Elin, but still beautiful, pure as ice and radiating dozens of perfect points like light shining from a star. Her throat tightened.

Someone had left it there.

For the widow? But if so, why hadn't they knocked?

Her mind flew back to the blue sphere. She'd assumed that was from Elin, but this . . . no. It had to be a coincidence. Maybe it had fallen out of Widow Gri's pocket. It was just the sort of thing the strange old woman would be carrying with her. That was it. Just dropped from the old woman's pocket.

Lizbete placed it on the ring of bricks surrounding the hearth. The crystal caught the orange light from the fire and refracted it around the room. Twinkling lights danced upon the low ceiling. Lizbete stared at the crystal in amazement. It was so beautiful. Like nothing she'd ever seen before.

The rain continued its constant beat over her head as the fire crackled and the crystal lights danced. With nothing she could do and in a place of calm, Lizbete found her eyelids drooping. One hand still in the fire, she closed her eyes and drifted off to sleep.

Chapter Nine

"Up, Spirit Girl! Up!" Someone shook Lizbete.

She awoke with a gasp.

Light flooded into the pit-house from the open door, silhouetting the looming figure of Widow Gri. The older woman squinted down at her.

The memories of the earthquake, of Auntie Katryn's episode, and her long, cold run to the widow's house jolted through Lizbete. She leaped out of her chair.

"Auntie Katryn?"

"She's resting. Exhausted but stable for now."

Relief flooded through Lizbete, weakening her knees. "Thank you."

"She's not out of the blizzard yet. She needs to rest, avoid stress, and drink the teas I left her for the pain in her chest." Widow Gri tossed a log on the fire which had died to a few coals since—how long had Lizbete been asleep?

Glancing through the opened door she tried to get her bearings on the sun. Her throat tightened. "Is it morning?"

"Yes. I stayed with her all night—and it stormed most of the night as well." Widow Gri fed some dried grass to the seedling flames, which roared up to consume the fuel. She reached for her kettle which sat beside the hearth, but paused mid-motion.

"What's that?" She nodded at something sitting beside the growing flames. Lizbete's crystal.

Her mouth suddenly dry, Lizbete stared at the lovely object. "I found it on the doorstep. I thought you must've dropped it."

"I've never seen it before." Widow Gri shook her head.

"Oh." Lizbete's stomach twisted. "Maybe someone left it there for you?"

Again the widow shook her head, wrinkles deepening across her face. "No. I have a feeling this is meant for you." She took Lizbete by the wrist, forcing her hand out, and placed the crystal in her palm. "I'm not sure what it means, but I'd keep it secret for now. Just until things calm down around Brumehome."

"Calm down?" Lizbete stammered. "How so?"

The widow sighed, crossed to the still open door, and closed it. She then turned to Lizbete, her expression grave and eerie in the firelight. "The townsfolk like to talk. Yesterday we had an earthquake, a storm, and the sudden illness of an important community member. Such misfortune over such a short time period has them looking for a cause, something—or someone—to blame."

Lizbete's breath left her. "But none of those things could be caused by a person."

"A human person, no." Widow Gri's lips quirked in a wry smile.

Lizbete's stomach flip flopped.

I'm human.

I'm at least not not *human. I can't be.*

Widow Gri gripped her shoulder. Lizbete tried to jerk away,

but the old woman's grasp was surprisingly strong. "Keep your head down and your ears open. Also, here—" Widow Gri released her and walked to the back of the room. A moment later she returned carrying a small tin pail which she filled with coals from the fireplace. She held it out to Lizbete by the handle. Heat rose off the metal. "Carry this with you down the cliff path. It'll stop you from freezing up, but be sure to dump it before you come in sight of the village. You don't want to do anything that might draw attention to you, all right?"

"All right." Lizbete nodded, trying to ignore the lump in her throat.

"Good." Widow Gri gave a curt nod. "I don't know what you are, girl, but whatever it is, I don't think it is an evil thing. I don't think you mean to hurt anyone."

"I don't!" Lizbete burst out. "I would never. I'm not dangerous. I swear."

Widow Gri chuckled. "Oh, I wouldn't say that. I wouldn't say that at all."

With the widow's bucket of coals cradled close to her chest, the walk back to Brumehome didn't feel quite so draining. By the time she reached the bottom of the cliff, the coals had died to cold black lumps, all their heat absorbed into Lizbete's body. She dumped them on the side of the path and sprinted the last leg of the walk.

As she entered the village, her pace flagged. Debris littered the usually neat pathways of Brumehome. Men on ladders worked to hurried patch damaged roofs, and children chased after loose chickens. The storm had hit the already shaken town hard.

In spite of Widow Gri's worries, no one gave Lizbete a second look. She reached the tavern and slipped inside.

She stopped short.

Hangur sat at the bar, flagon in hand, a hazy look in his eyes—more so than usual. A bottle stood next to him . . . with another toppled on its side, apparently empty, next to it.

Lizbete scowled. Her Auntie was sick, and this fool was drinking away her stock of burning wine.

Hangur's gaze fell on her. He flushed, then scowled. "So, you're finally back."

"Yes." She crossed her arms. Should she berate him for his debauchery? It most likely wouldn't do any good, and he wouldn't like it—oh, but she so wanted to give him an earful. "It's not even midday. Should you really be drinking now? With Auntie ill abed and so much to do?"

Rage contorted his features.

Panic spiked in Lizbete's chest as he lurched to his feet. He extended a shaking finger in her direction.

"Don't you lecture me, you worthless girl!" he slurred. "You ran off, disappeared. I've been here all on my own, patching up, cleaning up, working while worried out of my mind about my poor sister." He staggered towards her. Lizbete quailed back. While a wastrel, Hangur boasted his family's impressive physique, as tall as Brynar and as broad-shouldered as Mayor Sten. Even drunk out of his mind, he was an imposing figure, perhaps more so as Lizbete wasn't sure what he'd do or if he'd have the good sense not to murder her.

She braced herself against the wall. "You need to calm down."

"No! I won't." He loomed over her, the stench of sour liquor and unwashed man nauseating. Her stomach churned. "How dare you begrudge me a drink when all you've ever done is leach off my family? My sister's home is my home, and you will not sass me beneath my own roof—"

His hand clenched into a fist which he brandished beneath her nose.

Heart in her throat, Lizbete grabbed him about the wrist. Heat rushed from him to her with a wave of dizzying senselessness. Her head swam. He stared at her, wide-eyed then fell back, teeth chattering, lips blue.

Horror stole Lizbete's voice. What had she done?

"What did you do to me, you little witch?"

Footsteps pounded on the staircase that linked the common room to the upstairs bedroom.

"Uncle Hangur! Stop it!" Brynar burst into the room.

Hangur whirled about to face him, lost his balance, and crashed into a table. Brynar half-sprinted, half-leaped across the common room and skidded to a halt between Lizbete and Hangur.

"Don't you touch her," he growled.

Hangur gawped at his nephew. Drops of spittle clung to his beard, further sickening Lizbete.

"She—she did something to me!" he spluttered.

Brynar crossed his arms. "The young woman who isn't even half your size did something to you?"

"She . . . she's a witch! She has foul powers!" Hangur squared his shoulders, or tried to. He still swayed like a man crossing a ship's deck in a storm.

"You're drunk," Brynar said simply. "Go lie down and sleep it off before you embarrass yourself further.

Hangur's nostrils flared. "Don't you sass me, boy. I spent all night with your aunt—"

"I know. I was here too, but that doesn't excuse—"

"But where was she?" Hangur jabbed his finger at Lizbete who shied behind Brynar again. "Chaos breaks out, the woman who has raised her, took her in when no one else wanted her cursed presence, nearly dies, and where does she go?"

"I went to get help!" she squeaked out, somehow finding her voice again. "I went to get Widow Gri."

"Aye, but Widow Gri came yesterday, and you just mosey on in here now, mid-morning. Where were you? Why didn't you come back with the widow?"

Lizbete's teeth clenched. She couldn't tell the truth, but there was no excuse she could give that wouldn't make her sound awful or be an obvious lie. She'd fallen asleep? She'd lost her way? No, all of that would be nonsense. The truth was Auntie Katryn had needed her, and she hadn't been there.

Her heart shattered and she darted around Brynar and up the stairs.

"Liz!" Brynar shouted.

She didn't look back. She rushed into her bedroom and slammed the door.

His footsteps crashed after her but slowed as he approached her room before stopping altogether. Lizbete sank to the floor sobbing, head in her hands.

"Liz?" his voice called gently through the door.

She held her breath, willing herself silent. She didn't want him to hear her cry.

"Can I come in?" he pressed.

Lizbete closed her eyes. Yes, she wanted him to come in. She wanted to throw her arms around Brynar and hold on for dear life, to let him comfort her, so she wouldn't feel so alone. However, if she did, her blood would steal his heat. He'd notice. Even if it didn't hurt him irreparably, he'd notice, and he'd know. However, if she had to face him right now, the desire to embrace him would hurt too much. No, she needed to put a firm wall between them, to establish the distance, establish that she could care for herself.

After an anxious silence, he gave a great sigh. "I can't make you open that door, but Liz, I'm your friend. We both know the truth, all right. Don't take what Hangur said to heart. He's an idiot even when he isn't as full of alcohol as a wine-sopped sponge."

In spite of herself, she smiled.

Another long silence passed. "Look, I told Auntie I'd make sure the tavern continued to serve patrons. We're already too late to get food for the midday rush, but I want to be sure we serve dinner. If you need me, I'll be in the kitchen with Falla. She said she'd come in and help out until Auntie is better."

The floorboards creaked as he moved away from the door. A pang of agony shot through her.

"Thank you!" she burst out. He paused in his retreat. She wiped her nose on her sleeve then continued, "I'll be fine. Take care of Auntie's business. That's what matters."

"I will." Warmth returned to his tone. She wished she could absorb it from his words as well as his body. "I'll see you soon, Liz."

"You, too." Her voice came out harsh and reedy.

Brynar's footsteps faded down the stairs as Lizbete pressed herself against the door, longing to be near to him for as long as possible. She could hear muffled shouting as Brynar confronted Hangur again. Even though she hadn't wanted to get Brynar drawn into the drama between her and Hangur, she was glad he'd intervened, if only so that fool stopped drinking all of Auntie Katryn's best wine.

Weary-hearted, she cast an aimless glance around her room. Something shiny and blue caught her eye. Her sphere, the one she'd found outside the chicken coop, rested on the windowsill. Someone, probably Brynar, must've found it in the common room and brought it up to her bedroom. She reached into the pocket of her smock and pulled out the crystal from Widow Gri's doorstep. Turning it over in her hands a few times, she examined every spike, every glinting facet, of the beautiful discovery before rising and placing it next to the sphere.

Someone had to be leaving these treasures for her. The one outside the chicken coop could've been anyone in the village. The crystal left in the middle of a storm outside of an isolated pit-house—that one took a little more explaining.

It couldn't have been Elin. Her mother would never let her wander outside in weather like that. Brynar, likewise, would've been too busy with Auntie's care to do it. Auntie Katryn, of course, wasn't a possibility due to her sickness. Who else even liked Lizbete enough to give her presents? The only other person who was decently friendly with her was the widow. Could it have been her?

It would've been easy enough for the widow to plant the second crystal outside her own cottage and then pretend to know nothing when interrogated, but she couldn't have made the scratching noises that had drawn Lizbete's attention to the stone. Also, would she have been able to drop the sphere outside the chicken coop then make it back to her house before Lizbete arrived to find her? With part of the walk taking place during an earthquake? Maybe. But why?

Well, Lizbete wouldn't find the answers sitting in the bedroom. If she didn't want Hangur to be right about her, she needed to make herself useful. She could always find work to be done around the tavern, doubly now that Auntie was abed.

She left her bedroom and started down the hall. As she passed her auntie's bedroom, Lizbete paused. It wouldn't hurt to look in on her, if she were quiet and careful not to wake her. After everything that had gone wrong lately, she needed to see Auntie's face, to know that she was okay.

Lizbete eased the door open a notch. She could see the foot of Auntie's bed. She pushed the door open a little wider. The hinges gave a cringe-worthy squeak. Lizbete winced. She should back out now before—

"It's all right, Lil' Liz. I'm awake," Auntie's weary voice greeted her. "Bored out of my skull, but awake."

Lizbete stepped inside. Auntie lay, partially propped up on a mountain of pillows, her face wan and the wrinkles about her eyes deeper than ever. Lizbete came to hover awkwardly at her bedside.

"Are you feeling better?"

"Mostly." Auntie's eyes fell shut. "Widow Gri's teas seem to help, but they also make me sleepy, and I don't like that. There's so much that needs to be done."

"You need to rest!" Lizbete said quickly. "Brynar is here, and I'm here, and Falla is coming back to work."

"I suppose, but I don't like people being put out because of me."

"We want to help, though." Lizbete brushed her hand across Auntie's wrist, careful to keep the contact brief enough that she didn't steal her heat. "We all owe you so much."

"You've all repaid it in a multitude of ways." Auntie smiled faintly. "I suppose a day or two of rest won't close the tavern. Make sure Brynar doesn't overwork himself, or you. Also, that Falla doesn't stay away from her new babe for too long. If she needs to bring him into work, we'll figure that out. Wouldn't be the first time there was an infant in the tavern." Auntie chuckled.

Lizbete dropped her gaze to her feet. She'd been an infant in the tavern, sleeping next to the cooking fire to stay warm as Auntie bustled about. In the whole town only Auntie Katryn had been willing to risk taking in the strange foundling who may have killed a barn full of animals just by sleeping near them.

"I have something for you." Auntie wriggled into a seating position, bracing herself against the pillows behind her back. "I meant to give it to you closer to the First Frost, but now feels like the right time." She pointed towards the wardrobe in the corner. "In there. You'll see it when you open it."

Brow furrowed, Lizbete crossed to the wardrobe and opened the door. Her breath left her. Hanging from the back of the drawer was a sky-blue dress trimmed in ribbons and lace—real lace with delicate twists and knots. She glanced from it to her guardian and back again. "It's . . . beautiful."

Even as her heart swelled at the joy of the extravagant gift, a lump formed in her throat.

"It's for the First Frost. I had it specially made by Madam Yalyn. You'll be the best dressed girl at the festival." Pride lit Auntie Katryn's face, and for a moment she didn't look so tired.

Lizbete touched the fabric of the dress. It was soft, so much softer than her usual work smocks. She longed to try it on, to feel like a lovely lady, but she couldn't accept this. No, doing so felt like a promise to attend the First Frost and there was no way she could.

"Auntie, I can't go." Her throat ached and the words came out cracked.

"Why not?" Auntie frowned.

"They don't want me there!" Wasn't that obvious. No one wanted her, least of all the happy young folk in their finery who would flock to the First Frost looking for an evening of delight, unmarred by the presence of freaks of nature like her.

"Who is this 'they' who you ascribe so much power to?" Auntie gave a weak smile.

"Everyone!" Tears blurred Lizbete's vision. She took off her spectacles and pretended to clean them on her apron.

"Now we know that's not true. Brynar at least—"

"Brynar is kind, but I don't need his charity." She set her mouth into a firm line.

"Is that what you think he—Lil' Liz, there are people who love you."

"Not many." Lizbete squared her shoulders. "But I don't need more. I have you and Elin."

And Brynar? No, I don't have him. At least not how I'd like. Still, friendship is something, even if the root of it is pity, not affection.

"You have me for now." The bed creaked as Auntie swung her legs over the side and staggered to her feet.

"What are you doing?" Lizbete rushed to her. "You need to rest."

Auntie held up her hand. "If I can't stand for a moment to hug my own daughter, what good is breathing?"

Lizbete's heart gave out. Daughter? She didn't think Auntie had ever called her that before.

The older woman's calloused hand stroked Lizbete's cheek. "Lil' Liz, I won't be here forever. With how things have been lately . . . well, I don't want you to worry about my health right now."

Lizbete swallowed. Easier said than done.

"Still, you need connections. You need friends. Family." Auntie drew Lizbete into a hug.

"Stop!" Lizbete squirmed as she felt her blood stealing from Auntie. "I'll hurt—"

"Shush." Auntie squeezed her closer. "I know the risk. I'll be all right for a minute."

Auntie's warmth tasted of care, of concern, of comfort. A dull ache filled Lizbete's stomach. "I'll be all right, Auntie. Please, don't worry about me."

"I can't help it, child. I always do." Auntie withdrew. She shook with cold, but she still hovered near Lizbete, her hands just over Lizbete's shoulders, not touching, but as close as she could be without Lizbete's blood taking more heat. "I need to talk to Sten. There are things that need to be sure before—before it's too late."

"I'm sure he'll be by to see you soon," Lizbete said. "If not, I'll tell Brynar to send for him."

"Yes, we should do that." Auntie plopped onto the side of the bed and drew several deep breaths. Lizbete waited until Auntie lay down then pulled her blankets up around her chin. Auntie's eyes fell shut, and she breathed a deep sigh. Her whole body melted into the mattress.

With a smile, Lizbete left the room.

She stopped halfway down the stairs. Murmured voices rose to her. Two men, Brynar and . . . his father? From their hushed tone, they were likely trying to avoid anyone overhearing them, but it only took a little focus to bring their conversation to where she could hear it.

"I know you want to help your aunt, but the rest of the town is in bad shape too, and as the mayor's son, you can't show favoritism—"

"So I can't help my own family because it might look bad?" Brynar shot back. His voice held an edge, sharp as broken ice over dark water. Lizbete suspected he was on the verge of losing his temper.

"I didn't say that." Mayor Sten kept his voice level, failing to rise to his son's challenge. "However, you can't help her to the detriment of all else. She has employees, and Hangur is willing to—"

"Hangur is sleeping off a bottle and a half." Brynar's tone tightened, speaking through clenched teeth, probably. "He's in no shape to help with anything."

"Be that is it may, you still need to be available—"

Someone pounded on the tavern door. The noise jarred Lizbete's ears. Wondering who it could be, she crept the rest of the way down the stairs and peeked around the landing.

Brynar opened the door, and a red-haired man who Lizbete recognized as a local herdsman—Trin, if she remembered correctly—popped in, face contorted in anger.

"Where's your father? I need to speak with the mayor!" He pushed past Brynar and shook his fist at Sten who didn't flinch. "We have a thief among us. I went to check on my flock this morning, and I'm missing three head. Two fine ewes and my best ram."

Sten frowned. "Are you sure they didn't just get spooked and run off during the storm? No one in town would be that brazen. We have too many busybodies who would notice if someone were hiding three whole sheep or suddenly feasting on mutton."

"The fence was intact, and there's no way they could've jumped it." Trin scowled. "We need to investigate, search everywhere—"

Sten let out a long breath, his posture slackening for the span of a blink before he returned to his usual commanding presence. "We'll see what we can do, Trin, but everyone is busy patching up homes and businesses from the storm and the quake."

Brynar's face softened and he came to stand beside his weary father. "I'll ask Einar if he can get together a few of his friends and look around. I'm sure they'll be happy enough to get out of roof patching and trash gathering."

Trin's shoulders relaxed and his hands dropped to his side. "That would be appreciated. I can't afford to lose my ram. Not with the damage the storm did to my cottage and the chickens so upset they've stopped laying."

"We've all been hit hard by circumstances, Trin, but we'll do our best to help you out." Sten's expression changed to a sympathetic smile. He patted the other man's shoulder.

"A foul business. So much misfortune in a short span speaks to dark forces at work in our village." Trin narrowed his eyes and cast a glare around the room. He caught sight of Lizbete, and his scowl deepened. "Maybe we should be more careful about what we allow into our midst."

Fear washed through Lizbete and she shied back into the stairwell.

The door slammed shut behind Trin.

"Son, you promised to get Einar on that. You'd better follow through," Sten said.

"I will."

Remembering that Auntie wanted to speak with Sten, Lizbete squared her shoulders and entered the common room.

Brynar's eyes widened, then he grinned. "You feeling better?"

She nodded. "I spoke to Auntie. She wants to talk to you, Mayor Sten, but she fell asleep before I left the room. I'm not sure if we should wake her."

"Thank you. I'll let her sleep, then drop by this evening." The mayor gave a sigh. "I wish I could stay and wait for her to be up, but unfortunately, I need to be everywhere at once today." He narrowed his eyes at Brynar. "Remember what we spoke about?"

Brynar gave him a stony nod, not saying anything as his father departed.

"You need to go do something?" Lizbete prodded.

He rubbed his forehead. "Yeah, apparently I'm turning into my father."

She laughed. "There are worse people you could be . . . like your uncle."

He snorted. "Skywatcher willing, I will never stoop that low."

"No, you never will," she said firmly. "You're too good a man."

"I hope you're right." He gave her one last heart-quickening smile. "I'll see you in a bit, Liz."

Lizbete rubbed her arms to warm herself as he left. Maybe Mayor Sten was right. Maybe spending so much time with her and Auntie would hurt Brynar's standing with the community at large, but having him there meant so much. The idea of him fading from her life again chilled her worse than the cold sea breeze.

Forcing the worry from her head, Lizbete turned towards the kitchen. Her place in the community was with her pots and pans, helping her Auntie, even as Brynar's was preparing to replace his father one day. They belonged in different worlds, even if both worlds happened to be contained within the tiny village.

Chapter Ten

Determined not to let Auntie Katryn down, Lizbete threw herself into preparations for the evening meal. The chaos of the previous day had prevented Auntie from completing her usual errands, and other businesses had likewise stopped their trade. There had been no trip to the butcher or market, no delivery of fish or dairy. Thankfully, they had a large stash of potatoes, dried herbs, and butter. Lizbete proceeded to quarter the potatoes, cover them in melted butter and dried herbs, and place them in the oven. A delightful savory smell soon filled the kitchen.

The door opened and Falla walked in, her blonde hair a loose bun, baby strapped to her ample chest and her seven-year-old son, Pike, following close behind. "I brought my boy. He's old enough to wash dishes and clear tables, and he's willing to help."

Pike stuck his chest out. "I'm getting paid in pie."

His mother groaned. "By 'willing' I mean there was some negotiation involved."

"Thank you, and I'm sure I can arrange pie." Lizbete added another item to her to do list. They had no fresh fruit, but they had enough eggs to make a decent custard pie if they could get a hold of some cream. "If Pike is ready to run an errand for me, we can get started."

Falla and Lizbete barricaded themselves in the kitchen, rolling out pie crusts, baking sweet black bread, and cooking down their stash of vegetables into a delicious, onion-forward soup. After he returned from fetching Lizbete a jar of heavy cream from the dairy down the street, Pike set about sweeping up and wiping down tables.

Brynar wandered back in and beamed at the women's progress. "This is amazing. What do you need me to do?"

"You'll be serving tonight." Lizbete was glad to have someone else to pass that duty off to. She loved working in the kitchen, but every time she'd dealt with customers it seemed to end badly. Most simply didn't like her or want her anywhere near their tables.

By the time the first customers of the evening arrived, the common room was filled with delicious smells and lit by a roaring fire. As Brynar brought dishes of roasted potatoes out to their first patrons of the night, Hangur wandered in, still bleary and slow-moving but apparently ready to work. When Lizbete poked her head out of the kitchen to check on Brynar, Hangur cast her a disgusted look, but took his place behind the bar. Within minutes he was chatting up the patrons, pouring drinks, and laughing boisterously. Lizbete blinked. Then she saw him turn his back to the bar and take a swig from a tumbler.

She wrinkled her nose. Apparently he worked better with a little alcohol in him. The patrons seemed to enjoy his company, though. Maybe it would be all right.

Lizbete retreated to the kitchen and checked on the custard pies. She'd made six, some slices of which would be set aside for Pike, but the rest would be served to any customers who were interested. The crust was golden brown and the custard had a creamy yellow finish, like clouds in sunlight. Lizbete grinned. Everything was running smoothly. Auntie would be so proud.

The door to the common room opened, and Sten's familiar voice called out. "Hello, son."

Lizbete slipped the pies out from the oven one at a time.

"Hello, sir. Did Einar and his friends take care of Trin?" Brynar asked.

"They calmed him in that he was glad to see someone looking for his missing sheep, but they never found the animals, and I don't think he's very happy about that."

Lizbete finished with the pies and placed them in front of the kitchen's lone glass window to cool. Auntie loved that window. Glass being such a luxury, she'd had to save for months and send away to the capital for it. With the pies done, Lizbete filled her arms up with baskets of bread, one in each hand, one in the crook of each elbow, and pushed her way into the common room.

Sten looked up at her approach. "How is my sister?"

Lizbete set down the first basket on a table for some customers, then allowed Pike to take two more off her hands before approaching Sten still holding the final basket.

"Still sleeping. I haven't wanted to bother her."

Sten's eyebrows melted together. "Surely someone should at least check on her though."

Lizbete's throat closed in on itself. She'd been so busy making sure that the tavern stayed in business that she hadn't even considered that.

Brynar eased up behind his father and cleared his throat. "I don't think Lizbete's had a chance to leave the kitchen all day, Father. You know how Aunt Katryn is about this place. If Lizbete didn't see to running the tavern, Aunt Katryn would push her way down here and do it herself."

"I suppose." Sten sighed loudly. "I need to speak with her anyway. I'll go see if she's awake."

Lizbete passed Brynar the last basket of bread. "Wait, you should bring her some broth." She hurried into the kitchen and ladled out a steaming bowl of vegetable soup. She returned to Sten as quickly as she dared without splashing the liquid, but the steam had cooled off by the time she reached him. Hopefully it would still be warm enough for Auntie.

Without a word, Sten took the soup and stomped up the stairs.

Lizbete shuddered. "He really doesn't like me."

"He's just overwhelmed," Brynar assured her. He placed the basket of bread she'd given him in front of a young couple who had just sat down.

Hangur's raucous laugh echoed over the common room. Every seat at the bar had a customer in it and the common room was swiftly filling. Laughter, boisterous conversation, and even singing mingled in the air.

"We're going to be busy tonight," Lizbete said. She mentally tallied the number of customers and compared it to the number of servings she'd prepped.

"A day spent fixing roofs and searching for lost sheep has the entire village hungry." Brynar smiled. "I hope you made enough potatoes." His words echoed her own worries, and she snapped to attention.

"I'll get started on another batch."

She turned and took a step towards the kitchen. A faint cry from overhead froze her in her steps. The cheerful customers continued to eat and talk around her, but Lizbete knew what she'd heard. It was a cry of distress, of pain. She spun on her heels and took a step towards the stairs.

"Hey, Lazy Liz!" Hangur shouted over the crowd. "My friends here want bread. What's taking so long?"

Lizbete looked from him to the stairs and back again.

"Leave her be," Brynar snapped at his uncle. "She's got a whole kitchen to look after. If you're in such a hurry, you can run and get a basket yourself."

Hangur glared at him but stayed behind the bar. He lowered his head towards the nearest patron and whispered, "Young folk these days have no respect. Lazy lot, all of them."

Brynar hadn't caught his words—probably other than Lizbete and the one he'd whispered directly to, no one had. He continued to go about his rounds, greeting new arrivals. Lizbete's hands clenched. Lazy? That a drunken freeloader Hangur would dare suggest such a thing sank into her soul like burrs in her sock.

She took a step closer to him, ready to snap at him for drinking on the job and for acting like he owned the place when his sister was sick in bed, but creaking from the stairs drew her attention.

Sten descended, his steps slow, his gaze on his feet. Lizbete's heart withered. He didn't need to say anything. She knew.

Auntie Katryn was gone and life would never be the same.

Chapter Eleven

If I'd checked on her yesterday afternoon, would she have been all right? Would there have been something I could've done to help her?

Would she at least not have died alone?

The musing was pointless. From how Sten had found her, Auntie had passed away in her sleep. Her last memory would've been talking with Lizbete before drifting off. She hadn't died alone.

But she had died, and Lizbete felt lost without her.

Now she sat in the corner of the common room as well-wishers drifted in and out. The family had a large table in the center of the room, but Lizbete didn't feel comfortable sitting among them, especially not since Brynar had left to take Elin home. The young girl had cried through the burial and then fallen asleep in her brother's arms. Brynar's mother had volunteered to stay with Elin so that Brynar could return to the mourning room, but he'd said he wanted to at least carry the girl home rather than force her to walk. He'd promised Lizbete he'd return shortly, and she found herself glancing at the door often.

Various villagers wandered in and out to pay their respects or offer kind words to the family, but other than Falla, no one addressed Lizbete. It was as if she didn't exist. The rejection ate at her. Each pair of eyes that passed briefly over her before snapping back to the "real" family pushed Lizbete deeper into her own sorrow, making her feel more and more alone, as if the town had dug a hole for her alongside Auntie's grave and couldn't understand why she hadn't disappeared into it. Why she still bothered to exist when no one wanted her.

Finally, the crowd died down, the family sat around the table, sipping tea and wine and sharing stories of Auntie.

Lizbete longed to join them. She had so many stories of her own. Of misadventures in the kitchen, like the time a fisherman had sold Auntie a large eel that proved to be not quite dead and the creature has objected to being filleted, slapping Auntie across the face with its slippery tail. Or how Auntie single-handedly broke up a fight between two drunk brothers, forced them to clean up the mess they'd made, and had them sobbing and apologizing to each other before the night was over. She'd been an incredible person.

But why couldn't Lizbete join them? She was just as much Auntie's family as they were. Hadn't Auntie called her "daughter"? Resolve strengthening, she stood and took a step towards the table.

The door sprang open and Witta breezed in carrying a basket. Lizbete grimaced. What was she doing here? If she tried to do more party planning now, Lizbete would freeze her blood and leave her an ice sculpture.

Witta glanced around the room. Her brow furrowed before her face hardened into a determined expression and she strode up to Sten.

"Mayor Sten, I'm very sorry for you loss." She offered him the basket. "I made these for your family. Currant tarts."

Lizbete choked. Those were Brynar's favorite. Auntie had always made them on his birthday.

"Thank you, Witta. That was sweet of you." He took the basket and placed it on the table. "Currant tarts are actually my son's favorite."

"Oh really!" Witta laughed, tossing her hair. "I didn't know."

Sure you didn't.

Witta scanned the room as if thinking Brynar would pop out from a trap door or slither out from under a rug. When her gaze fell on Lizbete, her nose wrinkled.

"I'm sorry I missed Brynar," Witta said. "I know he was close to his aunt, and I wanted to express my condolences."

"You can wait for him." Sten pulled out a chair for her—at the family table. "He is just escorting his mother and sister home for the night and should be back shortly."

Lizbete's skin crawled as Witta settled into the midst of Brynar's family and immediately began a conversation with one of the aunts. She slipped right in, fitting like another egg in the nest. Something Lizbete could never hope to do.

The door opened again. Brynar strode in, and Witta popped out of her chair like a gopher peeking out of its hole.

He froze. "Witta. I wasn't expecting you."

She rushed to him, hands clasped in front of her chest, her expression overwrought. "I'm so so so sorry about your dear aunt, Brynar. You must be devastated. If you need *anything*, if there is *anything* I can do to comfort you, please, please, *please* let me know."

She put her hand out towards his chest, but he stepped around her. "Thank you. I'm doing all right. The real loss is Liz's." He crossed the room to where Lizbete stood, dumbfounded. "Are you hanging in there?"

She started to nod but her bottom lip quivered and tears blurred her vision. She shook her head.

He reached for her, but she couldn't accept the hug no matter how nice it would've been. Not now, with everyone looking. Even if she managed to pull away before her heat-stealing hurt him, someone might notice if Brynar were suddenly shivering after embracing her. She stepped back.

"I'll be fine. There's work to do, you know." She cleared her throat.

Sten stood. "I'm glad you're back, Brynar. Your uncle and aunts and I have something we need to discuss. You can keep an eye on the door. Make sure if any more well-wishers come by, they're properly greeted." He placed his hand on Witta's shoulder. "Let Witta help you. She brought some of your favorite currant tarts."

"Thank you, but I'm not hungry." Brynar frowned.

The siblings, Sten, Hangur, and their two married sisters—Agga and Jeski—retreated to the private dining area off the main common room. It was separated from the public space by only a curtain, which they left open. Lizbete angled away from them, not wanting to appear to be listening, though they had stationed themselves within range of her sensitive ears.

Sten cleared his throat. "I hate to ask this of you, Hangur, but the tavern needs to keep running. It was important to Katryn. She spent her life building it as a business after she inherited it from Uncle Ivar. It would dishonor her memory to let it close just because she's gone. All of us have our own lives, our own families and businesses. We don't have time to run it, but maybe you've returned to the town for this purpose. Will you take it over?"

"I can do that. I was practically running things while she was ill, after all." Pride studded Hangur's tone. Lizbete bristled. If by "running things", he meant drinking and jaw-flapping while Lizbete and Brynar did all the work, sure. "However, if I'm to do that, I want something in return."

Lizbete's shoulders hunched to her ears.

"You all right?" Brynar asked.

"Shh!" She put her finger to her lips and stepped closer to the discussion. Brynar followed with a puzzled Witta right behind.

"I've lived my life as a wanderer," Hangur said. "No trade of my own, no home to settle down in."

Lizbete had a bad feeling about where this was going. She glared at the back of Hangur's head, but no one in the family meeting seemed to notice.

"If I am to take over this business, I wish to do it as its owner, not as a glorified employee. I think that's what Katryn would've wanted, for it to stay in the family."

Rage swelled within Lizbete like a pot boiling over.

"No, it is not!" she shrieked.

Every head snapped to look at her.

"Liz, what is it?" Brynar frowned.

Her breath left her as her gaze bounced from the wide-eyed family to the concerned Brynar to Witta who had arched her eyebrows in smug amusement at Lizbete's outburst. Of course, Brynar hadn't heard what his family was talking about. Lizbete wasn't *supposed* to be able to hear it. Still, this was too important. She couldn't let fear of her oddness stop her from protecting what should be hers, what *was* hers.

"Auntie Katryn wouldn't want *him* taking over her business! He drinks at the bar. He's barely been here a week. She . . . she wanted me to have it," she stammered.

"There's no way she would trust this lazy child with her busi-

H. L. Burke

ness," Hangur murmured, angling towards his siblings and away from her.

Lizbete's vision blurred with anger. "I can hear you."

He started, flushed, and glared at her. "Well, then I'll say it again," he spoke louder this time. "You're an immature child who hides in the kitchen when there's work to be done—"

"Considering it's a tavern that serves food, the work to be done is usually in the kitchen, Uncle," Brynar said. The edge returned to his voice, and his eyes hardened. Hangur stiffened, then squared his own shoulders as if ready to fight. Lizbete's chest tightened. Were they about to come to blows? Right here? The whole family would blame her. Take it as another sign she was bad for Brynar. She needed to do something, to defuse the situation. Oh, but she also needed to protect the tavern from Hangur's greed.

Witta glanced anxiously between the quarreling family members. For a minute, Lizbete dared to hope she would leave, but instead the girl slunk to the bar and took her seat, watching quietly.

"Lizbete's right," Brynar continued. "Aunt Katryn never said anything that would lead me to believe that Hangur should inherit the tavern."

"But did she say anything about Lizbete doing so?" Sten strode out of the private dining area, eyes focused on his son.

She meant to, Lizbete realized, remembering their last talk. That had to be what Auntie had wanted to speak with Sten about, to make sure someone she trusted knew her intent for Lizbete and the tavern.

Brynar shifted from foot to foot. "No, but Lizbete is her daughter. A daughter should have priority over a brother in matters of inheritance."

Agga and Jeski exchanged a look, and Hangur snorted.

"She's not a daughter. She's a charity case. Katryn only took her in because no one else wanted her, and she could never stand to see a stray starve."

Rage twisted Brynar's face. "Talk about Liz like that one more time, Hangur, and uncle or not—"

"Brynar," Sten said sharply.

"Father, are you really taking his side in this?" Brynar turned on his dad. "Lizbete has lived under this roof her whole life and worked in the kitchen with Aunt Katryn every day. Hangur? He showed up less than a week ago after years of doing who knows what and now he's just supposed to slip into Aunt Katryn's place while Liz does what? Starves on the street? You know no one else in this town will employ her or take her in."

Lizbete's heart seized. She'd been so concerned about the injustice of losing the tavern that she hadn't even considered the possibility that she could be homeless.

Sten's stony expression melted, and he rubbed at his beard with the back of his hand. "I don't want any harm to come to the girl."

"Please," she said. "This is my home."

"What kind of a man do you think I am?" Hangur stomped towards Brynar.

A drunk. A freeloader. Lazy. Lizbete clamped her mouth shut, knowing that calling him out wouldn't gain her any points with the family.

"One who would steal an orphan's inheritance out from under her," Brynar shot back, apparently having no such qualms. His cheeks flared red, and his eyes flashed in a way that made Lizbete shiver.

"I wouldn't do that." Hangur's tone softened, and he addressed his brother. "I'm not a monster. I am better equipped than the girl to take care of this business. For one thing, the locals actually like me. For another, I'm not a child." His face softened into a more sympathetic expression, fake as gold-tinted paint on cheap tin. "Still, I wouldn't deprive her of her home. She can keep her job and work for room and board like she always has. Nothing will change for her other than instead of working for Katryn, she'll work for me."

"That seems more than fair." Sten nodded. "Agga? Jeski?"

The two women exchanged a look then nodded.

"The girl does need a home," Agga, the older of the two, said. "I can't take her in. I have my own children to look after and so does Jeski. I also wouldn't ask you to burden your Nan with an extra child, what with her needing to care for your poor, sick little one."

"Yes, Hangur taking charge of the tavern *and* the girl seems the best way to deal with things," Jeski put in. "Nothing will change for the girl. She'll be no worse off. It's fair."

No, it isn't. Tears ran down Lizbete's cheeks, but she knew it was no good to fight. The family had made up their mind, and with Mayor Sten against her and the whole town unlikely to care for her plight, she had no recourse. Not wanting to cry in front of Hangur, she fled into the kitchen without a word.

"Liz!" Brynar started after her before the door even closed, but his footsteps paused.

"We need to talk," Sten said.

Lizbete settled beside the fireplace, her toes in the ashes, and tried to draw comfort from the flames.

"No, I need to see to Liz. She just lost her only family. Skywatcher knows the rest of us never stepped up to care for her."

"This is important, and it involves Liz, but I don't want to have this talk in front of everyone else."

"We were just leaving," Agga said.

"We're walking home together," Jeski added. "Witta, did you want to come with us? Your home is on the way."

Lizbete shuddered. She'd forgotten Witta was even there. Great, now the whole town would hear how she'd been rejected by the family in favor of the drunken idiot, Hangur.

"I was really hoping I could talk with Brynar—"

The girl just couldn't take a hint.

"It's really not a good time—"

"No, you'll be a gentleman and walk Witta home tonight," his father said sharply. "Wait in the private dining room, Witta, dear. I need to talk to my son alone for a moment. Hangur, can we have some privacy?"

"I'll walk our sisters home."

Footsteps crossed floorboards and doors opened and closed. Lizbete pressed herself into the brick casing of the fireplace and wondered if she should try not to listen. Was it right? Then again, it wasn't her fault the family hadn't learned their lesson about her keen hearing yet.

Sten coughed. "You need to stop it with this girl. When we talked about her this spring, I thought you'd come to a sensible conclusion, and I supported your choices because they were the right ones. But now?"

"They weren't the right choices," Brynar growled. "Sir, I tried. I really did, but I can't. You're asking me to cut off my friendship with a person who has been there for me, and Elin, my entire life."

"I'm not asking you to ignore the girl. Doing so the first time was your choice, not mine."

Shock jolted through Lizbete. Her whole being collapsed in on itself, and she found herself unable to breathe.

"It was, but I've regretted it every moment since then."

"But it might've been the right choice considering you don't seem to be able to handle yourself around her. You neglect your duties to the town to be with her and help her. You take sides with her against the rest of the family—"

"Liz is family!"

"No, she's not, and she never will be." His father's voice harshened.

Lizbete winced.

"Son, our family has overseen this village for five generations. The people here depend on us, and to honor that dependency we have to be worthy of the citizens' trust. That means associating with people who build us up and bolster our position, not who drag us down."

"You act as if Lizbete is a criminal. She's just a girl, Father."

"We both know there's more to her than that. While I will not have her persecuted for things she cannot help or change, I also will not have you give up everything I have worked to pass on to you for the sake of a foundling who deserves our pity and our charity but who would never be an acceptable bride for my son."

Shame rippled through Lizbete. Did Sten think she had designs on Brynar? She didn't. She knew where she stood as much as he did. Being with Brynar as a friend had been an unexpected blessing. Being with him as more had always been an impossible dream no matter how much she…

She loved him.

Even as Lizbete tried to deny it, the words settled into her chest and took hold. She loved Brynar. It was the only thing that explained how terrible she felt when Witta fluttered around him like a moth circling a lantern. How her heart leaped when he appeared in the tavern door. How much it ached when he was gone.

But apparently he'd been gone by choice. Oh, why had he done that to her?

"Father, maybe I'm not cut out to be what you want me to be," Brynar's beloved voice continued. It was a voice that she trusted completely. Trusted in a way that maybe he didn't deserve.

"You are. You just need time to clear your head and get your priorities straight." Sten let out a long breath. "Look, after the burial, Hangur mentioned to me that he was regretting that he'd left his wife behind in the capital. Says that losing Katryn made him realize the value of family."

"Well, considering our family just gave him an established business just for showing up and being related to us, I can see why he'd value that."

In spite of everything, Lizbete laughed.

"Would you just listen to me for a minute without the sarcastic commentary?" Sten snapped. "My point is, if Hangur had his wife here, if he had his own family to look after, it might anchor him. A tree doesn't stay in place without roots, and Hangur's sense of place and duty—let's just say he could use more roots."

"So have him fetch his wife then."

"I want you to go fetch her."

Lizbete blinked. Sten had just spent the past two weeks berating his son for how often he was away from Brumehome, and now he wanted him to leave?

To get away from me. I'm a greater threat to Brynar's future than the prolonged absences.

"Me? It's *his* wife! I'm not the one who abandoned her—"

"Look, if the transition with him owning the tavern is to go smoothly, he needs to be here. You're familiar with the capital, and I need you to take some time to think. This is the perfect opportunity for that."

"What if I've already thought all I need to on the matter and come to my own conclusions?"

"Then I have no way of changing your mind, but consider this: your choices don't have consequences for you alone, Brynar. You're a part of a family and a community, and there are people who need you. Far more than just one girl. Are you really going to abandon all of us for her?"

The room fell silent. Lizbete's pulse hammered in her ears. She would've given anything for the sense of community Brynar had behind him. To be a part of a whole, to have friends, to be loved by a large, sprawling family that would help and support her. She couldn't ask Brynar to give that up to be with her.

Oh, but to lose him again! The pain of his first departure spread through her like venom in her veins.

"Look, think about it." Sten's voice took on the diplomatic tone he employed when settling disputes between his constituents. "The trip might do you some good. Let you clear your head."

"I really should get home," Brynar's tone grew stiff, sulky even. "I'm tired."

"Well, I promised you would walk Witta home. You won't make a liar of me, will you?" His father laughed, but joylessly.

Lizbete bit down on her bottom lip until she tasted blood.

"I guess not. I need to get my coat, though. I left it in the kitchen."

"All right. I'll start home without you. I'll tell Witta you'll just be a moment."

Lizbete jumped to her feet as the door to the kitchen swung open and Brynar walked in.

She frowned at him. "Your coat isn't in here."

"I know. It's on a hook by the door, but I wanted to talk to you, and I knew Father would fight me on that..." He let out a sigh and brushed his fingers back through his blond hair. "Things are getting complicated—"

"What did your father mean when he said it was your choice to ignore me?" The words slipped out before Lizbete could stop them.

Brynar swallowed audibly. "You . . . you heard that."

"I heard everything. He said you—What did he mean by that?"

Brynar stared at her like a rabbit caught in a snare. Then with a sigh, he hung his head. "This spring, Father . . . he took me aside and questioned me about the time I was spending with you, about my intentions, about—about whether or not I had feelings for you."

A lump formed in her throat. "And you told him no?"

"I wanted to." He shifted from foot to foot. "I had every intention of saying we were just friends, good friends, close friends, but only friends. Yet, I couldn't get the words out. It—it scared me."

The light from the setting sun danced across his face, glinting eerily on his blue eyes. Eyes which she'd always adored, but which now unnerved her in their sincerity. Her heart opened to him, only to immediately snap closed again. He cared for her, but he'd left her. Whatever he felt for her, no matter how much she longed to believe it was real, it hadn't been real enough to keep him near her.

"I couldn't say that I didn't feel for you because I knew I was starting to." He drew closer to her. She shied back, for once not just because she feared taking his heat. Pain crossed his expression, but he continued, his tone growing in desperation. "I knew that every time I left you, I wanted to go back, that every time I saw you, it felt like coming home, and . . . and the thought of what that meant was terrifying. Liz, my family has always had my life planned out. The things I would learn, the friends I would have, the type of girl

I would marry."

"And the future mayor of Brumehome could never be with the local Ash Lizard." The words tasted bitter on her tongue.

"That's not what—" He closed his eyes. "Father strongly suggested that for the good of the family, I pursue other girls, and I—I couldn't. Not when I couldn't stop comparing them to you, to your smile, your laugh, your kindness towards Elin. I thought—I thought it would be easier if I just didn't see you for a while."

A gaping wound formed deep within her chest. It hadn't been her imagination, the way he'd disappeared. The feeling that he was avoiding her, the loneliness and loss of a good friend suddenly gone.

"You left me," she whispered.

"It was a mistake!" Pain rippled across his face. "I should never have done it, or at least should've been honest about why I was doing so. But I thought if we just didn't see each other anymore it would be easier for both of us."

Grief hardened into a red-hot point of rage. She glared at him. "Easier? You left me all alone, Brynar, without so much as a goodbye. I was confused and I was hurt, and I had *no one.* You have your family, your friends, the whole village, but me? You were my only friend, the only person my age I thought cared for me and you— you left me like I was nothing."

"That's not true!" He reached for her hand, but she shied away. "Liz, I made a mistake. I was wrong, and I'm so sorry, but I never stopped caring for you."

"Yes, you did!" she snapped. "Maybe you didn't stop feeling or thinking you cared for me, but in action? You stopped. You stopped completely. You can say you cared all you want, but you didn't act like you cared, and what else matters? Nothing!" Tears blurred her eyes and she turned away. "You left me all alone, Brynar." And how could she be sure he wouldn't again? With the whole village against her and his family seeing her as a threat to his future, what place did she have in his life?

None. His parents were already doing everything they could to get rid of Lizbete. Taking her inheritance, sending Brynar away from her, forcing that stupid Witta in his face. There was only one way this could end, and it wasn't happily. "I need to—I have to go."

She turned and rushed back into the common room.

"Liz, wait!" His footsteps pounded after her.

"Brynar!" a feminine voice squealed. Witta barreled past Lizbete and crashed into Brynar.

Lizbete froze. Common sense told her to keep moving, to leave. Some morbid fascination caused her to stop and stare as Witta clung to Brynar's arm, halting his pursuit of Lizbete.

The young lady widened her eyes and plumped her lips in a pout. "What's this I hear about your leaving Brumehome? We're supposed to be working on the First Frost together. Will you even be back in time?"

"I'm not sure I'm leaving. I don't want to." Brynar's eyes sought Lizbete. She frowned at him. What did she care if Witta snatched him up? It was better for them both if they ended any foolish notions right now.

"Just go," Lizbete said, holding his gaze. "You—I don't need you. I'm fine by myself. I did fine the first time you left, and I'll do fine this time. Just go!"

Witta arched an eyebrow at her, and shame rippled through Lizbete. Biting down on her tongue to stop herself from screaming, she rushed from the room and up the stairs. In her bedroom, she collapsed onto her mattress and burst into tears.

Oh, how could she have been so stupid? Why had she allowed

herself to fall in love with him?

Chapter Twelve

"Lizbete, you lazy girl!"

Up to her wrists in bread dough and covered in flour, Lizbete winced.

Hangur stuck his head into the kitchen and glared at her. "Why haven't the chickens been fed? I can hear them cackling from my bedroom. If you starve the steam-blasted things, they'll stop laying. Is that what you want?"

You're just mad because their clucking woke you up before midday. I've been up working since dawn.

"I'll take care of it as soon as I'm done with this," she said. "If I had some help I wouldn't be so far behind."

He scoffed. "Don't think I don't know what you're doing, trying to get out of work. You don't need help. This kitchen functioned just fine without extra employees before my sister died."

"Because Katryn did as much work as two employees!" Lizbete protested. "You..." She clamped her mouth shut when her eyes caught Hangur's. Accusing him of laziness wouldn't make her day any better, no matter how true it was. Instead she punched down as hard as she could into the dough, folded it over, and punched again.

Hangur grunted, as if to signal he was done with her, and left the kitchen. The door slammed behind him. Lizbete's whole being felt tired, but she continued to knead the bread until it was finished. With that accomplished, she covered the dough with a cloth, brushed as much flour as she could from her garments as well as removed a smudge from her spectacles, and took up the basket to collect the eggs.

Before she left the kitchen, she wrapped herself up in an oversized cloak that had once been Katryn's and stood beside the fireplace trying to absorb as much heat as possible. Though the First Frost Festival was still over a week away, the literal first frost had come several days before, coating Brumehome with a layer of white icing. When Lizbete stepped outside in this weather, the cold pricked at her like a thousand needles. Her breath fogged before her, and she moved as quickly as possible to get back inside in her warm kitchen again.

However, when she reached the chicken coop, she stopped short. Something green glinted in the harsh morning sun. She let out a breath.

This again?

Drawing closer, she discerned that this time the anonymous gift was an oblong green stone the color of fuzzy sage leaves. Someone had drilled a small hole in the top of it and threaded a rough bit of twine through the hole so the stone could hang from a nail in the door. She sighed.

"Thank you, whoever you are. Honestly, I'd rather just know why you're doing this." She didn't shout. Someone not involved with the gifts might hear her and have questions. The village already thought she was strange enough without adding in the element of a mysterious benefactor who only gifted interesting rocks.

The gifts had grown more frequent. After the blue sphere and the clear crystal, she'd continued to find stones and crystals left where she would inevitably stumble upon them. Her windowsill collection now included a chip of obsidian, a cracked geode with sugar crystal insides, and a lump of yellow metal she suspected was gold but was afraid to show anyone to verify. No more of the precious red crystals that could help Elin, however. Whoever—or whatever—was leaving the gifts apparently didn't know what she truly wanted. Still, the stones were pretty, and they were an act of kindness, presumably. With Auntie dead and Brynar gone, she didn't experience enough kindness nowadays to reject such a gesture.

She hung the twine about her neck, making sure the stone lay beneath her collar before continuing her work with the chickens.

The rest of that chore went without incident, allowing her to return to the kitchen before her blood chilled to a painful level. Once there, she started chopping onions for the stew she planned to make. Falla had brought her some stew meat from the butcher the night before, and Lizbete had set aside bones for stock. Altogether enough ingredients to make something savory and rib-sticking.

The common room door swung open. Lizbete paused to listen. It was too early for customers.

"What are you doing in here?" Hangur spluttered. "This isn't a place for children to play!"

"I'm here to see Lizbete."

Lizbete put down her knife. Elin? And by herself, it seemed. Hangur would never dare snap at her if Sten or Nan were there.

"She's working." Hangur's tone suggested this should be the end of the discussion.

"At least someone is."

Lizbete laughed and crossed to the swinging doors. She peered out, ready to come to the girl's defense if needed. Though it seemed Elin could handle herself.

Hangur stood behind the bar, an uncorked bottle and a tumbler beside him. His face glowed tomato red. "Don't you sass—"

"Does my father know you're drinking on the job?" Elin tilted her head to one side. "Should I tell him?"

The blood drained from Hangur's face. He slammed the cork back into the bottle, snatched it off the bar, and shoved it onto the shelf behind him. "I was just testing to make sure it hadn't gone bad, and you're not telling anyone."

"I'm going to see my friend now." Elin spun on her heel and caught sight of Lizbete. Her face lit up. "Hi, Liz!"

"Come on in." Lizbete held the door open for her. As Elin joined her, Lizbete murmured, "Blackmail seems to come naturally to you. Do you have any other skills I should be aware of?"

"If Hangur doesn't learn to shut up, I might try my hand at murder," Elin scoffed.

Lizbete thought about admonishing the girl for the dark comment but let it slide, in no mood to even try to defend Hangur.

They entered the kitchen together. Elin let out a long breath and dabbed at her forehead. Lizbete's throat tightened. In spite of the cold day outside, sweat beaded on the child's brow.

"Are you feeling all right?" she asked.

"No." Elin reached under her shirt and pulled out her crystal. At least Lizbete assumed it was the same crystal. The color had changed completely, from bright, vibrant crimson to a dirty gray like smoke-tainted clouds. "It's not working anymore. My fevers are coming back. My dreams are awful." She sank wearily into a chair beside the prep table. "I wish Brynar were here. Why'd he have to go to the capital right now?"

Lizbete shrugged. She'd spent the last week trying very hard not to think about Brynar's absence or wonder when he'd return. He'd tried to see her again the morning before he'd left, but she'd hid in the kitchen and pretended she hadn't heard him knocking at the inn's locked door. At the time, the pain had been too fresh. Even now, Lizbete wasn't she'd have the courage to face him again. She forced a brave face for Elin. "Hopefully he'll be back soon."

"Father promised that witless Witta that Brynar would be back by the First Frost. That's all that girl thinks about, her stupid dance. She has this idea that everyone should be wearing masks. She even designed one for Brynar. It's got rooster feathers all around it." Elin gave an exaggerated shudder. "He'll look so stupid in that. I hope he doesn't wear it just to keep her happy. Brynar does too much to keep stupid people happy."

"That's kind of the mayor's job." Lizbete smiled without humor.

"Maybe, but I wish he'd do more things to make himself happy." Elin tapped her fingers against the arm of her chair. "He deserves that."

"Maybe you can make him a mask that you think he'd really like. Something that fits his personality like . . . like a wolf." Lizbete wasn't sure where the thought came from, but once she said it, she was somehow certain it fit him and would please him.

Elin brightened. "I could!" She leaned forward in her seat. "I could make one for you too."

Lizbete's stomach twisted. "I'm not going to the First Frost, Elin." Regret filled her soul as she remembered the dress Auntie had purchased for her. Well, Auntie wouldn't be there to see her not atttend.

"Lizbete!" Hangur loomed in the doorway. "We have a customer. Is there any food ready?"

Lizbete's jaw dropped. "We're not open until midday. It's hardly mid-morning."

"Don't question me. I say we have a customer, and we have a customer." He stormed back into the common room.

Elin gave a low whistle. "He's a pleasant sort, isn't he?"

"I think he's just finding out that running a tavern involves more than serving drinks and telling dirty jokes to the local sots." Lizbete snorted. "Apparently the real job is stressful." She considered the kitchen. The bread dough was still rising. She hadn't made the stew yet. She did have the eggs she'd collected though.

She hadn't cleaned her frying pan from breakfast yet. A thick layer of bacon grease still coated the bottom. She heated this up until it melted and started to sizzle then added a few thinly sliced potatoes. Once these began to brown, she cracked three eggs directly into the grease. The grease spit and bubbled. A delicious smell rose from the pan, and Lizbete's mouth watered.

"That smells yummy." Elin came up behind her and gazed into the pan.

"If you stick around, I'll make you some." And hopefully also get a chance to absorb some of Elin's extra heat.

As soon as the eggs whitened and the potatoes looked sufficiently brown, she tipped the contents of the pan onto a wooden tray and carried it out into the dining room.

A man sat at the bar clutching a tankard in one hand while waving the other fist wildly in the air before him. Lizbete wrinkled her nose. Another early drinker. Lizbete vaguely recognized him as a regular, though what his name or profession was, she wasn't quite sure. She'd found since acquiring her spectacles she'd had to relearn a lot of faces that should've been familiar to her, people who had never gotten close enough for her to see them unblurred.

"It's not my fault the animals went missing, Hangur," he said. "But once the boss noticed them gone, he started poking around and found my stash of bottles. Couldn't convince him that I only drink to keep the cold away. I'm alert. Those sheep are my best friends, you know, besides you, Hangur." He took another swig. "But nope. And now I've lost my job."

"That's not fair, Erich." Hangur refilled his tumbler.

"What am I going to do?" Erich sank his head in his hands. "I don't want to work on a fishing boat. It's so . . . wet."

Lizbete's fingers tightened around the platter. She sincerely doubted that this man had anything to pay with. This was one of Hangur's drinking buddies, and he'd yelled at her to make him food.

Well, the eggs were already fried. She stomped to the bar and slammed them onto the counter before him.

"Easy!" Hangur snapped. He then inclined his head towards Erich and stage-whispered, "Good help is hard to find." A smile crept across his face. "Hey! You can work here. We always need servers."

Lizbete recoiled as if smacked. Was he seriously going to hire a drunk herdsman to wait tables? Afraid she'd scream, Lizbete headed back towards the kitchen.

Erich grunted. "It'd be better than herding. Living out there with the sheep, exposed to the elements, and with dark spirits lurking at the edge of the firelight, waiting to eat my soul."

Lizbete slowed her steps. Dark spirits?

"Dark spirits, eh?" Hangur chuckled. "You certain you weren't just hitting the bottle too often?"

"No, I saw them when I was dead sober. They're the ones that took the sheep. I'd bet my good teeth on it." Erich took another draft. "Gray as ghosts with glowing eyes, and silent as fog, slipping in and out of the herds, disappearing in the standing stones. All the workers saw them. Boss forbid us from talking about them, but that only stood when he was actually around."

Lizbete pushed through the swinging doors and leaned against the wall for a long breath. Elin's joke about murdering Hangur seemed less funny and more wishful thinking as the day progressed. Skywatcher help her.

I just need to keep my head down and push through the day . . . then the next day, and the next.

"You all right?" Elin asked.

Lizbete pulled herself out of her gloom spiral. In her frustration over Hangur's behavior, she'd forgotten Elin was waiting. "Fine."

"Good." The girl rested her chin in her hands, elbows on the prep table. "You still owe me eggs."

"I wouldn't dare forget." Lizbete threw another piece of bacon into the pan to re-grease the surface and got to slicing some more potatoes. Trying to distract herself from Hangur and his antics, she concentrated on slicing the root vegetables transparently thin. Elin fell silent, drawing in the flour left from Lizbete's bread making. The bacon curled at the edges. The grease popped and sizzled, and Lizbete inhaled the scent. Here, next to the fire, doing what she was good at, in her own home, she felt almost normal.

"Liz," Elin whispered.

Something in the girl's voice chilled her, and Lizbete turned to look at her. Elin had drawn a series of dancing skeletons in the flour, but was in the process of rubbing them out, one by one.

"Is something wrong?" Lizbete took the pan off the fire so it wouldn't burn before approaching the girl.

Elin drew a line through the neck of a particularly boisterous skeleton. "Why aren't you and Brynar—before he left he said something about you—about you not wanting to see him anymore."

Lizbete swallowed. "We had a fight."

"But you'll forgive him, won't you?" Elin gripped the edge of the table, sending a poof of flour into the air. "I know he makes mistakes sometimes, but he really likes you. You like him, don't you?"

Lizbete bit her bottom lip. She hadn't wanted to hurt Brynar. As much as he'd hurt her, the thought of him in pain still filled her with regret. It would be nice to get a chance to part on better terms, even if they could never love each other in the way she—and apparently, he as well—wanted to. For now, though, perhaps the distance was best. Perhaps it would give them both a chance to forget and move on.

How could she explain all that to Elin? "It doesn't matter if Brynar and I like each other, Elin. We're not the same. He's going to be the mayor after your father. The only place this village will allow me to occupy is this kitchen."

"Brynar likes this kitchen too," Elin pointed out. "He's happiest here, with you."

Lizbete's heart ached. "I wish it were that simple."

"It should be," Elin snorted. She smoothed out the flour and traced a snaky outline. Her hand then strayed to the pocket sewed onto her skirt, only to shy back as if bitten. Her gaze darted to Lizbete and back to her drawing again. "Liz, how mad at Brynar are you?"

Lizbete let out a long breath. "I'm not mad at him right now. Not really. Just—it's hard to explain. I think both of us were idiots to think we'd ever be able to keep things the way they had been when we were children. It was inevitable that we'd grow apart." She wished it didn't have to hurt so much.

"He asked me to give you something, but also said not to do it until you seemed ready." Elin pulled a folded piece of paper from her pocket. "Are you ready?"

Lizbete froze. "What is that?" she asked, like an idiot. She grimaced. "I mean, I'm assuming it's a letter, but why?"

"He said you wouldn't let him say before he left, but the idea that you'd go the whole time he was gone not knowing it ate at him." Elin pushed the letter towards Lizbete. "You don't have to read it right now, please, but promise me you will before he gets back. I don't know what it says, but he looked so miserable when he gave it to me. It has to be important to him. I know he wouldn't want to hurt you, so it's not something bad."

Lizbete's jaw tightened. Wouldn't want to, but he still had. Did he really think that could be fixed so easily? The anger she'd convinced herself had calmed returned with a vengeance. She moved to shove the letter away, but something in Elin's wide, dark eyes stopped her. With a sigh, she took the letter and stuck it in her apron pocket. "I'll read it soon."

"Good." Elin returned to her flour drawing.

Lizbete replaced the pan on the fire and concentrated on her cooking. A few minutes later she served Elin her eggs and potatoes. Elin's snake had grown into a full-fledged sea serpent, munching on the hapless stick-figure survivors of a shipwreck.

A little grim, but that was Elin. While the girl ate her eggs, Lizbete brushed her hand across Elin's head and drew away the sickly heat of her fever.

Elin's shoulders relaxed. "Thank you." Her eating slowed and her eyelids drooped shut. "I didn't get a lot of sleep last night. The nightmares, you know?"

"You mentioned them." Lizbete hung a cauldron over the fire

155

and half-filled it with water. She then dropped in the bones for stock. "Do you remember what they were about?"

Elin shook her head. "Not usually. Just the feeling. Prickly. Afraid. Off. Like my shoes are on the wrong feet, but all over." She plucked the crystal from around her neck. "This thing's useless now. I might as well throw it away."

Lizbete took the crystal from her. "Maybe we can find you a new one. I mean, if there's one, there's more."

An uneasy feeling itched at the back of her neck. The crystal pulsed with a last heartbeat of faint energy in her hand. She dropped it into her pocket. Unsure why she did, but maybe it could help somehow.

A scratching sound drew her gaze to the window. Red eyes glinted at her through glass fogged with early morning frost. She gasped. The face ducked out of view.

"What?" Elin stammered.

Lizbete sprinted out of the kitchen and through the side door to the back alley. She burst into the cold air and stared in the direction of the window. Nothing. No one. The passage was empty. She stood, shivering, trying to remember what she'd seen.

The eyes had given her the most immediate impression, but something had been off about the face as a whole. It had been narrower than a normal face, gray in pallor, even more so than her own. Beyond that, she wasn't sure what it looked like. It had vanished so quickly, and she'd been so surprised.

"Liz? What is it? Why did you run away?"

The cold wind bit at Lizbete's exposed skin. She shouldn't have run outside without her cloak. Quickly returning to the kitchen, she stationed herself beside the fire to thaw.

"I thought I saw someone looking in the window," she explained.

Elin's brow furrowed. "Watching us? But why?"

"I don't know."

Mysterious presents. Strange watching faces.

Gray as ghosts with glowing eyes.

Dark spirits?

No, such things weren't real. She drew herself up taller. Even if they were, they had no place here, in the warmth of Lizbete's kitchen. This was her home, her only sanctuary. Dark spirits wouldn't ruin that for her.

A little later, Elin's mother, Nan, came to claim her. The tall, willowy woman gave Lizbete an awkward thank you for looking after the girl, then hurried her out the door as if afraid her daughter would catch Lizbete's strangeness.

All for naught, Lizbete thought. *If there's anyone in Brumehome who could challenge my reign as queen of the freaks, it's Elin.*

Falla arrived just as the midday customers were coming in, and Lizbete's bread emerged dark brown and steaming from the oven. Falla had stopped by the market on her way to work and brought a basket of vegetables and a selection of fresh fish. Lizbete thanked her for these and set them aside to prep. The stock pot bubbled merrily, and the whole kitchen smelled of fresh-baked bread, roasted chicken, and sea-kissed fish.

Thankfully Falla's presence made it so Lizbete rarely had to leave the kitchen. She was glad for that. Hangur and Erich had planted themselves at the bar like noxious weeds. While Hangur at least attempted to serve other patrons, Erich only grew louder and more obnoxious as the afternoon progressed until a space formed around him, as no other customers wished to be close to his nonsense.

As afternoon trickled into evening, a scowling Falla approached

Lizbete and indicated Erich. He now sat, sloppy drunk, muttering to himself and sipping on his drink.

"Should we ask him to leave?" she asked, blue eyes snapping with anger.

Lizbete opened her mouth, then caught sight of Hangur who stood over a table, regaling the customers with some story to the detriment of their dining experience. What did she care if that idiot ran his business into the ground? It wasn't like he'd listen to her anyway. She set her mouth firm. "It's not our business. We don't own the place."

She refilled a basket of bread and threaded her way through the dining area, morbidly curious what nonsense Hangur was spouting. However, a few steps into the room, her sensitive ears caught another conversation.

"I am sorry about the sheep, Rawl, but I don't understand why you fired Erich."

Lizbete paused. Erich's former employer was here? That had to be awkward.

"Look at the poor sot," the first voice continued. "He'll drink himself into poverty. Considering how many of us have lost livestock over the last few weeks, do you really think it was his fault?"

"The sheep were just the last straw with the drunken idiot," Rawl snorted.

Lizbete continued around the dining room, passing out loaves, but always with an ear to the conversation.

"The fool thought he saw dark spirits everywhere. I blame it on the *liquid* spirits he consumed endlessly, but still, he was scaring the other men, making it hard for me to get them to take night watches."

Lizbete considered this. It made sense. There were no dark spirits, only intoxication and hallucinations.

That doesn't explain the face in the window.

"Well, that's been happening more and more, too. I've heard tales of strange figures lurking about town, eyes watching from the shadows, but vanishing when you give them a hard look." The first man dropped his voice to a conspiratorial whisper. "Though if Erich intends to escape them by hiding in a bottle here, he had best think again. They say this place is a magnet for them. Half the sightings have been within spitting distance of this building. I think it's the Ash Lizard. There's always been something off about that girl. She's probably drawing other creeps to her."

Lizbete nearly dropped her basket. She slammed it down on the nearest table, giving them four times the bread she intended, and scrambled for the kitchen.

Her arm brushed up against a patron, and her blood gulped for the heat. He pulled away, shivering, and rubbed his arms.

Lizbete bolted to safety.

The pounding of her pulse overwhelmed the cheerful voices drifting from the common room, the crackling of the fireplace, and the low moan of the wind outside.

They already think I'm a monster and now they think I'm in league with other *monsters. What am I going to do? Oh, what am I going to do?*

Her eyes fell on the basket of vegetables Falla had brought from market. She'd used about half of its contents, but a lot still remained—including a bright orange gourd with a bumpy shell.

I'll make pie. That's what I'll do. A great big sweet squash pie.

She grabbed her big knife and stabbed into the squash with a relish Elin would've appreciated. Soon she had it sectioned into cubes which she covered with water and left to simmer beside the stewpot.

With the pie baking to occupy her, Lizbete settled into the quiet bustle of a working kitchen. Falla darted in and out, fetching food, but no one else bothered her.

"Just me and the vegetables." Lizbete hummed as she rolled out pie shells.

As the last customers were leaving, the pies came out of the oven, steaming and beautifully orange. The tavern was already closing down, and the pies still needed to cool, but that was all right. Lizbete preferred her sweet squash pie to be cold when she ate it. Having them sit on the windowsill overnight would mean they'd be perfect for tomorrow's lunch rush.

The door to the kitchen swung open, and she turned to greet Falla. Instead, she found Hangur. Her mouth wrinkled.

"I sent Falla home. You can handle clean up on your own, right?" Hangur arched an eyebrow.

Lizbete coughed. On busy nights, she, Auntie, and Falla would often work together so they could all get to bed before midnight. At the very least, Hangur could help. She opened her mouth to suggest them, but Hangur listed to the side. He caught himself on the door frame, shook his head, and glared at her, as if daring her to mention his unsteadiness.

Drunk as always. He probably wouldn't be much help.

"I'll manage," she said simply.

"Good." He turned away, but then glanced back over his shoulders. "Oh, Erich was in no shape to see himself home, so he's sleeping here. We had some unexpected travelers from the pass take the paying rooms, so I gave Erich your room."

"What?" Lizbete stammered.

"I can't very well send him out in that." Hangur jerked his

thumb towards the window. The chill wind shook the pane. "He'd probably freeze to death trying to find shelter. Is that what you want?"

"No but—"

But there had to be another option other than her room. He could stay with Hangur, or sleep behind the bar, or in the kitchen next to the fire.

Knowing Hangur had made up his mind, and not wanting to test his temper when he'd been drinking, Lizbete clamped her mouth shut.

Just for tonight. Tomorrow he'll go. I need to get moving on this mess or I won't be sleeping tonight anyway.

"So it's decided then. Make sure you're up in time to feed the chickens. I don't want them bothering our guests if they want to sleep in."

Hangur departed.

Lizbete half-heartedly stacked some dishes, but her heart felt like a boulder, pressing her into the floor. Her vision blurred, and tears smudged her spectacles. At last, she collapsed in a pile of ashes next to the fireplace, put her head in her hands, and wept.

Chapter Thirteen

Lizbete woke with a crick in her neck, ashes all over her clothing, and a dry throat from breathing in wood smoke all night. Her grief hardened into a hot ball of rage in her chest. She stomped her way through her chores, slamming cabinets, rattling crockery, and sweeping up with such ferocity that the dust flew into the air and settled back onto the floor rather than be corralled into neat piles for collection.

There has to be something I can do about this. I can't just let him walk all over me. If he's giving away my room after only a week, what's next? My food? My clothes?

What recourse do I have?

The chance of Hangur's family siding with her over him in any dispute was as thin as her fried potatoes. With Mayor Sten the arbitrator of most village conflicts, it left her without a lot of options. If she had someone else on her side, maybe, someone who could attest to her ill-treatment…

The obvious answer was Brynar. No. Even if he hadn't been away on his father's bidding, her pride stung at the thought of crawling to him for help after learning that he'd intentionally abandoned her.

Also, she wasn't sure she could look him in the eye again, knowing what she knew now. She loved him, and he'd at least flirted with the idea of loving her, but that it didn't matter. They could never be together. No, any interaction with Brynar would be like standing on the wrong side of a window, watching a cheery fire burn without any benefit of the heat. It would only remind her of something she could never have. Her hand slipped into her pocket where his letter still hid. Whatever he had to say, it couldn't change how things were. She'd read it, eventually, because she had promised Elin she would, but not now. Now she needed a clear head and determination. Brynar couldn't help her now.

If she were going to improve her lot—or at least stop it from worsening any further—she'd have to take some action herself.

But how?

Leaving Brumehome wasn't an option. Maybe at the height of summer with the long days and warmer weather, but in the winter? When the water was already freezing and falling sleet would put out campfires? She'd have no way to survive the journey to anywhere else. She'd freeze on the road. Some unlucky traveler would find her, a human ice statue, miles from home.

Maybe she didn't have to leave Brumehome, just the tavern. Still, as Brynar had said, no one else would offer her a job which, in turn, meant she'd have nowhere to live, nothing to eat, no way to keep warm. Maybe Widow Gri could take her in, train Lizbete in healing, let her sleep beside the fire in the pit-house.

The widow isn't afraid of me, but I hate to ask her for charity. What can I offer her in return? Maybe crystals. I was able to find them in the caves when no one else could. One, anyway. She said they were valuable. Also, it would be nice to find more for Elin.

That was at least a plan. If she could find more of the crystals, she'd give some to Elin, then take the rest to Widow Gri and negotiate an apprenticeship.

A smirk curled the corners of Lizbete's mouth. If there was any trade she was cut out for, local witch was it.

Footsteps crossed the common room. Discerning they were coming in her direction, Lizbete put her broom aside and faced the kitchen door.

Hangur entered, recoiled when he found her gazing directly at him, then scowled. "Are we ready for the midday customers yet?"

She shook her head. "We need someone to go to the butcher, the dairy, and the market. Or if not the butcher, then the docks to see what the fishermen brought in."

"And why haven't you done that?" Hangur pointed an accusing finger at her.

Lizbete pursed her lips. That had never been her job. Auntie Katryn recognized that the local merchants often treated Lizbete unfairly and always did the market runs herself or sent Falla if the woman was working an early shift. Falla wouldn't be in until midday today.

"With what money?" Lizbete pointed out. "I have no access to the coffers."

"You'd think after we've served the town for so long, the merchants could let us have a few days' worth of goods on credit," Hangur grumbled.

Lizbete's jaw clenched. Had he been Katryn, they probably would have done so, but even if they had chosen him over Lizbete, the village still wasn't about to trust Hangur with their livelihoods. They'd want coin.

"I'll take care of it," he finally said. "Just make sure to wipe down the common room while I'm gone. It smells of sour ale."

Lizbete nodded stonily. She couldn't really begin cooking in earnest until he fetched her more ingredients anyway.

Once Hangur departed, Lizbete heated a bucket of water over the fire before grabbing a handful of washclothes and heading into the common room. Through the swinging door, Lizbete shivered. The room was cold and poorly lit. Hangur hadn't bothered to start a fire in the hearth or light any of the lanterns. She quickly set about doing both, bathing the room in a pleasant, golden light. She then took the table in the farthest corner and began to wipe it down with a mixture of hot water and vinegar.

For the time it took to clean about a half dozen tables, Lizbete's world was a mix of hot water, repetitive motion, and the acrid but not unpleasant scent of the vinegar. Her blood mostly drew from the warmth rising off the fireplace, but sometimes also from the bucket of water. To counter this, she kept a second bucket sitting on the hearth. Every time her bucket grew too cold, she swapped it with the one warmed by the fireplace's flames.

The seventh table had a smear of dried gravy across the top that took a little more elbow grease than the rest of the task. As she scrubbed at it, her back to the bar, a gentle creaking of feet on floorboards caught her ears. She cast a furtive glance in that direction.

Erich crept down the stairs, hugging the wall. Lizbete angled away and pretended to be engrossed in her work. She worked around the table in a circle, moving to where she could watch him out of the corner of her eye.

Unaware of her awareness, the man continued to sneak forward, slipping across the common room and behind the bar. His hand extended, quivering, towards the shelf of liquor.

Lizbete opened her mouth, ready to shout at the man for stealing, but hesitated. It wasn't her liquor. Wasn't her tavern. Wasn't her problem. Hangur had stolen her inheritance and allowed this wastrel into the bar. Let him suffer the consequences in stolen booze.

She set her back to him and whistled as she worked. She heard him sneak back up the stairs.

Idiot. Well, maybe Hangur will learn a lesson when he comes back to find his friend blackout drunk before noon.

Lizbete continued her task. Once the tables were complete, she fetched a mop and started on the floors.

Another faint scratching noise echoed about the common room. She looked up, wondering how Erich could've possibly finished off his bottle so quickly.

The room was empty.

Lizbete stood as still as stone. With her sensitive hearing, she was used to sounds of foundations settling, of wind scratching at rooftops, of distant voices and footsteps . . . but this hadn't been that. It had been close. Quiet, but close.

Maybe a mouse or a rat had found its way into the tavern? She hoped not. Rats nibbling on their already understocked pantry items was the last thing she needed right now. Disgusting things. Auntie always fed the local stray cats generously to avoid such an incident, but had Hangur been doing the same?

Lizbete swallowed. She'd have to put out some scraps that evening to buy the protection of the local felines. Her ears twitching, she continued to mop the floor. The sound didn't repeat, but she couldn't shake the strange feeling that she wasn't alone. She opened her mouth to call out, only to shut it again.

This is ridiculous. You're just anxious for no reason. Erich's drunken stories are getting to you.

She finished her work and dumped the bucket of dirty water

down the drain that Katryn had installed behind the bar for easy cleaning of spills.

Something thumped overhead. She paused. Unlike the scratching, this was undeniable. Another thump soon followed. What was going on up there?

Lizbete chewed thoughtfully on her bottom lip. They'd had a few travelers in the rented rooms the night before, a group of farmers from the In-Lands who had come to Brumehome to sell their crops and livestock. However, she'd personally checked them out that morning. She didn't mind dealing with visitors. They tended to lack preconceived notions about her. Apparently no one had gotten to these ones with tales of her strangeness and possible deadliness, as they'd smiled and chatted when she'd taken their money and sent them on their way.

If those men were gone, and Hangur was still at market, that only left one possible culprit.

"Erich?" she shouted up the stairs.

No answer, though the rustling and thumping continued. Groaning inwardly, she strode up the stairs. The door to Erich's room—her stolen room—stood open. With a deep breath she strode in, and her knees turned to jelly.

Bedclothes lay tossed about the room. Her wardrobe doors hung open and clothing items flowed out of it like honey spilling from a tipped pot. The room smelled of vomit. Her eyes darted about taking in the chaos before alighting on Erich. The man swayed before the window, pawing at her collection of crystals.

"Stop! Those are mine!" she gasped.

He picked up the blue sphere and tossed it over his head. She cringed as it descended. He reached to catch it, fumbled, and stared dumbly as it struck the floor with a great crash. It rolled across the floor. Lizbete dove for it, praying it wasn't damaged. Erich's foot swung forward, knocking the sphere under the bed and coming so close to her teeth that she could smell his rancid socks.

She fell backwards onto her elbows.

He picked up the star-shine crystal she'd found outside of Widow Gri's and squinted at it. "These aren't yours. They're too pretty. Too valuable. I could get good money for these at the market." His words slurred like a slug slipping over a garden path.

"They *are* mine." She jumped to her feet and stamped her foot, hoping to jolt some sense into him. "Everything in this room is mine!"

"No, everything in this room, in this whole tavern, is my friend's." Erich waved the crystal under her nose. "You're a beggar who owns nothing. If Hangur weren't the generous sort, you'd be out on the street." He grinned, flashing yellowed teeth. "You still might be when he hears how you treat his guests."

Rage expanded in Lizbete's chest, and she clamped her jaw tight to keep from screaming. "Put my belongings down."

His grin hardened to a glare, then slowly morphed into an unnerving smile. He extended his hand as if offering her the crystal. She reached for it. Erich released it before her hand could grasp it, sending it crashing to the ground.

A strangled cry escaped her, and she dropped to her knees. Several perfect points had broken off the crystal. Lizbete clutched it to her chest. Her vision blurred with tears. She blinked to clear it before tucking the broken crystal into her apron pocket and scrambling up again.

She snatched up the green stone and the chip of obsidian. The gold nugget was missing—probably in Erich's pocket, but at least she'd reclaimed some items. She turned to rush out of the room, running past him, and her breath left her.

Erich reached into her wardrobe and pulled out the blue party dress with its lace and ribbons.

"Don't touch that!" she wailed.

He held it up to his chin and fluttered his eyelashes. "Oh, does the Ash Lizard like to dress up pretty? You might as well put this on miller's old mule. It'd look just as good."

Lizbete's throat tightened. To see the last gift Auntie Katryn had given her manhandled by an unfeeling drunk, it was the final snowflake that collapsed the roof. The last of her strength left her, and she just whimpered, "Please, stop. That's—that's mine. It's special."

"In fact, I think I'll go put it on the mule right now." He pushed past her and out the door.

She blinked. Did he really intend to—no, that made no sense. She bolted after him.

He danced down the hall, singing loudly and off-key, "Put a dress on a mule, you still got a mule, tie a bow round a lizard, you still got a lizard, plant a kiss on a shrew you still got a shrew..."

"Give it back!" she shouted.

Her hand clamped down on him. Even though she was warm, her blood latched onto his heat. Ravenously. The rush of heat leaving his body must've been tangible, as he jerked away, spun around, and backhanded her.

His fist hit her chin, knocking her into the wall. The world swam. Her ears rang, and blood throbbed in her head.

"What—what was that? What are you?" He loomed over her. He swayed on his feet. "You're a . . . what did you do?"

Lizbete swallowed the blood that seeped from her teeth. She struggled into a standing position, or at least a leaning one, bracing herself against the wall. Her beautiful blue dress lay crumpled at his feet.

Panic and desperation surged through her. She snatched the garment up and sprinted down the stairs away from him.

"Come back, you witch!" He lumbered after her. His heavy footfalls shook the stairs.

She hit the common room just as the door opened on the other side of it. Hangur stepped in, and his eyes widened.

"What under the sky—?"

Lizbete didn't stop. She shoved past him into the street.

I need to get away. I need to get somewhere safe. Not here. Anywhere but here.

"Come back, witch! Give me that!" Drunk and enraged, Erich barreled after her. A handful of citizens looked up from their errands and stared as Lizbete fled the angry man. The cold air reached for her. It snaked into her mouth and up her nostrils. Dizziness overtook her, and her run turned to a stagger.

"What's going on here?" a masculine voice called out. Mayor Sten stepped out of the blacksmith's shop across the street and glared at the insanity before him.

Undeterred, Erich snatched at the dress and started to pull it from Lizbete's hands.

"Stop!" she screamed. "He's robbing me!"

"She's a witch! We need to tie her down. She tried to freeze my heart!" Erich growled.

Sten shook his head wearily. "Erich, you're drunk. Don't be—"

"No, he's telling the truth." Hangur stepped out of the tavern, his eyes flashing. "I'd let it slip by me, but the girl's done it to me before too. A touch from her hand and your blood turns cold."

People abandoned their tasks and stopped to gawk many drawing closer. Lizbete hunched into herself as the circle of onlookers closed in around her. Murmurs spread through the crowd.

"That's what she did to those sheep, remember?" Hester, the cobbler's wife, whispered. "All those years ago? Dead in their stalls as if they'd been left out overnight in the cold instead of safe in their barn."

Lizbete shivered. She wanted to run, but somehow she couldn't bring herself to drop the dress. The dress Auntie had given her before she'd died. Erich clung to the other end of it with a grip like a hard-shelled crab.

"We should've left the monster out in the wilds to let the beasts and frost take care of her years ago," an old man snarled.

Sten stiffened. While his hearing wasn't as keen as Lizbete's, it didn't take catching the words of the crowd to sense their mood. The murmurs grew louder.

"Whatever she did to you, either of you," he narrowed his eyes at his brother who shut his mouth, "you both seem fine. I won't have this town fall into disorder over drunken fancies. Erich, give the girl back the dress."

Lizbete's shoulders eased. The wind still snaked about her, stiffening her joints. She wasn't sure how much longer she could stand, let alone maintain her hold on the garment.

Erich's lower lip quivered. The crowd lingered but made no move to support him. He frowned and released the dress.

Lizbete let out a relieved sigh and gathered it tightly against her chest. She took a step towards the tavern door. Maybe she could collect her belongings before making the walk to Widow Gri's.

Erich reached under his shirt and yanked out something that glinted in the sun. "If no one else in this town has the courage to kill this witch—"

"He has a knife!" someone shouted.

"Erich, no!" Sten yelled.

Lizbete whirled. The blade loomed over her head. It would strike in a heartbeat.

She was going to die.

A streak of gray rushed from the entrance to the alleyway and collided against Erich. The figure moved fast. Too fast to be human. It knocked the man to the ground and hunched over him, hands gripping him by the neck.

A woman screamed.

"What is that?" another man cried.

Lizbete stared. Red eyes glinted at her from an ash gray face. The creature looked human in form with a slender, sinewy body clothed in some sort of rough black cloth. It blinked at her, then darted its gaze around the stunned crowd.

"Stop it! Get it!" Sten barked. He lunged for Erich's knife, which lay abandoned on the cobblestones. The creature leaped up and dashed away as quickly as it had come. Two men took off in pursuit, but Sten stayed, stooping over Erich.

The drunken fool stared blindly up at the sky. Frost scaled his eyes and lips, and his skin carried a ghostly pallor.

"He's dead," Sten said simply.

Fog closed in on Lizbete's vision. What had just happened?

Chapter Fourteen

The voices of the frightened villagers turned into an unintelligible rattle, like dried leaves in the wind. Lizbete's whole body shook. The cold air ate at her, but even worse, terror gripped her. What had she just seen? What had just happened? Nothing made sense. The world spun around her, and she swallowed down bile, trying not to throw up.

"It was a dark spirit!" A shrill voice shoved her out of her panic and back into the present. A present somehow even more horrifying than her previous confusion had been.

"There's no such thing!" Mayor Sten barked. Panic laced his tone, and his hands clenched and unclenched as if trying to get a hold on the situation. "I've spent my life trying to keep this town from reverting to superstition and ignorance. I will not have that overturned by one . . . admittedly . . . very odd incident." He let out a long breath, and his voice calmed to his usual manner.

"Odd incident?" Hangur stomped towards his brother. "Sten, are you mad? Or blind? We all saw that monster. It was not human."

"The girl is in league with it!" Hester stormed out of the crowd, eyes wild. "It appeared when Erich threatened her! She must've summoned it somehow."

"Maybe she *is* one of them," someone in the crowd hissed. "Look at her complexion."

Whispers from the onlookers struck Lizbete like stones, one after another.

"She's always been odd."

"Don't forget those animals…"

"What if she killed old Katryn too?"

"Yeah, that never sat right with me, how quickly she died. The blacksmith's daughter said the girl tried to claim the tavern as her own right after the funeral. Would've taken it too if the family hadn't stepped in."

Lizbete shook her head. "I didn't! I—I don't know what that was. I've never—" she stopped short. She *had* seen it before. Peering at her through the kitchen window. Had it been following her? Watching her? Was it the source of the anonymous gifts?

"We should toss her in the sea before she has a chance to kill any more of us!" an elderly man shouted.

"That's nonsense." Sten stepped between Lizbete and the growing mob. Lizbete inhaled sharply. Was he really protecting her? "The girl has lived in our village for over sixteen years without incident—"

"Without incident?" Hangur jabbed a finger at Erich's corpse.

"What about the livestock that keeps going missing?" It was Rawl, Erich's former employer. "The herdsmen and farmers have lost more in the last month than they have in previous years combined."

"And the earthquake!" Hester added.

Lizbete shied back. What was she going to do?

"There's no way this child could've caused an earthquake," Sten scoffed.

"Her dark spirit guardians could, though."

Lizbete opened her mouth to defend herself, but Sten grabbed her arm. She gave a squeaking protest as her blood pulled a burst of heat from his body. He released her and staggered back, wide-eyed.

Shame rippled through her. Horror washed over his expression followed by confusion and then, pity.

"Get inside, stay out of sight," he whispered, angling himself between her and the crowd. "I will calm them down. I don't know what is going on here, but my son trusts you. You're not a murderer."

Befuddled by this unexpected mercy, Lizbete nodded and bolted for the tavern door.

"What are you doing letting her into my tavern?" Hangur snarled as she slammed the door shut behind her. "I don't want that little freak—"

Lizbete paused, her keen hearing able to hear Sten's response in spite of the shut door and growing noise of the angry crowd.

"As I said, the girl has lived peaceably in this village for over a decade and there is no proof she has ever harmed a soul. Compared to you, who just waltzed back into town after years spent doing Skywatcher knows what. In fact, from what I can tell, there's more correlation between your sudden reappearance and all this strangeness than there is with anything involving Lizbete."

A slight twinge of pleasure spread through Lizbete at the thought that *Hangur* was the cursed one.

"Do you want me to go around spreading rumors that *you* killed off our sister to get her tavern? That you're jinxed and have caused an earthquake, and storms. That you made livestock go missing?"

"Of course not, but I—"

"Then don't go spouting that nonsense about a young woman with no family to speak up for her. You may be my brother, Hangur, but I have a whole town to look after, and Lizbete is just as much a citizen as you are."

The crowd fell silent. Lizbete couldn't name the sensation within her chest. It was a mix of comfort and fear, confusion and gratitude. Mayor Sten was protecting her. The man who didn't see her as good enough for Brynar, who had allowed Hangur to take her inheritance . . . he still wanted her to live and saw her as worthy of safeguarding. Why?

She considered peeking out again but feared someone would see her and rile the mob again. Glancing down, she realized she still gripped the fancy blue dress. Mud streaked the fabric and at some point during the struggle, the sleeve had torn away from the bodice. She sighed. It wasn't as if she'd ever get a chance to wear it.

"But what are we going to do about this?" Rawl asked.

"Did Erich have any living family?"

"Pordi, the butcher's wife, is his sister, but they don't speak. She doesn't like to acknowledge him."

"Well, someone needs to inform her and see if she wants to claim the body."

"But what about the monster?"

"It wasn't a—whatever it was, we'll find it and deal with it. It couldn't have gone far. Einar, I see you in the back there. Get up here."

"Sir?"

"We need to search the village."

Lizbete stepped away from the door. The immediate danger had passed, but too many people had witnessed the chaos for her safety to be guaranteed. Her position in the village had already been tenuous, but now everyone had proof that she was inhuman and dangerous. Even Mayor Sten couldn't protect her for long.

She needed to get to Widow Gri's today. Even if she couldn't provide her the crystals in exchange for her apprenticeship immediately, the widow wouldn't turn her away. Would she?

Lizbete entered the kitchen. Never having journeyed outside of Brumehome, she'd never had need of a knapsack or other means to carry her belongings. The rough sacks that they received potatoes or flour in would probably serve. She had a stash of them saved up. She also wanted a metal bucket she could fill with coals. That trick had kept her warm on her last trip from Widow Gri's. It should work again today.

As she gathered these things, she couldn't help glancing repeatedly out the window. She half expected to see that strange, gray face looming there, watching her with its eerie red eyes. Still, considering her two quick glances at the creature, it wasn't really frightening. While the color was off, its features were mostly human. A little gaunt, but not monstrous. Just a skinny, gray-skinned, red-eyed person.

Lizbete paused, clutching her flour sack in one hand.

She matched two out of those three traits—three traits if she counted the apparent ability to freeze at a touch.

Oh, Skywatcher. Am I also whatever that thing is?

Her mind scrambled for differences. The creature appeared to be hairless, and she had hair, stringy ash-brown hair that wasn't much to look at, but hair nonetheless. Her eyes had an amber tint to them, more like a cat's than a person's, but not like the creature's.

Person.

She set her jaw firm and crammed her ruined dress angrily into her flour sack. Whatever the being was, human or not, it was still a person. She wouldn't let herself demonize it as a monster. Especially not after it had saved her life from that awful Erich.

Glancing out the window, she noted the sun was descending in the sky. Already after midday for sure. She shook her head. The tavern hadn't opened for lunch, and she doubted it would be open for dinner.

Wait. Hangur had gone out to get groceries for the meals. He'd come back empty handed. Had he not bought anything at all? Auntie Katryn would be so disappointed. How could Lizbete abandon her auntie's beloved tavern to fall into disrepute and disrepair at the hands of the lazy Hangur?

A tavern isn't a person, she assured herself. *It might remind you of Auntie Katryn. It might have been important to Auntie Katryn, but it's not Auntie Katryn. Auntie would care far more about me being safe than she would about this business continuing.*

She set aside her small tin bucket, a spare that she sometimes used to feed the chickens with. She'd fill it with coals closer to departure so it would stay heated for her journey. With her flour sack, she slipped out of the kitchen but immediately shied back.

Hangur stood behind the bar, his back to her, one hand grasping the neck of a bottle.

"First the stupid merchants won't give me food on credit, then I lose my friend, then my idiot brother bosses me around in front of the whole steam-blasted village," his voice a growled slur. "Force me to live with a girl who might freeze me solid in my sleep. I see how it is. Some brother."

Lizbete grimaced and crept towards the stairs. She managed to get up them before Hangur noticed she was there.

When she reached her bedroom, her legs almost went out from

under her. She owned so few things that to see them all strewn about like flotsam and jetsam after a storm nearly brought her to her knees again. She took off her spectacles. The amount of crying she'd done recently had left them hopelessly smudged. Focusing on cleaning them with her tunic seemed to help. The simple act of removing spots from her vision somehow brought clarity to life as a whole.

She scrounged up her clothing, her spare shoes, and the blue kerchief Auntie had given her and placed them all in her sack. This accomplished, she got down on all fours and fished under her bed for the sphere. Most of her other presents were in her pocket. The only missing one was the gold lump. She morbidly mused about whether Erich's estranged sister would find it on his body before he was buried. Well, let her have it.

Her fingers met with the cold stone of the sphere, and Lizbete added it to her small stash of treasures. She considered a box of childhood trinkets at the bottom of her wardrobe that Erich had missed in his ransacking. Not that they were anything of value. Small wooden animals that Auntie had purchased from a local vendor, a collection of pretty pebbles, and some sea glass that had washed up on the shore near the village. Her flour sack was already getting full, and she didn't really need any of childhood trinkets. After some hesitation, she selected her favorites of the carved animals—a family of foxes: mother fox, father fox, and three kits—and tucked them into her bag.

She paused and looked over the chaos Erich had created in her tiny room. Lizbete's throat tightened. Auntie had taught her to keep things neat and tidy. She couldn't stand to leave her childhood room in such a mess. She picked up any remaining items off the door, fixed the toppled bedside table, found the candle and candle holder Erich had knocked to the ground, and made the bed.

A great weariness overcame her. She had a long walk before her without any sure promise that Widow Gri would take her in. Also, she'd have to walk through the village, filled with people who feared and hated her. The whole thing made her want to worm under her covers and close her eyes to the world.

I'll just lie down for a moment. Say good-bye to my bed, to my home.

She rested her head on the pillow. She remembered sleeping in Auntie's arms as a child. Although Auntie had swiftly discovered the dangers of holding young Lizbete for any length of time, she'd learned tricks to mitigate the risk. Her favorite was wrapping Liz in several layers of blankets so that they had no direct contact, but she could still cradle the girl in her arms and rock her to sleep. Lizbete missed being that close to someone, the pressure of arms around her, the sound of breath and heartbeat. Auntie had been willing to go through so much to keep her safe and help her feel loved.

I'll never have that again, but the memory will be mine forever.

The comfort of her blankets and the softness of her down-stuffed pillow reminded her of Auntie's embrace. Her body melted into the mattress as the world softened to gray with her.

A shaking woke her what felt like only moments later. Her bed vibrated beneath her, the doors to her wardrobe trembling as if someone inside were trying to get out. She gripped the sides of her bed and prayed until the earthquake ended.

Another one? What is going on with this town?

Her spectacles sat crooked on her face, and she quickly righted them. Lizbete blinked. Her room was dark.

Oh no.

How could she have slept so long? She hurried to the window

and peeled back the corner of the thin layer of animal hide that served to let in light but keep out the cold. Her fingers tightened on the windowsill.

Good news, it wasn't night yet.

Bad news, a thick layer of fog had rolled in over Brumehome. It cloaked the building across the street.

"Steam-blast me. Why did I dawdle?"

Lizbete snatched up her bundle of belongings and dashed downstairs. She needed to grab her bucket, fill it with hot coals, and sneak out of town.

This could be a blessing. The fog will make it so no one sees me leaving. After what happened today, some vigilante might take it upon themselves to finish what Erich started.

"Whadya think yer doing?"

Lizbete froze with her hand on the kitchen door.

Hangur lurched out of the private dining room. "When I felt the tavern shaking, I should've known you were about." His gaze fell on her sack of belongings, and his eyes narrowed. "What do you got in that bag, girl? You trying to steal from me?"

"No, these are mine." Lizbete clutched the sack to her chest.

Hangur's hair stood up in unruly tufts, and he staggered more than walked. "Nothing here is yours," he sneered.

She squared her shoulders. "These things are."

And the rest of it should be too.

"I can't afford to have you robbing from me." He extended a shaking hand in her direction. "I've already lost too many customers because you're here. The butcher, the fisherman, even that worthless miller who married my sister—none of them will do business with me without cash up front." He stomped his foot. "How can I make money if I don't have food to sell my customers, huh?"

Lizbete shrank away from him. "I don't know, but I won't be here much longer. I'm leaving."

His eyes widened. "But—but I won't have anyone to cook tomorrow. You can't just run out on me, you little traitor!"

"You just said I'm costing you—" Realizing it was pointless to argue, Lizbete stopped. "I won't be here to scare off your customers any longer." She took a step towards the kitchen, but he cut her off.

"Drop the bag!" he ordered.

She tightened her hold on it. "No. It's my clothing. My personal items."

"Then empty it out and let me see!" He lunged for her. She dodged, but his hand caught her by the wrist.

"Stop!" she gasped as his sickening, dizzying heat rushed into her. He screamed and pushed her as hard as he could. She fell against the nearest table. The edge of it hit her hard in the ribs, and the air left her lungs in a woosh. The sack crashed from her hand onto the floor.

Hangur snatched it up. "You tried to freeze me again! Just like Erich! You little ice witch! This time my brother will have to listen." Still holding her belongings, he rushed from the tavern.

Lizbete rubbed her bruised side with a whimper. She needed to get out of here now. Even if Sten didn't listen to him, it was only a matter of time until Hangur escalated his nonsense until either he got her killed, or she accidentally froze him to death.

She limped to the kitchen and wrapped herself in the spare cloak she kept on a hook there. With her bucket, she scooped up as many hot coals as she could carry. Trailing her hand lovingly across the bricks of the fireplace, Lizbete whispered a good-bye to the building that had been her home for as long as she could remember. She'd grown up here, toddled around Auntie's ankles as she cooked. Losing her home, her place in the inn, ached like losing Auntie all over again. Tears escaped her eyes before she hardened herself.

I have to get out of here. As much as I hate it, I can't stay.

Losing her belongings was a small price to pay for freedom.

With a whispered goodbye, she slipped out the back door and into the alley way.

The soup of fog rose to greet her. She shivered and pushed onward. Her vision was obscured beyond the reach of her arm, but she put one hand on the outer wall of the tavern and used it to guide her way.

Particles of ice floated in the fog, stinging against her face as she staggered forward. She tightened her hands around the tin bucket. The coals within gave off a pleasant smoky scent.

Small joys. Cling to those. I'll make it through this. Just a short walk to Widow Gri's, and I'll be safe.

Lizbete reached the corner of the tavern and swallowed. She knew her way around town well enough, but the fog made everything look strange and unnerving. Pausing, she listened. In the distance a cow lowed. Somewhere to her right came a constant pounding of metal against metal. The blacksmith's shop? Possibly, if he were working late. She angled in that direction.

Her glasses fogged over, and she had to stop to clean them. When she placed them back on her nose, they immediately fogged over again. With a groan, Lizbete took them off and put them in her apron pocket. In this weather, she couldn't really see past a few feet anyway. She bit her bottom lip. Should she have brought a lantern? Well, it was too late to go back now. For all she knew Hangur already had a mob out looking for her.

She reached the end of the alley. With the fog she could probably risk going by the main streets. No one would see her.

Ice crystals stung against her neck, and she stuck one hand directly into the bucket of coals. The heat sizzled against her skin before spreading through her body. Fortified by this, she took off at a brisk walk across the town square. Ahead a beacon of light pierced the fog. Someone had lit the watchtower at the harbor. Did that mean there were still boats out in this? She certainly hoped not.

Unable to see much else in the way of landmarks, Lizbete clung to walls and fences that she recognized, but that wouldn't work once she got to the edge of town.

This is ridiculous. What am I thinking? She paused, gripping her bucket and praying that the fog would lift. *Even if I'm lucky enough to find the path up the cliff face in this soup, I'd be an idiot to climb a narrow track up the side of a sheer cliff in it. I'll break my neck.*

She glanced back in the direction she'd come. Maybe Hangur would have calmed down. Maybe she could sleep in the kitchen.

Or what about Mayor Sten? Elin would advocate for her. If Lizbete made it clear it was only for the night and that she'd willingly sleep out of the way, maybe in their kitchen. Maybe if she was clear that she had nowhere else to go.

No pride left, she turned around and started towards the mayor's house.

The ground trembled beneath her. She fell back against the wall of the nearest building. The tremor ceased as quickly as it had started. She let out a long breath. Again? That was two in a day. At least these ones were weak—

The ground heaved. Lizbete crashed to her hands and knees. Her bucket of coals scattered on the ground before her, sending sparks of red through the fog. She gasped and curled up into herself as the world continued to shake. In the distance a woman screamed. Something crashed against something else. Vibrations ran through

Lizbete's body. Debris crashed down on her, bits of plaster and thatch from the house she cowered next to.

Skywatcher, save me! She closed her eyes.

Then as quickly as it had begun, the shaking stopped.

For a long moment, she didn't dare to unfold. Voices echoed through the fog. People cried out in confusion and fear. Finally, she lurched to her feet. Her knees shook. What was going on?

The wind sprang up around her, and terror gripped her by the throat. Her blood thickened and her muscles stiffened. She'd lost her coals. She was out alone in the chilly fog and she'd lost her only source of heat. She needed to get to shelter, fast.

Lizbete tried to run, but the fog disoriented her. The familiar streets and buildings of the tiny village seemed strange. Her hand found the end of the building she currently guided herself. An alley stretched out before her.

She bit her bottom lip. If she was where she thought she was, the mayor's house was at the end of this alley.

Almost there. They have to give me shelter. They have to.

The wind howled, and as if in answer, hard bits of ice pelted her. They hammered down, at first only a few, then all around her, a torrent of tiny balls of cold. Each time one struck her, heat leached from her body. She quivered.

Almost there.

She staggered a few feet forward and collapsed against a fence. A wooden fence, roughly hewn. Her throat closed in on itself. This wasn't the mayor's yard. Her hands clenched about the fence rail started to stiffen and seize from the cold. Where was she?

Over the sound of the sleet pounding against the nearby buildings and cobblestone streets, she caught a gentle snuffling and grunting. Pigs. This had to be the pig farm one street over from the mayor's house. She must've turned one alleyway too soon.

"I . . . c . . . can make it," she forced the words through chattering teeth. She needed to hear them. Needed to believe them. Needed to trick herself into going onward.

Lizbete staggered through the storm, her leaden legs slowing her to a slug's pace. After a few yards, she stumbled.

"Somebody help," she whimpered.

No one came.

Squinting through the driving ice and lingering, she looked for any sign of hope. An outline of a building loomed before her. She stumbled up the short path and collapsed against the door.

She pounded upon it until her fists hurt. "Please let me in! It's so cold."

No one answered, though light seeped under the crack in the door. Desperate, she tried the handle. The door shook but appeared to be latched from the inside.

"Please!" she wailed.

"It's the Ash Lizard. Don't open the door." The frantic whispers barely carried over the chaos surrounding her and the throbbing of her own pulse. "If she's here the dark spirits can't be far behind."

A young child whimpered.

Lizbete coughed. "Please. I'm not a monster. Hangur threw me out. I'll die out here."

No one came.

Lizbete collapsed, lying on their doorstep, shivering. Her body grew numb. She felt heavy, absent, drifting away...

She heard footsteps. Someone was coming for her? In her haziness, she wondered if it could be Brynar. Had he returned to save her? To protect her as he'd offered what seemed like so long ago?

A slight scent of sulfur tickled her nose. She opened her eyes again. A dark figure loomed over her. Red eyes glowed in its otherwise indiscernible face, terrifying and definitely not Brynar's.

Lizbete tried to scream, but nothing came out. The creature swooped down and gathered her up as if she'd been a small child.

She jerked and twitched. Too weak to fight but still desperate to free herself before it harmed her—but then it happened.

Heat flowed from the creature's touch into her. Her scream turned into a sigh of relief, and she melted into him. Darkness and weariness overtook her. She vaguely felt the movement as someone ran carrying her, the bumps of hurried footfalls through the back paths of the freezing village, then the welcoming embrace of warm air. Wherever he was taking her, whoever—or whatever—he was, she was warm again. Even if he killed her, at least she wouldn't die cold.

Chapter Fifteen

"Grimir, what were you thinking?"

The voice echoed through Lizbete's restless dreams. It had a feminine quality to it, but with a raspiness, as if the speaker had a severe cold.

"If the others find out you brought her here . . . if the Ravenous One finds out—"

"They won't, Naasha." A deeper, gravelly voice interrupted her. "She won't be here long. I just couldn't let her freeze. She's—she's mine."

Lizbete's eyes snapped open. Fear surged through her, bringing her to instant consciousness. Where was she? How had she gotten there? She almost leaped to her feet, but forced herself to stay still. If the people who had brought her here knew she was awake—especially Naasha, who did not seem to want her there at all—they might do something to her. Lizbete needed to take stock of her whereabouts, find out what she was up against, and if possible, who she was with. That would all be easier if her captors thought her still asleep and unaware.

She lay on a bed that crinkled beneath her when she moved. A blanket of some coarse cloth covered her and a sheet of the same material rested beneath her. Before her was a wall of stone bathed in firelight. Upon the wall, like characters in a children's shadow puppet play, were two thin silhouettes, both human. At least, she could clearly discern the correct number of limbs and a head of roughly the right shape.

"I worry about you, though," Naasha continued. "You've taken so many risks lately. Even with your family's influence, there is only so much the council will put up with."

"You forget, I'm also a member of the council," Grimir chuckled.

"You won't be if they find out about *her*." Displeasure tainted Naasha's tone.

"They won't. Like I said, I couldn't let her die out there, but I have no illusions about . . . I know I can't keep her."

A trace of agony crept into Grimir's words. In spite of her anxiety over her unexpected relocation, Lizbete found herself pitying him. Whatever he was, he'd done her no harm. In fact, he'd saved her. For that alone, she could allow him some trust.

"The storm is over, though. Can't you put her back now?"

"She's sleeping. Also, the villagers almost killed her yesterday. If I hadn't intervened—"

"Yes, we all know about that. The other council members aren't pleased with how you revealed yourself."

"It could not be helped. If I hadn't acted immediately that beast would've stabbed the girl."

A shiver cut through Lizbete. Her rescuer was the one who had killed Erich?

"Perhaps, but if you're wrong and they find out—please, be

careful, Grimir. You have just started to regain the trust of our people. Do not throw it away on another human you cannot save."

Soft, shuffling footsteps faded in the distance. Face to the wall, and not wanting to draw attention to herself by rolling over, Lizbete focused on her other senses to gather information about her surroundings. Sounds echoed oddly, and between that, the warmth, and the stone wall before her, it was easy enough to deduce that she was in a cave. Someone moved about in the cavern with her. She assumed it was Grimir. Water dripped steadily somewhere in the room, and in the background roared a constant crackling fire. Not close. Not in this chamber. It had to be a large fire to be heard here where she could neither see its light nor feel its warmth.

A sort of warmth did fill the chamber. However, it was an ambient heat, not radiating from any particular area. There was also a slight humidity and heaviness to the air, along with a scent of sulfur which at first wrinkled her nose, but which she then came to tolerate and even like. She rubbed her fingers against the surface beneath her. The cloth was softer than canvas but coarser than wool. She worked her hand beneath it and found dried plant-like material. Moss? It was hard to be sure without examining it visually.

Lizbete strained her ears for more information, but nothing new presented itself. Grimir's shuffling and bustling stopped, leaving the room silent except for the distant sound of flames and the constant drip, drip, drip of water on rock. She needed to find out more.

She rolled over and her breath went out of her lungs.

The light she'd assumed was from a fire radiated from a riot of red crystals. They grew in bunches like flowers in a garden all over the stone wall opposite her bed.

Those are the crystals that can help Elin. She stood. For a moment her knees wobbled, but she braced herself against the wall, inhaled, then walked forward a little steadier. A delightful energy hummed around the crystals. It prickled against Lizbete's skin and enlivened her senses. She reached towards one particularly large bunch of red.

"Stop!"

She cowered, covering her head with her hands. What would this strange being do to her? If he saw her as *his* somehow, could she hope to escape?

A gray shape dashed from the far side of the chamber. The shadowy figure shimmered like smoke in sunlight as it moved with breathless speed to block Lizbete from the crystals with his body. She blinked. The figure solidified into an ash-gray skinned man with hollow cheeks, red glowing eyes, and no eyebrows or hair.

He held up his hand. "I do not mean to frighten you, but please. Don't touch the crystals. They're sacred to the Ravenous One. If you—it's dangerous."

Lizbete frowned. She'd handled one of those crystals before and not been harmed by it. In fact, the crystals had helped Elin. What did Grimir mean by 'dangerous'?

"I'm sorry. I was just…" She swallowed. He did not seem unkind. Could she convince him to help her with Elin? "I have a friend who could use some of them to make her feel better."

He dropped his gaze. "I wish I could give you one, but if I did people might get hurt. I made that mistake once already, and I can't risk it again."

Confused, Lizbete took a step back from him. He wore a rough garment made of what appeared to be the same dark cloth she'd slept upon. His feet were bare, his red eyes unnerving, but not frightening. In spite of his claim of ownership towards her, he did not move in a way she found threatening nor speak to her like a possession. What did he mean, though, that she was *his*?

"They're beautiful, and there are so many of them." She motioned towards them. "How are there so many?"

"I grow them." He smiled. Reaching under his garment, he pulled out a pouch that hung around his neck by a twisted cord that appeared to be made of the same moss that stuffed her mattress. He tipped the contents of the pouch into his hands. Tiny shards of glinting crystal glowed against his gray skin. "You can seed an area with crystal fragments, and if provided with heat and the right mix of elemental energy, they will grow. That's my profession. I'm a crystal gardener."

A whole series of questions blossomed in Lizbete's mind. Could she find a way to grow crystals for Elin? Why did Grimir consider them dangerous? But other questions screamed them down. She didn't even know where to start. Well, that wasn't true.

"Thank you for saving me," she said. "Twice now, apparently."

Grimir dropped his gaze to the fragments in his hand. Holding his pouch open with one hand, he returned the shards to it with the other. "It—it was not at great cost to myself."

"But it was a great gift to me." She forced a smile, wanting to be kind and not show him her fear. "What…" She hesitated. Asking *what* he was might seem like an insult. She didn't know he wasn't human. After all, humans came in more than one shade, from Widow Gri's dark skin to the pale skin of the villagers. She decided on another first question. "I heard another person talking to you. Are there many people living in these caves?"

"A few hundred of us at any given time. Our population ebbs and flows."

She glanced at the bare walls of the cavern. They'd have no way to grow crops or raise animals. So little lived down here. "How do you survive? I mean, what do you eat?"

"For the most part we live off the energy that rises from the steamvents themselves." He moved away from the crystal wall towards an alcove, where a series of shelves had been carved into the rock itself. A dozen or so small containers—clay jars, boxes fashioned of what appeared to be driftwood, and even some glass—sat upon these shelves. He opened one and held it out to her. "We do sometimes eat, of course. Some animals can be hunted within the caves, and when we can, we emerge from our caverns to gather food from the Over-Lands."

Lizbete peered into the jar he offered her. Inside were a series of pale yellow flakes about the size of coins. She took one and examined it. Was this cave-people food?

"Try it," Grimir prodded. "I promise, it will not harm you. You may even like it. It's hair root, a type of root we gather, slice thin, and prepare for consumption. These ones are dried in the heat of the lava pits so that they can last for long periods without spoiling."

"That doesn't sound so bad." Lizbete gave a nervous laugh before popping the flake into her mouth. It had a slightly earthy taste, but no more so than other root vegetables she tried. It had a mix of sweetness and bitterness, somewhere between a carrot and a radish. "It's good."

He pushed the rest of the jar towards her. "Do you need more? You are used to living among the humans and must be accustomed to eating like them."

She froze. *Like them? I am them!*

She shied away from the offered food. "I . . . I am one of them."

"Partially." He cleared his throat, avoiding her eyes again.

A thought struck her as she remembered his conversation with Naasha. *She's mine.*

What if—but no. That couldn't be.

I'm human. I'm human.

I'm human...

"What are you?" she braved the question. Even if it insulted him, she needed to know. She needed to know what he was to be sure she wasn't it.

"We call ourselves simply cavers. We have lived in this land a long time, for generations before your people came here on ships to settle in the shadow of the mountains and fish in the waters." He replaced the jar on the shelf.

"So you're not . . . human."

"We are not overlanders." He shrugged. "To put it in terms you might be familiar with, we are as similar to humans as sheep are to goats or dogs are to wolves. We function in similar ways and..." He coughed, as if suddenly uncomfortable. "And we can interbreed, though it happens rarely and when it does the children are often sickly and unable to survive. In all of history, I think there have been a half-dozen hybrids that lived into adulthood. That was in the days when our people intermingled which is a time none living now remember. For the last several generations, my people have chosen to stay to our underground paths."

"So none of the villagers know you are here, then?" Lizbete swallowed. "They think you are dark spirits."

He laughed. "I have heard that. We hear much. It's a quirk of our bodies that our ears are far more sensitive than those of humans."

A tremor of doubt cut through her, even as her mind slowly loosened its grasp on her determination to believe that she was completely human. "I do as well."

"And poor vision?" He tilted his head to one side.

Her hand strayed to her apron pocket. Her spectacles lay there, safe and sound. In the dim-lighting and close quarters of Grimir's crystal garden, however, she had no need for them. Her throat tightened, but she managed a nod. Oh, why had he brought her here? Why was he telling her these things? She had been happy to be human. Happy to believe she was the same thing as the villagers. Even if they didn't accept her, they were still the only community she'd ever known.

"Why did you—why did you save me?" Tears blurred her vision. "You allowed the villagers to see you, and from what I can tell, you cavers don't do that. You—you must've had a reason to be there, to be watching me . . . twice."

Wrinkles deepened around his eyes. He reached into the pouch around his neck again and pulled out a strand of blue ribbon tied around a lock of hair, rich brown in color. "Because I loved your mother. Together we created you."

Her muscles gave out. Lizbete had to brace herself against the wall.

"Easy!" Grimir grasped her by the shoulder and led her back to the bed. "I did not mean to . . . I know this must be a lot to take in."

"You're my father?" she stammered. Her tongue felt thick in her mouth.

He hung his head. "I am . . . unworthy of that title. A father is one who cares for a child. Who provides love and sustenance for it, who protects it."

"Well, you at least did that."

"Two times? In the whole of your life?" He grimaced. "No, you may call me Grimir. I do not deserve to be called 'father.' However, if we are speaking in terms of simple fact, I suppose it is true."

Lizbete's heart quickened. She had a father. She wasn't truly alone. Perhaps he could give her a home, tell her what she was and how to control her thirst for warmth. Questions flooded her brain, and she tried to sort them by priority. "And my mother? She was a human? No one in the village could tell me who she was."

"I doubt anyone in the village ever knew her." He sighed and stared across the room at the fire crystals. "Your mother grew up on a small farm on the other side of the mountain. Some of the passages from this cave system extend that way, but to humans who must go around rather than under the mountain, it is a very long walk. As far as I know, neither she nor her parents ever made the journey."

A hollow formed in Lizbete's chest. She'd often wondered who her mother had been, what she'd looked like, why she'd abandoned Lizbete. Now she finally had someone who could tell her. "What was her name?"

"Leala," Grimir whispered the name with reverence. "Her parents were miserable people. Poor beyond belief and resentful towards their child and her needs. They often chased her in tears from the house, leaving her to fend for herself. She took to hiding in caves, and that is where we met." He stroked the lock of hair before tucking it away again. "I was likewise young and very much alone. My father was a crystal gardener overseeing a small patch in a remote area where there were few other cavers. While I knew we cavers were not supposed to speak to humans, I was intrigued by this strange girl who would hide in the shadows, singing to comfort herself." He sighed. "Leala had a beautiful voice. Eventually I summoned the courage to introduce myself and tell her about our hidden world."

He stood and paced to the other side of the cave. "And so began a friendship that lasted for many years, eventually growing into love." A slight smile played across his thin lips before rage contorted his face. "When her parents found out she was in love with a mysterious 'dark spirit' from the caverns, they would have none of it. They locked her away, tried to keep us apart, not knowing she was already pregnant with my child." The fierce light in his eyes dimmed to a moody glow. "With you."

"What happened to her?"

"With my help, she escaped and fled into the caverns with me. Unfortunately, my people were no more accepting than hers of our love. I was forced to hide her from the other cavers." He shook his head. "Perhaps they were right and our union was doomed. She grew ill away from the sunlight and fresh air. Finding her food to eat was a constant struggle, and the pregnancy—" His voice cracked. "She died a few days after your arrival. My father, who had done what he could to help us, pointed out that you resembled her race more than mine. We both knew you would never be accepted by my people, but I thought the humans might take you in as one of their own." He cringed. "Apparently I was wrong."

"So wrong." Lizbete winced.

"Well, at least the humans allowed you to grow to near adulthood among them." He scowled. "If my people had discovered you, there is a high chance you would've ended up a sacrifice to the Ravenous One."

That name again. What did it mean?

"I watched you for the first few years," he continued. "To make certain you'd found a home and were being cared for. It looked as if you had, so I withdrew rather than risk being sighted. However, when you stumbled into the caves recently with your tall, human friend—"

Brynar?

"—I happened to see you from the shadows. I followed you. Saw how you could see through the caver magic we use to mask our hidden ways, how you had an affinity for the warmth. I realized you were the child I had left behind so many years before, and I—I started taking stupid risks in order to be near to you." Grimir winced. "Risks that have regained me the scrutiny of my fellows and even incurred the wrath of the Ravenous One."

"You were the one leaving me presents?" Her hand strayed to the green stone hanging about her neck.

"Yes." He beamed. "Though I assumed you were too accustomed to life among humans for me to dare to approach you. Apparently, I was wrong again." He narrowed his eyes at her. "If you don't mind me asking, after sixteen years, what caused them to suddenly turn against you?"

She sighed. "They've never liked me much, honestly. They only put up with me for the sake of Auntie Katryn before she died. I think it was only a matter of time until they found something to blame on my strangeness, and with the earthquakes, the livestock thefts… a bunch of little things swarming together like bees. A single incident wouldn't have been noticed, but three or four, one on top of the other? They started looking for someone to hold accountable. Why not that odd, ugly girl who no one ever liked?"

"Ugly? Don't be ridiculous." Grimir peered at her, his red eyes glinting strangely in the light of the crystals. "You are beautiful, Lizbete." In spite of their shared blood and his kindness to her so far, the hairs on the back of Lizbete's neck stood on end. Eyes simply weren't supposed to be that color—or glow that way.

Cut it out, she mentally chided herself. *It's not like you're a paragon of normalcy. This is his world. You are easily as strange to him as he is to you.*

"It's amazing," he said, his gravelly voice oddly soothing, like the purr of a large cat. "I can see your mother in your eyes, your face, so very human." He stroked her cheek. The sensation of being touched without fear or hesitation sent a jolt through her, and Lizbete stared up at him, bottom lip quivering, closer to tears than she had been since her arrival in this strange underground world. "But I can still see the traits of my people. You can draw off heat? But you can't bestow it?"

She shook her head. "I've never tried, in all honesty. It never feels like my blood has had enough. It always takes. The idea that it could ever *give*, that seems strange and impossible."

"We of the caves have the ability to hold a little more heat than we need which we, in turn, can give to others through these." He held up his hand revealing thick black pads of what appeared to be fur on the tips of his fingers. "May I see your hands?"

She exhibited her quite furless digits.

"Ah, I wonder what else you didn't inherit from me." He narrowed his eyes. "Can you turn into smoke to camouflage yourself and ride upon drafts of warm air?"

She coughed. "Can you?"

In response, his body shimmered, growing so transparent she could see the crystals shining through him.

Lizbete gaped. "No, I certainly can't do that."

"Interesting. It's as if you maintained human flesh while somehow still having a caver's essence. The drawing of heat, but not the bestowing of it." He tapped one finger thoughtfully against his chin. "Also, you say you can't control how much heat you take in?"

"No." She swallowed. "But you said you can. Is it something I can learn?"

"Unfortunately, it isn't something I can teach. It comes naturally to us as soon as we are born for if not, mothers would die with their children within them." A look of pain crossed his face.

"Your mother almost died many times when she carried you. She was always so cold. It was only by constant administration of the fire crystals that I managed to keep her alive long enough to…" His voice broke.

Shame flooded through Lizbete. She'd killed her mother. The first person to love her, to give her care, to even know of her existence, and she'd died because of what Lizbete was.

Grimir's eyes widened, and he gripped her wrist. "No, little one, do not grieve. Your mother, she lived long enough to hold you, and her death . . . she was not meant to live here in the dark and the smoke of my world. It weakened her." He sighed. "Add that to the stress of having to hide from my fellow cavers and the Ravenous One." His voice dropped to a hiss as he spoke the name.

Lizbete wanted to ask about this being that apparently inspired such fear, but she also wanted to ask about her mother, about the fire crystals. She needed to know if she could stay in the caver world rather than risking the human village again. The most important thing, however, was learning how she could stop herself from ever hurting anyone else.

"You can touch me without pulling away my heat, but in the village you drew away *all* of the heat from the man who attacked me. Is that because he was fully human and I'm not?"

"No, that is because I fully intended to steal away as much heat as possible from him, and with you, I have no such intention." Grimir's face grew darker. "I suppose I could've injured rather than killed the brute, but I would not be able to watch over you at all times lest the man tried again. I would have no assurance that he wouldn't simply try again Seeing as he showed himself to be willing to take your life, I have little regret."

Lizbete rubbed her upper arms. Grimir didn't sound bloodthirsty, but his surety in his own rightness unnerved her. Of course, there were times she wanted to condemn Hangur to a similar fate, if she were honest. "But you hardly know me. For all you know, he had good reason to want me dead."

"You are my child and you have your mother's eyes," Grimir whispered. "Leala had the gentlest spirit. She took pity on me in spite of my oddness to her, loved me even when it cost her her family, and bore no ill will towards my people even when they proved as prejudiced against her as her family was against me." He sighed. "No, you could not be worthy of such treatment."

Events suggested otherwise. Lizbete dropped her gaze to her hands. She had at least animal lives on her conscience—and one human life if she counted Erich who had died because of her, even if she had not herself done the deed.

"So you can choose not to draw to the point where you hurt someone? But I can't seem to help it."

He furrowed his brow. "That shouldn't be. We cavers are not able to absorb infinite heat. If we take too much upon ourselves, we will burn." He examined her skin. "I wonder if the combination of your two heritages has caused some of your caver traits to, for lack of a better word, malfunction."

Bitterness rose within her. Not only was she a reject from two different worlds, she was apparently a faulty reject. A botched creation who had inherited the worst rather than the best traits of both halves of her family tree.

"It is strange." He ran his fingers up and down her skin. "I can feel you leaching from me even though you are completely warm and surrounded by other sources of warmth."

"But I can still touch you without you freezing?" She could feel his heat filtering into her, but faintly. It carried affection, something she hadn't felt since Auntie Katryn's death, but also confusion and regret. Perhaps because he'd abandoned her? Or perhaps because he'd fathered a daughter so worthy of abandonment? "I can't do that with humans."

"I'm capable of absorbing heat from my surroundings quickly enough to make up for the draw," he explained, releasing her hand. "Humans can't do that, the poor things."

"So it just can't be helped? There's no way to fix me?" A hollow pit formed within Lizbete's chest. Even here she wouldn't find comfort.

"I'm not sure if 'fix' is the right word." He turned to his collection of fire crystals. "However, I might be able to help you moderate your unique traits." He took one of the crystals from the basket. "This one was broken from its cluster when a rock fell from the wall on top of it, which means it is one of the few I can give away without angering the Ravenous One. He has already counted it as lost and will not recognize its absence." He turned back towards her. "My guess is that your body chooses the easiest source of heat to draw from. When you are in physical contact with another living being, they are that easiest source." He held out the fire crystal. "Take this."

She extended her hand, and he dropped the crystal onto her palm. Immediately energy flowed into her blood, spreading down her arm, and into her core. Her whole being melted.

Grimir leaned closer and rested his hand on her arm. Her blood ignored him, latching onto the crystal like a suckling infant.

A grin spread across Grimir's face. "Yes, that will do. As long as this crystal maintains contact with your skin, your blood won't be tempted by the faint heat of humans."

Lizbete let out a relieved sigh, only for concern to immediately overtake her. "But how long will it last? When we fetched a crystal for Elin, it faded within a few days, and you can't keep giving me them. You said the Ravenous One will take vengeance if he notices them stolen."

"What was the human girl using it for?" Grimir frowned. "When I left it in your path, I understood that you wanted it but not why."

Lizbete explained about Elin's sickness, her constant fevers, and how the crystal had offered her temporary relief before losing its light and turning a sickly gray.

"I see." He clicked his tongue. "To start with, the crystals do not produce heat. They are simply conduits for it. Gatherers of it. They suck it from their surroundings even as we do and use it to grow, but their absorption increases rather than depletes the warmth. It turns it into a different sort of energy, one that cavers can absorb, but humans can't. We cavers, simply by existing beside the crystals, gather from it. My guess is it drew heat from the girl, but she could not absorb the energy it produced as you can. With nowhere for the energy to be dispersed, the crystal expended its ability to conduct heat and died."

"But it won't do that with me?" She rolled the crystal in her hand.

"It won't. It will feed into you and flourish as if it were still rooted within its subterranean home." He brushed his hand through her hair. "And with it to pull from, your blood will never need to pull from a human or caver again."

Her vision blurred as hoped swelled within her chest. "You . . . you fixed me?"

"Fixed, no? Found a solution for you to manage your gifts, yes." He tilted his head. "This ability of yours to keep drawing after you are filled, it intrigues me. I wonder what your limits are."

Lizbete furrowed her brow. "You call it an ability like it is something I can control. I can't and it's not. It's a curse. It prevents me from interacting with other humans, from touching people. From loving them." A sob captured her words.

He rested his hand on top of her shoulder. "Believe it or not, I know something about being alone in the world."

They stood in silence, only broken by the continual drip of water from some area of the cavern and the constant, distant roar that pervaded this place. Lizbete thought she could get used to this strange underground realm with its dim lighting and quiet. She'd miss the sun. She'd miss humans— but she would never be cold and she'd have Grimir. Her father.

She gazed up at him. "Can I stay with you?"

He winced. "Lizbete, I wish you could, but if my people find you here—"

"Grimir! We need to talk to you!" Voices echoed from the passage. Grimir stiffened, then pulled Lizbete into the corner of the room. A smaller tunnel branched off from his chambers here.

"Get inside and stay quiet," he hissed.

Panic spiked in Lizbete's chest as she wormed her way into the cramped passage. The low ceiling forced her onto her hands and knees, but it was wide enough to turn around in, if she were careful. She scooted a few feet in, then turned back so she could see the shadows moving about Grimir's chamber.

"What were you thinking? Showing your face in the human village?" This caver's voice was higher pitched. Perhaps female, though it still carried that rasp that made Grimir's voice so distinct. "What if they come poking around here?"

"We have nothing to fear from the humans," Grimir said simply. "They could never navigate the caves to find us, even if they had the courage to try. They see us as dark spirits, and dark spirits cannot be defeated by human weapons."

"Even so, now they'll be watchful," a second caver, this one with a voice even deeper than Grimir's, added. "It will be far harder for us to take sacrifices for the Ravenous One without them seeing us. Otti is right to be concerned. They've already increased their guard over their livestock."

"I've never been comfortable with us taking the human's livestock for the sacrifices, and you know that, Dravish. The amount we've stolen recently has been pushing the limit for what the town will tolerate." Grimir sighed.

Lizbete blinked. The cavers were behind the recent animal thefts? For sacrifices? She shuddered. The whole thing sounded ominous.

"But what choice do we have?" Otti snapped. "Even now, with the animals we can provide it, it's restless, angry. It quakes the earth, ready to emerge and take if it is not given."

"If we cannot appease it, the humans will have far greater problems than missing sheep," Dravish intoned dryly. "We all know it prefers human flesh. In the days of our fathers, a human child would keep it pacified for months at a time. We'd have to feed it a few times a year instead of a few times every month."

Lizbete's blood grew cold in spite of the warmth around her.

"The council would never stand for that!" Grimir snapped. "We're not barbarians."

"Better the death of one or two children—or maybe some old sickly woman or unwanted beggar if that would be less odious to the council—than the whole village, and likely our people as well." Somehow even while talking about human sacrifice and the value of beggars compared to children, Dravish still managed to sound bored. "Also, considering what I heard about your 'interactions' with the humans recently, I wouldn't be so self-righteous. You killed a man to save a single girl. I'm suggesting killing a single girl to save hundreds of humans and cavers. Mathematically, I would say that puts me on firmer moral ground than you."

Lizbete's jaw clenched. As uncertain as she'd been about Grimir's choice, he hadn't killed Erich in cold blood, hadn't planned to do so, and didn't treat it with the flippancy Dravish did. She longed to leap out and shout at the infuriating caver. Instead she tightened her hand on the fire crystal Grimir had given her and kept quiet.

"Either way, the current situation is not sustainable," Otti said. "We can't keep stealing chickens and sheep to delay the inevitable. Eventually we will have to do something. If we don't want to feed it humans and we can't get more animals, then perhaps the time has come for us to abandon this land to its ravages. Evacuate the caverns before the Ravenous One will emerge, and get as far from here as possible. There must be other caves, other steamvents."

"And leave the humans to face its ferocity when its hunger and rage explode from neglect?" Grimir snarled.

"Do you have another suggestion?" Otti snapped. "You are quite free to tell us what we cannot do, Grimir, but give no indication of what we can."

"I will think on it. I just feel we should only pursue paths that would avoid loss of life."

"It's not your decision, anyway. You are only one member of the council, and a junior member at that." Dravish snorted. "I plan to discuss things with the other members tonight. If I get enough support from them, I won't need you. In fact, with how you've comported yourself of late, I can't imagine that you'll remain on the council for long."

Lizbete waited until two sets of footsteps faded in the distance before crawling out of the passage into Grimir's chamber. He now sat with his face in his hands, shoulders slumped.

"Are you all right?" she whispered.

"No." His voice cracked. He looked up and steam rose from his eyes. She recoiled before realizing this was probably the caver version of tears. Well, at least in that way she was more human. "Lizbete, I . . . I have spent the last sixteen years separated from you, wondering what it would be like to speak with you, to tell you that you are my daughter, to know you as my child. But now?" He stood, his mouth forming a firm line. "You can't stay here. If Dravish and his supporters find you, they'll see it as a sign from the Creator of All that they are meant to sacrifice you to the Ravenous One. It will be hard enough convincing them not to kidnap a human now, but if one—even a half human—falls into their grasp, I will not be able to stop them."

Her heart gave out. "What is this Ravenous One and why do you and your people give it so much?"

He scratched at his chin. "In the dark days there were many like the Ravenous One who lived throughout the Within-Earth. Not all of them are dangerous. Many sleep for decades, centuries even, before awakening to devour all that they can over a period of a few violent days, then returning to sleep. The cavers learned that we could delay their outbursts and the destruction they caused by feeding them." He glanced through the entrance to his chamber. "They're gone." He gathered up several items off his shelves and bound them within the blanket from his bed into a bundle. He then beckoned to her. "Come with me. Staying here is too dangerous, but I know a more isolated area of the caverns where you can hide for a little longer before you have to go back to the human village."

Heart in her throat, Lizbete followed him. Would she never find a place to settle? Even here, among people who should understand what she was, she was an outsider. She was in danger due to no fault of her own.

They silently left the chamber and took a side passage that descended down a steep tunnel into darkness. Grimir offered her his hand. Guided only by the faint light of the crystal Lizbete still clutched in her free hand, they plunged into the inky black depths of the earth.

"Different fire beasts demand different feeding," Grimir's words tickled her ears in the darkness. "Some are satisfied with wood to burn or stone to melt. The one at the bottom of our cave system, however, craves meat. It is said once upon a time only human flesh would satisfy it, due to an old grudge, but a great hero of old chased it under the mountain and caused it to become diminished in power to where a pigeon or a rat could just as easily satisfy it. Many of the fire beasts were defeated in this way, being chased deep within the earth, imprisoned, or even slain, but it has been many years since a hero has existed mighty enough to slay a fire beast."

"And this one is waking up again?" Lizbete shuddered. The idea of a giant fire monster didn't seem remotely real, but from the reactions of the caver, it had to be. Would they really go to such extreme lengths for a mere fantasy? "Why? After so many years, what is bringing it back now?"

"It could be simply that its time of sleep is up, or somehow it sensed that the humans who were its sworn enemies have grown complacent and prosperous." Unease crept into Grimir's tone. "It does not help that in the last several decades some humans have entered his realm. Your friend searching for his crystals . . . my Leala

. . . even some fool in a boat who found one of the sea caves that reaches towards its chambers and was roasted alive for his boldness."

Lizbete's chest tightened. "Do you think it knows I'm here?"

Grimir's hold on her hand grew firmer. "I hope that your caver blood is enough that it will not sense you as an outsider."

He took another turn. A faint red light shone before them, growing brighter as they approached. The air also grew hotter. Lizbete winced as something wet dripped into her eyes, stinging them. She quickly swiped her hand across her brow. It came away damp.

Sweat? I'm sweating?

She gawped at the liquid clinging to her skin. An odd lightness crept through her. Intellectually, she knew being able to sweat was an odd thing to take pride in, but the lack of it had always been one more thing separating her from the other villagers. With everything strange going on, she'd take any inkling of normality.

Grimir glanced at her, the crimson light revealing a strange smile on his face. "A human would be dying in this heat. Your caver blood will keep you safe, but it might be a little uncomfortable. Here we are."

The tunnel opened up into a wide chamber, and her jaw dropped. The stone beneath her was hot to the touch, almost unbearably so. Massive stalactites dripped from the ceiling and stalagmites rose from the floor like bars of a cage. Behind this cage stretched a lake of molten rock. A black crust covered the surface. Cracks spidered across the crust, like the top of a baked pudding, revealing fierce orange fire beneath. The constant roar of flame was louder here than in Grimir's chamber. Loud enough that she wondered if it was coming from the lake itself.

Grimir shifted from foot to foot. "I hate to leave you here, but I need to see to the council. Try and convince them to continue with the animal sacrifices for a while longer. This isn't the first time the Ravenous One has grown restless, but usually it can be calmed with proper deference."

"Can you reason with it?" Lizbete sat cross-legged on the hot stone floor. Her clothing stuck to her skin. She'd never felt too hot before. The sensation was quite novel. She didn't mind it—for now—but saw how it might eventually grow tiresome. "You speak of it as if it is an intelligent being, able to hold grudges, aware of its surroundings."

"It is and it isn't," Grimir answered. "The short answer is, no. You cannot reason with the Ravenous One. For one thing, it doesn't speak, not that I've ever heard. Though I shudder to think what its voice would sound like if it did." He gave an exaggerated shudder for emphasis. "For another we mortals are so low to it that it would be as if ants tried to convince a human to spare their nest. It does not prefer the cavers as food, otherwise I'm sure it would have devoured us all ages ago, but even us it will destroy if we stray into its chamber. We have to leave the sacrifices outside of it and wait for it to come and claim them." He set the bundle of belongings he'd brought from his lair on the ground and started to work at the knots holding it shut. "All stories of people—human or caver— attempting to approach it end in the same way. With the mortal incinerated and the Ravenous One returning to its lair."

He exhibited its contents of the bundle one at a time. First, he held up an earthen jar. "More dried hair root, in case you grow hungry." He exhibited a glass bottle. "This is elemental water. It flows from a spring deep within our caverns. It has a sulfurous taste, but it resists boiling and evaporating, which means you will still be able to drink it here where other water might turn to steam." The next item was a series of small, interlocking metal hoops. "This is for your amusement." He turned away from her and fiddled with it before turning back and exhibiting an intricately woven ring with four different metal strands twined together. Spinning around so the ring was again out of view, he then faced her again holding the interlocking metal hoops. "You see, you have to puzzle how these hoops fit together to make this ring. These sorts of puzzles are a popular way to pass time among cavers, both crafting them and solving them." He passed her the rings. "See if you can figure it out." That done, he spread out the blanket on the ground next to the jar of food and bottle of drink. "I must ask that you stay in this chamber. It's too dangerous for you to wander the caverns alone. Even if you managed to avoid my people, there are pitfalls, vents that belch poisonous gasses, and the chance of getting lost."

"I will stay," Lizbete agreed. She didn't exactly savor the idea of slinking through this maze of passages in the dark, anyway.

"I will try to return to you as soon as I can. No one will come here. It's too close to the Ravenous One's lair."

Lizbete started. "You—why am I here then?" Her pulse throbbed. This creature was some sort of unapproachable monster and she was within shouting distance of him?

"The beast won't even know you're here," Grimir assured her. "The passages into this section of the caverns are too small for it to get through."

She settled onto the blanket, which provided some relief from the hot stones beneath her.

Grimir knelt beside her and brushed his hand through her hair. The mundane expression of affection, something she hadn't experienced since the loss of Auntie, sent a pleasant chill through her. "I'll be back as soon as I can. I want to tell you more stories of your mother before you have to go." He hesitated, his eyes flitting over her face. "I am not very good at this whole—I mean . . . I . . . I hope you don't hate me for abandoning you, Lizbete. It ached. I swear it ached so much."

Pain pinched his face, and pity swelled within her. Whatever mistakes he made, she believed fully that Grimir cared for her and had done what he felt was best for her. Wanting to express this, but unable to find the words, Lizbete impulsively leaned forward and kissed his cheek. "I forgive you."

Steam rose again from his eyes, and he angled away from her. "Stay safe, Lizbete. Rest if you can."

He stood. His being shimmered into transparency, and he flew up the passage they'd emerged from.

Lizbete sighed. Here she was, sitting under the earth near a massive fire beast that might eat her, waiting for her long-lost father. All next to a lake of lava with just a jar of food, a bottle of un-boiling water, and a puzzle ring.

If the villagers who think I'm strange could see me now, they'd lose their collective minds.

Chapter Sixteen

Lizbete bent one of the silver rings around to lie on top of the other. A gap between them very clearly marked a space for the remaining two rings, which, based on the way they twisted, were meant to nest together. However every time she tried to slip the two remaining rings up into the spot, they pushed the first two apart. She squinted at the steam-blasted puzzle. The sweat stinging her eyes wasn't any help. Ironically, she'd often wished she could sweat. She'd gotten strange looks as she strode through the marketplace in high summer, completely dry and unfazed by the blazing sun.

Of course, I also got strange looks when I shivered through the marketplace on cold days or walked through normally on temperate ones. Sweating probably wouldn't have changed anything.

She crunched down on another hair root chip. After the first six or seven, they'd began to taste like paper, bland and just as hard to chew and swallow. She wondered if anyone had even noticed she was missing yet. Elin at least might worry about her, or Brynar when he returned. Though seeing as she couldn't stay with the cavers, she might be home before he was. Grief gripped her soul. If anything, Grimir's doomed romance with her mother proved even further that she and Brynar had never had a chance together.

With a groan, Lizbete shoved the puzzle rings into her apron pocket next to her spectacles. As she did, her hand brushed against Brynar's letter. She drew it out. With everything that had happened since Elin had given her the letter, Lizbete had never felt it was the right time to read it. Now she had nothing else to do and nowhere to go. She started to unfold it and found her hands shaking.

What if it was a goodbye? She deserved a goodbye. They couldn't be together. The last time she'd seen him, she all but told him to go away forever. Maybe this letter would explain that he'd finally come to his senses and realized how he shouldn't see her anymore, how caring for her at all was a mistake—

Even as the fear of this gripped her, she remembered Brynar's smile, how kind he'd been, the way they laughed together. No, he wasn't cruel. Even if they couldn't be together, he'd be kind to her about it.

And I want to hear from him. I need to know.

She opened the letter.

Hello Liz,

I don't have a lot of time. I tried to come see you at the tavern this morning, but no one would answer the door. I know Hangur is rarely up before noon, but I hope you were also just sleeping. Chances are you were awake but didn't want to see me. I deserved that. I'm sorry.

I am going to try and get back quickly this time. When I do, please, consider going to the First Frost with me as your escort. Openly. I don't want to hide that you're the one I want anymore. I can't walk with one foot in the life my parents want for me and one in the life I want any longer. I need to choose, and I choose you.

I do. I swear. I just pray to the Skywatcher that I haven't lost my chance.

Please, Liz, my Liz, one more chance.

Please.

Brynar.

Lizbete's hand tightened around the letter until it crumpled. Unable to look at it, she shoved it back in her pocket.

He wants me. He wants to be with me in public. . . . oh, but he wrote this before Erich's death. It's one thing for him to be with a girl the whole village hates, but to be with one who is in communication with murderous dark spirits? No, that can't happen.

Tears leaked from her eyes but immediately turned to steam. She cringed. She really was an inhuman monster.

No. Don't say that. You might not be human, but you're not a monster because Grimir isn't, and he's what you are.

She closed her eyes. Grimir was kind and intelligent. Monsters weren't those things. Cavers weren't monsters, therefore she wasn't a monster. Yet, they still weren't human.

Brynar and I can't be together, but he deserves to know why. I need to tell him what I am, what a danger I am to him, but also that I love him. When he understands that, he'll accept that we can't be together. He has to.

Her throat grew dry and scratchy. Lizbete took a swig of the elemental water. It soothed her thirst, though the taste of sulfur was a little off-putting. She set it aside and let out a long breath. The air pressed down on her, and she wiped her face with the hem of her apron. So hot...

She peeled her apron off but kept her smock on, unwilling to go completely naked even alone in a room so sweltering that she was basting in her own juices.

With her resolution about Brynar made, she grew even more restless to get out of there, but time crept on with no sign of Grimir. She wanted something useful to do. Something to clean or cook. When was Grimir going to come back?

Anxious, she pulled her spectacles out of her apron pocket to survey the room. A quick scan didn't change her impression of it much, and her own sweat running into her eyes made it too hard to see anyway. Aggravated, Lizbete removed the glasses, wiped her eyes and forehead, and then put the glasses on for one last look.

Something glowed in the rock wall near the lava lake. She squinted. No, it wasn't glowing. It was backlit. An opening in the stone was allowing in even more light. From the surface? She was certain they were too deep for that, but what if they weren't? It was easy enough to get turned around in the dark, twisting tunnels.

Maybe it's a way out. I could start back to the village on my own, leave a letter for Brynar.

She took a step towards it, but then stopped. Grimir had asked her to stay put for her own safety. If she got herself killed poking around the tunnels, Brynar would never know the truth, plus dying like that was simply an idiotic way to go.

Grimir said not to leave the cavern, but looking through that window wouldn't be leaving. I'd still be in the chamber. Just gazing out. Perfectly safe.

Her spectacles slipped down the bridge of her nose, and she set them back in her apron pocket with a grunt of frustration. Well, Lizbete just wanted to see if that was the surface. She didn't need perfect vision for that.

Wiping her hands on her smock, she crossed the chamber. The lava bubbled and burped, sometimes sending up sprays of orange sparks. She kept a good several yards away from the edge. She wasn't sure what would happen if she fell in, but even with her innate fire resistance, she couldn't imagine it would be good. That pool was hot enough to melt rocks and metal. One half-human, half-caver girl wouldn't stand a chance. Thankfully, while close to the pool, the window was directly over a section of rock floor, not lava. Setting her hands to the wall, Lizbete found it as hot to the touch as the ovens in Auntie's kitchen. Not more than she could bear. Cracks in the wall made for easy handholds. She wedged her fingers into one and hoisted herself up.

The heat rising off the lava pool buffeted her face, but she kept climbing. Gripping crevices and clinging to ledges, she spidered her way up towards the window in the rock, perhaps ten feet above the floor of the cavern.

Lizbete had to stop constantly to wipe the sweat from her palms lest they become too slippery to hold on. After several minutes, she caught the edge of the window and pulled herself up to look out of it.

Her heart sank. Another chamber stretched before her, clearly still deep inside the mountain. A high ceiling disappeared into darkness, but below it glowed another lake of lava, this one far larger than the one in her sanctuary. Molten rock dripped down the walls of the chamber into a series of smaller pools before coming to rest in a sea of lava too wide for her to see the other side. The glow from the lava cast shadows around stalactites and spires.

Bubbles that had to be the size of cows or even horses rose to the surface of the pool before bursting in a spray of orange and red. Lizbete clung to the window ledge, mesmerized by the colors and lights. Even with her poor vision, it was a lovely sight.

Time slipped away. Her arms grew tired, aching slightly from holding her up so long. Time to go down.

Before she could act upon this plan, something stirred in the lava below. A great rasping noise like boulders grinding together rose from beneath her, and the wall of stone she clung to trembled. Her whole body stiffened. The surface of the fire lake churned like a sea in storm. Her breath left her. What was in there?

Her grip tightened on the ledge until her knuckles ached. Then as swiftly as it had begun, the churning stopped, and the lava lay still as stone again. She let out a long breath. Maybe it was some sort of odd natural phenomena. Gas bubbles rising through the lava? A small earthquake? Whatever it was, it was over now.

A towering whip-like appendage broke the surface of the lake. Lizbete bit her tongue to keep from screaming. Another followed, then another, until five arms waved above the surface of the pool, feeling amongst the rocks on the shoreline.

Lizbete held her breath. The creature's hide appeared crusted black like the lava, but with veins of red and orange revealing a red-hot interior. Even though the arms rose from the center of the lake, they still easily reached the shore, perhaps a hundred yards from where it had emerged. She could see no head, no body, only searching tentacles.

If the arms are that long, what does the rest of the beast look like?

Common sense told her to get away from the window for fear of it sensing her somehow. However, she couldn't help but watch. The tentacles found an opening in the wall—thankfully not in the wall perpendicular to the wall she currently gazed through. A high-pitched scream rose from that direction, and Lizbete cringed. Was there a human in there? A caver?

The tentacle sprang back. A large goat struggled in the monster's fiery grasp. Smoke already rose from the poor beast's hide. It thrashed for several seconds, its cries growing fainter, before its head lolled to one side and it lay limp and lifeless.

A rounded protrusion with what appeared to be a beak broke the surface of the lava. The tentacle dropped the smoldering remains of the goat into the beak before disappearing back under the surface of the lake. The rest of the tentacles following like fleeing snakes.

Lizbete remained frozen in place long after the lava had ceased its roiling.

That has to be the fire beast Grimir spoke of. Why would that thing be satisfied with a goat? It would be scarcely a mouthful for it. Oh, to think of that thing *so close to the village. They don't even know.*

An image of the monster slinking out of the caverns and into the streets of Brumehome, of it devouring and destroying all in its path, froze her heart. As cruel as the villagers had been to her in the past, she didn't want to see them harmed like that. Also there were still a few people she truly cared about in their number. Falla, Elin, of course Brynar, and by extension the rest of Brynar's family.

Even if they knew of the danger, what could they do? Grimir said heroes used to fight those monsters, but how could any human, no matter how heroic, hope to stand against something like that?

Shaking her head, she started her descent, feeling with her toes for a foothold right below her.

"Lizbete! What are you doing up there?"

Lizbete gasped and whipped her head in the direction of the voice. Her hands slipped. She flailed as her toes clung momentarily to their foothold, then the air rushed about her. Hot air. Unbearably hot.

"Lizbete!" Grimir shrieked. She landed against the pool of lava with a crash.

Chapter Seventeen

Fire raced through Lizbete. Her greedy blood guzzled the heat, but there was too much. Far too much. Searing pain flared in every particle of her being.

The lava had a consistency more like tar than water, and she found herself lying on top of it rather than sinking. Her clothing burst into flames around her. She pushed against it and somehow caught the rock at the edge of the pool. She yanked herself out and lay in agony on the stone.

"Lizbete!" Grimir caught her by the wrists and dragged her away from the pool. He gaped at her. "You—you're alive? How are you alive? Let me see." Grimir yanked her arm towards him, running his fingers over it. Heat fled from her as he pulled it away into his body, but for once she was glad for the loss. Her hair felt like it might burst into flames. Her insides stung. After a moment under his care, though, the temperature reached a manageable level.

"This is impossible," he hissed. The fabric of her garments fell to ash at his touch. He averted his eyes, breezed away in his smoke form, and returned with the blanket from the other side of the cavern. He wrapped this about her but continued to examine her exposed skin. He withdrew, shaking his head. "Not a burn on you. Lizbete, you should be dead."

She blinked at him. "But, I've never burned. I thought—I thought that was a caver thing? Something I inherited from you?"

Wrinkles deepened across his forehead. "Cavers are *resistant* to heat. We can still burn in high enough heat or from long enough exposure. The heat of that lava is high enough that even a caver would've been dead in seconds. Extremely painful seconds." He narrowed his eyes at her. "But you are unharmed?"

She pulled her hand away from him and held the blanket closer about her body. "Well, it wasn't a pleasant experience."

"This doesn't make sense. If anything, your human blood should make you more vulnerable to fire not less." He glanced at her. "Where is the crystal I gave you? Did you lose it in the lava?"

"No." She pointed towards the corner where her remaining belongings rested. "It's in my apron pocket, with my spectacles. Thankfully I took them off before. They're unharmed."

"That's good." He led her away from the lava pit and handed her the apron.

She grimaced. It would hardly cover her body sufficiently, but it was now all she had left. Her hold on the blanket tightened. She fished her spectacles and the fire crystal out of the pocket.

"Here." She exhibited it to him. "Would it have been destroyed in the lava too?"

"No." He smiled. "The crystals can absorb vast amounts of heat, but if it had fallen into the lava, it would be impossible to retrieve. You know, when your mother was pregnant with you, I had her surrounded by these constantly trying to channel warmth into her— oh, Creator." He slapped the top of his head. "You were inside her.

You must've absorbed so much of the crystals' energies while you were still being formed. You have *their* properties. Not caver traits. Not human traits. *Crystal* traits."

"What does that mean?" Lizbete frowned.

"I'm not sure." He handed her back the crystal. Regret crossed his face. "I'll need to get you some garments to wear before I take you back to the human town."

Her heart faltered. "Can't I stay here a little longer?"

"It's too dangerous." He shook his head. "Dravish is still campaigning for us to take a human to sacrifice to the Ravenous One. One of our people brought in a goat, which bought us a little more time, but we can't keep stealing livestock to feed the monster. We need to find a way to satisfy it long enough that it falls back asleep."

"And a human sacrifice would do that?" She furrowed her brow.

"According to tradition. Thankfully it has been decades since we have had to stoop to that level." He stroked her cheek. "Either way, the Within-Earth is unsafe for you as long as the Ravenous One is awake. Maybe if it sleeps again, we can find a way to be together as a family." A pleasant warmth, not related to the heat from the lava, spread through her.

"I think I'd like that," she whispered.

"In the meantime, do you have some place you can stay in the village?"

Lizbete bit her bottom lip. She still had Widow Gri, but even if that didn't work out, she wanted to find someone who would trust her and warn them about the Ravenous One. Maybe there was nothing the villagers could do against something that huge and powerful, but at least if they knew, they could prepare for the worst. Maybe evacuate if the quakes didn't stop. Though she wasn't sure if he'd listen to her, Mayor Sten made the most sense. He tended to be reasonable. If Brynar were there, she could tell him, and he could tell his father. That might be the surest way to get someone to listen.

"I do, at least in the short term." She fiddled with her apron. "I can't go there looking like this, though."

He laughed. "I suppose you can't. I will get you one of my moss-cloth smocks. It'll look odd, but it will at least cover you until you can find something that suits you more."

He hurried out of the cavern, then returned carrying a dark colored garment that resembled the one he was wearing. Lizbete slipped it over her head then tied her apron on over it to at least give it some semblance to human clothing.

Grimir nodded his approval. "That won't provide you much warmth, but having the crystal next to your skin will help. May I see it?"

She took it out of her pocket and offered it to him. He reached into the pouch at his neck and took out a thin wire. He wrapped the wire around the crystal before attaching it to a string. Then he looped the string around her neck. The crystal rested against her chest, spreading delicious warmth through her. Grimir took a second crystal from his pouch. "The Ravenous One has a connection to the crystals. If they are stolen, he knows of it. However, during the earthquakes, some break naturally from their clusters, allowing me to harvest them. Your sickly friend can use this one. It won't last her long, but it will offer some relief."

"Thank you." Lizbete tucked it into her pocket.

"There are some tunnels that lead all the way to the village. I can take you through those so you don't have to walk in the cold air." He offered her his hand. "Come. We have a way to go."

Lizbete remained silent during the walk through the still corridors under the earth. Only the glowing crystal about her neck provided any light, and she clung to Grimir's hand for fear of falling or getting lost. Finally, the air around her grew cool. A crack of faint light appeared before them, and after a minute more of walking they emerged through a narrow chasm in the cliff face into the cold, fresh air.

Lizbete did a quick turn to get a sense of her surroundings. They were a stone's throw down the beach from the village. The sun hovered low over the bay, bathing the horizon with yellows, pinks, and purples. From the town the gentle sound of distant music floated. Lanterns spangled the houses, giving the tiny village a look of fairyland. Lizbete's heart squeezed.

The First Frost is tonight.

The thought stirred memories of Brynar, of what could never be. Still, she wanted deeply to be with him. Not on the fringes of his life, but as an essential part, something that couldn't be shaken off with ease. *But that can never be.*

"Will you be all right from here?" Grimir asked, his hand trailing across her shoulder.

She nodded, pushing away her regret. With the crystal's pulsing energy against her skin, Lizbete didn't feel cold even with the chill of the evening breeze. "It's not far to walk."

"Good. Take care." He started to turn away. The thought of possibly never seeing him again, of losing the first family she'd had since Auntie Katryn's death, caught her like a punch to the gut, and she grabbed his arm.

"Father!" she gasped.

He wheeled to look at her, red eyes widening.

She dropped her gaze. "You . . . I will see you again?"

Grimir nodded. "I promise, my Lizbete. I stayed away from you for too long. I won't make that mistake again." He leaned close to kiss her forehead before smiling and disappearing into the tunnel.

With a sigh, Lizbete trudged into the village. She kept to the back ways, the narrow side alleys where no one had bothered to hang lanterns and streamers. However, her sensitive ears caught laughter, singing, music . . . Her heart ached to just once be a part of the joy the other young folk in the village experienced on a daily basis.

To belong. To be wanted. To be part of a whole.

Her hand strayed to the crystal hanging around her neck. She longed for a chance to test it with a human, to see if she could actually touch someone without harming them now that she wore it. A deep regret grew in her chest, like the roots of weeds working their way between cracks in a brick wall. She feared her willpower would crumble and she'd have to stop to cry. She would've loved to have more memories of hugging Auntie. She would've liked to have friends she could walk arm in arm with. She would give so much just to kiss Brynar.

The last thought came out of nowhere and struck her hard. She stopped and closed her eyes.

Silly Lizbete, she chided herself. *Brynar isn't meant for you. He's met for someone who his family likes, who the village approves of as their future mayor's wife. The gap between you and Brynar is far wider than your curse. It's as wide as every man, woman, and child in Brumehome.*

No. Brynar would marry someone like Witta, but that didn't mean Lizbete didn't have a place in his story. Even if she couldn't be with Brynar, she wanted him to be safe, wanted the people he cared about to be safe—Elin, his parents, even the villagers who he considered himself responsible for as the mayor's son. All of that was important to him, and because of that, important to her.

And he didn't know about the threat lurking beneath the mountain.

She needed to warn him, warn the village, about the Ravenous One. Once that was done, she'd leave for Widow Gri's and never look back.

The mayor's house loomed up ahead. She skirted the back of it and fished around in the alleyway for a few pebbles. She knew which window was Elin's. Now she just had to hope the girl was there and paying attention. Concentrating on the second story window, she cocked her arm back, then let fly. The pebbles pattered against the treated animal skin window. Lizbete held her breath, hoping it was Elin who answered and not her mother or someone else less friendly.

The window creaked open. A dark-haired head poked out, eyes wide.

"Hello?" Elin managed to call in a loud whisper.

"Over here!" Lizbete waved her arms.

Elin jumped, then grinned. "Liz! You're not dead!"

Lizbete grimaced. "Last I checked. Can I come up?"

"Oh, yeah, give me a second!" Elin disappeared inside. Lizbete rubbed her arms, half-expecting Mayor Sten or his wife to run around the corner and chase her off with a broom.

The house's back door opened.

"Hurry!" Elin hissed from the shadows inside. Lizbete scampered inside. They stood in a back hall of the large house in the light of a single candle Elin grasped in her hand. Elin glared at Lizbete. "Where have you been?"

Lizbete examined the girl. Her complexion was pale but her cheeks flushed. Lizbete could feel the heat rising off her even though they weren't touching yet. The crystal Grimir had given her would help that. First things first, she needed to warn the mayor about the Ravenous One.

Lizbete exhaled. "It's a long story. Is your father home?"

"No, he's at the First Frost." Elin cocked her head to one side. "With Brynar."

Lizbete's knees wobbled, and she immediately hated herself for the weakness. "Brynar is home?"

Elin nodded and motioned for Lizbete to follow her. They took the stairs at the end of the hall. "He came in yesterday morning. Apparently he found Uncle Hangur's 'wife' almost immediately, but the woman had moved on and wasn't interested in returning with Brynar. Can't say I blame her."

"Wherever she is, considering it's where Hangur isn't, it's got to be an improvement." Lizbete wrinkled her nose. "So Brynar's at the First Frost?"

"Under protest." Elin opened a door and let Lizbete into her bedroom. "When he got home and you were nowhere to be found..." The girl whistled. "He was mad. He was so mad. He was madder than mad. He was burning hot, blazing—"

"I get it." Lizbete's cheeks warmed. The sensation gave her pause. She'd never had that happen before. "What—what did he do?"

"Oh, he shouted at my uncle for turning you out in the cold, then at Father for not stopping it. Then Father shouted at him, and he shouted back, and they screamed back and forth like a couple of crows fighting over a scrap of bread." A ghoulish glint crept into Elin's eyes as if recalling the chaos gave her great pleasure. "Best of all was when that idiot Witta showed up in the middle of it. She wanted to pout at Brynar because she'd prepped a matching mask set for him and her, a rooster and hen, but he wouldn't wear it. He pretty much told her to go lay an egg." Elin giggled madly. "Best day I've had in a long time."

Lizbete cleared her throat. "But he did go to the First Frost?"

"It was a compromise. Father's pride finally broke, and he practically begged Brynar to make an appearance at the party to save face. Brynar agreed on the condition that he wouldn't be pressured into seeing Witta anymore. Father also said that you'd just run off to Widow Gri's and were just there waiting, safely. He probably made that up, but it got Brynar to stop raging. Brynar told Father he's leaving immediately after to go ask Widow Gri about you, but now that you're here—" Elin bounced up and down on her toes, then rushed over to the wardrobe on the back wall of her room and tossed it open. There, hanging inside, was Lizbete's dress—but somehow not her dress. Elin beamed at her. "Brynar collected your belongings from Uncle Hangur, who was trying to claim they were his. I've been feeling poorly for the last couple of days. Mother wanted to keep me cooped up inside, so I took the time to finish it up for you. I hope you like it."

Lizbete blinked, trying to figure out what she was looking at. The blue fabric with the ribbons was exactly as she had remembered it, but Elin had sewn white fur around the hem and collar, creating a ruff. Beside it hung a mask of snowy fur with eyes rimmed with bits of pure blue seaglass and tufted ears.

"It's a snow fox," Lizbete whispered. "It's—it's beautiful, but what am I going to do with it?"

Elin took the mask from the hook and held it out to Lizbete. "You're going to the First Frost. You're going as the girl with the prettiest mask. You're going to dance and you're going to laugh and no one will say anything about it because you're not going to be the Ash Lizard tonight. You're going to be the vixen queen, and if anyone says anything about it, well." Elin smirked. "I might know a young man fox who would love to sink his teeth into the first person who insults you."

Lizbete gaped. "Oh, I can't! Elin, this is amazing. This is one of the most wonderful things anyone has ever done for me, like something out of a story, but the whole town hates me. If I show up at the First Frost, they'll—"

"All whisper, 'who is that mysterious foxy fox woman?'" Elin held the mask over her own face and winked through the eye holes. "So foxy."

Lizbete took the mask and stroked the soft fur. Elin had a point. It covered up most of her face, and the dress would hide almost all her grayish skin. She could walk right up to Brynar and talk to him in front of everyone. It would be the fastest way to get the information about the Ravenous One to him. Also, she'd be there, in the middle of the lights and the music and the laughter. A sharp pang stabbed through her empty belly.

It won't be real. If any of them figure out who I am, they'll turn on me in a heartbeat. Oh, but even if it is make-believe, I'd be there, at the First Frost, with Brynar.

Swallowing down the lump in her throat, Lizbete nodded. "All right. I guess I'm going to the First Frost tonight."

Chapter Eighteen

The white fur ruff brushed up against Lizbete's neck and face as she slipped from the mayor's house. She glanced back at Elin, who gave her a thumbs up from the door. Lizbete's stomach quivered, but she managed a weak smile.

She'd given Elin her extra crystal as the girl had helped her dress, and Elin already looked better. Maybe if the Ravenous One could be dealt with, they could find some sort of system to trade with the cavers, or Grimir could teach Lizbete the secret of growing the crystals. Either way, Elin's future had hope. If nothing else, Lizbete had given her that.

"Don't let my brother get too handsy with you at the dance!" Elin called out. "If he does, knee up, fast. That always cools an amorous mood."

"Elin!" Lizbete's cheeks heated wildly. Oh, that was a strange sensation. She reached under her collar and touched the crystal hanging from her neck. Was this what it was like to be fully human? Hot blood rushing around one's body at the slightest upset? *It'll take some getting used to, but I prefer it to drawing heat off people and constantly shivering.*

Whatever Lizbete thought of Witta, the girl had spectacularly transformed Brumehome for the party. Every street in and out of the town square was lined with paper lanterns, streamers dyed blue and green, and dried flowers carefully preserved to maintain their color and scent. Music drifted through the village, and Lizbete caught herself swaying as she walked. Scents of frying food, sugary cakes, and roasted apples tickled her nose.

Lizbete paused when the lights of the square came into view. A roaring bonfire reached towards the evening sky as a group of young people joined hands and danced around it. All around the square sat tables and benches heaped with food, tankards of drink, and more of Witta's stunning decorations. Everyone wore their finest, and most wore masks. Lizbete's hand strayed towards her own mask which sat oddly over her spectacles. Would it be enough? She could identify some of the village young people, even with their masks on.

Einar had surrounded his face with black feathers to imitate either a crow or a raven. The mask left enough of his features visible that Lizbete was able to spot him as he and Marget, who wore a similar get-up of white feathers, danced and kissed in the firelight. Other villagers she knew by voice, recognizing Tieren's harsh tone as he shouted and laughed over his drink at a nearby table. Lizbete wouldn't have recognized Witta, except for Elin's warning about the hen mask. The young woman stood, arms crossed, observing the festivities and occasionally snapping at the younger boys who were running food back and forth from the tavern across the square.

Lizbete shied back. This was a bad idea. None of these people wanted her here. She needed to run and hide before someone figured out that she didn't belong—

She turned to go, and her eyes caught a flash of vibrant orange.

Her heart fell into her stomach as Brynar stepped out from behind the fire. He wore a similar mask to hers, only with red fox fur rather than white, with flecks of gold around the eyes. Even with his face obscured, she knew it was him from his posture and the way he moved. Bryanar was always somehow both hesitant and confident, as if he were taking great care but still knew what he was doing.

Witta looked up from bullying a serving boy, crossed to Brynar, and said something. With the roar of the fire and the chaos of dozens of voices, the words were lost even to Lizbete. When Brynar responded, Witta threw up her hands and stomped away.

Brynar's shoulders slumped, and he shook his head.

He looked up. Straight at Lizbete.

Her heart galloped within her as his blue eyes stared at her through his mask.

She wanted to run. She wanted to run and never look back, but she couldn't. She couldn't look away from him. As if of their own choice, her feet took a stumbling step forward.

Brynar pushed through the crowd and met her before she could go more than a few feet.

"Liz?" he whispered. "It is you! Are you . . . are you all right?"

Her tongue stuck to the roof of her mouth, but she managed a nod.

His shoulders rose and fell in a great sigh. "Thank the Skywatcher. When I came home and no one had seen you for over a day—" He grimaced. "My uncle, that idiot. I swear, I almost strangled him on the spot. All that talk about caring for you the way Aunt Katryn would want, and in less than two weeks—"

She found her voice. "It's all right. I'm fine."

"I was so worried." He stepped closer. "Father said you were probably at the widow's, but without knowing for sure, it was eating at me."

She could feel his heat calling to her, but for once her blood didn't try to steal it. Instead her whole being savored it like a cat basking in a sunbeam, not taking, but still enjoying. Her insides melted, and without thinking, she took his hand. His grip tightened immediately around hers. Warm, solid, so real. Her soul inhaled the contact like a drowning man gasping in a breath.

Brynar stared down at their entwined fingers. He swallowed. "You're—I don't think you've ever touched me before without immediately pulling away."

Her heart twisted. "Let's just say, I figured something out."

The music grew louder. Someone beat a drum in a merry rhythm while a flute and a fiddle harmonized over the roar. Everyone rushed to the other side of the square where a platform had been set up for the musicians, leaving Lizbete and Brynar alone.

Lizbete shivered as he stroked the back of her hand with his thumb. He drew her closer, one arm slipping around her shoulders. "Are you cold?"

She shook her head. "No. For once, I'm not." This felt so good, but this wasn't why she was there. She needed to tell him, to warn him. Then she needed to end this, to wake up from the dream before she was yanked out of it or it turned into a nightmare. "Brynar, there's something important I need to tell you—"

"Can it wait?" He brought his face closer to hers. The warmth of his breath intoxicated her, and it was all she could do to keep standing. "Liz, I thought I'd lost you. Even before I came home to find you gone, I wasn't sure you'd ever speak to me again. I made a mistake, and I'm sorry. Please, Liz, no matter what else you have to say, before you make any choices about what I deserve, just right now, here—can I have one dance with you?"

"Yes." Her heart pushed out an answer without consulting her brain. A smile spread across his lips, so brilliant and beautiful that she lost all hope of escaping. He gathered her into his arms, and before she could breathe, she found herself flying across the square, holding fast to him. Her heart in her throat, her eyes consumed by him as they moved to music she couldn't quite hear, surrounded by people she couldn't quite see, in a world that didn't matter anymore except in that Brynar was part of it. Brynar was part of it, and she'd cling to him like an anchor chain to keep from getting swept away.

Head so light Lizbete feared she wouldn't be able to stand, she relied on his arms to support her. She could hear his heart beating and his every breath. Her soul soaked up the contact with him even as her blood used to absorb warmth. For the first time in too long, she felt whole. Safe, happy. The music slowed, but he kept moving, drawing her away from the crowds. Then they stood at the mouth of an alleyway leading off the square, just out of sight of the bustle of the party though still within the reach of the lights and the music. Alone, Brynar abandoned all pretense of dancing and just held her, rocking slightly on his feet, his cheek pressed to the top of her head.

The position pushed Lizbete's mask off her face and up into her hair, but she didn't care. No, this moment was fully for them, whatever that meant.

But like rust creeping into metal, doubt eroded her happiness.

Her fingers tightened on his shirt. This wasn't meant to be. Brynar belonged to his village, to his family, to everything and everyone who would never accept her. Even with the crystal allowing him to hold her without freezing, it was only a temporary reprieve. She was still dangerous. What if the cord broke? What if the crystal stopped working? What if she hurt him?

Tears streamed down her cheeks. She wanted this. She wanted him. Wanted the way he made her feel when he looked at her—but she couldn't have him.

"Liz?" He ran his fingers across her cheek, brushing away tears. Removing his mask, he stared down at her, his beautiful blue eyes sincere and worried. "Oh, Liz, please don't cry. I want you to be happy."

"But I can't be. Not like this. This isn't meant for someone like me." She pulled away from him. "Brynar, you're the prince of this village, the future leader. You're smart and handsome and everything any girl could want, but you deserve so much better than me. You should be with someone your family will approve of, who the village won't hate, someone . . . beautiful." She glanced down at her hands. Her pallid gray skin looked sickly and ashen compared to his, compared to anyone's. Even now, knowing it was because of her caver heritage, she couldn't expect him to accept her like this.

"But you are." He placed his hands on her shoulders. "Liz, you are the best girl in this village, and no matter the mistakes I've made, part of me has always known that. I've known it since you gave your time to helping Elin when everyone else wanted to turn their back on her. You're kind and good, and that has more value than anything the rest of the village might hold in high regard."

"But I'm not..." Her voice cracked. "You say I'm kind and good and that gives me value, but that's not beauty. Not really. What people mean when they say beautiful is perfect skin that isn't corpse-gray, cheeks that aren't sunken in, a body that isn't all angles and bones." She choked. "'Beautiful on the inside' just means not beautiful at all. If you are honest, Brynar, if you compare me to any other girl in this village with a healthy complexion and appealing figure, can you truly say I am beautiful?"

"Liz—" He stepped closer.

She staggered away from him. "No, you can't, because for all your kind words about my goodness, that's not what beauty means. Beauty means outside. It means that when a boy looks at me, he actually would want to touch me, and that . . . that isn't what I am."

His expression softened, and he reached for her. She didn't have the fight left in her to pull away. His hand caressed her cheek, her blood drawing on his heat ever so slightly, just enough to taste the stability of his presence. "If that's what it means, if it just means that I want to touch you, then yes. Liz, I can honestly say you are beautiful. In fact, you are the most beautiful woman I've ever seen."

Her breath went out of her as his arms twined about her body. Her feet left the ground, and her lips rose to meet his. They touched, softly at first. When she didn't pull away, he brushed his fingers through her hair and intensified the kiss. Her arms found their way around his neck and she drew herself even closer to him, holding on for dear life. Their closeness nudged her spectacles cockeyed, but she didn't care.

At last, his lips parted from hers. His mouth remained close, hovering over hers, their breaths intermingled.

"I love you, Liz," he whispered. "I love you, and I don't care what anyone thinks about it. Please, give me one more chance."

"I love you, too." The words broke down the last of her resistance, and she pressed her lips to his again, hungry for him. This time as her mouth parted from his, her eyes caught movement in the shadows down the alleyway. She paused, looking over his shoulder. A small, dark-haired head peeked around a stack of barrels, locked stares with Lizbete, and immediately ducked behind the barrels again. Lizbete smirked. Well, Elin had practically orchestrated this moment. Let her enjoy the view.

She released Brynar to look him in the eye, still smirking.

"What?" He arched an eyebrow.

"Nothing."

He took both her hands and let out a long breath. "Do you want to be there when I tell my parents? It might be easier if I break the news by myself and then bring you in once they've had time to process."

She blinked at him. "Time to process what?"

"That I'm in love with you, not their carefully chosen candidate." He snorted. "Though Witta isn't going to be too broken up about it. I swear she cares more about this festival than she ever would about me. I think I was just the escort she thought would look best in her chosen costume."

"Cocky of her," Lizbete chuckled.

"Yeah. Wait," he scoffed. "Was that a chicken pun?"

"Yep." She grinned.

"Ah, I see. Well, she shouldn't have counted on those plans before they hatched." He winked at her. "Come on. I at least want to spend the rest of the festival with you on my arm."

A wave of emotions crashed through Lizbete, stealing her sense. Fear of being seen publicly with Brynar and the derision he might face collided with pride and delight over actually being with him, of being his chosen companion. She was overwhelmed and . . . oh, this wasn't even what she'd come here for!

"Brynar, I want that too, but first, when I said there was something I needed to tell you, it wasn't about us. I found out something—"

The ground heaved beneath her feet, sending her crashing into Brynar's chest. The earth shuddered and everything around them turned to chaos.

Chapter Nineteen

"Hold on!" Brynar barked. He sheltered her with his body as the whole world seemed to shake. Crashing, screaming, shaking. Oh, so much shaking! Lizbete's fingers tightened into Brynar. Would it never stop?

As quickly as it had begun, it was over. She cracked open one eye.

"Are you all right?" he stammered.

She nodded. "You?"

"Yeah." He staggered to his feet and looked around. The barrels down the alleyway had toppled.

Panic shot through Lizbete. "Elin!"

"What?" Brynar's eyes widened.

Lizbete sprinted down the alley. The girl huddled against the wall of the nearest building, trembling.

"Oh, Skywatcher!" Brynar dashed to her and scooped her up in his arms. "What are you doing out here?"

"Getting shook to death." Elin pushed him. "Let me go, Brynar. I'm fine."

He let her down to walk but kept one hand on her shoulder. "We should go check on the others. Come on."

They hurried into the town square. Logs had escaped from the bonfire and set one of the table displays aflame. Young folk beat on fire with sacks, and the flames grew steadily weaker. Chairs and tables were toppled, food scattered, drinks spilt. Still, at least at a glance no one seemed to be hurt.

"Everyone all right?" Brynar shouted over the chaos.

"I think so." Einar emerged from the group of fire-fighters. "Almost everyone was in the square when it happened. Not a lot to fall on people here, thank the Skywatcher." Einar's gaze fell on Lizbete. His brow furrowed, but he didn't speak.

"That's good." Brynar nodded.

"Where were you?" Witta stomped up to him. "The whole festival is ruined, and you were nowhere to be seen!"

Elin rolled her eyes. "He was busy causing an earthquake just to annoy you and ruin your little party."

"Quiet, you brat!" Witta's cheeks reddened. "It may not be his fault, but he's not helping anything."

"What's going on here?" Mayor Sten and his wife, Nan, approached. Nan caught sight of Elin, and the older woman's eyes narrowed. Elin, who flushed and shrank behind her brother. Lizbete wanted to disappear too. This looked like it could turn into a family fight, and she wasn't ready to face the mayor's disapproval just yet.

"What's going on is that your son was supposed to help me make this the most memorable First Frost ever, and now it's ruined and he's not even here to help pick up." Witta thrust a finger at Brynar. "This town is getting worse and worse, and you're just sitting by and letting it happen. You aren't fit to be mayor."

Anger kindled in Lizbete's chest. She took a step forward, but Brynar held up his hand.

"Maybe not. I'm not even sure I want to be, honestly."

Mayor Sten choked. "Brynar—"

"We'll talk about it later, sir." Brynar squared his shoulders. "Right now, we need to make sure everyone is safe. Einar, you want to help me?"

Einar started. "Me?"

"You know the town better than I do." Brynar smiled.

Einar glanced at his father, but the older man just shrugged. The tension in Lizbete's shoulders eased. Perhaps this wouldn't be the disaster she feared.

Something hit her between her shoulders, knocking her to the earth. Her breath rushed out of her. The cobblestones tore her hands, leaving them stinging.

"Hey!" Brynar yanked her to her feet and pulled her against his chest.

Lizbete stared down at a stone about the size of a man's fist, a stone that mirrored the sore spot now throbbing on her back.

"Who threw that?" Mayor Sten shouted.

A group of townsfolk stepped out of the twilight at the edge of the square, shoulder to shoulder. Lizbete's gaze flitted across their faces. She saw several she knew. Hester. Hangur. Tieren and his father. Witta's parents. All carried expressions of fear and anger.

She shrank against Brynar, wishing she'd inherited her father's ability to simply disappear as a wisp of smoke.

"It might as well have been all of us, brother." Hangur stepped forward. "We all would've liked to. All see the need to. Everyone but you and your brood knows what has to be done here."

Sten narrowed his eyes at his brother. "Have you been drinking again, Hangur?"

Hangur snorted. "No, for once I am dead sober, and might be for a while considering how many of my liquor bottles were crashed in that shake up. Who is going to pay for that?"

"The earthquakes are no one's fault," Nan broke in. She grasped her husband's arm as if she could prop him up against his constituents' displeasure.

"We're all hurting, and we'll all help each other get back on our feet," Einar added. "That's what we've always done when hardship has hit our village, and it's what we'll continue to do." The youth drew himself up taller. Lizbete couldn't believe the change in his tone. Maybe there was more to Einar than she'd thought.

"You say it's no one's fault, but we all saw that little witch consulting with dark spirits!" Hester aimed a finger at Lizbete. Lizbete's heart jumped into her mouth. She couldn't speak, couldn't think.

"Liz hasn't done anything." Brynar gripped her tighter.

"Tell that to Erich's frozen corpse!" Hangur growled.

"We're losing animals," Tieren's father added. "The town has been hit by storms and shaking, and this girl lurks among us, consulting with monsters. If she's not causing the disasters, perhaps it is the Skywatcher punishing us for having her in our midst."

Einar glanced at Lizbete out of the corner of his eye and took a subtle step away from her. She winced. That was the Einar she knew.

Nan took Elin's hand. "Darling, let's go home and let your father deal with—"

The child yanked away. "No. I'm staying here. I'm not going to let them hurt Liz!"

"His girl's always been spirit-touched," Hester hissed at Hangur. "No wonder your brother won't listen about the Ash Lizard, with that demon child in his very household."

"Elin is just a sick child!" Lizbete gasped. "If you're turning on her, then you must be mad."

Hester recoiled, and everyone else stared at Lizbete. She cringed. She'd done it again, responding to things she shouldn't have even been able to hear. Things were going bad fast, and she didn't want Elin around for whatever might happen.

Lizbete turned to Elin. "Please, let your mother take you home. I'll be all right. I promise."

Elin glanced from Lizbete to her mother to the angry crowd then finally to her brother. "Brynar, if you let them hurt Liz—"

"I won't. Go on." He nudged her towards her mother.

Nan wrapped her arms around Elin and scurried from the square.

"The storms and the quakes are just that. Storms and quakes." Sten crossed his arms. "It's not as if we've never had them before."

"But they're worse now! Have we ever had three within a year, let alone a month?" More people gathered around until Lizbete was certain the entire village was staring at her.

"And what about that dark spirit? It killed Erich right in front of us at the girl's bidding!"

"I didn't ask him to do that," Lizbete said. "But Erich was about to kill me. Grimir only acted to save me."

A gasp spread through the crowd, and even Brynar's hold on her loosened.

Lizbete bit her bottom lip before stepping away from Brynar to stand on her own. She had meant to tell Mayor Sten or Brynar in private, but the whole village needed to know the danger they were in.

"Yes, I know him. His name is Grimir, but he isn't a dark spirit, and he and his people aren't causing the quakes." Though they were stealing the livestock, but she'd leave that out for now. "They're called cavers, and they live in the steamvents beneath Ash Mountain."

"Liz?" Brynar frowned. "What are you talking about?"

"I'm . . . I'm one of them. Half, anyway." She angled away from Brynar. Might as well get it all out now. "My mother was human. I didn't know until Grimir—my father—found me. They don't mean the village any harm. They've lived here longer than the village has stood, and they have no need for us, but . . . but they aren't the only thing living under the mountain."

Her voice rose in volume as her confidence grew. "There's a monster beneath the mountain. Not like me or even Grimir, but a true monster, a creature massive enough to cause an earthquake with its stirring. It has slept for generations, but now it's awakening. That's why the town is shaking."

Mayor Sten took a step back from her.

"Can we kill it?" To Lizbete's surprise, Einar had asked the question.

She shook her head. "It is massive. A beast of fire and stone. It can't be destroyed or reasoned with. The cavers try to placate it by feeding it, but it only grows hungrier."

"What do you expect us to do then?" The youth scowled.

"I—I don't know. I just felt you should be warned." In all honesty, she thought they should run, abandon Brumehome and find a place to live that wasn't within spitting distance of an ancient horror so insatiable it was called the Ravenous One. However, she knew the villagers would be resistant to fleeing the only home they'd ever known, and she'd already pushed her luck enough for one day as far as upsetting them.

Murmurs spread through the crowd. Brynar shifted from foot to foot. She could sense his unease. What she'd just revealed was a lot to take on faith, even from the girl he'd said he loved.

Finally, Brynar faced his father. "Sir, if she's telling the truth—"

"How are you even entertaining this nonsense!" Witta pushed her way between Brynar and Lizbete and shoved him in the chest. "Don't you see what this girl is doing? She tried to steal the tavern out from under your family, and now she's trying to steal you from me."

"I was never yours in the first place, Witta." Brynar said, his tone stern in a way that very much reminded Lizbete of his father.

Witta's lower lip went slack before her glare hardened to a snarl. "You're bewitched! This little demon girl, this Ash Lizard, has gotten into your head. Honestly, I wouldn't be surprised if she did call down the quake somehow, just to ruin the First Frost so that you wouldn't have a chance to leave her." She rounded on Lizbete with a snarl. "Quake aside, you're a thief, and the proof is right in front of us." She grabbed the fur that Elin had sewn around the neck of Lizbete's dress. "How else could you have gotten this?"

Lizbete cried out in horror as Witta yanked so hard the dress ripped. She clutched at the torn segment. Witta's eyes fell on the exposed crystal hanging from her neck.

"And jewelry? Who did you nip that from?" She snatched the crystal from Lizbete's neck, snapping the cord.

"Cut it out!" Brynar dove forward and gathered Lizbete up in his arms.

"No!" Lizbete gasped.

It was too late. Separated from the crystal, exposed to the cold air of twilight, and spurred by panic, Lizbete's blood screamed for warmth.

Warmth it quickly found in Brynar.

She felt the draw from him come like a blast of hot air from an oven. It washed over her bringing with it everything she loved about him, but also confusion and fear. His eyes widened. His lips turned blue.

"Stop!" she wailed, pushing him as hard as she could, but his cold limbs seized around her. "Let go!"

"Brynar!" Einar yanked his brother away from her.

Lizbete gaped as Brynar collapsed, shivering madly, his eyes half shut. Witta screamed and took off running, still clutching the crystal. No one stopped her.

"She killed him!" Hester shrieked. "Just like Erich!"

"Brynar?" Sten knelt beside his son.

"I—I'm . . . I'll b—be fine." Brynar's teeth chattered.

Lizbete's voice left her as relief that he was alive mixed with terror over how quickly she'd harmed him. The villagers glared at her, looking as if they wanted to tear her to pieces but didn't dare touch her. For the best. If anyone laid a hand on her right now, she wasn't sure she could stop her already agitated blood from draining them completely.

"I didn't mean to," she whimpered.

Sten touched his son's face, worry deepening the wrinkles around his eyes. "You feel like ice." He leaped back to his feet. "Einar, can you get your brother home and warmed up?"

"Do you finally see it?" Hangur growled. "We're trying to save you, save the whole town, Sten. You must see it. Now that she harmed your own son—"

"We don't—I don't know what is going on, but I'm not going to let this town descend into anarchy." Sten grabbed his brother by the arm. "You want to save me? Then help Einar with Brynar. It'll be easier to carry him between the two of you."

Brynar gave some sort of mumbled response, but his words were too slurred for even Lizbete to decipher. Her whole body shook. What had she done?

"But the girl!" Hangur protested.

"I'll take care of the girl." Sten grabbed Lizbete by the collar, only touching cloth, not skin. "She won't hurt anyone." He faced the crowd. "Please. I've served this town for over a decade, and my father before me. I know things have been difficult lately, but I still have your best interest at heart. Please, trust me one more time."

The villagers mumbled among themselves but did not move to attack Lizbete. Hangur's gaze flicked from Lizbete to Brynar then back to his brother. He gave a stony nod. He got behind Brynar and hoisted him up. The young man stumbled, but between Einar and Hangur's urging, he didn't protest as they more carried than led him away.

Sten let out a long breath, then narrowed his eyes at the crowd. "All of you, get back to your homes and families. I'll see that she's put away where she won't be able to . . . whatever it is that she does." As the crowd began to disperse, the mayor focused on Lizbete. His blue eyes, the eyes Brynar had inherited, shone hard and cold in the light of the bonfire. "Are you coming willingly, or do I have to bind you?"

"Willingly," she whispered. "Please, don't touch me, though. I don't want—"

"I won't." He still kept hold of her garments, but Lizbete managed to lean away from him enough that he didn't come into contact with her skin.

They walked through the dark streets. Lizbete could feel the eyes of the village following her, though none approached.

Where is he taking me? Oh, what am I going to do? What if Brynar isn't all right? What if . . . Skywatcher, please, let him thaw out. Let me not have hurt him permanently. I'm so sorry. I'm so, so sorry.

Sten led Lizbete to a storage cellar dug right into the hillside near his home. "This is the closest thing we have to a prison. I hate to leave you in here, but for your own protection as well as the village's peace, it's best to keep you away from people for now." He opened the door.

She drew a deep breath. It was cold and dark. She shivered. "I'll freeze to death in there."

He eyed her torn garments. "I'll bring you some things to help you keep warm." He nudged her towards the door. "I honestly don't believe you meant to hurt Brynar, but I also cannot deny that you did. Do you want to explain how to me? Now while we're safe?"

Resigned to her fate, she stepped into the cellar. Maybe this was what she deserved. "I don't have the ability to stay warm on my own, and when I get cold, I steal heat from other sources. If I'm touching a human, they will be that source. It is usually just a little bit, but . . . but sometimes it's more."

"I see." He shifted from foot to foot. "And you can't control it?"

She shook her head.

"That explains what happened when you were an infant, as well as my brother's ravings." He sighed. "My son cares for you a great deal."

Tears trickled down her cheeks but hardened to ice before they reached her chin. "I know."

"And you for him, I'm guessing?"

She managed to nod.

He let out a long breath. "I disapproved of the match because it would have made life more difficult for Brynar and possibly prevented the locals from accepting him as their next leader when it came time for me to retire. However, seeing how he obviously has affection for you—I admit, I was softening to the idea."

The tightness in Lizbete's chest eased, and she drew closer to Sten.

"However, after tonight—"

She shrank back. Here it came.

"If you really care for my son, you must realize you cannot be with him. You're dangerous. A marriage involves trust, and no matter how much you love him, no matter how you would loathe hurting him, you cannot be certain that you won't. What if he fell asleep beside you? Could you be sure he would awaken?"

Her insides dissolved into aching, searing pain. She shook her head. Even with the crystal's power, it was too easy for something to go wrong, for the chain to break and for her to be left at the mercy of her blood's hunger for heat.

It was a fool's dream. I'm a monster, and Brynar deserves so much better.

Sten sighed and rubbed the back of his neck. "It will be hard on him in the short term, but in the long term, it's best if you get as far from him as possible. I'll see if one of the fishermen is willing to give you transport down the coast. I have a cousin in the village of Rivermouth who will take you in until you can get on your feet. Brynar will accept it after a while." He reached out as if to touch her, but drew back and shook his head. "I am sorry. I believe you have a good heart, Lizbete. I know you can't help what you are, but for the good of Brynar, the family, and the village—"

"This is how it has to be," she whispered. "There's no place for me here."

"I'm glad you understand." He stepped outside the cellar. "I should be able to find passage for you by morning. In the meantime, I truly am sorry. For you, but also for my son."

Lizbete sat between two barrels and pulled her knees against her chest. Remembering Brynar's kiss, the warmth of his arms around her, the adoration in his eyes and the sincerity in his voice when he'd said he loved her. He loved *her* . . . It all cracked her open and left her bleeding out into her own soul. The door closed behind Sten, and Lizbete wept in the darkness.

Chapter Twenty

Sten kept his promise. Before Lizbete's body could seize up from cold, he returned carrying a metal brazier with a fire inside, a fresh tunic and leggings, and a warm cloak. As soon as she was alone, Lizbete quickly dressed, then rolled up her sleeves and stuck her hands right into the flames. The heat washed over her, and her muscles slowly untensed.

Finally thawed out, she lay beside the fire and tried to stop crying.

Look at me. What would Auntie Katryn say if she saw how I've given up? I'm lying here like a baby. Stop crying. Stop it. Stop it. Stop—oh.

She clenched her jaw until it hurt. This was so stupid. She had lost everything. Why couldn't she give herself permission to cry about it?

Shut up, me. I'll cry if I want to. She squeezed her eyes shut. *What else am I supposed to do? I'm stuck here. It's not like I can do anything to make this better. Not like I can fix it. I'm the problem.*

Or was she?

A big fiery monster who can cause earthquakes and demands sac-

rifices seems like much more of a problem than I am. My heat-stealing is a danger to those closest to me, but the Ravenous One endangers the entire village.

She rolled over and tried to think about something else.

It's not like I can do anything about the Ravenous One. I'm not a great hero. Grimir said they are all dead, probably because they did stupid things like fight the Ravenous One. No. I can do no good. I am no good. There isn't anything left for me to do for anyone—

But what about Elin?

Lizbete swallowed. She had helped Elin. If she could find a way to get the cavers to trade peacefully with the human villagers, she could continue to help Elin. Also, if she could get her fire crystal back, or a replacement one from Grimir, she wouldn't be such a danger. It wasn't as if it was her fault.

But something bad could happen.

Fear made one last attempt to drag her into darkness. It paraded all the possible evil that she could cause. The harm to Brynar, to Brynar's family, to random villagers who happened to brush up against her in crowds. However, she'd lived in the village for sixteen years and for the most part, she hadn't hurt anyone. Bad things hadn't happened until tonight, and that had been Witta's fault, not hers.

Something bad could happen, but it could happen even without me. I wasn't the reason Auntie died. I wasn't the reason the earthquakes started or why the Ravenous One woke up or why Elin was born sickly.

Lizbete sat up.

And there is something I can do about it. I can tell Brynar that the villagers need to leave this place before things get worse. I can get the crystals for Elin, and for myself. For myself so I can hold Brynar again. I'll be honest about the danger, about the chance that things could go wrong, but I can't make the choice to abandon him based on that fear. If he decides it is too much danger for him, I'll accept that, but it isn't just up to me anymore. It's up to us.

The thought of her and Brynar as an "us" filled her heart to bursting. She stood.

Now that she wasn't going to merely sit back and accept her fate, Lizbete needed to figure out what to do with that determination. She approached the door and gave it a shake. It didn't give. Mayor Sten had locked it from the outside. She tried to remember what the outside of the door looked like. *It has a crossbar,* she thought. That would be hard to break down and impossible to undo.

I can just wait until morning and tell Mayor Sten I've decided not to leave. Would he accept that? He wouldn't force me to go, would he?

She'd never seen Mayor Sten commit an act of violence before, but with his son's safety and the peace of the village on the line, she wouldn't put it past him. Of course, if he tried to grab her, her blood might freeze him. She didn't want this, but it could be a deterrent to any manhandling. However, her blood couldn't stop someone from shooting her with an arrow or hitting her with a long stick.

Lizbete shuddered. Had it really come to the point where she was considering her chances in combat against the people she'd lived with her whole life? These were fishermen, blacksmiths, farmers and their wives, not soldiers.

All the more reason they need to listen to me and get as far away from the Ravenous One as possible. Maybe Brynar can convince them, or maybe I can convince Mayor Sten.

No, Brynar was a safer bet. Besides, she needed to apologize to him for almost turning him into a block of ice. There was a good chance Mayor Sten had already told him about her "condition." Regret tugged at her. She should've told Brynar herself, and a long time ago. Well, that was also something she needed to apologize for.

First she needed to get to him.

She put her shoulder to the door. Maybe it would give if pushed hard enough. The experiment gained her nothing but a bruised shoulder.

Lizbete screwed up her mouth. Now what? She tried to slip her fingers under the door and through the slight gap between the sides of the door and the frame. The door sat too tight. She could only get the very tips of her fingers through even the widest spot.

Maybe . . . could *I turn into smoke like Grimir?*

After all, she'd never tried. She held her hand in front of her face. If only Grimir had explained to her how he'd done it. Lizbete tried to imagine her hand growing thinner and lighter. She closed her eyes. She pretended the edges of her skin were soft. She was soft. Her whole body was smoke and mist and air. Nothing firm. Nothing heavy. Nothing solid.

Her mind took over, and she could feel the edges of her body lightening. She grew softer. Her head seemed to float above her body. She rose on her tiptoes, still touching the floor but barely. She was vapor.

She could do this. Her heart rate accelerated.

With a deep breath, Lizbete stepped into the door, and collided with solid wood.

She staggered back a step, rubbing her smacked forehead. Well, that hadn't worked. Letting out a frustrated breath, she started looking around the cellar for something she could use to smash the hinges.

Several minutes later, the only thing her search had turned up was an old board covered in splinters. Maybe she could wedge it into the cracks and get some leverage. She stuck the board into the space between the door and the frame, then leaned against it.

The board snapped in half with a loud crack. Lizbete gave a muffled shriek as she toppled against the wall.

Tears smarted her eyes. This was stupid. She had no way to get out. Brynar probably didn't even want to be with her anymore. Not after what she'd done to him. What sort of idiot would want to be with a girl who had nearly murdered him?

No, Brynar wasn't an idiot. She was. She was an idiot for ever thinking she could be with a boy like Brynar. For ever thinking she could be a part of this stupid village. For ever thinking she had a chance to save anyone from that monster under the mountain.

The door opened.

Lizbete squinted against the light of a lantern.

"Liz!" Brynar's voice sang to her ears, and her heart cried out for joy. He rushed forward. For a moment she accepted his one-armed embrace, too happy to see him to think of the consequences.

It only took a heartbeat, though, for her blood to pull from him.

"No!" She wrenched away and held her hand out to block him from trying again. "I'll . . . I'll hurt you."

He set the lantern down and gazed at her, his beloved blue eyes pleading with her. "My father told me a little about how. I don't understand, though. At the First Frost, I was holding you, I was touching you, and nothing bad happened." His cheeks reddened and a smile crossed his face, so charming it took her breath away. "Quite the opposite in fact."

She hung her head. "It was the crystal I was wearing around my neck. When I wear it, I pull from it rather than people. I just got it recently."

Understanding crossed his face. "And then that idiot Witta

ripped it off you?"

Lizbete wrinkled her nose. She'd been so panicked about hurting Brynar, so ashamed of her own blood, that she hadn't stopped to be angry at Witta. Now it hit all at once.

"If I'd killed you because of what she did, I swear, I would've . . . frozen her slowly and enjoyed every moment of it." Her words came out in an angry breath, and she felt better for it.

"Thankfully, I'm still here." He reached for her, but stopped less than an inch away from her face, hovering his hand near her skin without touching it. His warmth called to her blood. "I guess Witta must've taken the crystal with her. I lost track of it in the chaos. We could ask her to give it back, but she'd probably make another scene. We can't risk drawing attention from the townsfolk right now. Can we get you another?"

"Maybe, but does it really matter?" Tears blurred her vision. "This town will never let us be together, Brynar. Your father is already plotting to send me away to keep me from hurting you. In fact, how are you even here?"

He withdrew his hand. "Sneaked out the window. I made a show of agreeing with everything Father said when he explained why you and I would never work, how it was too dangerous, how he loved me too much to accept me in a relationship that could only end in heartbreak. Hard to stomach, but if I had argued with him he would've kept me under watch, and I already knew what I wanted to do." He drew a deep breath and dropped to one knee.

Lizbete recoiled, gaping at him. A bemused smile quirked his lips before his expression grew grave and sincere again.

"Liz, I love you. I don't care about the town or my father or anything but what I feel for you. The whole 'not being able to touch you' thing I'm not crazy about, but if there is a fix for that, even a temporary one, then I'll deal with it." Brynar took her hand. When she tried to yank away, he tightened his grasp, not painfully but enough that it gave her pause. "A moment won't kill me," he whispered. "I need you to know that I'm committed to this, to you, no matter what."

"But I'll hurt you," she stammered. She could already feel her blood drawing from him, taste the intoxicating warmth that seeped from him to her through their contact. Still, somehow she could not bring herself to pull away.

"I can feel it, and I'll know if it is too much, all right?" He kept his gaze locked on hers. "Lizbete, I want you to be my wife. If that means we leave this place and never look back, so be it. I would rather be a healer than a mayor anyway, and I know enough healing to make that my trade anywhere in the kingdom. I..." His teeth chattered, and he clenched his jaw. This time when she pulled away, Brynar didn't protest. "I love you. I'm not going to throw that away because of the opinions of others."

She bit her bottom lip. "But what about your family? What about Elin?"

Doubt crept into his eyes, but he still smiled. "We could take Elin with us."

She gave a half-hearted laugh. "No, we can't. Your parents will be broken-hearted enough losing you without losing Elin too. They love her just as much as we do."

He stood and rubbed the back of his neck. "Maybe we could just run away together for a little while then come back once we have, I don't know, a couple of children. They'd have to accept it then."

The thought of having a family—with him—filled Lizbete with a dull ache akin to hunger. She wanted it so much that for a moment she couldn't speak.

"We'll figure it out, somehow. For now, I just want to get you out of this hole and to some place safe." He picked up the lantern again and motioned for her to follow him. "We can stay at Widow Gri's tonight and decide what to do in the morning." He glanced at her. "I don't suppose you have a way to get another of those crystals right away? Just, you know, in case we, um…"

"I get it." She smirked. "There are many aspects of this situation that would be improved upon if I wasn't afraid of touching you."

"Exactly." He grinned.

Lizbete hesitated. There were many things she needed to figure out, including what to do about the Ravenous One. However, it would be easier to think from a place of safety. "I can't get a crystal tonight, but tomorrow we can try to make contact with my father and see if he can help us." She kicked herself for not setting up some way to leave messages for Grimir or let him know that she wanted to talk.

"I kind of want to meet him, anyway." He led her out of the cellar. The streets were dark and quiet. A bright half-moon drifted through the starry skies above. Lizbete shivered in the cold night air and drew her cloak closer about her. "I should ask for his blessing, after all."

The cold air snaked beneath her cloak, and she shivered.

Brynar's brow furrowed. "Are you going to be able to make it to the widow's?"

She squared her shoulders. "I'll be fine as long as we move quickly."

He hesitated. "Can you take from me in small doses? When I held your hand a moment ago, I got cold, but now that I'm moving again, I've already warmed up. I'm fine with loaning you a little of my warmth along the way."

She considered this. "We can try. Honestly, I normally take from people slowly. It only comes in a rush if I'm near freezing or panicked."

"I can see how having the entire town descend upon you like a swarm of angry hornets could lead to panic." He snorted.

Footsteps echoed in the alley ahead of them.

Lizbete inhaled sharply. "Someone's coming."

Brynar scowled and stepped in front of her. "My father probably found my room empty and figured out where I went. Well, we'd have had to deal with this sooner or later. They're my family. I'll handle it."

Lizbete nodded. Even though she trusted him, her heart stuck in her throat. The footsteps grew louder until there was no denying that whoever it was headed right for them. She clenched her jaw, determined not to allow her resolve to weaken. She was going to have a happy life. She was going to be with Brynar. She was going to help this town deal with the Ravenous One whether they liked it or not.

A figure emerged from the shadows and stepped into the puddle of light cast by Brynar's lantern.

Brynar blinked. "Einar?"

His younger brother's eyes flitted from Brynar to Lizbete. He swallowed. "Elin's gone. The dark spirits took Elin."

Chapter Twenty-One

Lizbete and Brynar stared at Einar.

"What are you talking about?" Brynar stammered. "There are no such things as—"

"Say what you want. Believe what you want, but I know I'm right," Einar snapped, his normally sullen eyes alight with a strange fire. Lizbete drew closer to Brynar.

"Are you sure she didn't just run away?" she whispered.

She knew from experience that the cavers weren't nearly as frightening as the villagers made them out to be. Also, Elin was Elin, more likely to cause trouble than have trouble acted upon her. Einar had to be just panicking. At least, Lizbete hoped that was the case.

Einar's gaze dropped to the ground. "That's what Father thinks, and Mother . . . Elin was upset when she heard about what had happened with you, that Father was going to send you away. Father went out to look for her, but he's just checking her usual hiding places. I know that's not what's happened. I just—I know it." His voice cracked.

Lizbete and Brynar exchanged a glance. She'd never heard Einar this upset. Angry, sure. Irritated, definitely. But upset? This was a first.

Brynar gripped Einar's shoulder. "Tell me exactly what happened."

Einar let out a long breath. "We—We were all sitting around downstairs. We all thought you and Elin were both asleep, and Father wanted to talk over what *she* had said about how you got hurt at the First Frost." Einar eyed Lizbete as if she might spontaneously turn him into a block of ice right then and there. "I heard something from upstairs. It was muffled, but it caught my attention over the sound of Mother and Father arguing about whether or not you would recover from a broken heart." Even in his distress, he stopped to roll his eyes. "I'd had enough of the conversation anyway. So I wandered upstairs and . . . Elin's door was open. Her bed was empty, and I found this in the middle of the floor." He reached into his pocket and pulled out the fire crystal, still attached to the wire and cord Lizbete had used to hang it around Elin's neck.

Lizbete's heart dropped into her stomach. "Oh, no."

Brynar's eyebrows melted together. "That's not good. She wouldn't have left that behind. Not willingly."

"That's what I thought, but Mother and Father are convinced she's just sulking because of everything that happened tonight." Einar passed the crystal to Brynar, who immediately handed it to Lizbete. In spite of the dire situation, she drew in the heat it gave her like the aroma of a good meal. "I went to wake you up, but when I found you gone, I figured you'd be here."

Brynar hazarded a hand on Lizbete's shoulder. Her blood, satisfied by the crystal, didn't immediately leach from him. She sighed in relief and leaned into him, happy to be able to touch him again without fear.

Lizbete slipped the crystal around her neck and tightened her hold around it. She could imagine Elin running away from her home—to help Lizbete, maybe, but also just to prove a point to her parents. However, she wouldn't leave behind the crystal that helped her feel better. Something that Einar had said further heightened her growing panic.

"Einar, you said *dark spirits* took Elin. What did you mean by that?" She stepped around Brynar to look him squarely in the eyes.

Unable to hold her gaze, Einar shifted from foot to foot. "It's— It's possibly nothing, but I swear for the last few weeks, since before Aunt Katryn died, I've seen shadows near Elin. Most of the time when we were near the tavern, so I blamed it on—on—"

"It's all right. You can say it." Lizbete crossed her arms. "On me."

"Yeah. Especially after what happened with Erich."

Lizbete swallowed. He was probably right to associate the shadows with her, assuming it was Grimir he was seeing. However, Grimir would have no reason to be specifically watching Elin. The only reason any other caver would be lurking around Brumehome would be to find opportunities to steal animals for—

Dravish.

"Oh, no!" Her stomach twisted.

Both brothers looked at her.

"Brynar, remember what I said at the First Frost? About the Ravenous One? About how the cavers try to pacify it by feeding it?"

"Yeah," Brynar said slowly.

"They've been doing that by stealing livestock from the village. That's why there have been so many missing animals lately. However, there's one caver who thinks the Ravenous One won't be satisfied with animal flesh much longer." She forced the words out though they sickened her stomach. "He wanted to kidnap a human to sacrifice to it."

Brynar's eyes widened.

Einar's lower lip hung slack. "Sacrifice? As in—to kill?"

Fists clenched, Lizbete nodded. If she was right, did that mean Dravish had gone rogue and taken matters into his own hands? Or had he finally managed to get the approval of the council?

"How long has she been gone?" Brynar glanced up at the sky. The moon was high, sailing above the sleepy village like a watchful sentinel.

"I'm not exactly sure. Since after Father came home. I saw her listening on the stairs when he told us about locking Lizbete in the cellar."

"We might still have time." Lizbete grabbed Brynar by the hand. "My father showed me a tunnel leading into the cavers' realm that starts just outside the village. They won't be expecting a rescue attempt, so if we hurry, we might be able to save her. We need to leave now, though."

"I'm coming too!" Einar burst out. When they both looked at him, his cheeks reddened. "I've always known our time with Elin would be short, that I'd lose her. I thought I'd accepted that, but— but it isn't meant to happen like this. She's not going to die being fed to some monster under the earth. Not on my watch."

A slight smile quavered at the corner of Brynar's mouth. "Let's go then."

Not wanting to deal with Brynar's father realizing Lizbete was free, the group sent Einar home to fetch supplies. He returned shortly with an extra lantern and oil, short-handled axes for each of the brothers, and a pack full of other items he thought might be useful. Lizbete then led the way swiftly around the edges of the village and out towards the crack in the cliff face, the crack she knew to be the tunnel entrance.

Einar grimaced as he stared into the darkness before them. In the light of the moon and their faint lanterns, it seemed even more impenetrable and foreboding.

"You bring the chalk like I asked?" Brynar glanced at him.

His brother nodded, dug in his pack, and tossed the requested item to Brynar.

"Good." Brynar stepped into the cave and made the first mark on the wall a few feet in. "Rescuing Elin won't do much good if we can't find our way out again."

Lizbete's chest tightened. She'd only traveled this route once, and in complete darkness. If there were too many forks or side tunnels, she wouldn't be sure they were headed the right way.

What other choice do we have? We can't abandon Elin, and we can't afford to wait.

Determined not to show her hesitancy, she strode after Brynar. Einar lingered longest at the mouth of the cave. Still, before Lizbete had turned the first bend, she heard his footsteps echoing behind her as he rushed to catch up.

"Shh." She set her finger to her lips. "We can't afford to be loud."

Einar cringed and slowed his pace to a shuffle. Lizbete took one of the two lanterns and forged ahead. She kept one hand on the wall, scanning for any side passages that might be large enough to be part of the route. Thankfully, this section of tunnels continued like a drainpipe, burrowing deep into the earth leaving no question as to the correct way to go.

"So, you've made up your mind about her, haven't you?" Einar's murmured question hit Lizbete's ear. She nearly whirled around to look at him. However, from the tone, it was clear he wasn't addressing her, or even intended for her to hear. She kept her eyes forward.

"Yes," Brynar answered simply.

"No matter what Father or the rest of us think?" Einar prodded.

"Do you really care who I marry, Einar?" Brynar snorted. "Father, I understand. He has this vision for my future that Lizbete doesn't fit into. But you? What difference does it make to you if I'm with Liz or Witta or no one at all for that matter?"

"I guess, I just wish I understood it. You could have any girl in the village, and look at her."

Lizbete's ears warmed, and her hold on the lantern's handle tightened.

"She's skinny as a bundle of twigs. Her hair's dirty brown, and her skin—I just don't get it."

Lizbete tried to push away her shame. After all, she didn't need Einar, or anyone besides Brynar for that matter, to find her attractive. Still, the plainness of his words smarted against her soul like salt in a wound. They weren't words chosen to hurt her. It was simply the truth of how he saw her, and that made it all the more painful.

"First off, what you call dirty brown, I just call brown. If you'd gotten your hands in it—which I have and you aren't allowed to, so you'll just have to imagine—it's feather-soft to the touch. Also, her eyes light up when she smiles, and I like that she's slender." Brynar's words soothed her. "More importantly, though, looks don't last forever. We all get old and wrinkly. Your Marget's golden locks will be gray before long. I'd rather pursue someone who makes me laugh and smile rather than someone who inflames other passions—which don't get me wrong, she does." He gave a low whistle. "She does plenty."

The warmth in Lizbete's ears spread into her face and down

her neck. She touched the crystal at her breast. Being able to blush continued to be an odd and unexpected side-effect to its powers.

"I suppose they are right when they say there's no accounting for taste." Resignation tinged Einar's tone. "I want you to be happy, Brynar, but I worry about you. Father's right. The village isn't going to make room in their hearts for the Ash Lizard any time soon."

"Well, if they don't want her, they don't want me."

As they walked deeper under the earth, the air around them grew hotter. Einar fell quiet, and when Lizbete glanced back, he seemed to melt under the weight of his pack and the heat. Sweat dampened both men's brows. Brynar's shirt stuck to his chest muscles in a way that made Lizbete do a double take, then intentionally keep her eyes anywhere else.

Talk about inflaming other passions . . . steamblast me, I hope I get to see him without a shirt before I die. That's something to keep going for, if nothing else. For now, eyes forward.

She quickened her pace.

After another turn, a red glow illuminated the passage ahead. Lizbete held out her hand for the men to stop.

"We're close now. We need to be extra careful."

Both men nodded, and Einar's hand strayed to the handle of his axe. Lizbete winced.

What does he think he's going to do with that? Try to protect himself from the cavers?

"Cavers can pull heat from you, just like I can," she said, "but unlike me, they can control it. This means that if they want to freeze you to a block of ice in seconds, they can." She narrowed her eyes at Einar. "If you do something stupid, it won't help Elin. It'll just give the Ravenous One a couple extra courses for his next meal."

"Why are you looking at me?" Einar hissed.

Brynar stepped between them. "We all need to be cautious. Whatever we do, I'd feel better if we had some sort of plan."

Pride glowed within Lizbete at the solid, stable words. "*That's* why I'm looking at *you*, Einar. Brynar doesn't rush in without thinking things through first. *You do.*"

"I just prefer actions to words." Einar craned his neck to look around her. "Do we even know where they are keeping her?"

She bit her bottom lip. "No, but I know someone who probably does. Come on. This way."

Instead of taking the fork that would've led to the fiery chamber where Grimir had left her to rest and which provided a view of the Ravenous One, Lizbete took the tunnel in the opposite direction. With Brynar's faith in her, she easily trusted her instincts with navigating the tunnels. Soon they ducked through a low doorway. The crimson glow of Grimir's crystal garden sent dazzling light refracting around them.

"Wow," Einar whispered.

"There's so many of them." Brynar reached towards the nearest crystal.

"Stop!" A hazy form rushed from the shadows at the back of the room. Grimir solidified in front of Brynar, blocking him from touching the fire crystals.

Einar yelped and tried to draw his axe, but Brynar's hand clamped down on his shoulder. "I'm all right. Easy." Brynar swallowed. "Grimir, I presume?"

Grimir tilted his head. His high, hairless brow furrowed. Lizbete stepped around the brothers.

"Lizbete!" Grimir's raspy voice tightened in tone. "You shouldn't be here. It's dangerous enough for just you, but if my fellow cavers find out that there are humans in our realm—"

"We had to, Father." Lizbete grabbed his arms. "They took a child from the village tonight."

Grimir's chin slumped towards his chest. "I know. I wish . . . I wish I could've stopped them, but by the time I found out anything about it, Dravish's plan was already in place. The last quake shook the whole mountain. Several tunnels collapsed and two cavers were killed—young ones." Steam rose from his eyes. "One of them was the child of an important council member. The loss was enough to sway his vote and get him to agree to this madness. They've convinced themselves that if the Ravenous One devours a human child, it will satisfy him for at least a year."

"Where's my sister?" Einar broke from Brynar's hold and darted for Grimir's throat. "If you ashy freaks have harmed her, I swear—"

Grimir caught Einar by the arm. The caver's eyes glowed, and the youth collapsed onto the ground, shivering.

"Don't!" Lizbete gasped. She knelt beside Einar. "Are you all right?"

"I didn't take enough heat to do him permanent harm." Grimir frowned. "Just to stop him from being a threat to me—or to himself for if he attracts the attention of the others, they *will* kill him. In fact, they'd certainly kill all of you." He shook his head. "You three need to leave, now. I just found you, Lizbete. It will break my heart if something happens to you."

"Sir, I'm not leaving without my sister." Brynar stepped closer. "I understand that Liz is your family, but Elin is mine."

"Liz?" Skepticism edged Grimir's voice. "And who are you to refer to my daughter so informally?"

"He's the man I love, Father." Lizbete placed her hand on Brynar's shoulder. "You . . . you know a little about loving someone when everything stands in the way."

Grimir's expression softened. "I do indeed." He sighed. "So, the boy you love just happens to be the brother of the young girl Dravish chose for his foul plans. I doubt very much that is a coincidence. He may have been watching me observe you this whole time. That would explain how he chose a child he thought would cause you pain, and me through you. I'm surprised he didn't try and take you instead."

"I might've been locked up at the time." Lizbete grimaced. It was very possible Mayor Sten's decision to hide her from the village had inadvertently hidden her from Dravish as well.

"Is she still alive?" Einar stammered from the floor. He still shivered, but color had returned to his cheeks. Brynar helped him stand. "Where is she?"

Grimir wrung his hands. "She's held in a small side cavern off the council chamber, and yes, she's alive. Thankfully, the Ravenous One is quiet now, and even Dravish isn't mad enough to wake it in order to deliver his sacrifice. The moment it stirs, however, they'll bring the girl to the sacrifice chamber. Once she's there, there won't be anything we can do."

"So we need to move quickly." Brynar nodded.

"I just don't see how this is going to work. If my people see you, they'll fall upon you in an instant." Grimir began to pace. "To our advantage, I don't think the young girl is under heavy guard. None of us would have expected you to find your way into our realm, let alone to the inner chamber where we have the girl hidden. To our disadvantage, they do have at least one guard assigned to the girl. If that guard shouts for help, a dozen cavers will rush to assist him."

"So we take him down before he can shout." Einar's hand strayed to his axe, his eyes glinting.

Grimir winced. "Perhaps, but my people are not easy to kill."

His being shimmered into a transparent haze. "In our smoke form, weapons pass right through us." He solidified again. "In our solid form we can kill a human at a touch. He will have a strong vantage point, so sneaking up on him isn't possible."

"Then maybe we can draw him away." Lizbete fiddled with the crystal about her neck. "Can you go up to him, distract him? If the cavers don't know we're here, he might be relaxed, believing he has won."

"I think the caver they have on duty is M'yil, Dravish's brother," Grimir said. "He doesn't trust me. If I approach him under any pretext, he will be immediately suspicious."

"But not if I do." Everyone spun to face the entrance. A caver in gaseous form drifted into the room. She solidified and gazed sadly at Grimir. "I see your daughter has returned. I should've known you couldn't keep away from her once you were reunited. Oh, Grimir, this could end so badly."

Grimir hung his head. "I know what I promised, Naasha, but she's mine, and—"

"Shh, I know." The female caver put her fingers to Grimir's lips. "I would not care for you as I do if you had Dravish's stone heart. The path my brother is taking our people down, the lines he is willing to cross to maintain our way of life, it frightens me."

Lizbete blinked. Naasha was Dravish's sister?

"It frightens me, too." Grimir took Naasha's hands. "If we allow him to murder this child, there will be no going back. Our people are already thieves, slaves to a monster who demands everything and gives nothing. I would not have us be killers as well."

Her brow furrowed. "I can draw M'yil away, distract him for long enough for someone to grab the girl, but once she is taken, you will have only limited time to escape. Dravish has too much support from the other council members, and this incursion of humans into our realm, even to save one of their own, will further his ends."

"Thank you." Grimir rested his forehead against Naasha's for a long moment before releasing her and turning back to the human observers. "We need to get started." He focused on Brynar and Einar. "If the Ravenous One awakens before we get your sister out of the caverns, there is no hope for any of us."

Chapter Twenty-Two

Following Grimir, the trio climbed an almost vertical tunnel that forced Lizbete to grip both sides with her shoes and shimmy up. At the top was a series of narrow passages, many too low for them to walk through standing up, especially Brynar.

"This will take us above the council chamber," Grimir explained in hushed tones. "This route is the best way to get there while avoiding notice. No one takes these paths."

"I wonder why," Einar grunted, dropping to his hands and knees to squeeze through a particularly tight spot.

They'd had to leave their lanterns and Einar's pack behind to fit through the passages, but Grimir brought along a faint light source made out of various crystals fastened together. A glowing red fire crystal was set in the center of a series of glass-clear crystals that magnified the light. The caver held this in one hand as he led the group through the tortuous backways of the cavers' realm. Finally, the area opened up, and they found themselves on a balcony-like ledge over a wide chamber lit by towering fire crystals. In the center of this space rose an oblong table carved out of the rock itself and surrounded by chairs of braided metal. These were empty, but against the back wall, a lone caver sat in front of an opening that looked more like a rabbit's burrow than a doorway.

Einar's fists clenched until his knuckles whitened. "That's where they have Elin?"

Grimir nodded.

Brynar scanned the rock walls. "How do we get down there?"

"I can show you how as soon as—ah, here we are." Grimir's tense posture relaxed as Naasha drifted into the room as smoke.

She took form before the guard, M'yil, and placed her hands on her hips. "You're really going to go along with this?"

M'yil's expression hardened. "What choice do we have? The quakes are growing stronger and closer together, like labor pains. I do not want to see what the Ravenous One will birth."

"But she's just a child, M'yil. An innocent!" Naasha grasped his shoulders. "You're a father yourself. How would you feel if someone snatched Laril or Ange out from under your care, for you to never see again?"

He hung his head. "Believe me, I feel for the grief of this child's family, but if we don't take action, many more children will die and many more families will grieve."

Naasha released M'yil and circled behind him, staring at the back of his neck.

"What?" M'yil snarled.

"I'm just trying to figure out how Dravish has attached the strings to work you as his puppet. Masterful job, how he manages to get his words to emerge from your mouth."

M'yil's scowl deepened. "Maybe I *am* following Dravish, but at least he has a solution. What would you have us do? Sit by and allow the Ravenous One to tear apart not only our realm, but the homes of the humans as well?"

Lizbete drew closer to Brynar. He stood, braced against the wall, every muscle in his body taut. She touched his arm, her eyes never leaving Naasha and M'yil. This was taking too long.

"Perhaps you are right, but once the humans find out that we've stolen one of their children—"

"They'll never suspect. They don't even know we exist in spite of that idiot Grimir's best efforts to expose us." M'yil scoffed. "Even if they did know about us, they'd never find their way through the tunnels. They're too light-dependent and stupid for that."

Einar gave a scornful sniff. Lizbete turned to glare at him for daring to make a sound. Would humans ever learn that not everyone was as deaf as they were?

"I wouldn't be so sure." Naasha shifted from foot to foot. "M'yil . . . there's something I need to tell you, but you must promise not to tell the others, especially Dravish and the council." She leaned closer to him. "Grimir has shown his half-human daughter the ways of our realm."

Lizbete stiffened. Was Naasha about to betray them? Einar and Brynar exchanged a worried glance, and even Grimir's brow furrowed.

"What?" M'yil snarled, his fists clenching. "Is that fool trying to get us all killed?" He glanced around. "She—she's not here, is she?"

"I don't want to get him in trouble, but I heard whispering in his chambers before I came here. Human voices. She's here, looking for the young girl. Apparently Dravish took a child she is attached to, and knowing the way—"

"How dare that idiot bring a human, or even a half-human, here?" M'yil stepped off the wall. "Sister, I know you care for the fool, but this is too far, even for him."

"M'yil, no!" She grabbed his arm. "If Dravish finds out—"

"He'll give that idiot exactly what he deserves. This is the second time Grimir has put his selfish attachments over the good of our people. You must go tell the others what Grimir has done. We need to put a stop to it."

Naasha stuck her chin in the air. "No. I will not betray the man I love. I want no part in this." Without another word, she shimmered and dashed from the chamber.

M'yil groaned and cast a nervous glance from the entrance to Elin's prison towards where his sister had exited. After a few tense seconds, he dragged a large stone across the cavern and wedged it into the opening. Then he shimmered and hurried after his sister.

Grimir let out a low whistle. "A risky move, but it did buy us some time. Come on." He reached under his smock and pulled out a coil of rope. After fastening one end to a stalactite he grabbed onto the rope and slid down to the level below. Einar and Brynar swiftly followed. Lizbete drew a steadying breath before wrapping herself around the rope and swinging down. Air rushed around her, and it took all her willpower not to shriek. She stopped with a jerk and tumbled into Brynar's arms.

"Easy," he chuckled into her ear.

In spite of the dire situation, warmth spread through her. She fixed her spectacles which had been knocked crooked in the descent.

Einar already strained at the large stone M'yil had placed in front of Elin's prison. It moved against the rocky floor of the cave with a grating noise that made Lizbete wince. As soon as the stone was out of the way, Einar wriggled halfway into the burrow before squirming out again, an unconscious Elin in his arms.

Brynar sucked in a sharp breath. "Is she all right?"

"I think so." Einar shook her gently. "Hey, Elin. Wake up." The girl moaned and stirred against his chest but didn't open her eyes.

"They probably dosed her with some slickleaf root." Grimir approached and brushed his hand across Elin's forehead. "A kindness. I'm sure she would've been terrified through this ordeal if they hadn't."

"Yeah, real charitable of them." Einar glared at Grimir before scrambling to his feet. "How do we get out of here?"

"This way!" Grimir motioned towards a side passage.

The group took off at a run—Grimir leading, Einar clutching Elin to his chest close behind, and Brynar and Lizbete bringing up the rear.

Away from the crystal-lit council hall, the passages grew narrow and dark. Squinting ahead, Lizbete could just make out Grimir's bobbing lantern, and she could hear the slapping of Brynar and Einar's boots upon the stone floors. She winced. Why did humans have to make such a racket?

Something crashed into Lizbete from behind. She toppled against Brynar, sending them both into the wall. He gave out a shout.

Hands found Lizbete. Grasping, clawing hands. She shuddered and punched out with all her might. Her fist impacted weakly against hard bone and sinewy muscle.

"Let her go!" Brynar snarled and swung.

In the dim light from the fire crystal around Lizbete's neck, she caught a shadow dodging Brynar's fist. Their attacker head-butted Brynar. He collided against the wall again.

"Brynar?" Einar shouted back.

"Keep going!" Brynar wheezed. "Get Elin to safety." He drew his axe from his belt and held it defensively in front of him. For a moment there was no sound other than Brynar's heavy breathing. Then Einar's footsteps started again, running after Grimir's fading light.

"You fools! We need that girl!" Dravish—Lizbete immediately identified the voice—lunged after the fleeing Einar.

Brynar swung for the enemy caver's head. Dravish shimmered, and the axe passed through him. He kicked out. Brynar dropped to the side, pushed off the wall, and rushed forward. Again Dravish faded to vapor. Brynar sank through him and hit the other side of the tunnel. He collapsed, gasping for air.

"If the Ravenous One doesn't taste human flesh, it will come for every living being within the shadow of the mountain." Dravish reached for Brynar. "But I suppose your flesh is as good as the child's—"

"No!" Lizbete snarled. She lunged for Dravish and grabbed him by the wrist, wrenching him away from Brynar.

He shook his arm furiously, trying to dislodge her. Lizbete hung on with all her strength.

"You little half-breed bastard!" Dravish's eyes glinted a cruel red. "You'll doom us all. I'll drain you of every drop of heat."

Panic surged through Lizbete. It couldn't end this way. She wouldn't die beneath the earth. Teeth clenched, she sank her fingertips into his skin. "Not if I drain you first!"

Wrenching the crystal away from her neck, she allowed her blood to inhale his warmth. It swept into her like a rush of tide bringing the peppery, foul taste of hatred and fear. Dravish's mouth dropped open. He gave a cry of agony as veins of cool silver spread through his body. His whole being went rigid as her blood found the end of his heat and stopped pulling.

Lizbete pushed Dravish away. His body shattered against the

cold stone like a chunk of ice.

Brynar gaped at her as she reclaimed her fire-crystal. Her stomach churned as she glanced at the pieces of Dravish's corpse. She tried to remember what Grimir had said about Erich's death. Dravish had likewise left her no choice. Even so, she wanted to scream or weep for being forced into the action.

"We need to keep moving." Brynar's hand gripped her shoulder. "There might be others."

"You're right," she said through gritted teeth. "Let's catch up."

They rounded a corner and ran smack into Einar.

"You all right?" He gasped, still clutching Elin to his chest. "I heard screaming."

"We're fine, thanks to Lizbete." Brynar nodded.

"Speed up!" Grimir barked. His light shone faintly in the distance. "They'll have figured out the girl is gone by now. We need to be safe in the village before they catch up to us."

For an aching forever, Lizbete stumbled after her father through the dark and twisting tunnels under the mountain. Everything was heavy breathing, pounding footsteps, and darkness. The hot air pressed around her. She held tight to Brynar, afraid if she let go, they'd become separated and she'd lose him forever in that hellish maze.

A breath of cool air slipped around her like a caress. A warm, yellow light overpowered the red glow of Grimir's cavern, and the tiny group burst into the light of a cold dawn. They staggered away from the cave entrance across an open stretch of beach awash with the sound of the waves and the scents of fresh sea air and woodsmoke.

The village sat a stone's throw before them, a quiet grouping of familiar buildings that looked somehow strange and unreal, as though a dream rather than a reality. Had they really escaped? Were they really home?

Brynar laughed. "We made it. I can't believe we made it."

Elin groaned in Einar's arms.

"Easy, little one," Einar whispered with uncharacteristic tenderness. He kissed his little sister's forehead.

"Let's get home." Brynar grinned and pulled Lizbete forward.

Her feet, however, wouldn't move. She gazed at her father who stood, staring at the distant village. For him, it wasn't home.

"I can't go any farther," he murmured. "If they see me, they will turn upon me . . . and perhaps on you, too."

"But can you go back to the caves?" She remembered how M'yil had reacted to Naasha telling him about Grimir and Lizbete. When the other cavers found Elin gone—and Dravish dead—they'd blame Grimir. "What will they do to you?"

He hung his head. "I'm not sure, but I don't have a place among your people any more than you do among mine."

Brynar stepped forward and offered Grimir his hand. "I can't make any promises on behalf of the other villagers, but you helped me save my sister's life and protected Lizbete before that. If there's anything I can do to aid you, any way I can convince the others to offer you shelter, I'll do it."

"If it's all right with you two," Einar broke in, "can we continue this conversation somewhere not right next to an entrance to a dreary underworld we might get dragged back into by vicious cave monsters?" He jerked his head in the direction of the village.

Lizbete focused on Grimir. "Father, where will you go?"

He let out a long breath. "There are enough caverns along the beach that I should be able to find somewhere to hide. I'll contact you tonight under the cover of darkness. We'll discuss our next steps. For now, stay safe."

With that he shimmered and drifted like smoke down the shoreline.

Hand in Brynar's, Lizbete trudged towards the village. They emerged into the courtyard to face a gathering crowd.

"Look! It's the girl!" someone shouted.

"Elin!" Nan rushed from the throng straight to Einar, her blue eyes bright with worry. The young man passed his mother the still-groggy child. Nan pressed her cheek to the girl's hair and rocked her like a baby. "Oh, I was so worried. Where did you find her?"

Brynar and Einar exchanged a glance.

"That's a very long story," Brynar said with an awkward laugh.

"Oh, it doesn't matter. She's safe now." Nan clutched Elin to her chest. "Oh, my baby. Never run away again." Sten hurried to join them, drawing his wife and daughter into a tight hug.

Lizbete swallowed. If the girls' parents thought Elin had just wandered way, it would be harder than ever to convince them, much less the rest of the village, of the danger from the Ravenous One. Even with Dravish gone, there was no guarantee the other cavers wouldn't to steal another human to use as a sacrifice. The Ravenous One was still very much alive and very ravenous.

"What is *she* doing out here?" Witta shouted from the crowd. She pointed an accusing finger at Lizbete.

Lizbete drew herself up taller. "I went to help Brynar find Elin."

"I thought you said you locked her up so she wouldn't hurt anyone," another villager shouted at Sten.

The mayor shifted awkwardly from foot to foot. "I thought I had." He narrowed his eyes at Brynar. "I'm guessing she had help in escaping."

Einar snorted. "You always been that perceptive, sir?"

Brynar crossed his arms, his expression placid.

"Brynar, I thought we'd come to an agreement—" Sten began.

"I intentionally let you think that because I didn't want you trying to stop me from running away with Liz, which I fully intended to do, and would have done had Elin not gone missing." Brynar slipped his arm around Lizbete's waist and drew her closer. Though the eyes of the village burning into her caused Lizbete's skin to crawl, the warmth of Brynar so close gave her strength. She kept her head held high as he continued to speak. "Lizbete has always been there for me. She's always helped Elin, but more than that, she's been a loyal member of this community, serving us in the tavern for years. She even tried to warn us about the cavers and the cause of the earthquakes, and in return we treated her like a snake in the hen house." His face blazed with certainty. "Well, I'm not standing for her mistreatment longer. I can't make you all behave decently to her, but I can decide how I'm going to treat her, and that's as my loyal friend . . . and the woman I love."

Lizbete's vision blurred as tears gathered in her eyes. She slipped her arm around Brynar.

"You're just going to ignore the fact that she almost killed you just last night?" Witta sneered. "Do you like being a block of ice?"

"Yes, Lizbete must drain heat to survive, but she has the fire crystal to mitigate her needs." He glared at Witta. "A fire crystal some idiot ripped from her neck in the middle of a temper tantrum."

"Hmph!" Witta squeaked out, her cheeks reddened.

"But what about the earthquakes?" Hangur pushed forward out of the crowd.

"Quiet, Hangur." Sten held up his hand.

"Try to silence me? Fine." Hangur scowled. "We all know she's behind the quakes."

Sten gave an exaggerated eye-roll. "Certainly. The teenage girl who weighs about as much as a sack of potatoes, and who probably can't lift as much, is the one stirring the very foundations of the earth to shake our village."

Villagers whispered among themselves and exchanged sheepish glances.

The ground rumbled beneath them. Lizbete gasped and tightened her hold on Brynar. Nan whimpered, clutching Elin closer.

The girl opened an eye. "Where am I?"

"See! See!" Hangur leaped into the air, pumping his fist in triumph. "She's doing it again!"

"Don't be ridiculous!" Lizbete stammered. "Even if I could control the earthquakes, why would I do it now? It would be in my best interest to hide any dangerous powers from you and your ignorant friends." The harsh words slipped out before she could stop them, and regret immediately filled her. She wasn't going to win any allies that way. She cleared her throat. "I told you why the earthquakes are happening. It's the Ravenous One. The monster under the mountain."

"You ask me to believe in a sleeping giant beneath our peaceful village?" Hangur arched an eyebrow. "And I'm the village idiot?"

She cleared her throat. How could she convince these fools?

"It's true." Einar stepped between her and Hangur. Lizbete gaped at him and even Brynar's eyes widened. "I thought it was nonsense too, but Elin didn't run away. She was kidnapped by strange gray people. They were going to sacrifice her to the monster. I was there. I saw it."

Gasps rose from the crowd. Mothers clutched at children and

men stood a little straighter.

Sten focused on his son. "You saw the monster?"

"Well, no." Einar rubbed the back of his neck. "I saw the people who took Elin to feed her to the monster. Why would they do that if there *wasn't* a monster, though?"

"Maybe because they are in league with this witch!" Hester burst from the crowd to stand beside Hangur. "They intend to fool us into believing her lies, into following her, leaving our town. They want us to leave our homes and belongings for them to do with as they please."

"And what good would that do me?" Lizbete stepped away from Brynar who released her reluctantly. "All my life, all I've ever wanted from you, from this village, was to belong, to be a part of things. To be accepted." Her voice cracked. "I know I never will. I know it is hopeless that I will ever be one of you. That you'll ever see me as anything but a freak and an outsider. It's still what I want." Tears ran down her cheeks. She pushed her spectacles back up her nose. "It's all I've ever wanted. It breaks my heart that you'd rather believe that I'm some sort of all powerful witch who can move the earth itself, rather than to believe that I mean you well and belong with you."

Brynar's hand caressed her shoulder. "You belong with me, Liz."

"And me!" Elin piped up, pushing her way out of her mother's embrace and coming to Lizbete's side.

Einar sighed and shook his head. "I can't believe I'm saying this, but you're not the monster I thought you were, Ash Lizard, and— and if you're what will make my brother happy, I'm all for that."

Nan approached her husband. "Sten, dear. If the girl really helped save Elin, and if Brynar loves her, then she's one of us. She's family."

Lizbete resisted to urge to clean her spectacles. This couldn't be real. What she was seeing—and hearing—couldn't be real. She had a family? A small family, admittedly. A family against overwhelming odds, judging by the glares still aimed at her by the majority of the village as a whole. Still, a family.

Sten let out a long breath, then turned a stern eye to the onlookers. "All of you, get to your homes. Hangur, that includes you. This is a matter for my household, not for the village as a whole."

Hangur glowered but kept his mouth shut.

Sten offered Liz his hand. "No matter what I decide, as the leader of this family or the leader of this village, you helped bring my Elin home. For that I am grateful."

With a weak smile, Lizbete slipped her hand into his.

The ground heaved, sending her toppling into Mayor Sten's chest.

Several villagers screamed.

Something crashed as loud as a rockslide. Lizbete fought to keep her footing.

"What was that?"

Everyone's gaze shot in the direction of Ash Mountain. Another great tremor shook the earth along with an ear-ringing boom. Two great tentacles of fire jutted into the sky, towering over the village.

"The Ravenous One!" Lizbete cried.

Chapter Twenty-Three

Rocks and dirt rained from the sky as more fiery arms burst out of the earth like foul seedlings. The ground shook madly. Screams erupted from the gathered villagers. Several collapsed, cowering into the earth, while others snatched up children and ran for cover. Sten stepped forward, as if instinctively wanting to confront the danger, before pausing, mouth agape, in the center of the of the courtyard, just staring at it. Brynar and Einar came to his side.

Lizbete's knees turned to jelly. Towering over the city, the creature seemed even more massive than it had contained within its mountain chamber.

Brynar, Einar, and his father exchanged a glance before Einar turned to Lizbete. "Hey, Ash Lizard, can that thing swim?"

She blinked. "Uh, I'm not sure."

"It seems our best chance. I've got an idea." Einar faced the crowd, arms waving. "We need to get out of here. Grab your children and get to the docks. They'll be safer near or in the water."

The few villagers who weren't lying on the ground shaking or running for their lives nodded. The mass of people started to move in the direction of the bay.

Brynar let out a long breath. "I hope that works."

Lizbete swallowed. She fought to standing in spite of the increasingly violent tremors shaking the earth around her.

"What if it doesn't?" Hangur grabbed Sten by the collar of his coat. "This girl has doomed us all!"

Brynar shoved his uncle away from his father. "Quiet, you idiot! After everything you've seen and heard today, including this," he jerked his finger towards the distant but looming monster, "how can you still—" He stopped, clenched and unclenched his jaw, then pushed Hangur in the direction of the fleeing villagers. "Go help Einar with the evacuation."

"Brynar, I'm scared." Elin pulled at her brother's hand. "We need to get out of here."

"It'll be all right. We'll keep you safe." He picked her up, kissed her forehead, and passed her to his mother.

Sten quickly kissed his wife's cheek. "Take Elin and follow Einar to the docks. Stay safe."

Her eyes widened. "But what about you?"

He squared his shoulder. "We need to figure out a way to stop this creature."

There isn't a way. Lizbete longed to shout the words, to get the men to run with the rest of their family, but she could see the quiet determination in Brynar's eyes mirrored in his father's. They weren't going to abandon their home without a fight.

Nan nodded and took off running with a protesting Elin clutched in her arms. Lizbete breathed a sigh of relief. At least the young girl was safe. Now if only she could convince Brynar to run as well. She turned to him.

The earth exploded around them. Lizbete shrieked as her feet left the air and a massive tentacle burst through the nearest house. She landed hard, her spectacles flying from her face and her breath abandoning her body. Squinting, she caught sight of both Sten and Brynar stumbling to their feet nearby. Brynar's gaze fell on her.

"Liz! Get out of here! It's not safe."

Her jaw clenched. "Not without you."

Sten pointed towards the dock. "Go. Take your girl and get out of here."

"And leave you to face this alone?" Brynar snarled.

The tentacle thrashed. Shards of wood flew. Lizbete dove for safety behind a short stone wall encircling the yard of the next house over. Brynar jumped over the wall and landed beside her, joined a heartbeat later by his father. They cowered together as tiny bits of house continued to rain around them.

"This isn't doing any good!" Lizbete shouted. "We have to run. There's no way to stop it. It's too big."

Brynar and his father exchanged a glance. "Sir, she's right. What are we going to do against *that*?" Brynar jerked his thumb behind them.

Sten winced but nodded. "Let's get to the docks."

Brynar took Lizbete's hand, and together they burst to their feet. He pulled her into a run, dashing through the back allies. Another building exploded. Lizbete glanced over her shoulder just in time to see the nearest tentacle snatch an unattended horse cart from the street and lift it high into the air.

"Look out!" she yelped.

Brynar hit the dirt, pulling her down with him. Sten dropped next to them.

The cart smashed into the alleyway in front of them. Lizbete cowered against Brynar whose arms tightened painfully around her.

The dust settled and she pried her eyes open. The cart blocked the exit to the alleyway.

"We need to break through." Sten got up and yanked at the boards.

A cloud of smoke crossed in front of Lizbete before solidifying into Grimir.

Sten stumbled back a step. "What is—"

"It's my father," Lizbete said quickly. She then faced the caver. "What are we going to do? Is there any way to stop it?"

"I—I don't know." He wrung his hands. "It's furious. It's destroying the caver village too. Collapsing our tunnels—"

"But why?" Sten stammered. "What does it want?"

"A sacrifice." Grimir scowled. "It wasn't fed this morning. The cavers were depending on the child and hadn't prepared a second sacrifice, and then to have its realm violated by humans?" He cringed. "Dravish was right. Only blood will satisfy it now. Human blood."

Brynar stood and swallowed. His hand traced Lizbete's face. "I can give it that. I wish there was another way. Liz, I'll miss…" His jaw tightened.

Lizbete's stomach sank. If he was thinking what she thought he was thinking, he needed to unthink it, and fast.

Before she could protest, he turned to Sten. "Father, get Lizbete to safety. I'll go with Grimir and take care of things."

"No!" Lizbete and Sten shouted as one.

Brynar winced. "Sir, you've said I need to learn to place the good of the village above my own wants. I can't think of a better time to put that into practice."

"You're just a boy." Sten gripped his son's arm. "Let me go."

Another crash as something hit the roof of the nearest house.

Bits of stone and dirt pattered around them.

"We need to get out of here." Grimir tugged on Lizbete's arm.

"I don't have a family that depends on me like you do. For Sky-watcher's sake, the whole village depends on you!" Brynar's voice cracked, and Lizbete's stomach twisted. "I love you all. Liz, I . . . I'm sorry, but if someone has to die today—"

Lizbete opened and shut her mouth, trying to find words, words that told him he was being an idiot and that he needed to live. However, the desperation in his clear blue eyes made it obvious she couldn't talk him out of this. The pain of potentially losing him gripped her, followed quickly by a resolution. No, if one of them was going to be a sacrificial fool here, it wasn't going to be him.

But how to stop him? Her mind cleared. She knew what she had to do, even if it hurt him. She had to keep him alive.

"I understand." She stepped closer to him, managing to keep her voice calm in spite of the roiling emotions in her chest. "Do I at least get a good-bye kiss?"

Sten gaped. "No. This is *not* decided."

Brynar ignored him and wrapped his arms around Lizbete. "I thought you'd never ask."

His mouth drew close to hers. Lizbete's heart rate quickened. She didn't want this, but it had to be. It was the only way. The right way.

His lips brushed against hers as her hand strayed to the chain around her neck. Needing the taste of him to steel her resolve, she savored his breath against her for a moment. At least she'd gotten a chance to be loved by him, if only for a short while.

Well, time to do what needed to be done.

Before she could reconsider, she yanked the crystal away from her skin and took in a great gulp of Brynar's heat.

He cried out as he fell, lips blue, whole body shivering uncontrollably.

"What did you do?" Sten gasped.

"I prevented him from doing anything stupid," she snarled.

"L-Liz…" Brynar tried to stand but collapsed immediately. Lizbete bit her bottom lip. Hopefully she hadn't taken too much.

She faced Grimir. "Father, can you make sure he gets warm?"

"What are you going to do?" the caver stammered.

Lizbete hesitated. She'd bought Brynar some time, but the village was being destroyed around them. If someone didn't do something soon, there wouldn't be anything left of Brumehome. The people would have no home, no livelihood, if they even managed to escape with their lives.

Grimir was right. There was only one thing that could stop the Ravenous One's attack, but she wouldn't let Brynar be the one to pay the price.

"I'm going to save my home and the people I love." She smiled at Grimir whose mouth hung open in distress and shock. "I'm so glad I got a chance to meet you. You—you're everything I wanted in a father."

"Lizbete, don't—" Grimir reached for her but she dodged.

"Don't make me freeze you too!" She held out her hand, keeping him from approaching her. "I'm sorry, Brynar."

"Don't!" Brynar lurched to his feet only to fall against his father. He stared at her, blue eyes stricken. Oh, how she loved those eyes.

The memory of his kiss at the First Frost strengthened her, and Lizbete's fear melted away like mist in the sun. For a short while, she'd had everything she'd ever wanted. That would have to be enough.

Without looking back, she turned and ran down the alleyway.

Her feet pounded against the cobblestones as the tentacles continued to lash into the village homes and businesses. Her sides and chest aching, she put on one final burst of speed. She dashed across the town square and down the street. At last, Lizbete burst onto the open stretch of beach between the cavers' caverns and Brumehome.

She skidded to a halt, her knees knocking together.

The Ravenous One protruded from a massive sinkhole in the center of the beach. Arms writhed from the hole, surrounding a snapping beak set in an eyeless face. Heat rising from the monster distorted the air which, combined with her own poor vision, smeared the whole view into a mess of fire and smoke and arms. So many arms.

The fear she'd thought she'd conquered returned in a heady rush. Her blurry sight spun.

It's going to kill me. If I don't turn and run, it will *kill me.*
I'll die.

She took a single step backwards. A tentacle whipped over her head, tossing a huge rock into the center of the village. The ground beneath her shook. The sand shivered beneath her like a frightened animal. Her jaw clenched. She'd come here to sacrifice herself, to die passively like that frightened goat she'd watched the Ravenous One devour. Now, facing the beast mindlessly wrecking everything she knew and loved, that wasn't want she wanted.

No. Lizbete wanted to fight.

I won't let that beast destroy the village. It's my home. It's where Auntie Katryn raised me. Where Elin accepted me. Where Brynar kissed me. It's the only home I've ever known, and I'm going to fight for it. Grimir said only a great hero could kill one of these monsters. Well, today I'll be a great hero even if it kills me.

Another massive rock flying overhead snapped Lizbete back to more practical matters.

Oh, Skywatcher, how do I even begin to attack a massive beast made of fire and stone?

She ducked behind a large driftwood log that lay upon the beach and tried to breathe. The crashing of rock and the quivering of the earth made it hard for her to think. She focused beyond them, to the distant pulse of the surf as the waves rushed in and out, oblivious to the monster's rampage.

The sea. Lizbete's breath caught in her throat. *If there's anything more powerful than the Ravenous One, it's the sea. Also, the enemy of fire is water, and I have all the water in the world right here.*

Lizbete closed her eyes and said a quick prayer. Auntie Katryn had believed the Skywatcher brought the souls of men into the stars with him, that she'd live among the stars after her last breath. Lizbete wasn't sure if half-human, half-caver girls had the same fate, but if so, she'd see Auntie again. That alone would be a gift.

Now or never.

She leaped to her feet and rushed towards the Ravenous One.

"Hey! Hey! Stupid fire-squid!" she shrieked. "I've made fish stew out of worse than you!"

The tentacles writhed in her general direction. Her throat closed in on itself, but she forced out another shout.

"If you want me, come and get me!" Turning, Lizbete sprinted in the direction of the water.

Her plan was simple. Draw the Ravenous One into the water and hope the ocean did her dirty work. She wasn't sure how much of the Ravenous One needed to be submerged before the creature would be extinguished, but hopefully however much she could tempt into the waves would be enough.

She didn't dare look back. Her feet pounded across the wet

sand. It sucked at her shoes, slowing her pace. The water beckoned, rushing to meet her in a foam capped wave. The ground lurched beneath her like an ancient beast rising from slumber.

Lizbete jumped.

She flew over the last stretch of roiling sand and splashed down on her hands and knees in two feet of briny freezing water. Her eyes stung. She coughed and spluttered.

The water turned, rushing back out to sea. Lizbete scrambled to her feet. She wasn't deep enough in or far enough out. The cold of the sea seeped into her. The icy seas around Brumehome were cold enough to stun a grown man. Even with her crystal's help, the water chilled her. She whimpered as her muscles seized and her blood thickened.

I have to keep going.

Jaw clenched, she forged onward.

Hot air guested. She instinctively dove to one side. A tentacle as wide as a tree truck slapped into the surf beside her. Steam hissed and scalding water sprayed Lizbete's skin. She struggled through the ebbing tide as the Ravenous One thrashed and flailed.

She pushed through the waves. The water, which originally had been painfully cold, began to boil. Lizbete laughed as her blood drew in the heat. The monster was *helping* her.

A furious roar shook the beach, echoing off the high sea cliffs. Lizbete spun.

The beach exploded in a shower of sand and stone. Lizbete threw her hands over her head as debris splattered around her. The whole of the monster now lay exposed, a formless mass of tentacles and molten earth as big as the village itself. Steam rose from it as it wormed across the shattered sands towards the roiling seas.

A lump formed in Lizbete's throat. Yes, she had led it away from the village, but just dipping its tentacles in the water wouldn't be enough to extinguish the beast.

How am I going to get it deep enough? I can't even swim!

Water dripped from her sodden clothing. Dead fish bobbed on the surface, cooked alive as they swam.

Another tentacle snaked forward from the monster's body, headed straight towards Lizbete. She gasped. She dropped to her belly, submerging herself in the hot water. The whip-like tip of the Ravenous One's arm snaked around her with a blast of heat. It yanked her from the surf. Warmth flooded Lizbete's blood. The creature growled and another wave of white hotness pulsed through her. Again, Lizbete's blood guzzled it.

The creature roared. A tremor ran through it, jarring Lizbete's teeth until her head ached. A third time, the blast of heat. Again, her blood devoured it.

Lizbete remembered the goat that had perished in the Ravenous One's grasp.

It's trying to cook me. To roast me to death, but I don't burn.

Something snapped in place in her brain.

It's absurd . . . but if it works?

She drew in a deep breath and set her blood free.

The Ravenous One gave a rasping growl like rocks grinding together. It buffeted her with inner fire. The air around her wavered and distorted. More heat. More fire. Lizbete's skin began to glow, then smoke. The wire holding the fire crystal turned bright red. The Ravenous One hissed and increased his assault.

Do your worst.

Lizbete smiled. After a life spent freezing, this was almost pleasant. The monster tightened its grip, and Lizbete began to sweat.

The Ravenous One gave a furious snarl. The tentacle loosened around her.

It's going to drop me. It realized it can't burn me, so it will crush me instead. Panic surged, causing her blood to absorb heat harder and faster. Lizbete shrieked as the temperature within her went from tolerable to searing in a heartbeat.

Her clothes burst aflame. The Ravenous One's hold slipped, but Lizbete caught herself. She wrapped her arms around its trunk-like arm and held on for everything she was worth.

Heat. So much heat. It raged around her. Flames danced along her body. The Ravenous One was no longer in control. Lizbete's blood had latched onto it and wouldn't stop until it had all the monster's warmth . . . or until Lizbete found the edge of her abilities and burst into a cinder.

Orange, red, yellow, white. Lights danced in front of Lizbete's eyes, blinding her to all else. The Ravenous One thrashed, trying to dislodge her. Lizbete couldn't have let go even if she wanted to. Her muscles, her blood, her bones were made of fire and she had no control over them. They only knew the heat. She could feel it coursing up the creature's arm from the dark, smoldering hellscape of its being. She was in the pool of lava again. There was no escape.

The fire rushed through her. Pain followed. Every nerve screamed in torment. She opened her mouth to shriek but only steam escaped.

She could see the monster's heart, see everything that happened within in. Her blood had found it, and she could feel her heat wrapping around the steady, beating pulse. Veins of silver-white crept across the massive organ. It beat frantically, then slowed, then stopped.

The tentacle holding Lizbete crashed into the earth. She rolled in the sand, which blackened beneath her.

The Ravenous One shattered. Its pieces flew into the air, impacting in the sand around her. Lizbete curled into a ball, expecting to be crushed at any moment. With the pain that still raged within her body, being crushed seemed almost a relief.

Then all was still except for the crackling of flames upon her. She struggled to her feet. Fierce red light bathed the world. Her skin screamed, and she tried to push off the heat. She flailed her arm in an attempt to release the fire crystal, but it fused to her hand, melting into her skin and down to her bones. It spread down her arm in veins of scarlet.

The fight was over, but Lizbete still burned. Steam rose from her eyes in place of tears.

The final remnants of her garments disintegrated to ash, leaving her naked except for a miasma of seething heat. She stood on the sand, which melted beneath her feet. Through her blurred vision, she saw figures emerging from the town in the distance, people cautiously emerging to observe the damage the monster had wrought.

Wisps of smoke drifted through the air, then solidified around her: cavers. She didn't know if any were ones she'd seen before. Her vision was too poor, her agony too great. They tried to approach her but shied back.

"You destroyed the Ravenous One," a female caver said. Lizbete knew her voice. *Naasha.*

"What's happening to me?" Lizbete wailed. She held forth her hands. Flames danced over them, licking her skin which remained whole, though it stung. It stung so badly that she wanted to die.

Naasha took a step closer but recoiled. "You are too hot for even me to approach. You somehow absorbed all of the Ravenous One's heat. How are you alive?"

"Lizbete!" Her heart leaped at Brynar's beloved voice. He burst from the village, his father and Grimir close behind. Lizbete put out her arms to greet him without thinking, only to immediately gasp and pull away.

"No! Don't come any closer!"

Naasha and two other cavers grabbed the young man by the arms. He stared at her from the edge of the circle. Even at that distance, the warmth rising off her reddened his skin.

Lizbete's throat tightened.

"Don't," she gasped. "I'm—I'm too hot. I'll burn you."

Agony crossed Brynar's face.

"Liz," he whispered. "What . . . what happened to you?"

The villagers joined the circle, eyeing the cavers with fear and suspicion.

"How do I stop it?" Lizbete wept. "It hurts. Grimir—Father! It hurts. How do I stop burning?"

Grimir's whole body shook, his face contorted in grief. "You absorbed too much heat, but your crystalline traits mean that you cannot be consumed. Lizbete, you need to expel the heat somehow. Can you?"

She focused on the heat, imagined it shooting from her. Imagined it leaching into the sand beneath her feet, imagined her body cooling. Nothing happened. The fire still raged within her, unquenchable.

"I can't!" she sobbed.

"You have to help her!" Brynar gasped. "She can't just burn forever."

"She has not the caver's ability to expel heat," another caver spoke, and she recognized the voice as M'yil's. "If she does truly have fire crystal in her blood somehow, then it is quite possible she could hold the heat indefinitely."

Panic spiked within Lizbete as she met Brynar's agonized stare. To always be on fire, to always be in pain, to never be able to touch another human or even come near them without harming them. She'd rather be dead. In this state, could she even die?

"You saved us all," another caver said. "The Ravenous One is no more. Both our people and the human village are safe now thanks to your great deed. We thank you, child of two worlds. We thank you."

"Don't just thank her!" Brynar snarled. "Do something!"

"Son," Sten came up behind Brynar and touched his shoulder, but the young man jerked away.

"No! She saved us all. Every sorry one of us, every person in our midst, no matter how many times they hurt and rejected her, she gave everything for us. I am not going to accept *this*."

Lizbete's heart ached. She longed to embrace Brynar if only for a moment. "I'm sorry," she whispered. "Brynar..."

"There is one thing we might be able to do to help," Grimir stepped closer. "No one caver could possibly absorb the amount of heat you have taken upon yourself, but all of us—if we all band together and help her—" He gazed pointedly at his fellow cavers. "We might have a chance."

M'yil recoiled. "But it is so much heat. If we are not enough, it could burn us alive. We would all be risking our lives."

"As Lizbete did by taking on the Ravenous One while we cowered in our caves." Grimir stepped closer. "Whether you join me or not doesn't matter. I have to try."

He drew closer to her but immediately winced as the heat buffeted his skin.

"Father! Don't!" Lizbete gasped. She staggered back a step but slipped on the molten sand. It clung to her feet like honey coating a spoon. "It's too much to take!"

"For one caver, perhaps." Naasha stepped to Grimir's side and slipped her hand into his. "For all of us? We shall see." She extended her hand towards her brother. "We owe her this, M'yil." She raised her raspy voice, "We all do. Call forth your friends, your brothers, your children. We must come to the aid of this child as she came to ours."

Cavers shimmered in and out of their smoke forms, dashing away then returning with more cavers. The human villagers gasped and retreated towards their village—though many lingered to watch. Within a few minutes a crowd of cavers stood around Lizbete.

"As one," Grimir instructed. He joined hands with Naasha who joined hands with M'yil. The cavers formed a ring around her, hand to hand. Lizbete's consciousness wavered. Gray fogged her vision. It hurt. It hurt so much.

"Hurry!" she whimpered. "I can't bear it much longer."

"Now!" Grimir shouted. He threw his hands forward, still clasped with Naasha's on his right and another caver's hand on his left. Heat rushed from Lizbete in a great gasp, but it was a single wave crashing off an endless sea of warmth and pain.

The agony stabbed into her bones. She shrieked.

"Liz!" Brynar tried to break through the line of cavers, but his father held him back. Lizbete managed to steady her vision enough to gaze at him. He strained towards her, his face drawn as if he could feel her pain.

"Again!" Grimir yelled.

The cavers' combined strength drew from her, and she felt her awareness flowing from her. The heat drained from her like blood seeping from a wound. Her legs wobbled, and she collapsed. Not into sand or even the molten mass she'd created with her heat. The surface beneath her was far smoother, far more so than stone or metal. The liquid sand hardened about her feet as the pain subsided to a low simmer. Voices echoed about her. Hands touched her, moving her. Her head swam and the world spun beneath her.

"Liz!" Brynar's words reached her as welcome as the first rays of sun after an endless night.

Her heart opened to him, even as darkness took her.

Chapter Twenty-Four

The blankets over Lizbete's body and the mattress beneath her were soft and warm, but not hot. Oh, thank the Skywatcher, they weren't hot. She'd had enough of hot for a lifetime. She nestled deeper into the nest of warm wool and smiled. From the distant smells of cooking food, she knew she was in the tavern again.

Home.

Where she belonged.

A hand brushed across her cheek and into her hair, a tender touch. Her blood tasted the warmth from the other person but didn't devour it as it once had. Even so, she still recognized the steady, comforting presence within the heat.

Brynar.

She considered opening her eyes and greeting him, but foot-steps on wooden floorboards distracted her.

A door creaked open.

"How is she?" It was Sten.

Lizbete stiffened. She still wasn't sure where she stood with the mayor as a citizen, let alone as a potential match for his son.

"Still sleeping, but I think she's going to be all right, sir." She could hear Brynar's smile in his tone. Joy expanded in her chest like flower buds opening to the sun. "Both Widow Gri and Grimir looked her over and said she was on the mend, though Widow Gri was admittedly distracted by Grimir."

"Yes, ah, Grimir and his fellows are . . . unusual." Sten laughed awkwardly. "To think we've lived beside them all these years without knowing it."

"I think that's how they wanted it to be. Obviously, things will change now."

"Yeah, a lot of things are changing in Brumehome of late." Chair legs scraped across the floor, stopping right next to Lizbete's bed. The furniture groaned as Sten settled into it. "Which is what I wanted to talk to you about, son. The village still doesn't know what to think of Lizbete."

"She saved their lives!" Brynar's tone sharpened. "If they can't see her value after that—"

"Steady, son!" his father soothed. "They aren't going to turn on her. For one thing, I think they're a little afraid of her after that show of power out there on the beach. At the same time, she'll never completely be one of them. I just want to be sure you understand that because I know what you're planning. If you go through with it, life won't be easy for you, or for her."

"The life most worth living is never the easiest, sir."

"Maybe, but the life I'd hoped to provide for you would've been." Sten sighed. "So, you're sure?"

"Yes, sir. It may not be easy. People might not accept us, but I love her. I would never forgive myself if I tossed her aside just because it might be hard." Lizbete's rib cage inflated with pure bliss. Tears trickled down her cheeks. He still wanted her. Things were going to be all right.

"And the rest of us? What about us?"

Brynar chuckled. "I'm not running away. I'll still be around, there to help out. It'll simply be a different path than you might've anticipated."

Lizbete's ears twitched.

"I've thought a lot about my future, and I've realized I never really wanted to be the mayor. I'd rather help people than lead them. While I know you do both, how I feel called to help is, well . . . I want to be a healer, Father."

"A healer?" Perplexity crept into Sten's tone.

"I've already talked to Widow Gri about training under her. I want to help people, to ease suffering."

"And the mayor's seat? Do we let that pass out of our family's care?"

"There's always Einar."

Sten snorted. Even Lizbete grimaced, glad she was facing away from the men so they couldn't see.

"I'm serious, sir. I've been watching him lately, and there's a leader under that thick layer of attitude and angst. He's got a way to go, but you're not retiring any time soon. Give him a chance."

"Hm, I'll think about it." The chair squeaked as Sten stood. "You coming downstairs? Falla is cooking something for the family."

"Maybe in a bit. I am hoping Lizbete will wake up soon, and I don't want her to be alone when she does."

"All right. I'll leave you to your watch."

As the door closed behind Sten, it took all of Lizbete's willpower not to jump up and embrace Brynar. She longed to, but if she did it would be clear that she'd pretended to be asleep to listen to his conversation. Instead she lay still and let the thoughts fizz within her like bubbles forming in a pot about to boil.

Brynar was going to be a healer. That made so much sense. He'd be an amazing healer, and maybe she could help him. She could learn too. She'd already thought about apprenticing herself to Widow Gri. Together they could do so much good, help so many people. Even if they didn't work together, he wanted to be with her, he wanted to love her, no matter what anyone else thought. Her heart sang within her.

She was wanted. She was treasured. She was loved.

Finally she felt enough time had passed that she could risk rolling over and opening her eyes. Brynar smiled down at her.

"Hey there." He held something out to her. She squinted before recognizing her spectacles. "You left these behind when you froze me in the village." He furrowed his brow. "Am I going to get an apology for that?"

She laughed. "Sure. How about, 'I'm sorry I didn't let you kill yourself and leave me bereaved and lonely and your mother and sister heartbroken'?" She slipped her spectacles onto her nose and winked at him. His eyes widened in bemusement. His beautiful blue eyes. She softened to him, momentarily sorry for her teasing, but before she could apologize, he chuckled.

"I guess that'll have to do." He clicked his tongue. "So, what do you think of my plan to be a healer?"

"It's wonder—" Lizbete stopped, flushed, and redirected. "I mean . . . what plan?"

"Don't bother. I know you were listening." He tapped her nose. "You made a face when I said I thought Einar would make a good mayor. Sleeping people don't react like that."

"How could you see me?"

"I'm tall enough to see around a small bed, Liz."

Ashen

"Oh." Her cheeks warmed. Wait, she was still blushing—and Brynar had touched her without her heat drawing off of him. Her hand strayed to her chest, feeling through the light cloth of her nightshirt. She wasn't wearing the fire crystal, so how was it possible? She glanced down and her breath left her. There, in her right palm, was a patch of red crystal embedded in her skin. Veins of the crystal flowed through her wrist and down her arm before ending just above her elbow. She traced the lines with the fingers of her opposite hand. "What—what happened?"

Brynar took her wrist in his hand and stroked the veins. "According to Grimir, you super-heated yourself to the point where you absorbed the crystal you were holding. He says it's permanently part of you, though he wasn't sure what that meant, not fully." He brought her fingers to his lips. "We did figure out that it means I can touch you without the threat of freezing to death."

"Oh…" For a moment, Lizbete couldn't catch her breath. It was too much. Far more than she'd hoped for. She might not be normal, not completely. Her skin was still gray. She could still taste Brynar's warmth even if she was no longer uncontrollably siphoning it off, but she could hold him. She could touch him. She wasn't dangerous to him. Tears spurted from her eyes, and she flung her arms around his neck.

Brynar embraced her, bringing his lips to hers. They kissed for a long moment, his hands rubbing up and down her back. She savored his warmth and strength before withdrawing to look him in the eyes.

"I'm—I'm so happy I can touch you," she whispered. "You don't know how hard it was living without being able to hug the people you love."

"You can hug me whenever you want." His words tickled her

ears, sending a pleasant shiver through her body. He caressed her cheek before releasing her. "Oh, there's something you might want to see." He turned to the bedside table and picked up two objects that sparkled in the light from the window. Lizbete blinked. They appeared to be made of glass but were shaped roughly like shoes.

"What are those?" she stammered.

He handed her one and turned the other about in her hand. "After your fight with the monster, you were so hot the sand beneath you melted and solidified to glass. There's a huge circle of it outside the village in the center of the beach. Where you stood it conformed to your feet, and when you cooled, it cooled. I was afraid it would shatter and cut you if we just broke you out of it, so I got the local bottle maker to come down with a glass cutting tool and cut your feet out of it. These remained after the process." He knelt before her and slipped the glass shoe onto her foot. "A perfect fit. Not very comfortable to walk in, but the bottle maker thought they were interesting. He filed them down into a more shoe-like shape as a gift to you for saving the town. Nice of him, though I can't see them being practical to wear." He took the other shoe from her and likewise fitted it to her. She twisted her ankle this way and that, admiring the way they glinted and shone.

"They're incredible." Lizbete swallowed. She'd been hot enough to melt sand into glass. How had anything around her survived?

A thought struck her. She glanced down at her nightshirt. That wasn't what she remembered being dressed in. In fact, the last thing she remembered being dressed in had crumbled away after burning.

"Oh no!" She jerked away from him, pulling the blankets up to her chin, as if she could recover her modesty and wipe out the memory by hiding herself in the present.

"What?" He tilted his head.

"On the beach. My—my clothes?"

His cheeks reddened. "Oh. They were pretty much burnt toast. I…" He cleared his throat. "Once you were cool enough to handle, I wrapped you in my coat and brought you here. My mother and Falla helped dress you in what you are wearing now."

"But you saw *everything*." Her stomach twisted. She was going to die. It was impossible to be this embarrassed and live through it. A second even more horrifying thought struck her. Half the village had been on the beach after her fight with the Ravenous One. "*Everyone* saw *everything*."

"I was more concerned about the fact that you were literally on fire than your lack of clothing, but . . . yeah." He avoided her eyes. "I'm sorry. For what it's worth, I have longterm plans that would've eventually involved me seeing all of you anyway."

In spite of her humiliation she smirked. "Oh, do you?"

"I'm not the most experienced, but I've heard rumors that marriage often involves such things." Brynar took her hand.

"And the rest of the village?" She arched an eyebrow.

His mouth wrinkled as if he'd tasted something sour. "Can't be helped. If they think poorly of you because they saw you unclothed and ignore the reason you were unclothed was because you saved their sorry skins in a fight with a massive . . . fire octopus?" He shook his head. "Whatever that thing was, if the clothes are the main focus rather than the bravery, then there's no hope for them." His hold on her hand tightened. "It feels rather anticlimactic to ask now, after I've already made my intentions so clear. Liz, you will marry me, won't you? I think I can make you happy."

"I know you can." She smiled and brushed her fingers up into his blond hair. "Yes. I will. I want to help you as you become a healer. I want to be with you every day of my life . . . and yes, you can see me unclothed whenever you wish."

His lips curled into a rakish smile. "Oh, really?"

"After we're married, of course," she quickly added. Heat raged beneath her skin.

Stupid blushing.

He laughed. "Good." He gently kissed her cheek. "Though I want to be a help to you as well. I haven't had a chance to talk it over with the rest of the family, but Liz, Uncle Hangur is driving this business into the ground. He's drinking his profits. The local merchants already won't deal with him because he won't pay for goods, and he threw a fit over the minor damage the tavern took during the Ravenous One's attack." He shook his head. "The whole town is rebuilding and repairing, and he expects Einar, myself, Father, and even my aunts' husbands and children to drop everything and help him with repairs because he's too lazy to thatch the holes in his own roof. I think he only wanted the prestige of being a tavern owner—and a place to drink with his wastrel friends. I heard him muttering how he'd be better off leaving Brumehome and going some place where he's properly appreciated."

Lizbete wrinkled her nose. "Good riddance." She then bit her bottom lip. "So, what does that mean for me?"

"I'm hoping it means that this tavern is yours as it should've been in the first place." He sighed. "That's what Aunt Katryn would've wanted."

Her heart fluttered within her. She'd have the tavern. It would be hers. She'd never have to worry about having a home because she *owned* her home. "Do . . . do you think I'll be able to do it?" She'd worked with Auntie her whole life, but always as a helper, never as the boss. To be the owner, the employer, was both thrilling and terrifying.

"You know the business, and you'll have help." Brynar nodded. "Honestly, if this were your place, I'd be more than happy to do that roof thatching for you."

"You can thatch my roof any time." She gave an exaggerated wink.

He frowned. "What does that even mean?"

She shrugged. "I don't know, but it sounded vaguely dirty, and I'm trying to get used to the idea that you've seen me naked now." She grimaced. "I'm kind of an awkward mess, all right? Are you sure you want to marry me?"

He laughed. "Yes, I'm sure. Maybe even more so." He leaned forward and kissed her again.

She wrapped her arms around his neck, holding on with all her might. The crystal embedded in her hand pulsed with an odd, prickling energy, and her feet felt strange within the cool glass of her fragile new shoes, but in spite of all that, she felt at home. Perhaps for the first time in her life, Lizbete knew exactly where she belonged, and she was never going to leave.

Chapter Twenty-Five

The scent of plump, sun-ripened blueberries drifted up to Lizbete's nose as she mixed together the butter-heavy pastry dough. Would a dozen cakes be enough? Had she set aside enough cream? Goodness, those blueberries smelled heavenly.

Taking a quick break from her baking, she popped a particularly fat one into her mouth and let the juice burst over her tongue. She closed her eyes. Perfect. Maybe the cakes were a mistake and they should just serve the berries fresh with cream and sugar. It would take the pressure off her having to both make that and prepare the fish bake.

The door to the kitchen swung open, and she turned to find Falla and Elin in the doorway, eyeing her skeptically.

"What do you think you're doing?" Falla frowned, putting her hands on her matronly hips.

"Cooking. We're going to be feeding half the village tonight." Lizbete dabbed at her forehead with the edge of her apron.

"I told you I'd take care of that!" Falla threw her hands in the air. "You're getting married in less than an hour, you're not dressed, and you're covered in flour."

"At least it's not ash." Elin sniffed, picking at her plain smock. It seemed she had won any battle her mother had tried to wage for her to wear fancier clothing.

"Whatever it is, this isn't where you should be. Your future mother-in-law is waiting for you upstairs." Falla pushed Lizbete towards the door.

Lizbete dragged her feet. Of course, she didn't want to be late, but there was so much to do. How long could getting dressed and wiping the flour off her face take?

She grabbed the door frame and muscled herself out of Falla's grasp. "Did you set aside the burning wine?"

"Enough to put the whole town under." Falla nodded, brushing a loose strand of blonde hair behind her ear. She gestured to the young girl beside her. "Elin, get your brother's bride out of her before I lose my temper!"

"Yes, ma'am." Elin grinned and yanked Lizbete through the door. Lizbete grunted in protest, but couldn't help admiring how much stronger her young friend had become. The last six or so months of constant crystal treatments had allowed the girl to finally flourish. She'd sprouted up several more inches over the winter and was now just as often found playing with other children her age as lurking by Lizbete's fire. Lizbete would let Elin push her around just for the delight of seeing her healthy—well, to an extent anyway.

Now Elin herded her through the common room, decorated with flowers and ribbons in anticipation of the upcoming ceremony, then up the stairs into her bedroom. Nan, her willowy frame clad in a pale yellow dress embroidered with pink flowers, waited there next to a full-length mirror.

"There you are!" Nan grinned, blue eyes warm. "For a moment

I thought you'd changed your mind about marrying my son after all."

Lizbete's face heated. "Oh, never!"

While Lizbete and Brynar had originally wanted to marry immediately, Sten had talked them into waiting until the town had rebuilt from the Ravenous One's attack and had time to adjust to the changes, such as Brynar no longer being the heir to the mayor's seat and Lizbete's ownership of the tavern. Though he helped out a great deal with the various town-fixing projects, Brynar had slowly handed off as much responsibility as he could to Einar. Over the winter, he'd divided his time between training with the Widow Gri and waiting tables for Lizbete. Having Brynar's familiar and respected face at the front of the house had eased the transition. Though Falla had joked that finding out Lizbete was as good of a cook, if not a better one, than Auntie had certainly helped too.

"You can win a lot of folk over with a good meal and a stiff drink," she'd pointed out.

Now, with the high summer sun, the couple had decided they couldn't wait any more. Lizbete didn't want to spend another night talking and laughing with Brynar as they cleaned up after the dinner crowd, only to have to bid him goodnight from the doorstep rather than a shared bed.

"You're covered in flour!" Nan clicked her tongue and brought out a handkerchief. "We all love your cooking, Liz, but today is not the day for that."

"Sorry." Lizbete cleaned herself off as Nan took something out of the wardrobe.

Nan held up a dark blue dress embroidered with red flowers. More woven embroidery bordered the skirt hem, the shoulders, and the neckline. There were even shiny brass buttons at the cuffs. "Let's get you ready."

Lizbete couldn't help but stare at herself in the mirror as Nan did up the buttons on the back of the dress. She'd never worn anything so colorful. She swallowed. "Are you sure this is a good idea? I disappear into the dress."

Nan shook her head, a soft smile crossing her face. "Hardly, my dear. You look lovely, and I imagine Brynar won't notice the dress at all anyway."

A short while later, red ribbons spangled Lizbete's braided brown hair. A necklace of crimson and clear crystals hung about her neck, a present from her father. While the cavers no longer hid from the villagers, the traditions that had kept the two races apart for so long continued to keep them from intermingling. The cavers simply didn't see a need to visit the village or the villagers the caves. Grimir was the lone exception to this, stopping by the tavern after close or bringing Lizbete—and sometimes Brynar and Elin as well—to explore mountain passages with him. He often told her stories of her mother and showed great amusement in trying food from the human's comparatively more varied diet.

Lizbete touched first the crystals, then the ribbons in her hair. Maybe it was the dress, or the ribbons, or the care Nan had taken in her grooming, but for the first time in her life, she felt truly beautiful. Her throat tightened.

"I wish Auntie were here," she whispered.

To Lizbete's surprise, Nan tackled her in a fierce hug. "I wish she could be too, Liz, but I'm honored that I get to stand with you now." Nan withdrew to arm's length. Tears misted in her eyes. "You look lovely, but more than that, my son loves you, and I've seen how you love him. This is the start of a very good thing." She brushed her hand down Lizbete's face. "It won't always be easy. It never is. A marriage is often two people thrust together like two bits of glass in the surf, battered by the waves of what life throws up against them, and sometimes against each other, but the end result?" She reached into her pocket and pulled out two pieces of polished sea glass, one clear blue and the other pearly white. She pressed them to Lizbete's hand. "It wears off our hard edges, brings out the character within. Some days it aches and stings and you're tossed about so much you don't know which way is up, but in the end, you're better and brighter together."

Lizbete stared down at the glinting glass. "I just want to make him happy."

"You already have." Nan kissed Lizbete's cheek.

Lizbete's heart warmed, and she smiled. Nan was right. This was the start of a good thing.

Nan started. "I think I hear something." She went to listen at the door. "Guests are arriving. Let me check and see if they are ready for you. I'll send Elin up to keep you company."

"Thank you," Lizbete forced a smile even though butterflies filled her stomach. As soon as Nan left, she sat on the edge of her bed and took deep breaths. She wanted this. She wanted to be with Brynar, but for some reason she felt like she were about to step off a cliff.

If I can just get through the ceremony, it'll be all right.

When she pictured life with him, she imagined laughing as they worked together, evenings spent by the fire in conversation, and much kissing. None of that scared her, even though she was sure Nan was right about the sting of losing her rough edges over time. However, the wedding feast, with everyone looking at her, would be pure torment, especially as many probably doubted Brynar's sanity for choosing to promise himself to the strange, ashen-skinned orphan. Thankfully, it would only be Brynar's family for the ceremony itself.

Because of his family's social status, they'd been forced to invite practically the whole town to the feast. For ease, they'd chosen to have a small ceremony with just their immediate families followed by a feast in town square. To their credit, several local business owners—butchers, farmers, dairy-owners—had donated food and drink. There would easily be enough to feed the entire town.

Someone knocked at the door.

"You decent?" Elin called out from the other side.

"As much as ever." Lizbete chuckled, pulling herself out of her doubts.

Elin entered and her eyes widened. "Look at you, all spangled and trimmed like a fancy cake."

"Tradition." Lizbete gave her a shrug.

Elin wrinkled her nose. "Tradition or no tradition, if I ever get married, I won't let them dress me up in fancy frippery. Nope, plain and sensible—unless maybe I can wear a full white bear skin." Elin's face brightened. "That's what you should've done!"

"It's a little warm this time of year for fur coats," Lizbete pointed out.

"True." Elin strode to the window. "Guests are almost all here. I think we're just waiting on a cousin or two. If you're going to run you better do it now."

"I'm good, thanks." Lizbete rolled her eyes at Elin.

"Are you sure?" Elin arched an eyebrow at Lizbete. "It's not too late to back out now."

"I'm sure." Lizbete focused on the mirror, not because she had any need to re-check her appearance but because she didn't want to look Elin in the eye and give away her nerves.

"He snores, you know," Elin pointed out.

"I think I can tolerate that." Lizbete snorted.

"And slurps his soup."

"So do you, you imp." Lizbete gently slapped Elin on the shoulder.

"And until he was eleven, he really believed that if he wasn't wearing new clothes on New Year's Day a giant frost cat would swoop in from the sky and eat him."

Lizbete paused. That actually surprised her. "Really?" She narrowed her eyes at Elin. "How do you know that? You would've been practically a baby then."

Elin shrugged. "My aunts like to tell the story at family gatherings. It embarrasses him, but I think that's probably proof that it's true."

"Probably." Lizbete had known Brynar when they were both children, but he was just enough older than her to always seem brave and responsible. The idea of him believing fairy tales about giant, man-eating cats would have to be addressed at some point when she needed the advantage in an argument.

Footsteps echoed in the hall outside and Nan peeked through the door Elin had left open. "It's time."

A chill cut through Lizbete, followed immediately by heart-quickening excitement.

Yes, it was time, and she was ready.

Fully dressed and primped, Lizbete followed Nan down the stairs into the common room.

She scanned the room. Roughly two dozen people, almost exclusively Brynar's family, though Falla's husband and children, Widow Gri, and Einar's girl, Marget, were also in attendance. For a moment, Lizbete's stomach tightened, but then she caught sight of a shimmering shadow lurking in the corner.

He had come.

Traditionally in Brumehome, weddings were performed by the fathers of both families, presenting their children to be joined. Cavers, however, had no such traditions, and while Grimir was less skittish around the villagers than he'd originally been, the idea of attending her wedding had obviously caused her father some anxiety. Seeing him, though, warmed Lizbete's soul. She wasn't alone. She had his support. She'd get through this.

The sea of visitors parted at her approach, revealing Brynar and his father standing in front of the unlit fireplace. In place of flames, a bouquet of flowers and bright red sheep sorrel blossomed in a vase.

Brynar's gaze snapped to her, and the butterflies in Lizbete's stomach erupted into her brain, making her head spin. He stared at her, mouth slightly agape, for an unending moment before a brilliant smile lit his face. Forgetting all sense of decorum, Lizbete rushed to his side.

He caught her up in a hug followed by a kiss as the onlookers burst into laughter. Lizbete's feet left the ground as the kiss deepened.

"Save it for tonight, boy!" one of Brynar's elderly great-uncles shouted.

Lizbete blushed but didn't break eye contact from Brynar as he withdrew from her.

"You look so beautiful," he whispered, brushing his hand down her cheek.

"You too." Her voice came out in a humiliating squeak, but she didn't care.

Grimir flitted across the room to stand before them.

"You look so much like your mother, my Lizbete," he said.

"Thank you." Her gaze dropped to her feet.

The crowd quieted, then Brynar laughed and offered Lizbete his hand. "So, we're finally doing this?"

"Took us long enough." She smirked.

Taking her hands, he turned to his father. "Can we start now?"

Sten nodded. "I think we can."

Lizbete's hold tightened on Brynar's long fingers. This was really going to happen. She was about to start her happily ever after.

About the Author

H. L. Burke is the author of multiple fantasy novels including *The Dragon and the Scholar* saga, the *Nyssa Glass* YA steampunk series, and *Coiled*. She is an admirer of the whimsical, a follower of the Light, and a believer in happily ever after. Married to her high school crush who is now a US Marine, she has moved multiple times in her adult life but believes that home is wherever her husband, two daughters, and pets are.

For information about H. L. Burke's latest novels, to sign up for her monthly newsletter, or to contact her, go to <u>www.hlburkeauthor.com</u>! Free eBook for newsletter subscribers!

MORE FROM
UNCOMMON UNIVERSES PRESS

A mortal alchemist.
A faeric king.
A bond that transcends death.

A deadly disease.
A vanishing remedy.
A breathless journey.

A healing touch.
A hideous face.
A looming curse.

Torn between two lives.
Reeve struggles to remember
what's real. Until night and
day collide, with a revelation
that threatens all of Acarsaid.

Ashen